STAR WARS
THE HIGH REPUBLIC
ADVENTURES

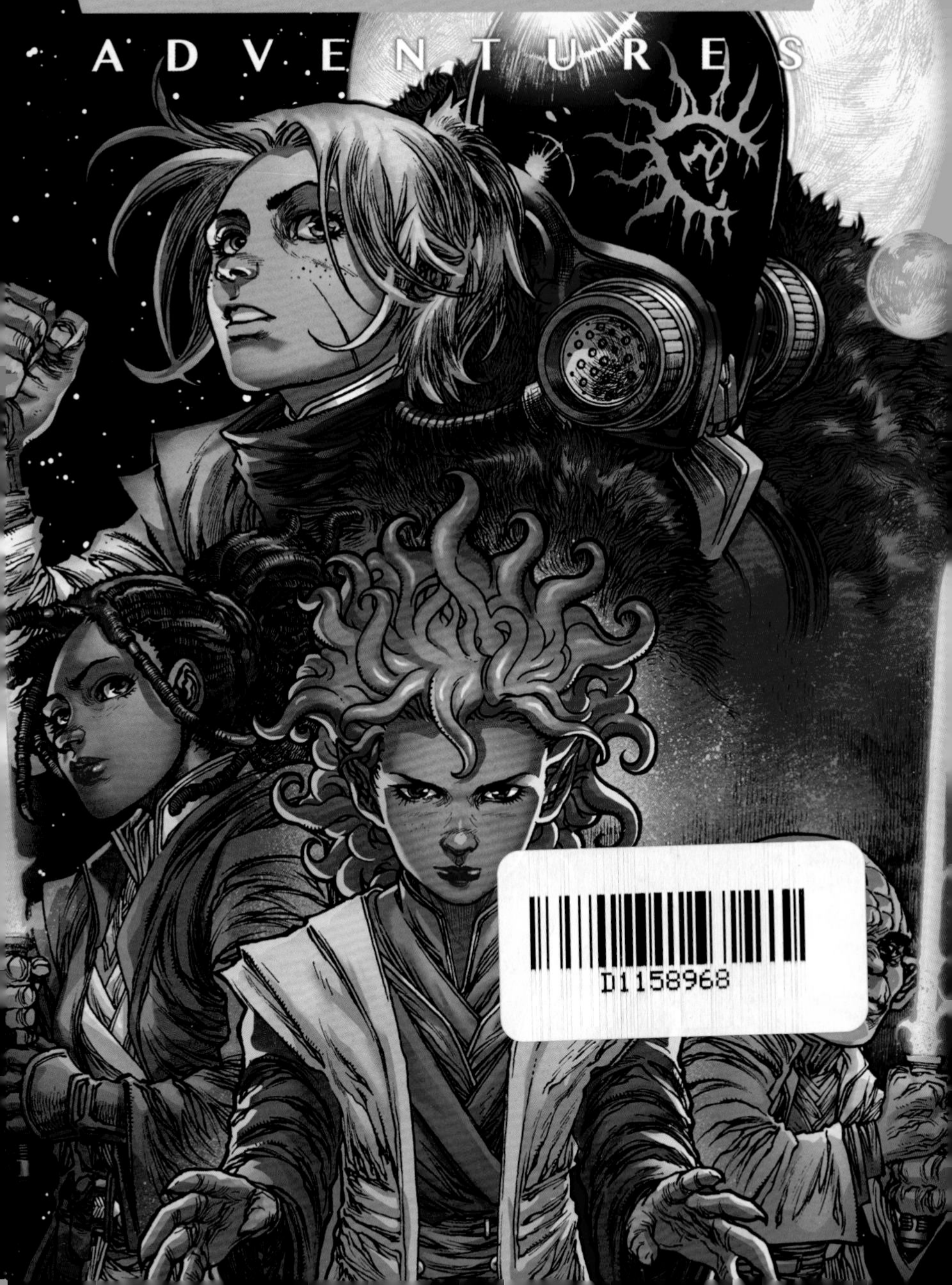

Facebook: **facebook.com/idwpublishing**
Twitter: **@idwpublishing**
YouTube: **youtube.com/idwpublishing**
Instagram: **@idwpublishing**

ISBN: 978-1-68405-853-2   24 23 22 21   1 2 3 4

Cover Art by
Harvey Tolibao

Cover Colors by
Kevin Tolibao

Series Assistant Edits by
Riley Farmer

Series Edits by
Elizabeth Brei and
Heather Antos

Collection Edits by
Alonzo Simon and
Zac Boone

Collection Design by
Nathan Widick

Lucasfilm Credits:

Senior Editor
Robert Simpson

Creative Director
Michael Siglain

Art Director
Troy Alders

Lucasfilm Art Department
Phil Szostak

Story Group
**Matt Martin, Pablo Hidalgo,
Emily Shkoukani,** and **Jason D. Stein**

STAR WARS: THE HIGH REPUBLIC ADVENTURES, VOLUME 1. NOVEMBER 2021. FIRST PRINTING. © 2021 LUCASFILM LTD. & ® OR ™ WHERE INDICATED. All Rights Reserved. The IDW logo is registered in the U.S. Patent and Trademark Office. IDW Publishing, a division of Idea and Design Works, LLC. Editorial offices: 2765 Truxtun Road, San Diego, CA 92106. Any similarities to persons living or dead are purely coincidental. With the exception of artwork used for review purposes, none of the contents of this publication may be reprinted without the permission of Idea and Design Works, LLC. IDW Publishing does not read or accept unsolicited submissions of ideas, stories, or artwork. Printed in Korea.

Originally published as STAR WARS: THE HIGH REPUBLIC ADVENTURES issues #1–5 and as "The Gaze Electric" in STAR WARS ADVENTURES #6.

Nachie Marsham, Publisher
Blake Kobashigawa, VP of Sales
Tara McCrillis, VP Publishing Operations
John Barber, Editor-in-Chief
Mark Doyle, Editorial Director, Originals
Erika Turner, Executive Editor
Scott Dunbier, Director, Special Projects
Mark Irwin, Editorial Director, Consumer Products Mgr
Lauren LaPera, Managing Editor
Joe Hughes, Director, Talent Relations
Anna Morrow, Sr. Marketing Director
Alexandra Hargett, Book & Mass Market Sales Director
Keith Davidsen, Senior Manager, PR
Topher Alford, Sr Digital Marketing Manager
Shauna Monteforte, Sr. Director of Manufacturing Operations
Jamie Miller, Sr. Operations Manager
Nathan Widick, Sr. Art Director, Head of Design
Neil Uyetake, Sr. Art Director Design & Production
Shawn Lee, Art Director Design & Production
Jack Rivera, Art Director, Marketing

Ted Adams and Robbie Robbins, IDW Founders

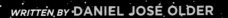

WRITTEN BY DANIEL JOSÉ OLDER

ART BY HARVEY TOLIBAO

ADDITIONAL ART BY NICK BROKENSHIRE (PROLOGUE),
POW RODRIX (PT. 2 & 5), *AND* MANUEL BRACCHI (PT. 5)

COLORS BY REBECCA NALTY

LETTERS BY JAKE M. WOOD

ADDITIONAL LETTERS BY JOHANNA NATTALIE (PROLOGUE)

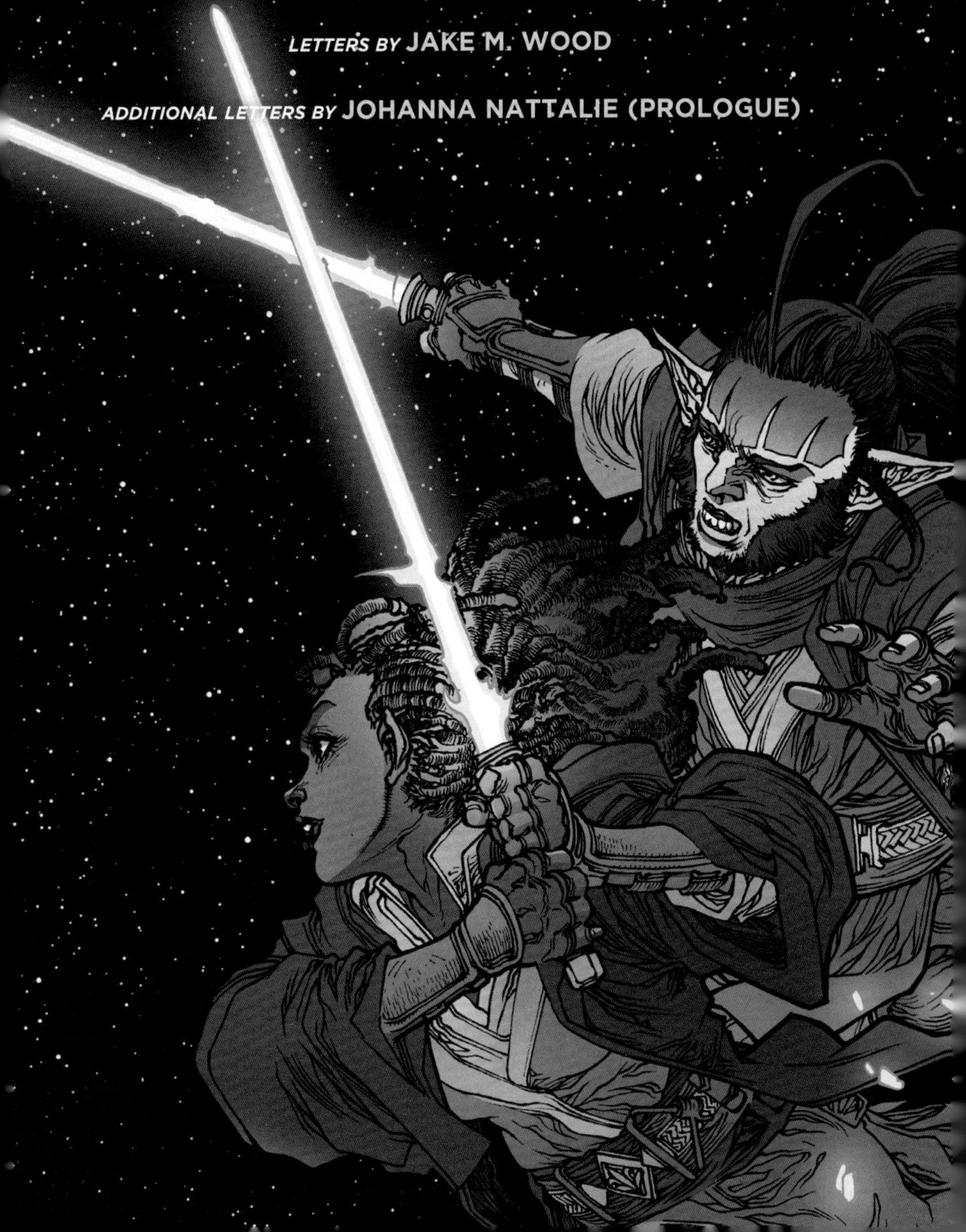

STAR WARS
TIMELINE

THE HIGH REPUBLIC

FALL OF THE JEDI

THE PHANTOM MENACE

ATTACK OF THE CLONES

THE CLONE WARS

REVENGE OF THE SITH

REIGN OF THE EMPIRE

THE BAD BATCH

SOLO: A STAR WARS STORY

AGE OF REBELLION

REBELS

ROGUE ONE: A STAR WARS STORY

A NEW HOPE

THE EMPIRE STRIKES BACK

RETURN OF THE JEDI

THE NEW REPUBLIC

THE MANDALORIAN

RISE OF THE FIRST ORDER

RESISTANCE

THE FORCE AWAKENS

THE LAST JEDI

THE RISE OF SKYWALKER

STAR WARS
THE HIGH REPUBLIC

The galaxy is at peace, ruled by the glorious REPUBLIC and protected by the noble and wise JEDI KNIGHTS.

As a symbol of all that is good, the Republic is about to launch STARLIGHT BEACON into the far reaches of the Outer Rim. This new space station will serve as a ray of hope for all to see.

But just as a magnificent renaissance spreads throughout the Republic, so does a frightening new adversary. Now the guardians of peace and justice must face a threat to themselves, the galaxy, and the Force itself....

PROLOGUE: THE GAZE ELECTRIC

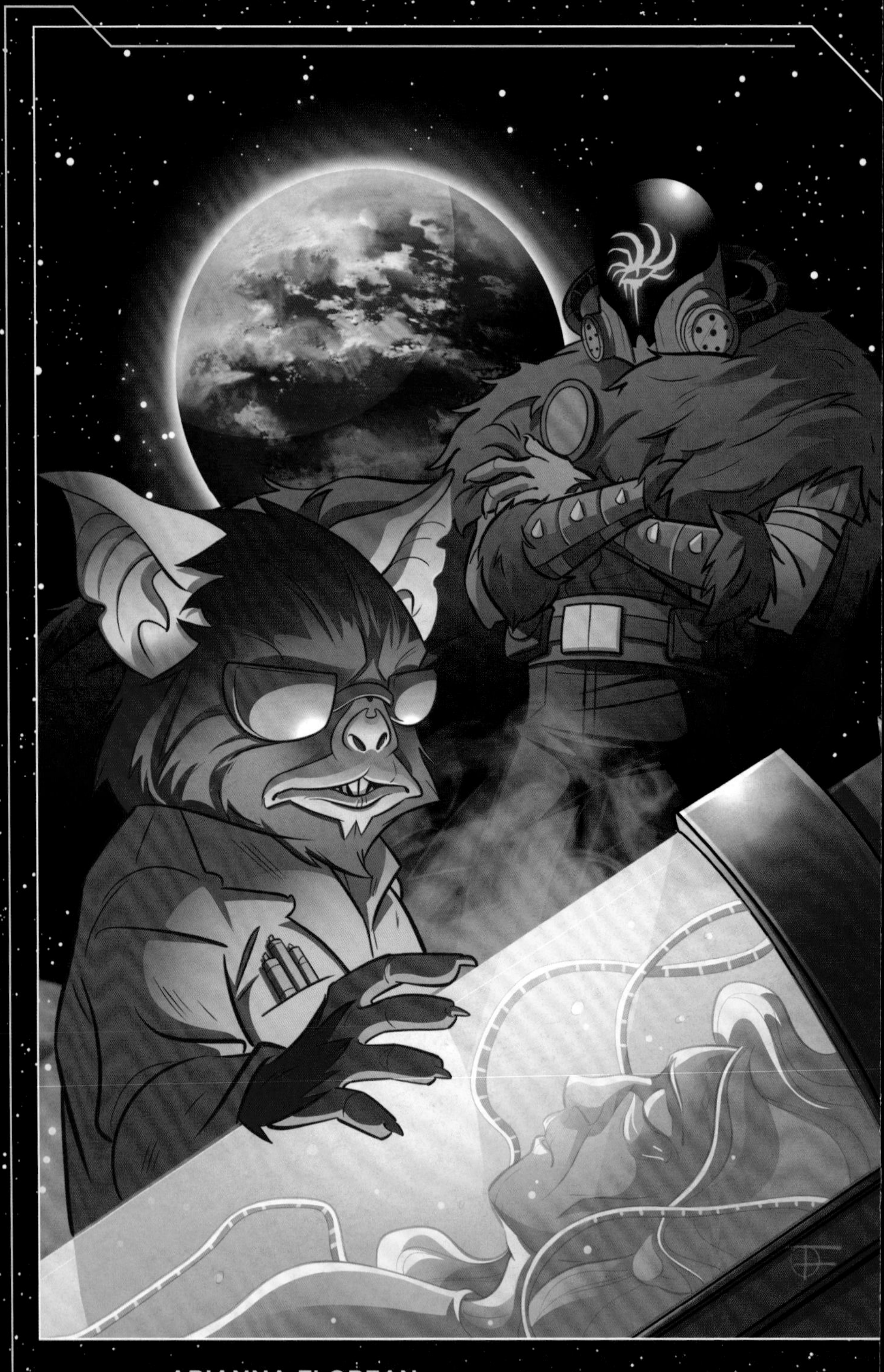

ART BY ARIANNA FLOREAN

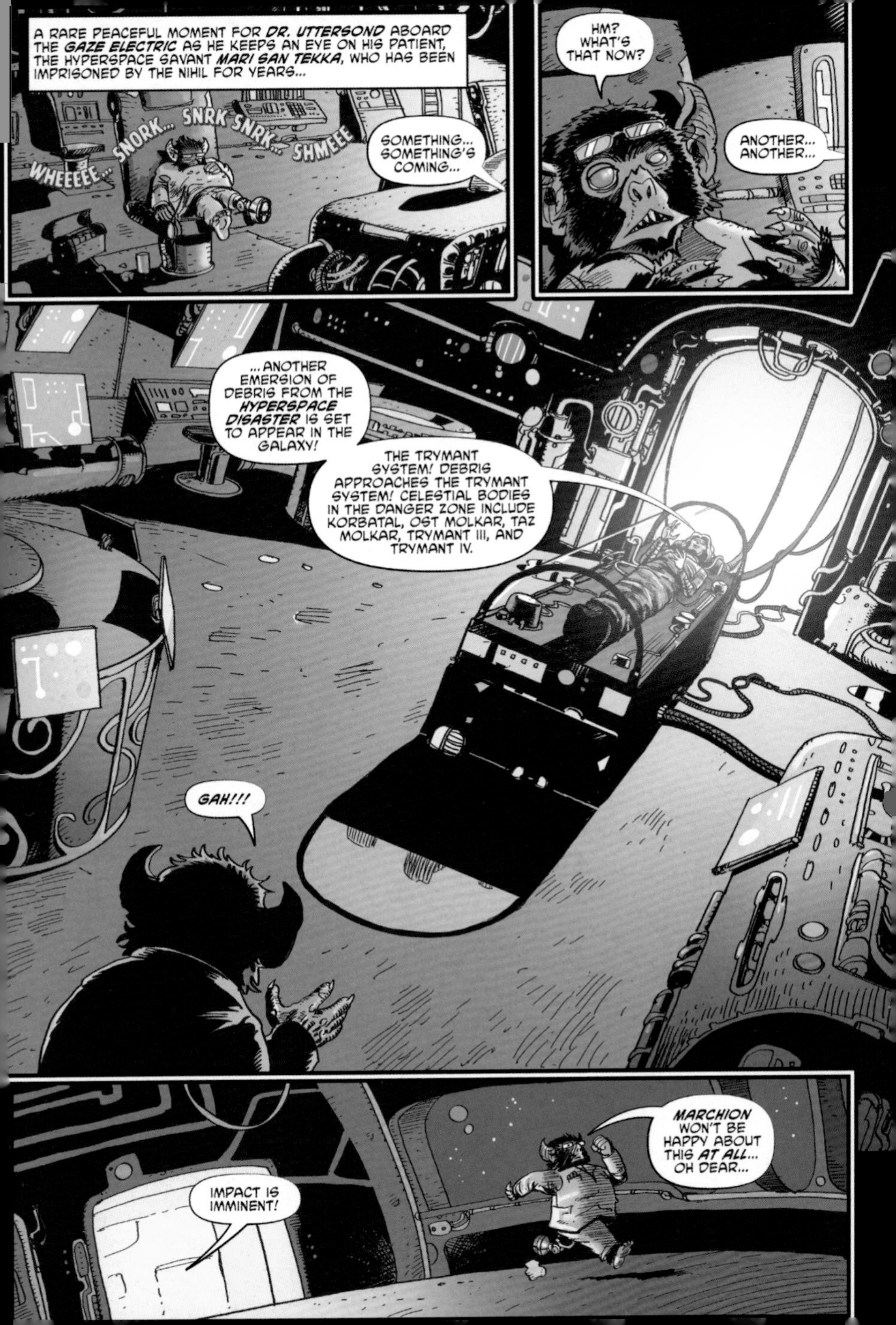
A RARE PEACEFUL MOMENT FOR DR. UTTERSOND ABOARD THE GAZE ELECTRIC AS HE KEEPS AN EYE ON HIS PATIENT, THE HYPERSPACE SAVANT MARI SAN TEKKA, WHO HAS BEEN IMPRISONED BY THE NIHIL FOR YEARS...
WHEEEEE... SNORK... SNRK SNRK... SHMEEE
SOMETHING... SOMETHING'S COMING...
HM? WHAT'S THAT NOW?
ANOTHER... ANOTHER...
...ANOTHER EMERSION OF DEBRIS FROM THE HYPERSPACE DISASTER IS SET TO APPEAR IN THE GALAXY!
THE TRYMANT SYSTEM! DEBRIS APPROACHES THE TRYMANT SYSTEM! CELESTIAL BODIES IN THE DANGER ZONE INCLUDE KORBATAL, OST MOLKAR, TAZ MOLKAR, TRYMANT III, AND TRYMANT IV.
GAH!!!
IMPACT IS IMMINENT!
MARCHION WON'T BE HAPPY ABOUT THIS AT ALL... OH DEAR...

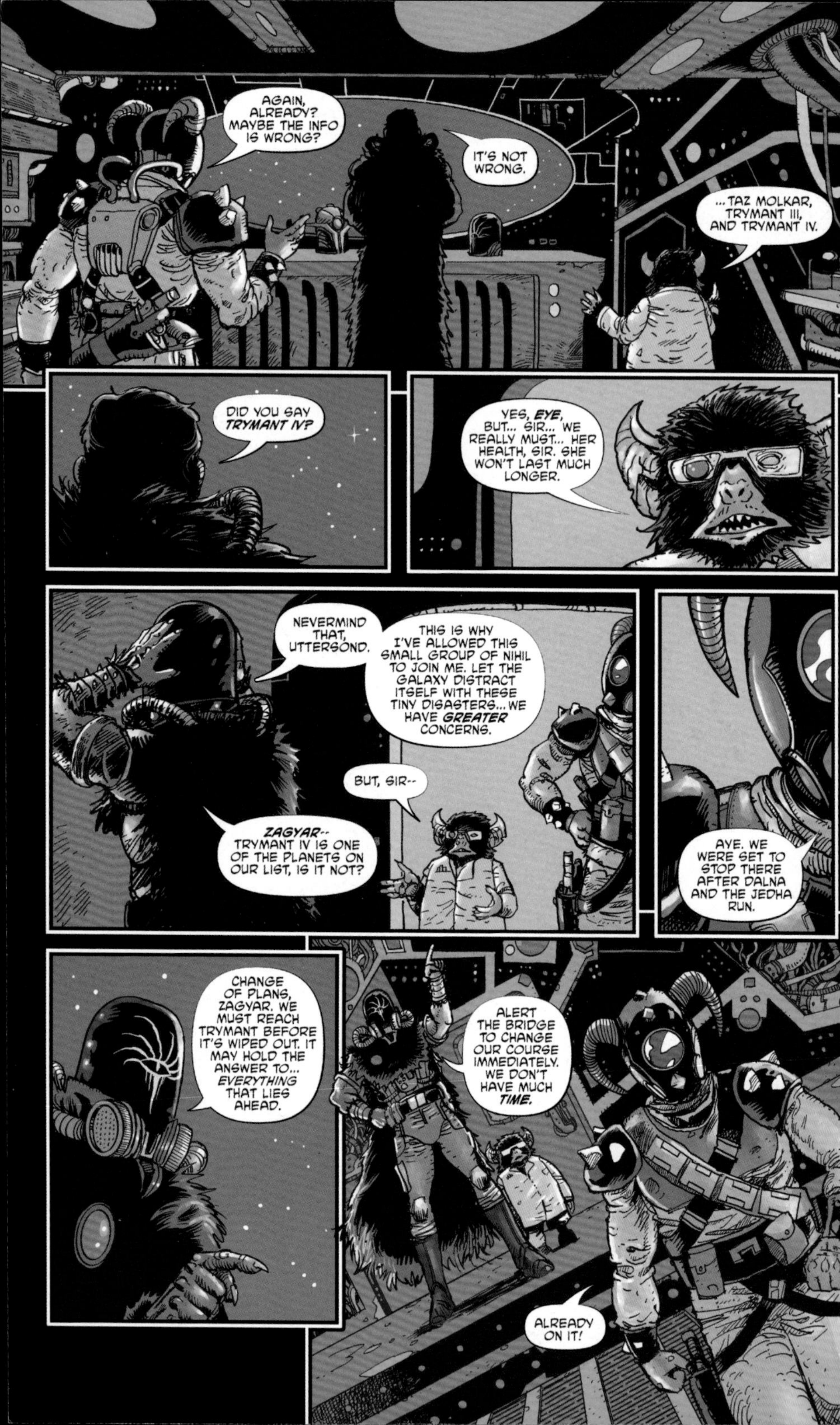
AGAIN, ALREADY? MAYBE THE INFO IS WRONG?
IT'S NOT WRONG.
...TAZ MOLKAR, TRYMANT III, AND TRYMANT IV.
DID YOU SAY TRYMANT IV?
YES, EYE, BUT... SIR... WE REALLY MUST... HER HEALTH, SIR. SHE WON'T LAST MUCH LONGER.
NEVERMIND THAT, UTTERSOND.
THIS IS WHY I'VE ALLOWED THIS SMALL GROUP OF NIHIL TO JOIN ME. LET THE GALAXY DISTRACT ITSELF WITH THESE TINY DISASTERS... WE HAVE GREATER CONCERNS.
BUT, SIR--
ZAGYAR-- TRYMANT IV IS ONE OF THE PLANETS ON OUR LIST, IS IT NOT?
AYE. WE WERE SET TO STOP THERE AFTER DALNA AND THE JEDHA RUN.
CHANGE OF PLANS, ZAGYAR. WE MUST REACH TRYMANT BEFORE IT'S WIPED OUT. IT MAY HOLD THE ANSWER TO... EVERYTHING THAT LIES AHEAD.
ALERT THE BRIDGE TO CHANGE OUR COURSE IMMEDIATELY. WE DON'T HAVE MUCH TIME.
ALREADY ON IT!

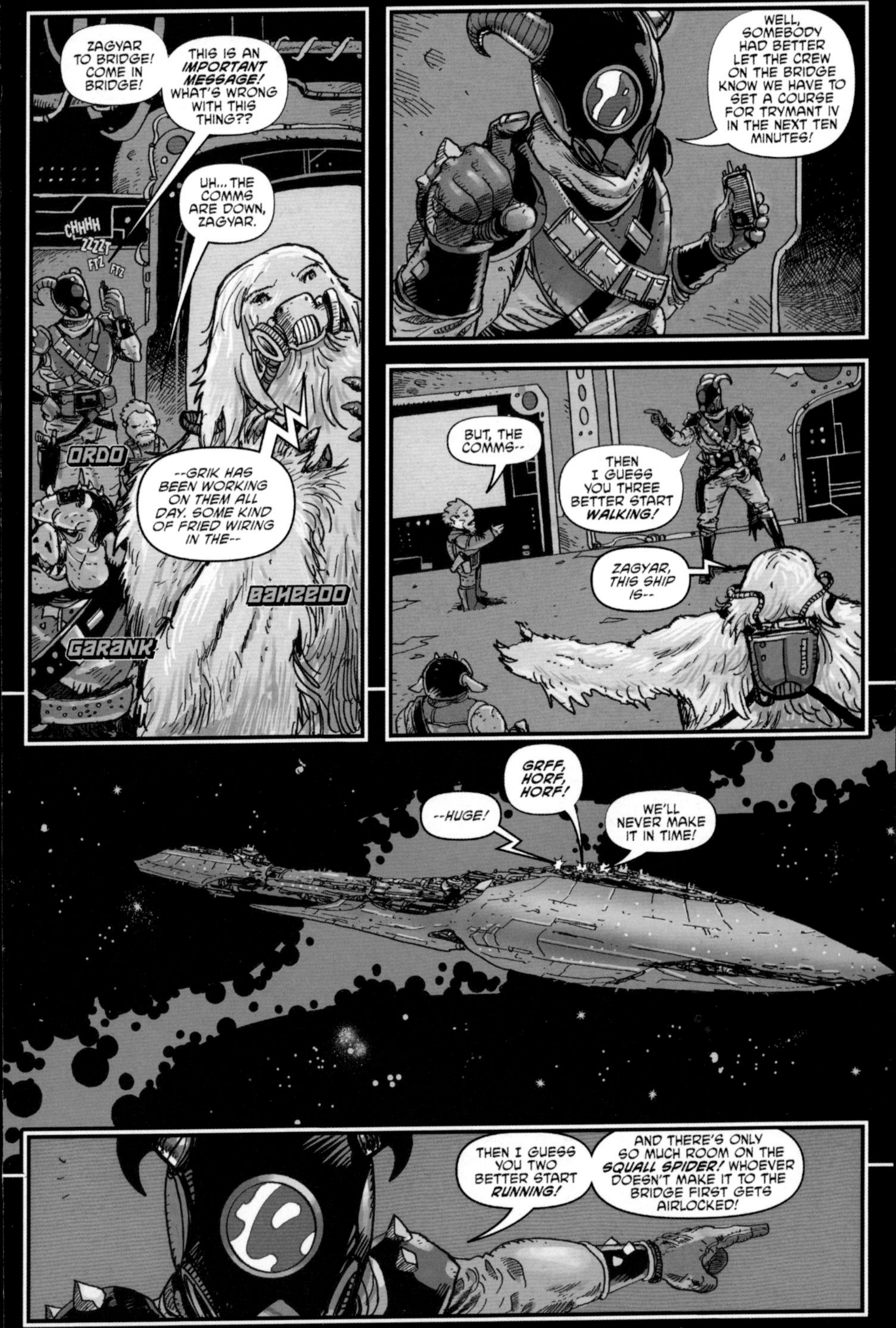
ZAGYAR TO BRIDGE! COME IN BRIDGE!
THIS IS AN IMPORTANT MESSAGE! WHAT'S WRONG WITH THIS THING??
CHHHH ZZZZT FTZ FTZ
UH... THE COMMS ARE DOWN, ZAGYAR.
ORDO
--GRIK HAS BEEN WORKING ON THEM ALL DAY. SOME KIND OF FRIED WIRING IN THE--
BAHEEDO
GARANK
WELL, SOMEBODY HAD BETTER LET THE CREW ON THE BRIDGE KNOW WE HAVE TO SET A COURSE FOR TRYMANT IV IN THE NEXT TEN MINUTES!
BUT, THE COMMS--
THEN I GUESS YOU THREE BETTER START WALKING!
ZAGYAR, THIS SHIP IS--
--HUGE!
GRFF, HORF, HORF!
WE'LL NEVER MAKE IT IN TIME!
THEN I GUESS YOU TWO BETTER START RUNNING!
AND THERE'S ONLY SO MUCH ROOM ON THE SQUALL SPIDER! WHOEVER DOESN'T MAKE IT TO THE BRIDGE FIRST GETS AIRLOCKED!

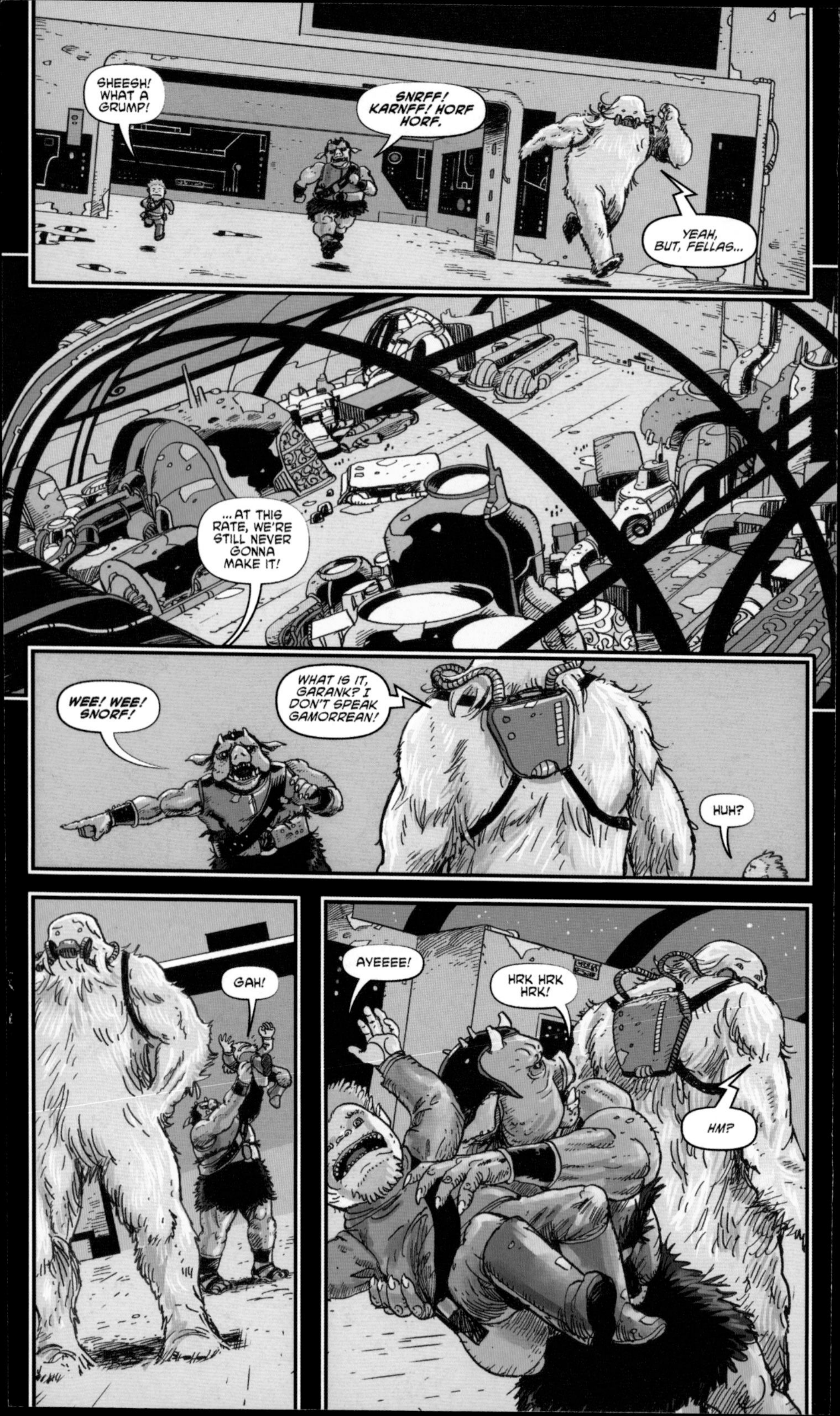
SHEESH! WHAT A GRUMP!
SNRFF! KARNFF! HORF HORF.
YEAH, BUT, FELLAS...
...AT THIS RATE, WE'RE STILL NEVER GONNA MAKE IT!
WEE! WEE! SNORF!
WHAT IS IT, GARANK? I DON'T SPEAK GAMORREAN!
HUH?
GAH!
AYEEEE!
HRK HRK HRK!
HM?

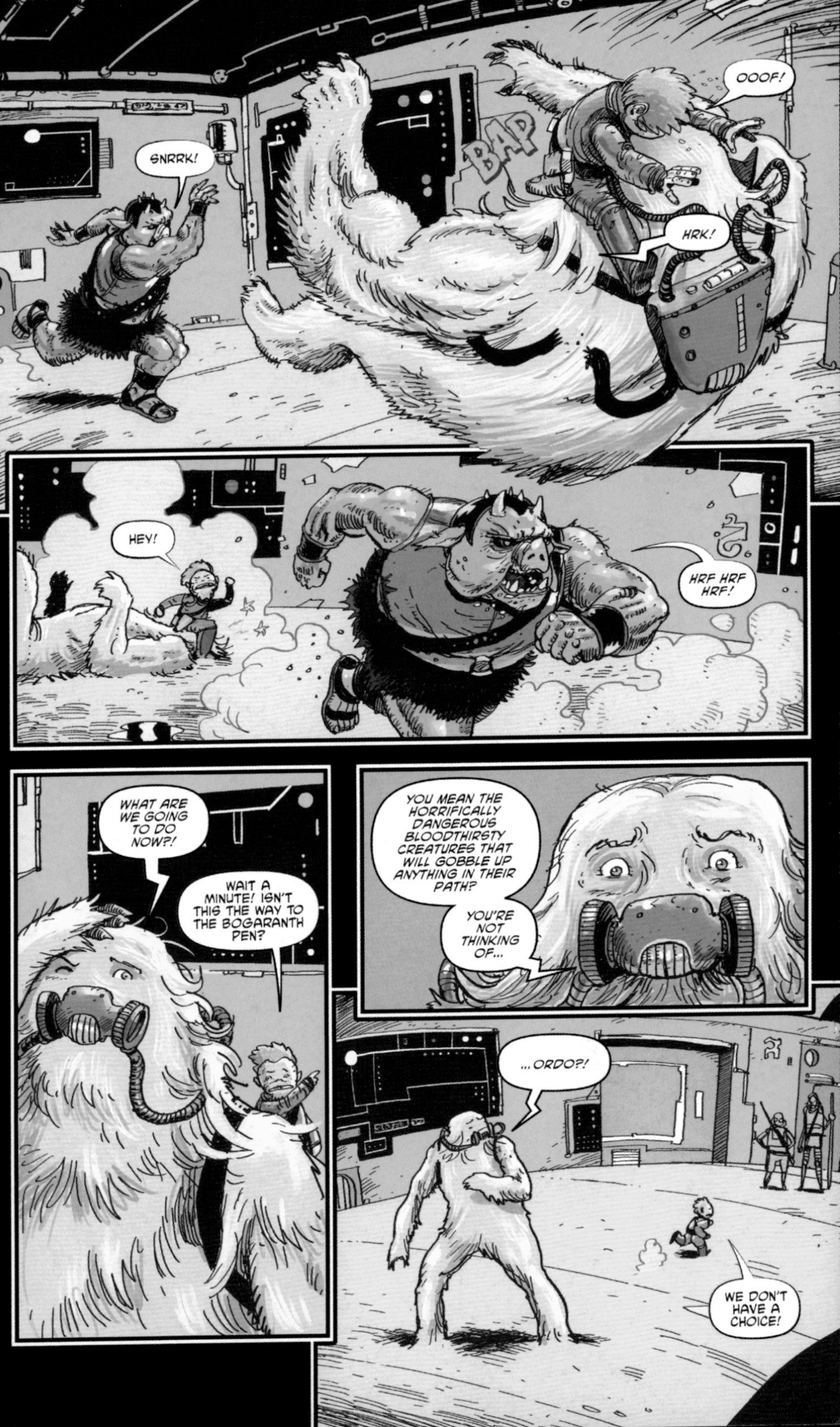
SNRRK!
BAP
OOOF!
HRK!
HEY!
HRF HRF HRF!
WHAT ARE WE GOING TO DO NOW?!
WAIT A MINUTE! ISN'T THIS THE WAY TO THE BOGARANTH PEN?
YOU MEAN THE HORRIFICALLY DANGEROUS BLOODTHIRSTY CREATURES THAT WILL GOBBLE UP ANYTHING IN THEIR PATH?
YOU'RE NOT THINKING OF...
...ORDO?!
WE DON'T HAVE A CHOICE!

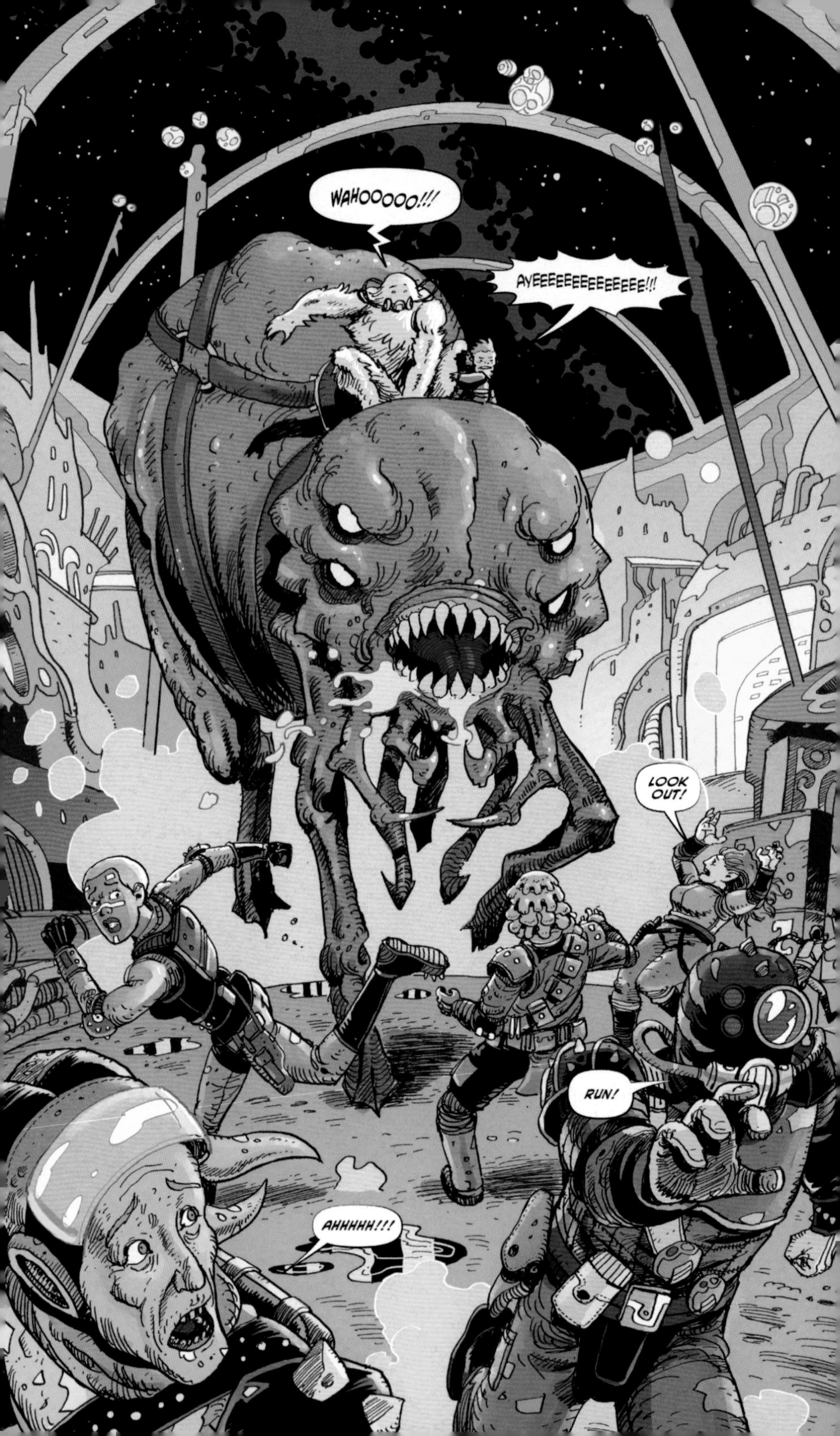
WAHOOOOO!!!
AYEEEEEEEEEEEEEE!!!
LOOK OUT!
RUN!
AHHHHH!!!

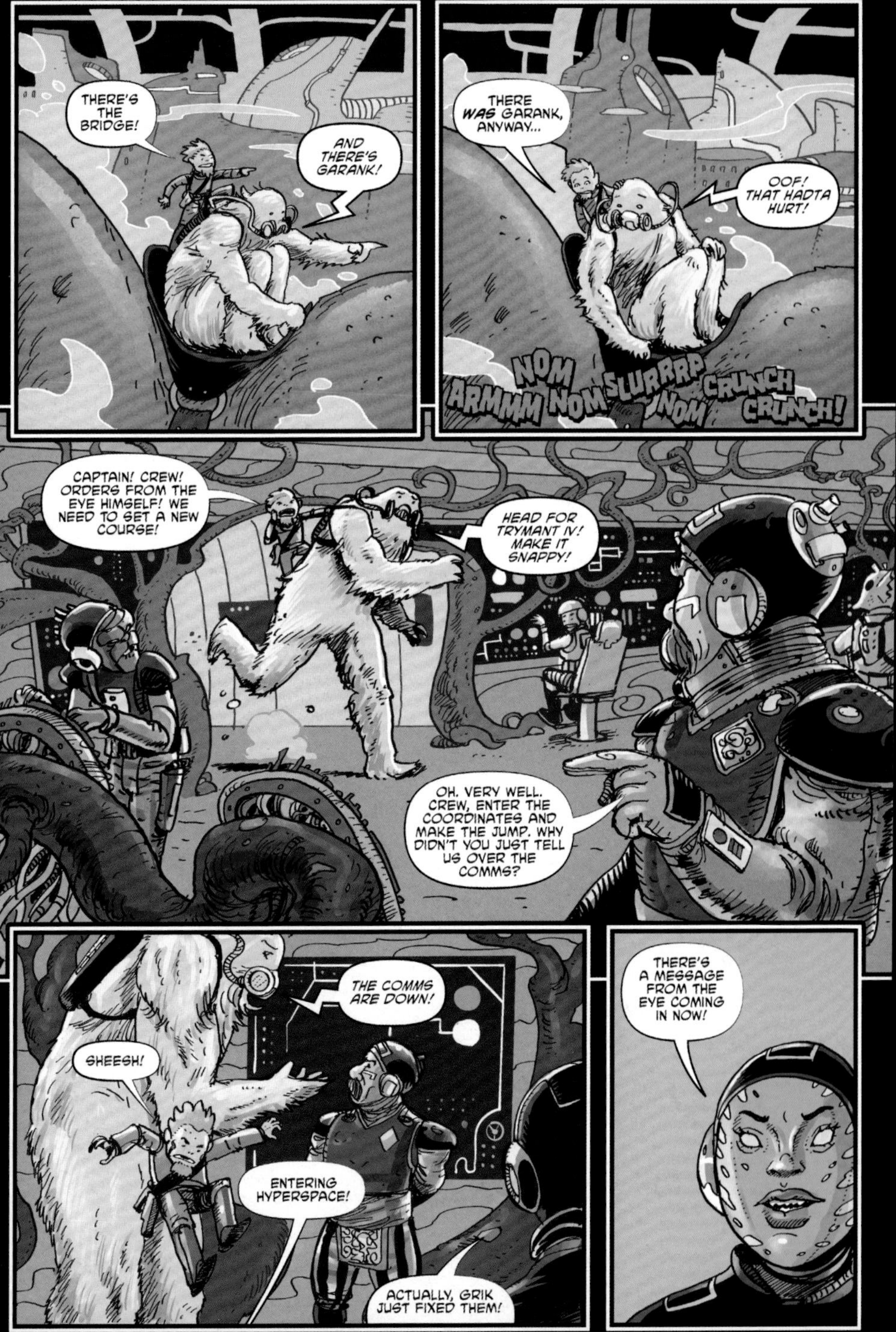
THERE'S THE BRIDGE!
AND THERE'S GARANK!
THERE *WAS* GARANK, ANYWAY...
OOF! THAT HADTA HURT!
NOM ARMMM NOM SLURRRP NOM CRUNCH CRUNCH!
CAPTAIN! CREW! ORDERS FROM THE EYE HIMSELF! WE NEED TO SET A NEW COURSE!
HEAD FOR TRYMANT IV! MAKE IT SNAPPY!
OH. VERY WELL. CREW, ENTER THE COORDINATES AND MAKE THE JUMP. WHY DIDN'T YOU JUST TELL US OVER THE COMMS?
THE COMMS ARE DOWN!
SHEESH!
ENTERING HYPERSPACE!
ACTUALLY, GRIK JUST FIXED THEM!
THERE'S A MESSAGE FROM THE EYE COMING IN NOW!

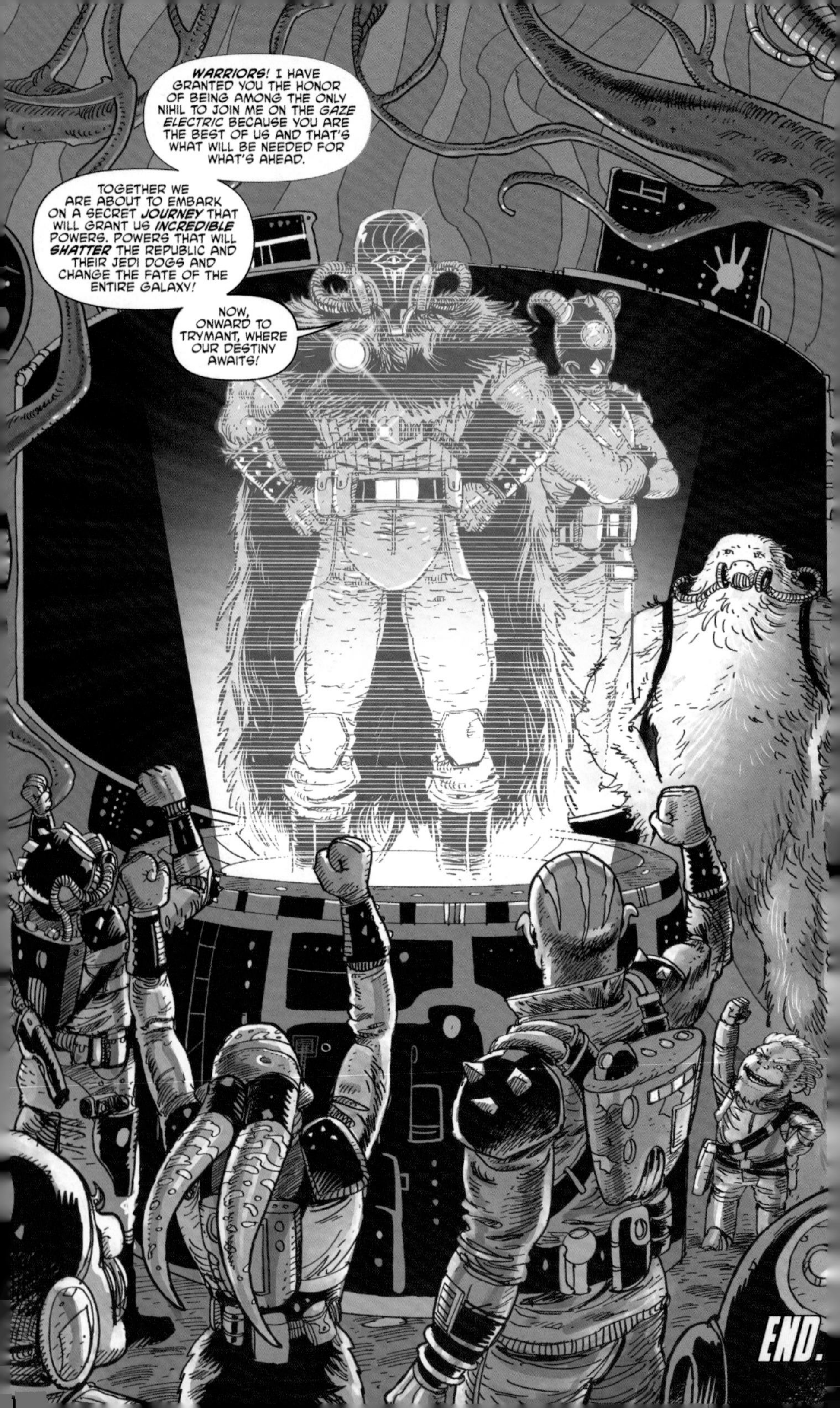
WARRIORS! I HAVE GRANTED YOU THE HONOR OF BEING AMONG THE ONLY NIHIL TO JOIN ME ON THE GAZE ELECTRIC BECAUSE YOU ARE THE BEST OF US AND THAT'S WHAT WILL BE NEEDED FOR WHAT'S AHEAD.
TOGETHER WE ARE ABOUT TO EMBARK ON A SECRET JOURNEY THAT WILL GRANT US INCREDIBLE POWERS. POWERS THAT WILL SHATTER THE REPUBLIC AND THEIR JEDI DOGS AND CHANGE THE FATE OF THE ENTIRE GALAXY!
NOW, ONWARD TO TRYMANT, WHERE OUR DESTINY AWAITS!
END.

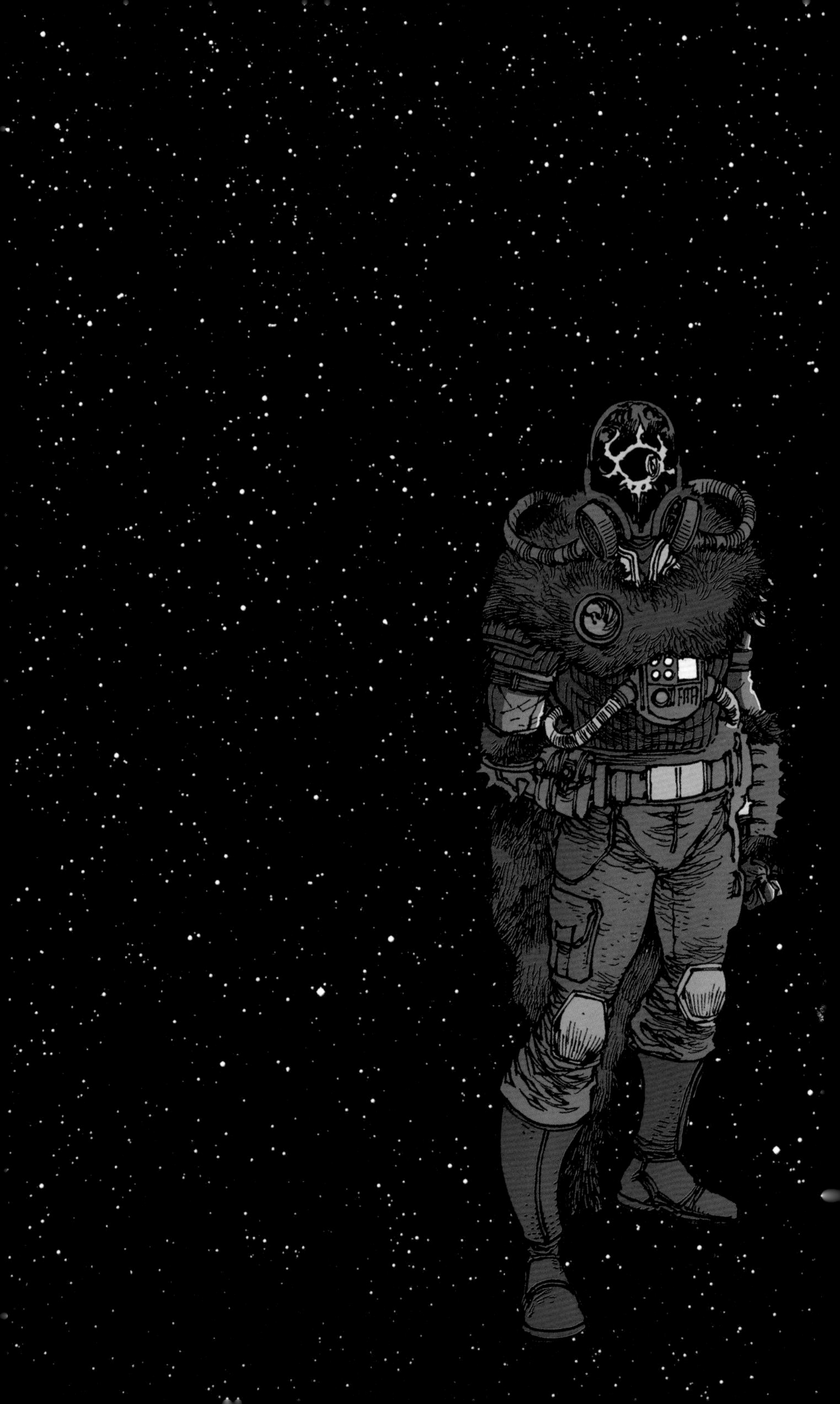

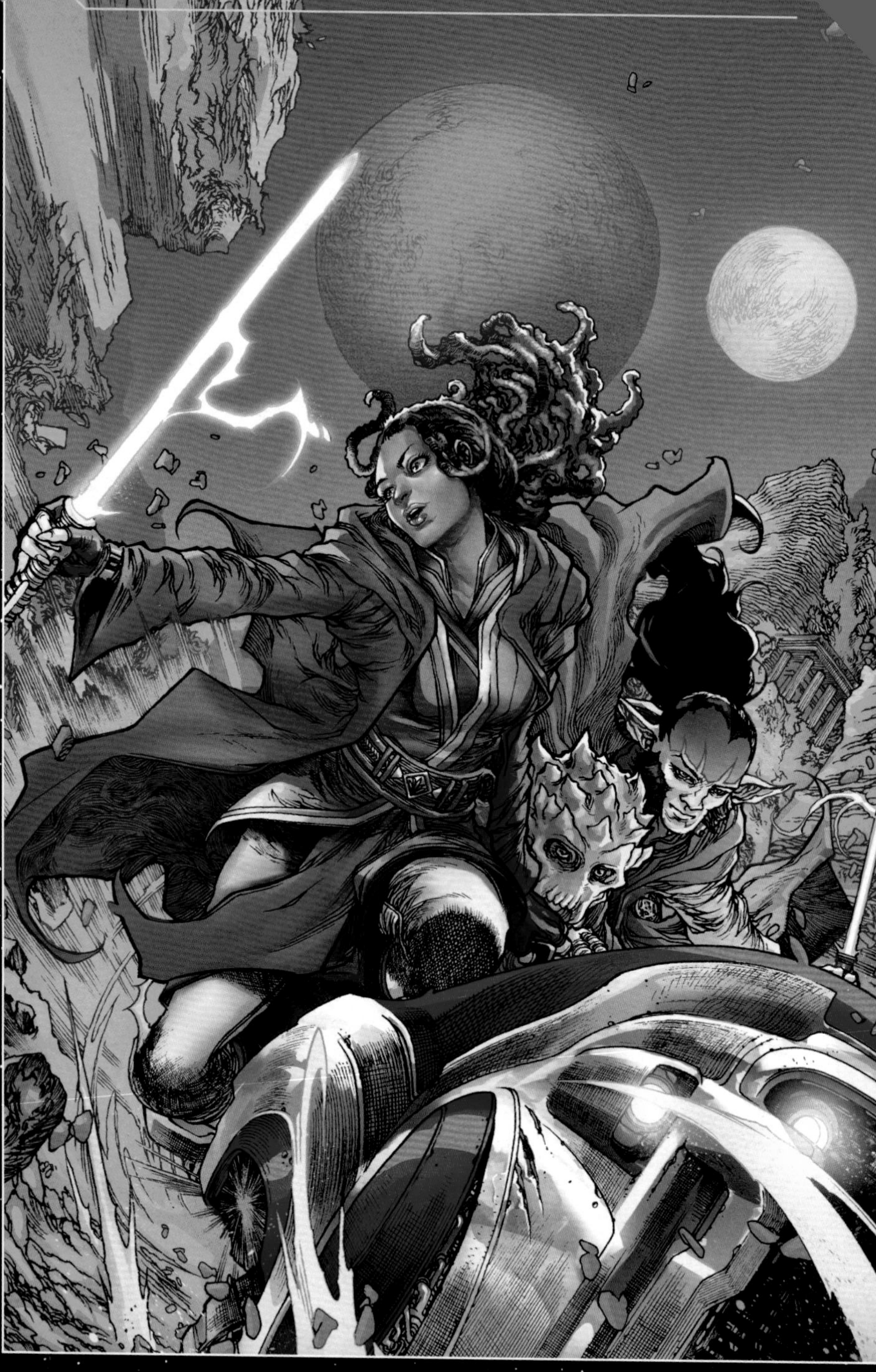

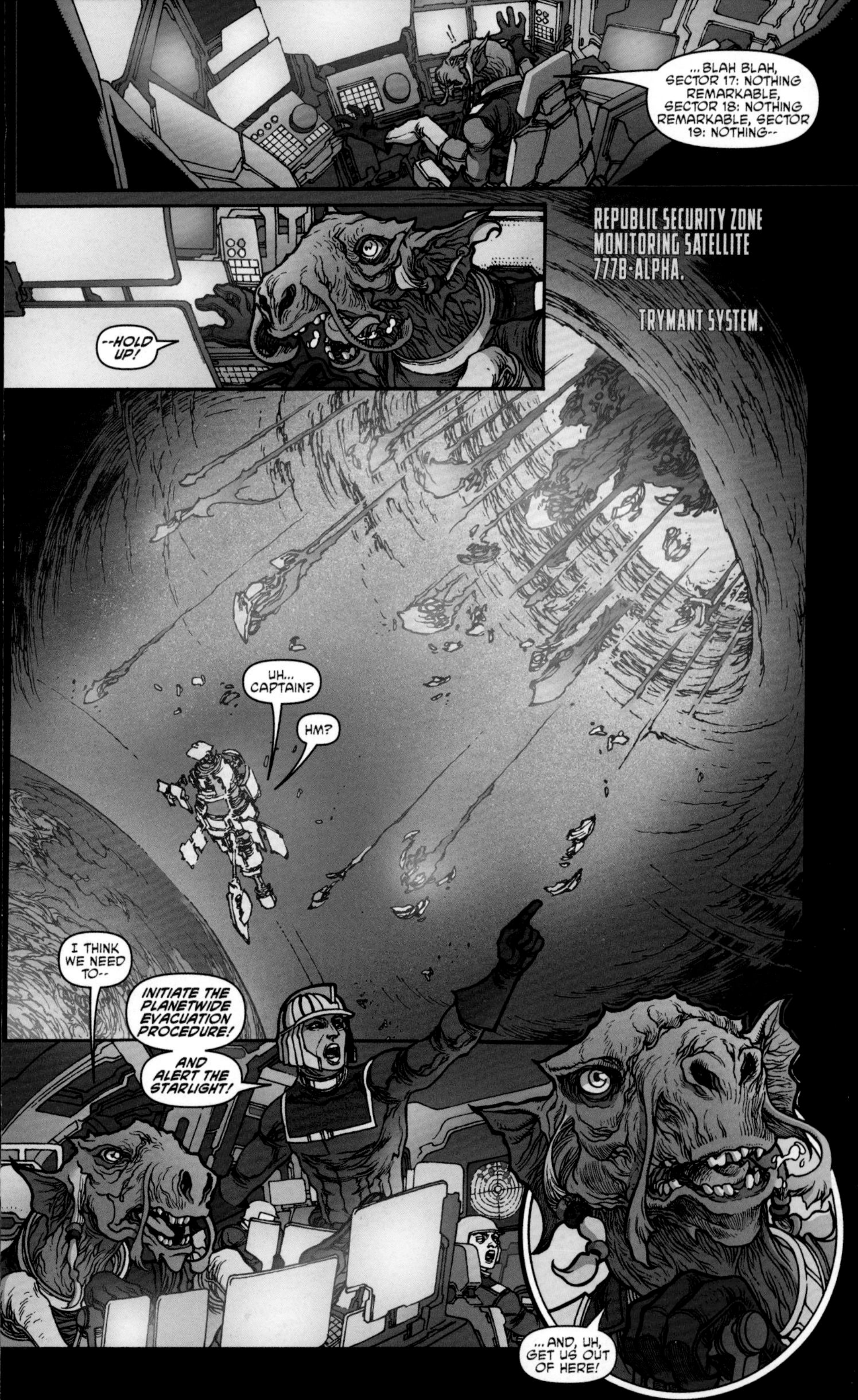
...BLAH BLAH, SECTOR 17: NOTHING REMARKABLE, SECTOR 18: NOTHING REMARKABLE, SECTOR 19: NOTHING--
REPUBLIC SECURITY ZONE MONITORING SATELLITE 7778-ALPHA.
TRYMANT SYSTEM.
--HOLD UP!
UH... CAPTAIN?
HM?
I THINK WE NEED TO--
INITIATE THE PLANETWIDE EVACUATION PROCEDURE!
AND ALERT THE STARLIGHT!
...AND, UH, GET US OUT OF HERE!

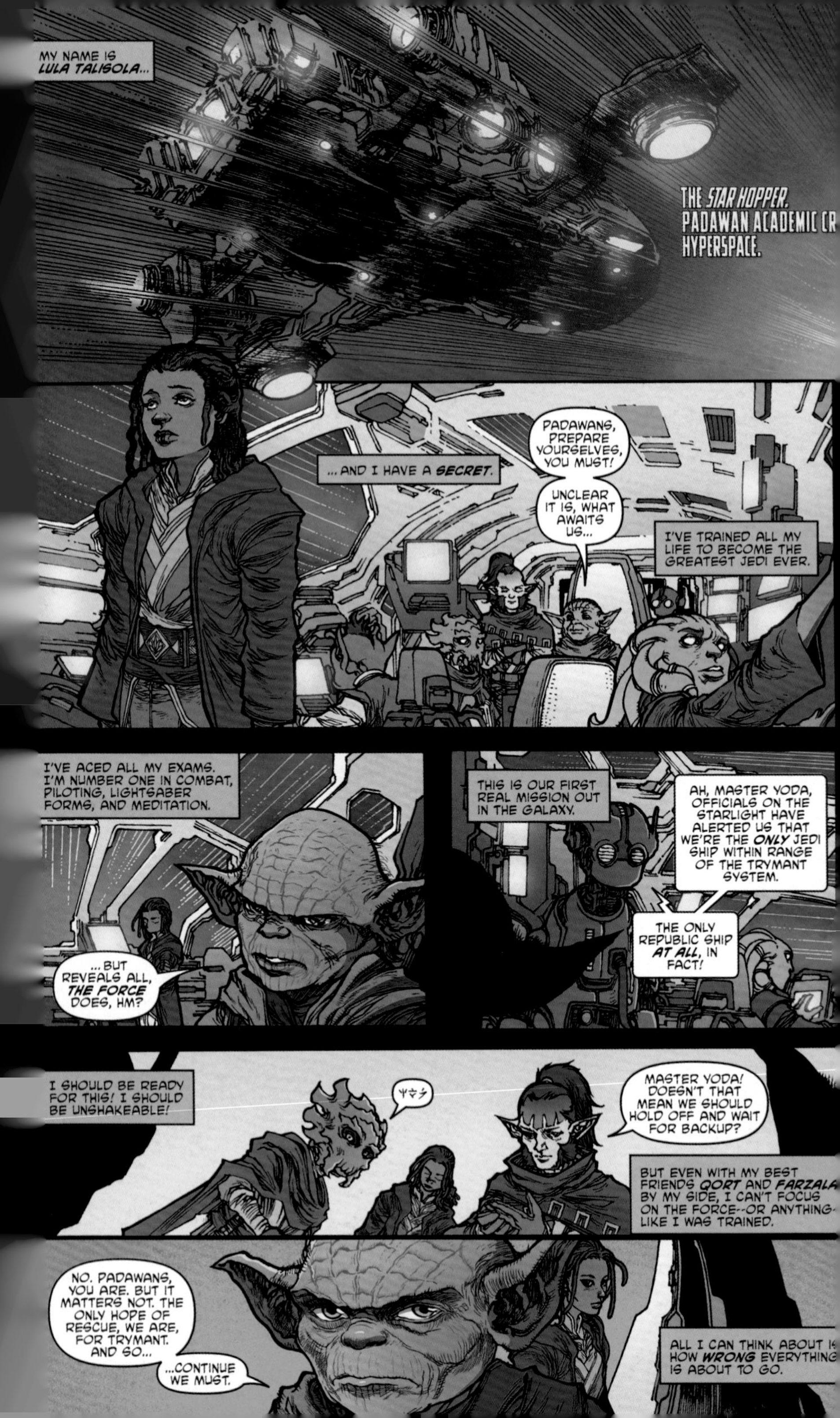

MY NAME IS LULA TALISOLA...
THE STAR HOPPER. PADAWAN ACADEMIC CR
HYPERSPACE.
...AND I HAVE A SECRET.
PADAWANS, PREPARE YOURSELVES, YOU MUST!
UNCLEAR IT IS, WHAT AWAITS US...
I'VE TRAINED ALL MY LIFE TO BECOME THE GREATEST JEDI EVER.
I'VE ACED ALL MY EXAMS. I'M NUMBER ONE IN COMBAT, PILOTING, LIGHTSABER FORMS, AND MEDITATION.
...BUT REVEALS ALL, THE FORCE DOES, HM?
THIS IS OUR FIRST REAL MISSION OUT IN THE GALAXY.
AH, MASTER YODA, OFFICIALS ON THE STARLIGHT HAVE ALERTED US THAT WE'RE THE ONLY JEDI SHIP WITHIN RANGE OF THE TRYMANT SYSTEM.
THE ONLY REPUBLIC SHIP AT ALL, IN FACT!
I SHOULD BE READY FOR THIS! I SHOULD BE UNSHAKEABLE!
MASTER YODA! DOESN'T THAT MEAN WE SHOULD HOLD OFF AND WAIT FOR BACKUP?
BUT EVEN WITH MY BEST FRIENDS QORT AND FARZALA BY MY SIDE, I CAN'T FOCUS ON THE FORCE--OR ANYTHING--LIKE I WAS TRAINED.
NO. PADAWANS, YOU ARE. BUT IT MATTERS NOT. THE ONLY HOPE OF RESCUE, WE ARE, FOR TRYMANT. AND SO...
...CONTINUE WE MUST.
ALL I CAN THINK ABOUT IS HOW WRONG EVERYTHING IS ABOUT TO GO.

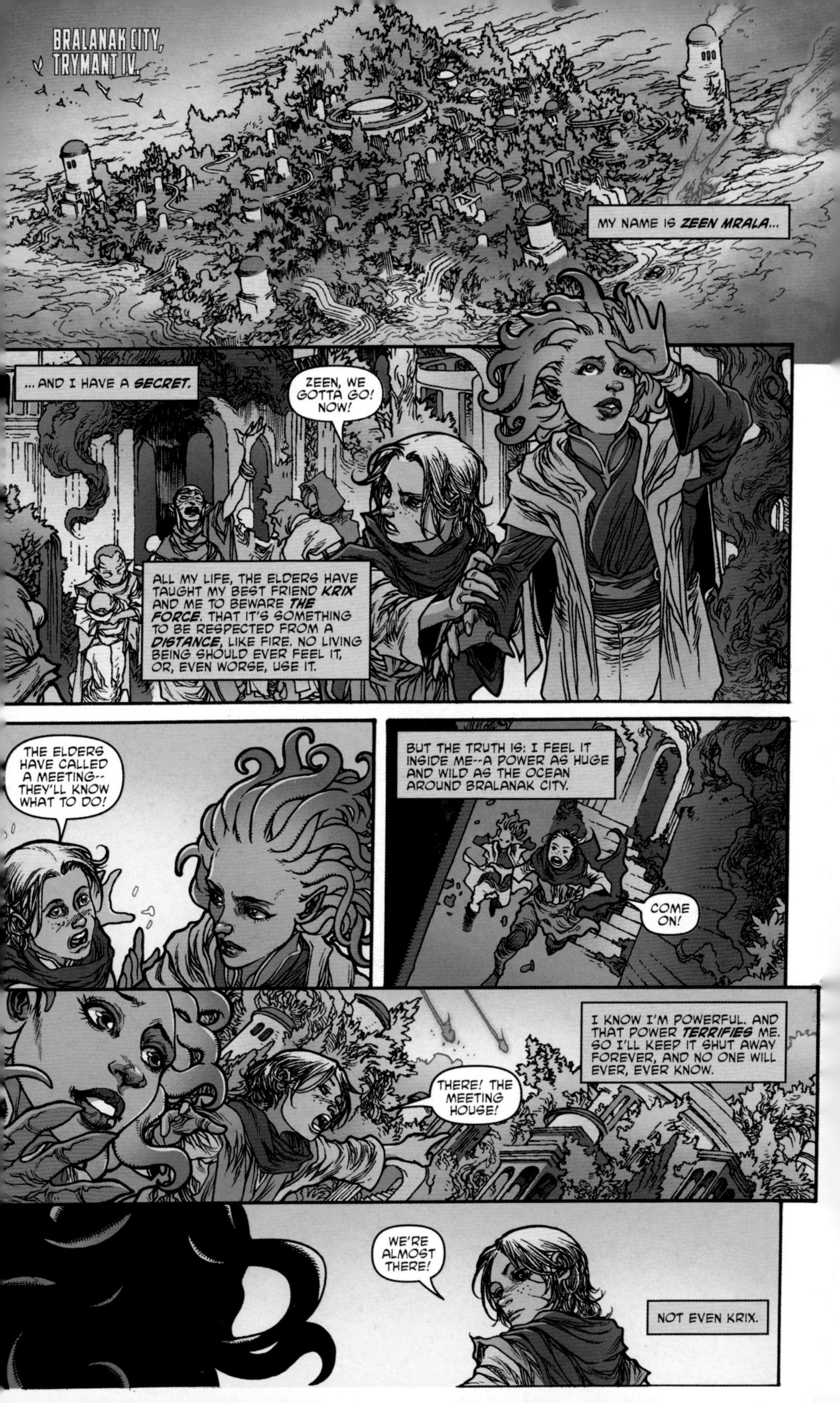
BRALANAK CITY, TRYMANT IV.
MY NAME IS ZEEN MRALA...
...AND I HAVE A SECRET.
ZEEN, WE GOTTA GO! NOW!
ALL MY LIFE, THE ELDERS HAVE TAUGHT MY BEST FRIEND KRIX AND ME TO BEWARE THE FORCE. THAT IT'S SOMETHING TO BE RESPECTED FROM A DISTANCE, LIKE FIRE. NO LIVING BEING SHOULD EVER FEEL IT, OR, EVEN WORSE, USE IT.
THE ELDERS HAVE CALLED A MEETING-- THEY'LL KNOW WHAT TO DO!
BUT THE TRUTH IS: I FEEL IT INSIDE ME--A POWER AS HUGE AND WILD AS THE OCEAN AROUND BRALANAK CITY.
COME ON!
I KNOW I'M POWERFUL. AND THAT POWER TERRIFIES ME. SO I'LL KEEP IT SHUT AWAY FOREVER, AND NO ONE WILL EVER, EVER KNOW.
THERE! THE MEETING HOUSE!
WE'RE ALMOST THERE!
NOT EVEN KRIX.

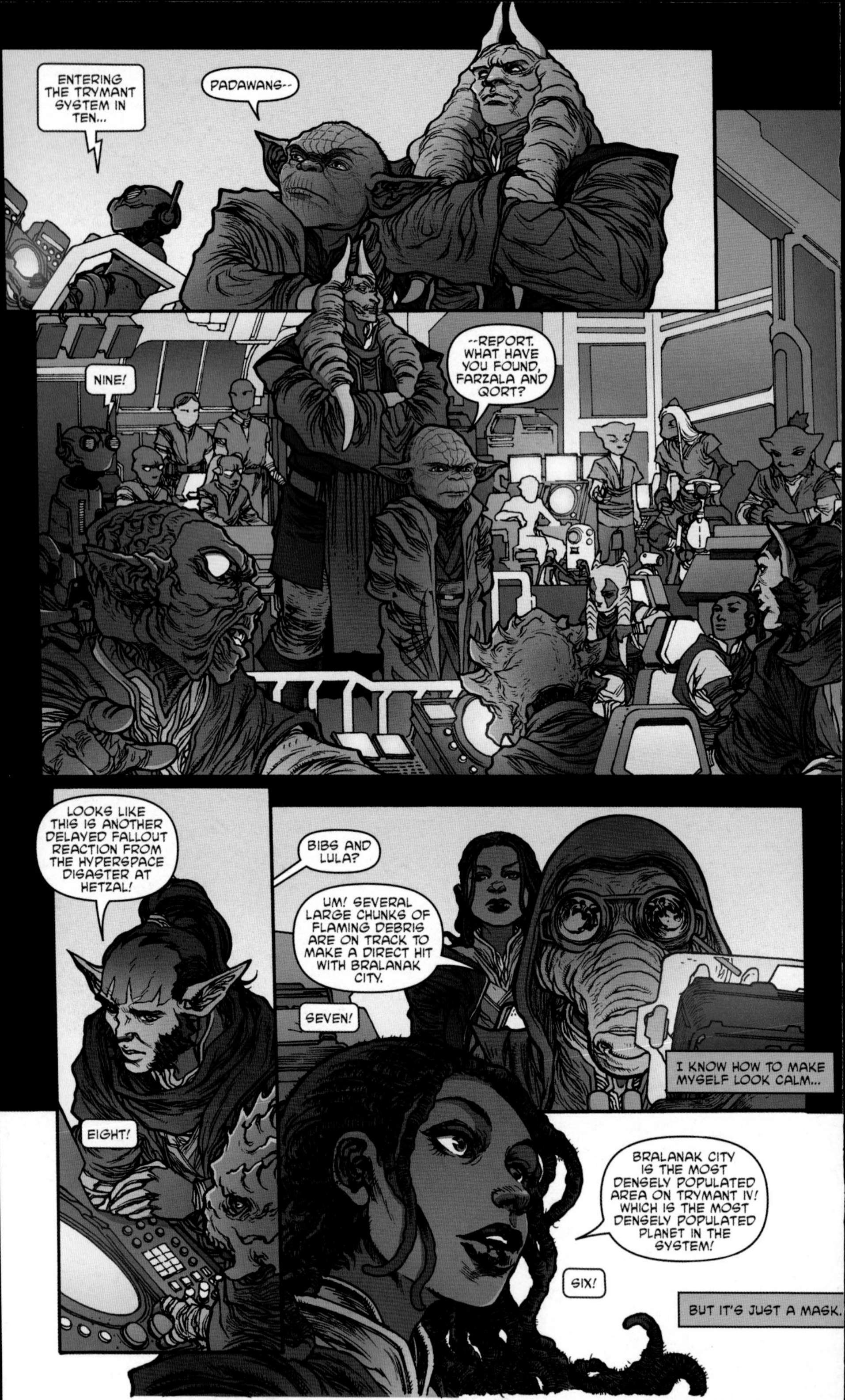
ENTERING THE TRYMANT SYSTEM IN TEN...
PADAWANS--
NINE!
--REPORT. WHAT HAVE YOU FOUND, FARZALA AND QORT?
LOOKS LIKE THIS IS ANOTHER DELAYED FALLOUT REACTION FROM THE HYPERSPACE DISASTER AT HETZAL!
EIGHT!
BIBS AND LULA?
UM! SEVERAL LARGE CHUNKS OF FLAMING DEBRIS ARE ON TRACK TO MAKE A DIRECT HIT WITH BRALANAK CITY.
SEVEN!
I KNOW HOW TO MAKE MYSELF LOOK CALM...
BRALANAK CITY IS THE MOST DENSELY POPULATED AREA ON TRYMANT IV! WHICH IS THE MOST DENSELY POPULATED PLANET IN THE SYSTEM!
SIX!
BUT IT'S JUST A MASK.

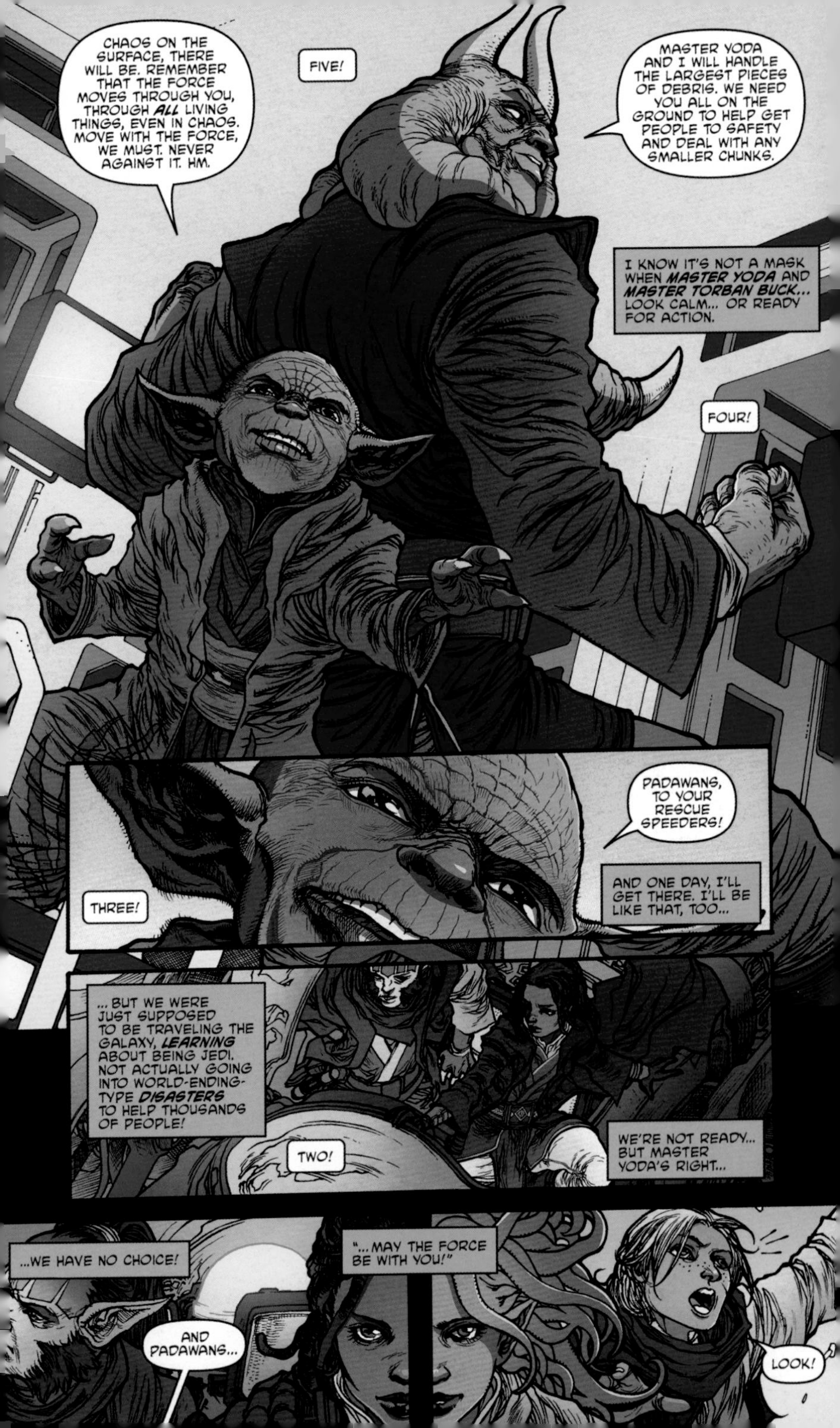

CHAOS ON THE SURFACE, THERE WILL BE. REMEMBER THAT THE FORCE MOVES THROUGH YOU, THROUGH ALL LIVING THINGS, EVEN IN CHAOS. MOVE WITH THE FORCE, WE MUST. NEVER AGAINST IT. HM.
FIVE!
MASTER YODA AND I WILL HANDLE THE LARGEST PIECES OF DEBRIS. WE NEED YOU ALL ON THE GROUND TO HELP GET PEOPLE TO SAFETY AND DEAL WITH ANY SMALLER CHUNKS.
I KNOW IT'S NOT A MASK WHEN MASTER YODA AND MASTER TORBAN BUCK... LOOK CALM... OR READY FOR ACTION.
FOUR!
PADAWANS, TO YOUR RESCUE SPEEDERS!
THREE!
AND ONE DAY, I'LL GET THERE. I'LL BE LIKE THAT, TOO...
... BUT WE WERE JUST SUPPOSED TO BE TRAVELING THE GALAXY, LEARNING ABOUT BEING JEDI. NOT ACTUALLY GOING INTO WORLD-ENDING-TYPE DISASTERS TO HELP THOUSANDS OF PEOPLE!
TWO!
WE'RE NOT READY... BUT MASTER YODA'S RIGHT...
...WE HAVE NO CHOICE!
AND PADAWANS...
"...MAY THE FORCE BE WITH YOU!"
LOOK!

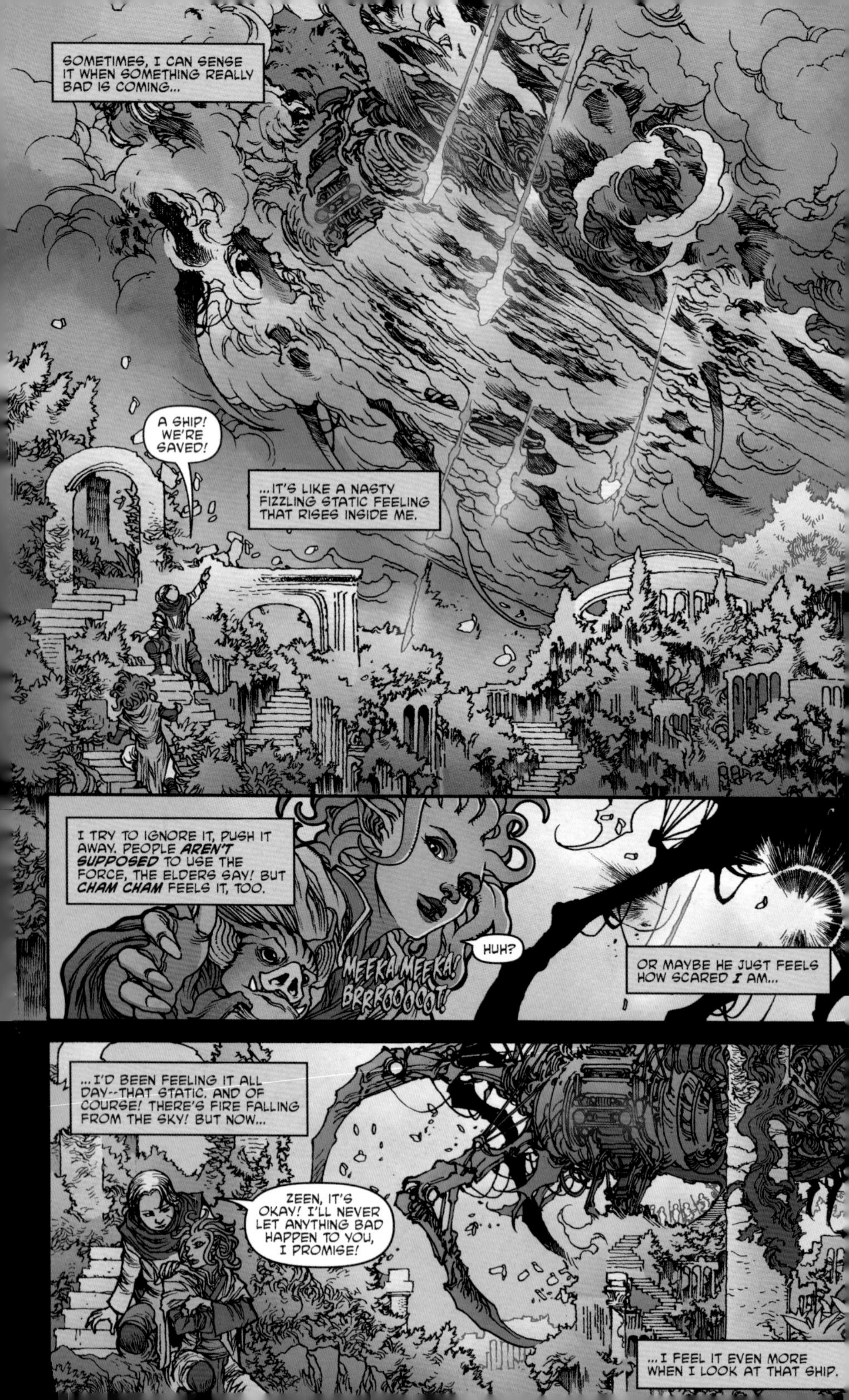
SOMETIMES, I CAN SENSE IT WHEN SOMETHING REALLY BAD IS COMING...
A SHIP! WE'RE SAVED!
...IT'S LIKE A NASTY FIZZLING STATIC FEELING THAT RISES INSIDE ME.
I TRY TO IGNORE IT, PUSH IT AWAY. PEOPLE ***AREN'T SUPPOSED*** TO USE THE FORCE, THE ELDERS SAY! BUT ***CHAM CHAM*** FEELS IT, TOO.
MEEKA MEEKA! BRRROOOOCOT!
HUH?
OR MAYBE HE JUST FEELS HOW SCARED ***I*** AM...
...I'D BEEN FEELING IT ALL DAY--THAT STATIC. AND OF COURSE! THERE'S FIRE FALLING FROM THE SKY! BUT NOW...
ZEEN, IT'S OKAY! I'LL NEVER LET ANYTHING BAD HAPPEN TO YOU, I PROMISE!
...I FEEL IT EVEN MORE WHEN I LOOK AT THAT SHIP.

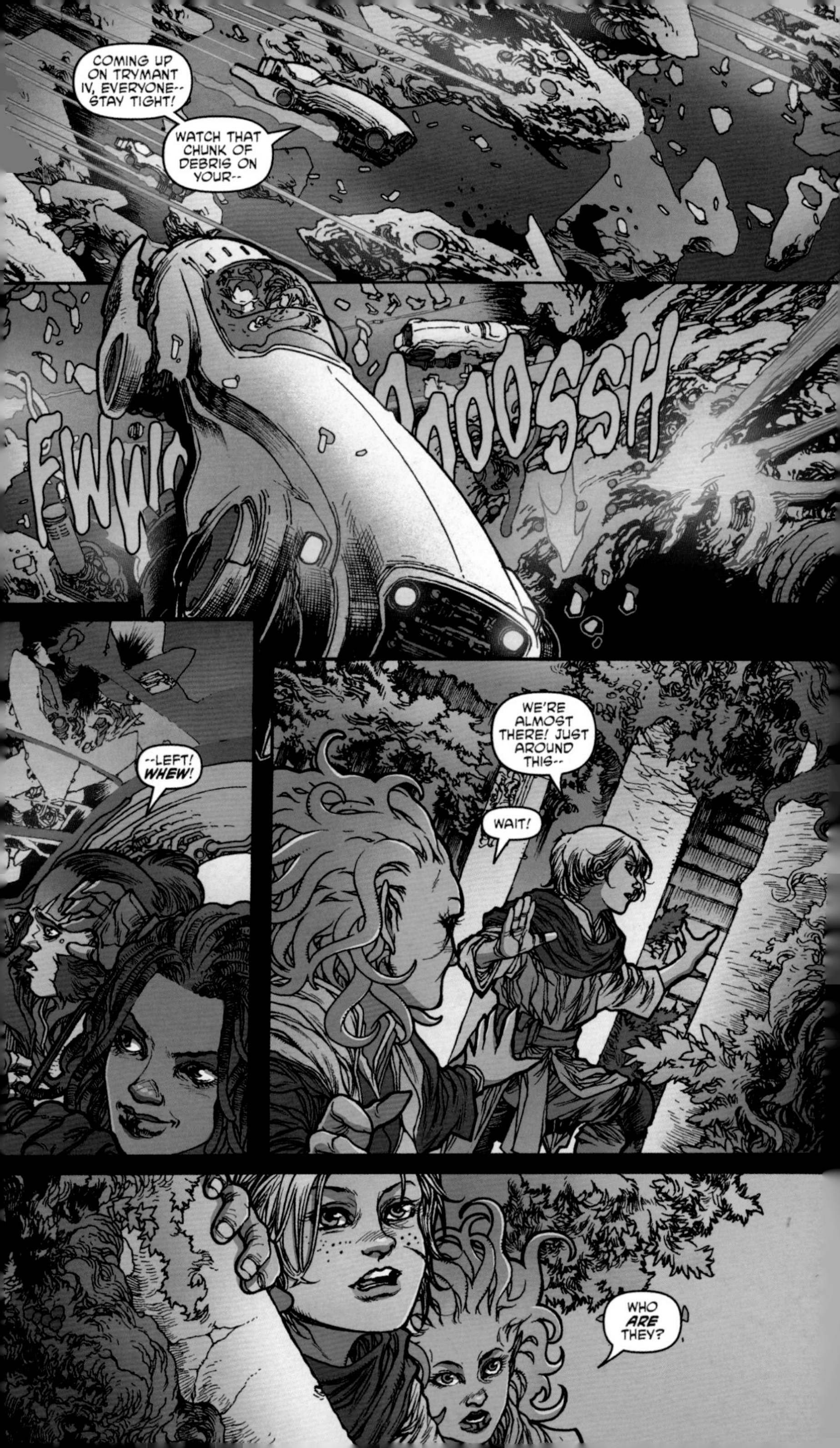
COMING UP ON TRYMANT IV, EVERYONE-- STAY TIGHT!
WATCH THAT CHUNK OF DEBRIS ON YOUR--
FWWOOOOSSH
--LEFT! *WHEW!*
WE'RE ALMOST THERE! JUST AROUND THIS--
WAIT!
WHO *ARE* THEY?

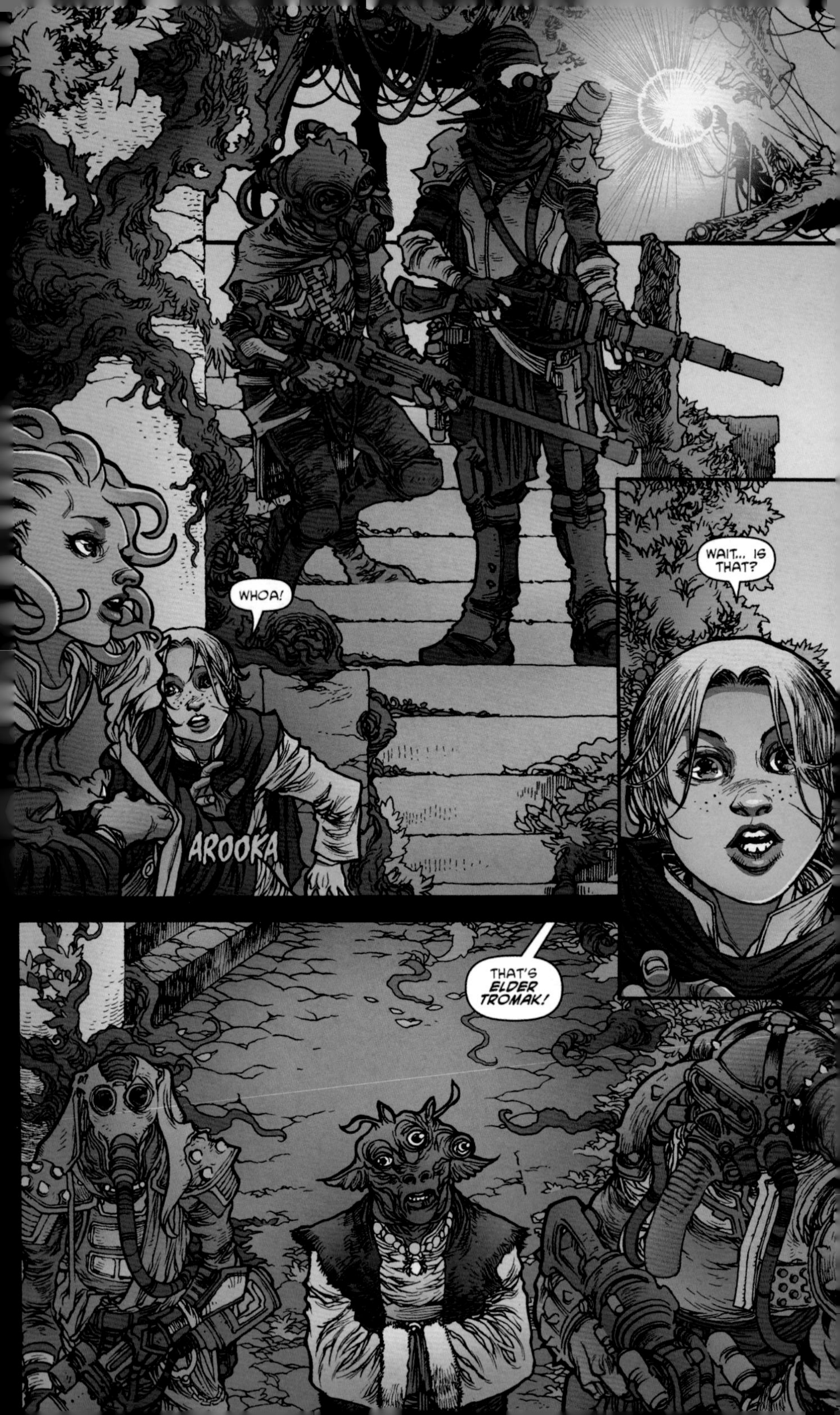
WHOA!
AROOKA
WAIT... IS THAT?
THAT'S *ELDER TROMAK!*

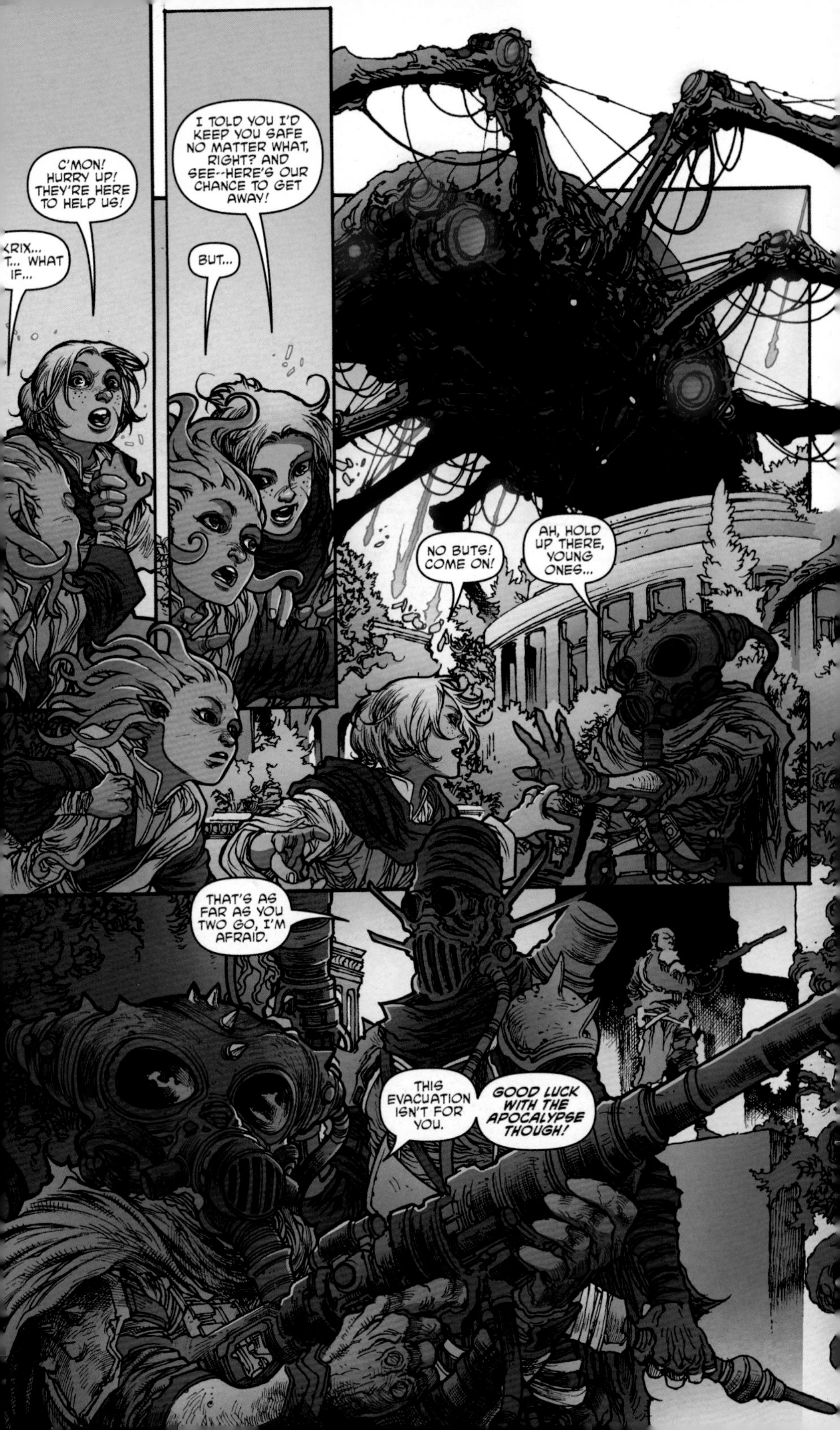
C'MON! HURRY UP! THEY'RE HERE TO HELP US!
<RIX... T... WHAT IF...
I TOLD YOU I'D KEEP YOU SAFE NO MATTER WHAT, RIGHT? AND SEE--HERE'S OUR CHANCE TO GET AWAY!
BUT...
NO BUTS! COME ON!
AH, HOLD UP THERE, YOUNG ONES...
THAT'S AS FAR AS YOU TWO GO, I'M AFRAID.
THIS EVACUATION ISN'T FOR YOU.
GOOD LUCK WITH THE APOCALYPSE THOUGH!

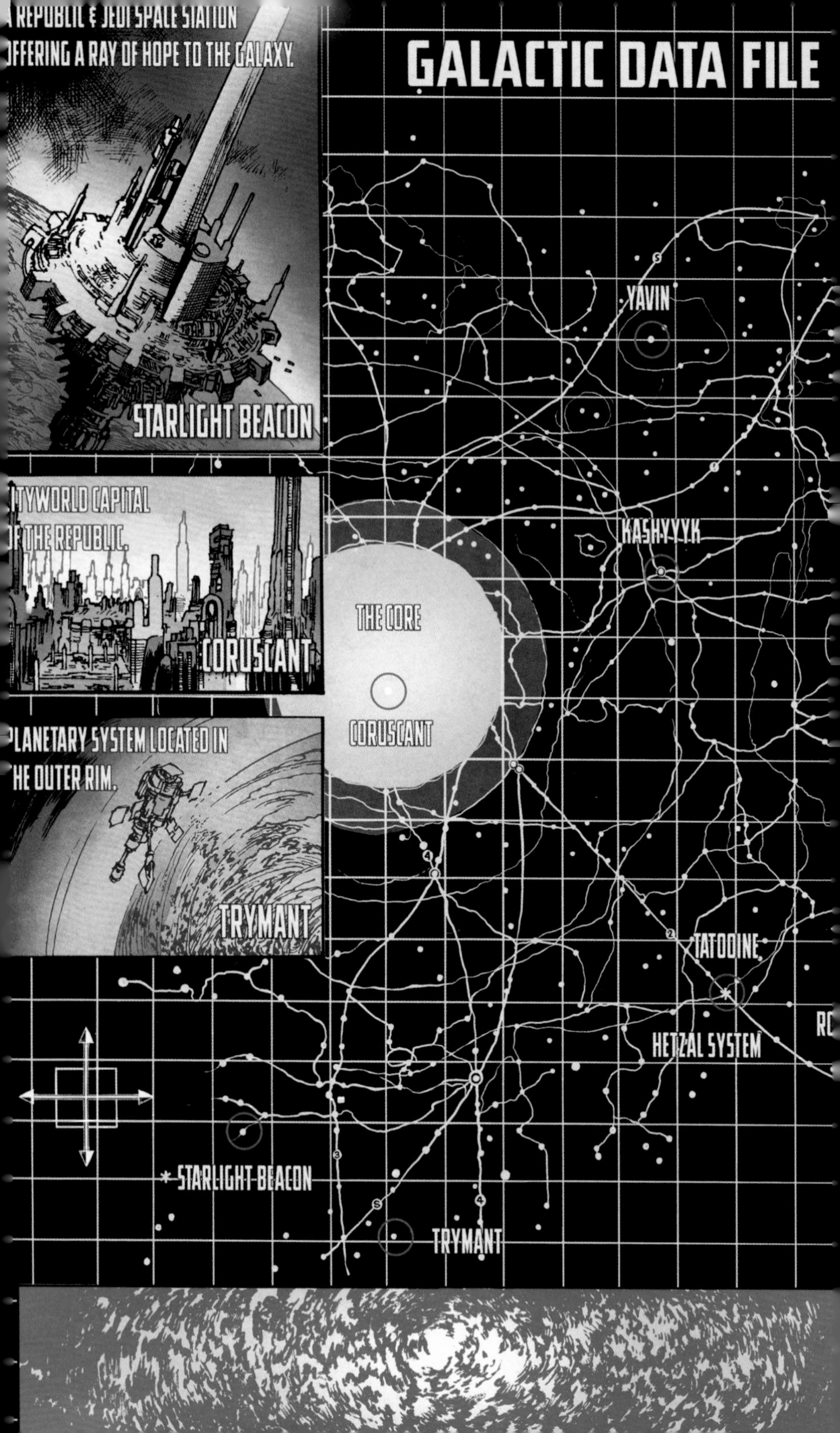
GALACTIC DATA FILE
A REPUBLIC & JEDI SPACE STATION
OFFERING A RAY OF HOPE TO THE GALAXY.
STARLIGHT BEACON
ITYWORLD CAPITAL
F THE REPUBLIC.
CORUSCANT
PLANETARY SYSTEM LOCATED IN
HE OUTER RIM.
TRYMANT
YAVIN
KASHYYYK
THE CORE
CORUSCANT
TATOOINE
HETZAL SYSTEM
* STARLIGHT BEACON
TRYMANT

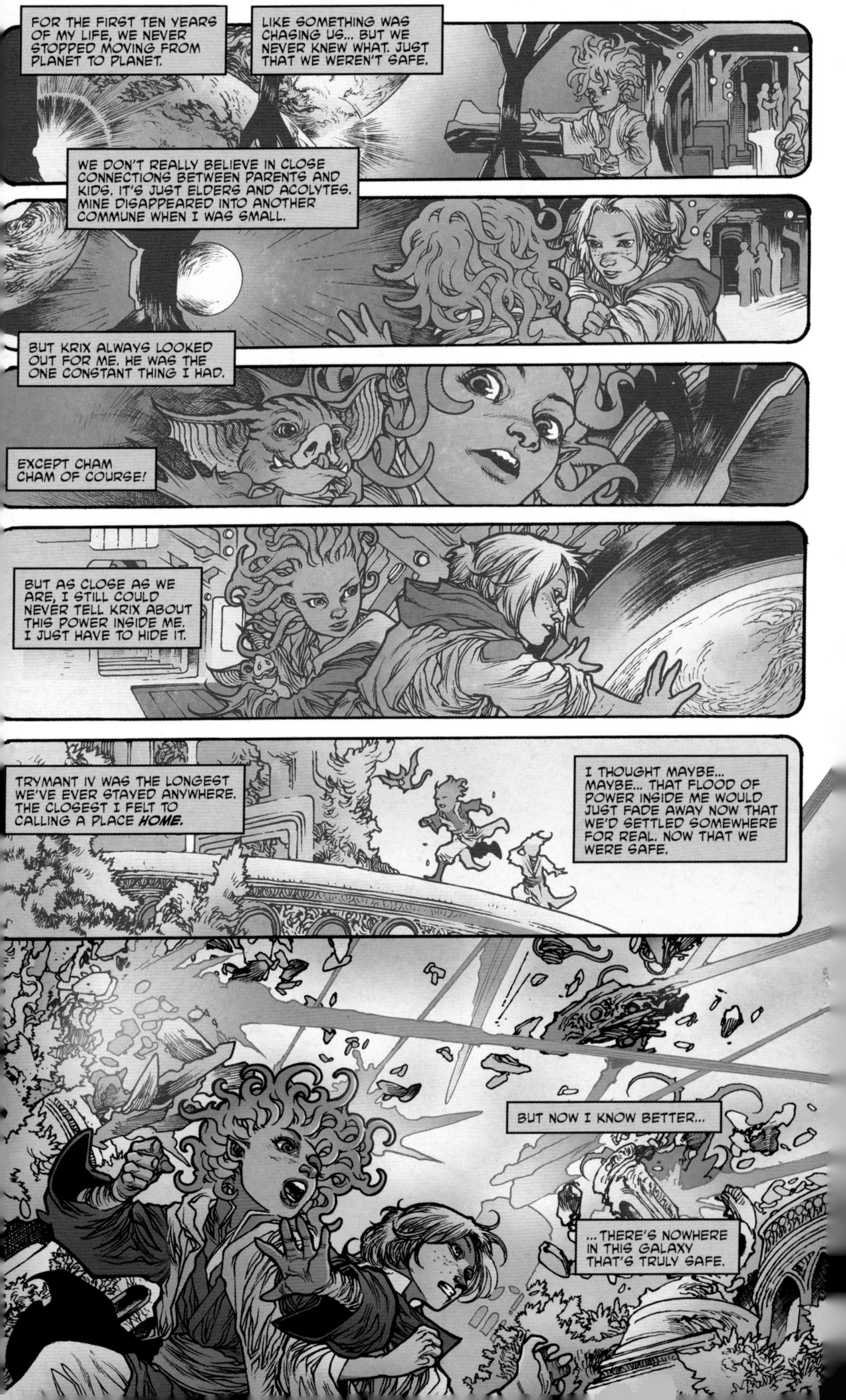
FOR THE FIRST TEN YEARS OF MY LIFE, WE NEVER STOPPED MOVING FROM PLANET TO PLANET.
LIKE SOMETHING WAS CHASING US... BUT WE NEVER KNEW WHAT. JUST THAT WE WEREN'T SAFE.
WE DON'T REALLY BELIEVE IN CLOSE CONNECTIONS BETWEEN PARENTS AND KIDS. IT'S JUST ELDERS AND ACOLYTES. MINE DISAPPEARED INTO ANOTHER COMMUNE WHEN I WAS SMALL.
BUT KRIX ALWAYS LOOKED OUT FOR ME. HE WAS THE ONE CONSTANT THING I HAD.
EXCEPT CHAM CHAM OF COURSE!
BUT AS CLOSE AS WE ARE, I STILL COULD NEVER TELL KRIX ABOUT THIS POWER INSIDE ME. I JUST HAVE TO HIDE IT.
TRYMANT IV WAS THE LONGEST WE'VE EVER STAYED ANYWHERE. THE CLOSEST I FELT TO CALLING A PLACE *HOME.*
I THOUGHT MAYBE... MAYBE... THAT FLOOD OF POWER INSIDE ME WOULD JUST FADE AWAY NOW THAT WE'D SETTLED SOMEWHERE FOR REAL. NOW THAT WE WERE SAFE.
BUT NOW I KNOW BETTER...
...THERE'S NOWHERE IN THIS GALAXY THAT'S TRULY SAFE.

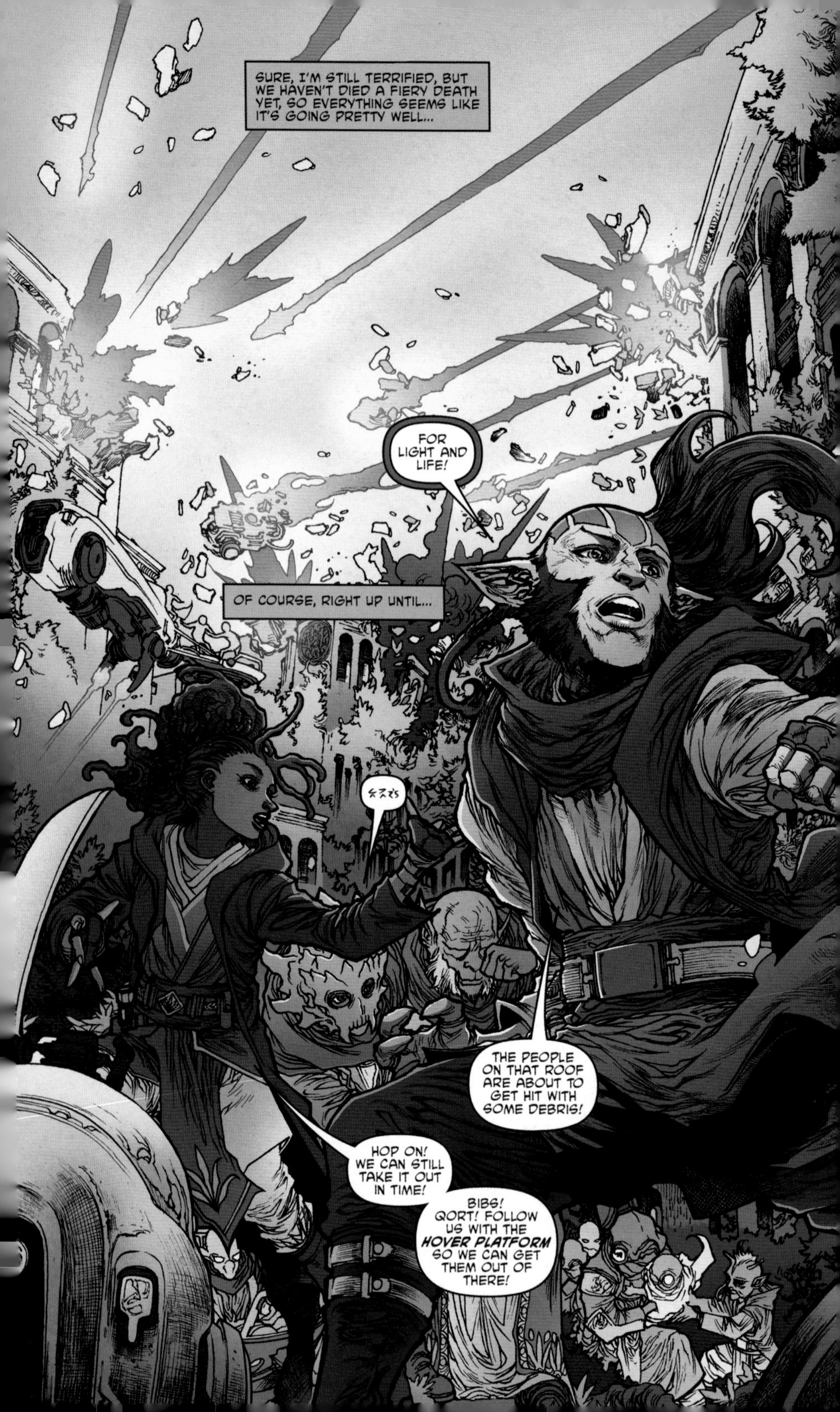
SURE, I'M STILL TERRIFIED, BUT WE HAVEN'T DIED A FIERY DEATH YET, SO EVERYTHING SEEMS LIKE IT'S GOING PRETTY WELL...
FOR LIGHT AND LIFE!
OF COURSE, RIGHT UP UNTIL...
THE PEOPLE ON THAT ROOF ARE ABOUT TO GET HIT WITH SOME DEBRIS!
HOP ON! WE CAN STILL TAKE IT OUT IN TIME!
BIBS! QORT! FOLLOW US WITH THE **HOVER PLATFORM** SO WE CAN GET THEM OUT OF THERE!

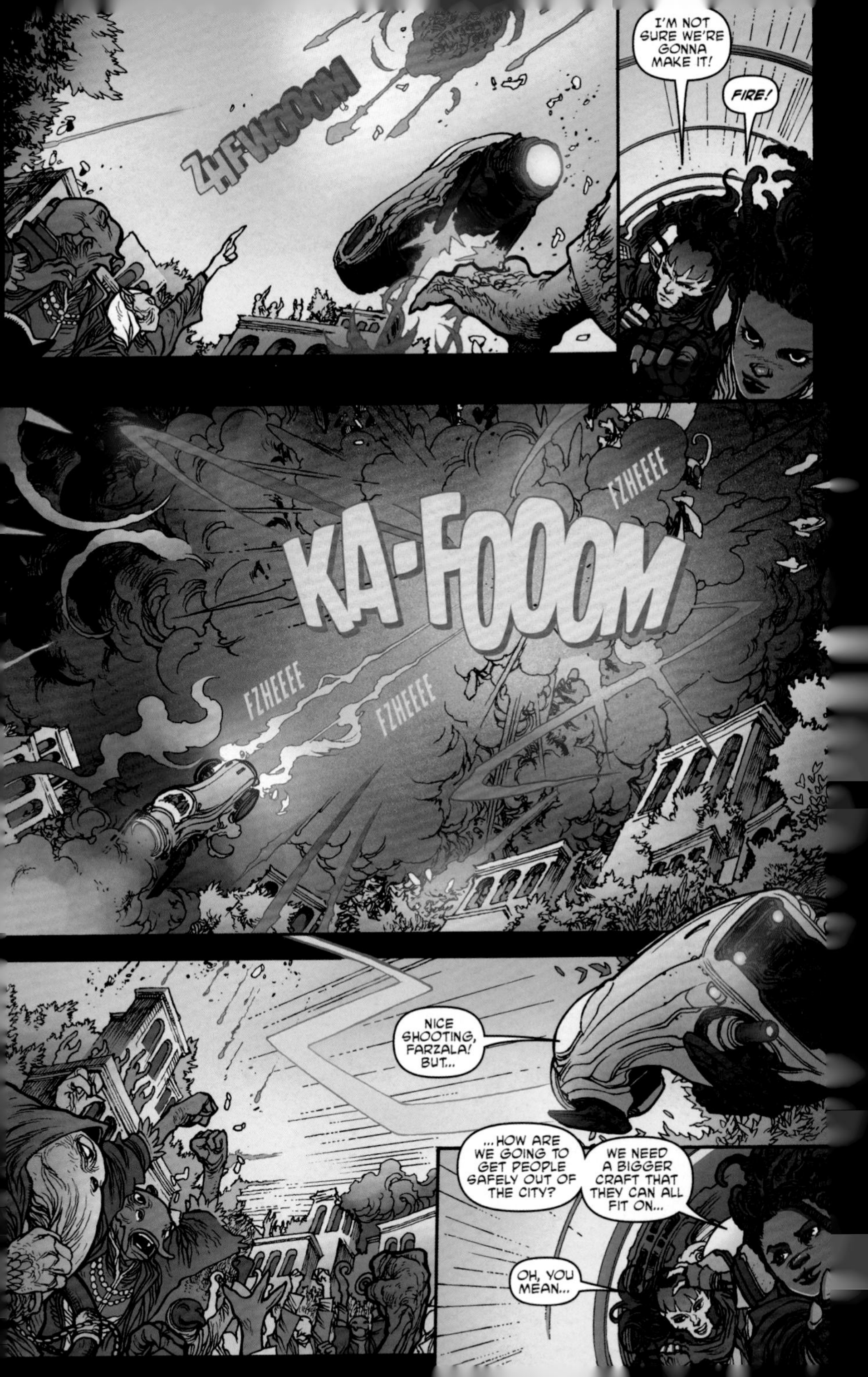
ZHFWOOOM
I'M NOT SURE WE'RE GONNA MAKE IT!
FIRE!
KA-FOOOM
FZHEEEE
FZHEEEE
FZHEEEE
NICE SHOOTING, FARZALA! BUT...
...HOW ARE WE GOING TO GET PEOPLE SAFELY OUT OF THE CITY?
WE NEED A BIGGER CRAFT THAT THEY CAN ALL FIT ON...
OH, YOU MEAN...

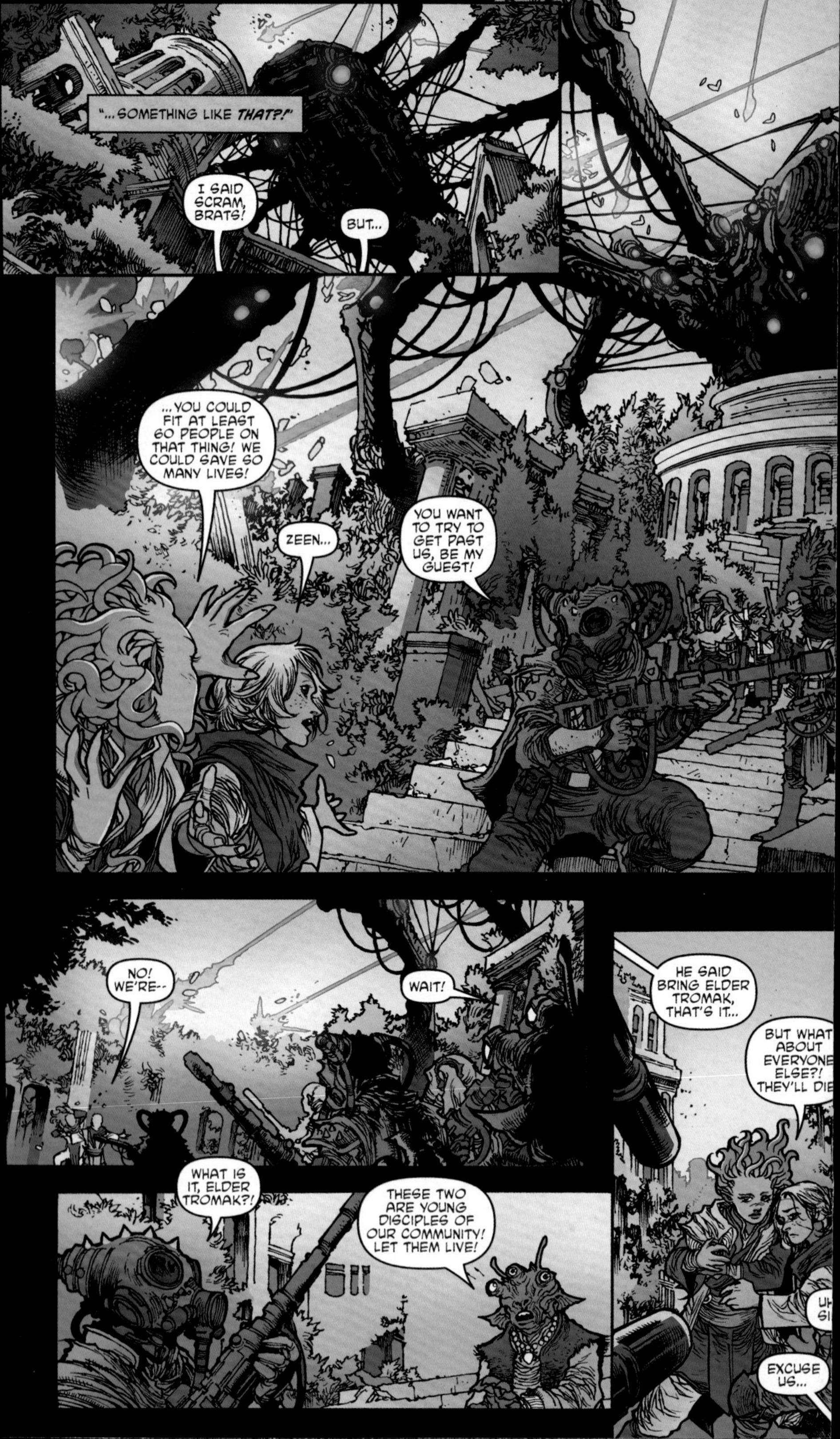
"...SOMETHING LIKE *THAT?!*"
I SAID SCRAM, BRATS!
BUT...
...YOU COULD FIT AT LEAST 60 PEOPLE ON THAT THING! WE COULD SAVE SO MANY LIVES!
ZEEN...
YOU WANT TO TRY TO GET PAST US, BE MY GUEST!
NO! WE'RE--
WAIT!
WHAT IS IT, ELDER TROMAK?!
THESE TWO ARE YOUNG DISCIPLES OF OUR COMMUNITY! LET THEM LIVE!
HE SAID BRING ELDER TROMAK, THAT'S IT...
EXCUSE US...

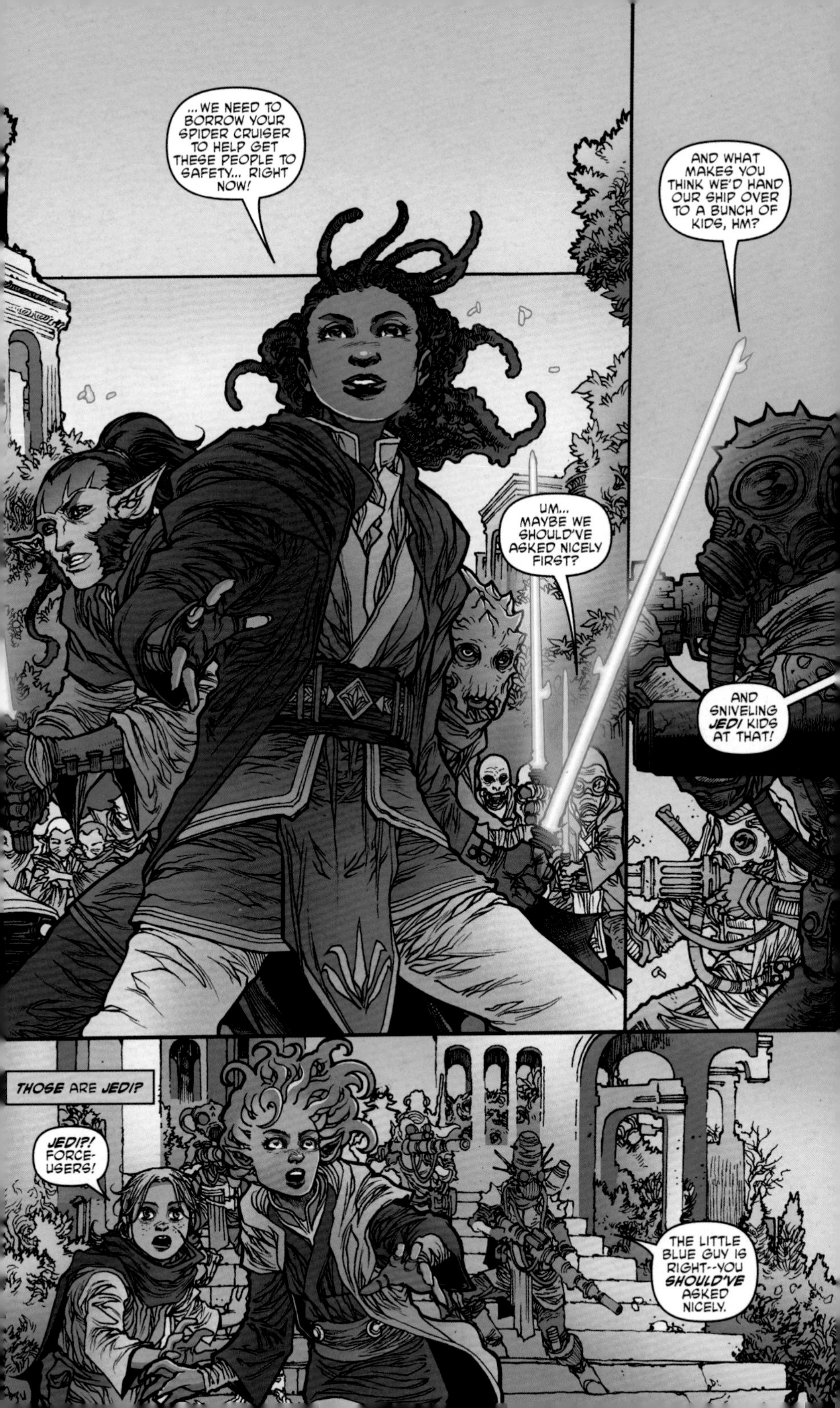
...WE NEED TO BORROW YOUR SPIDER CRUISER TO HELP GET THESE PEOPLE TO SAFETY... RIGHT NOW!
UM... MAYBE WE SHOULD'VE ASKED NICELY FIRST?
AND WHAT MAKES YOU THINK WE'D HAND OUR SHIP OVER TO A BUNCH OF KIDS, HM?
AND SNIVELING JEDI KIDS AT THAT!
THOSE ARE JEDI?
JEDI?! FORCE-USERS!
THE LITTLE BLUE GUY IS RIGHT--YOU SHOULD'VE ASKED NICELY.

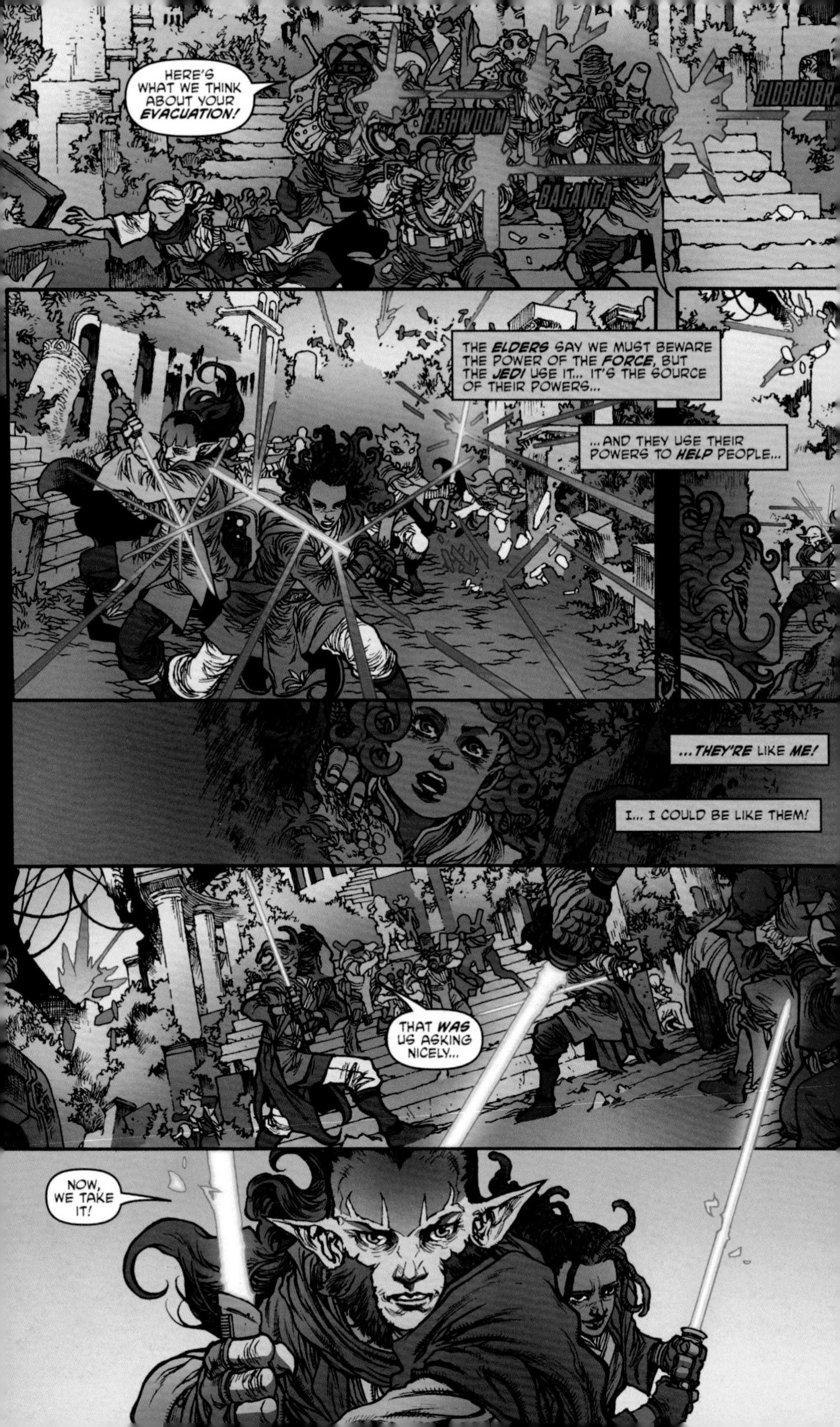
HERE'S WHAT WE THINK ABOUT YOUR *EVACUATION!*
FASHWOOM
BIDIBIBR
BAGANGA
THE *ELDERS* SAY WE MUST BEWARE THE POWER OF THE *FORCE*, BUT THE *JEDI* USE IT... IT'S THE SOURCE OF THEIR POWERS...
...AND THEY USE THEIR POWERS TO *HELP* PEOPLE...
...THEY'RE LIKE *ME!*
I... I COULD BE LIKE THEM!
THAT *WAS* US ASKING NICELY...
NOW, WE TAKE IT!

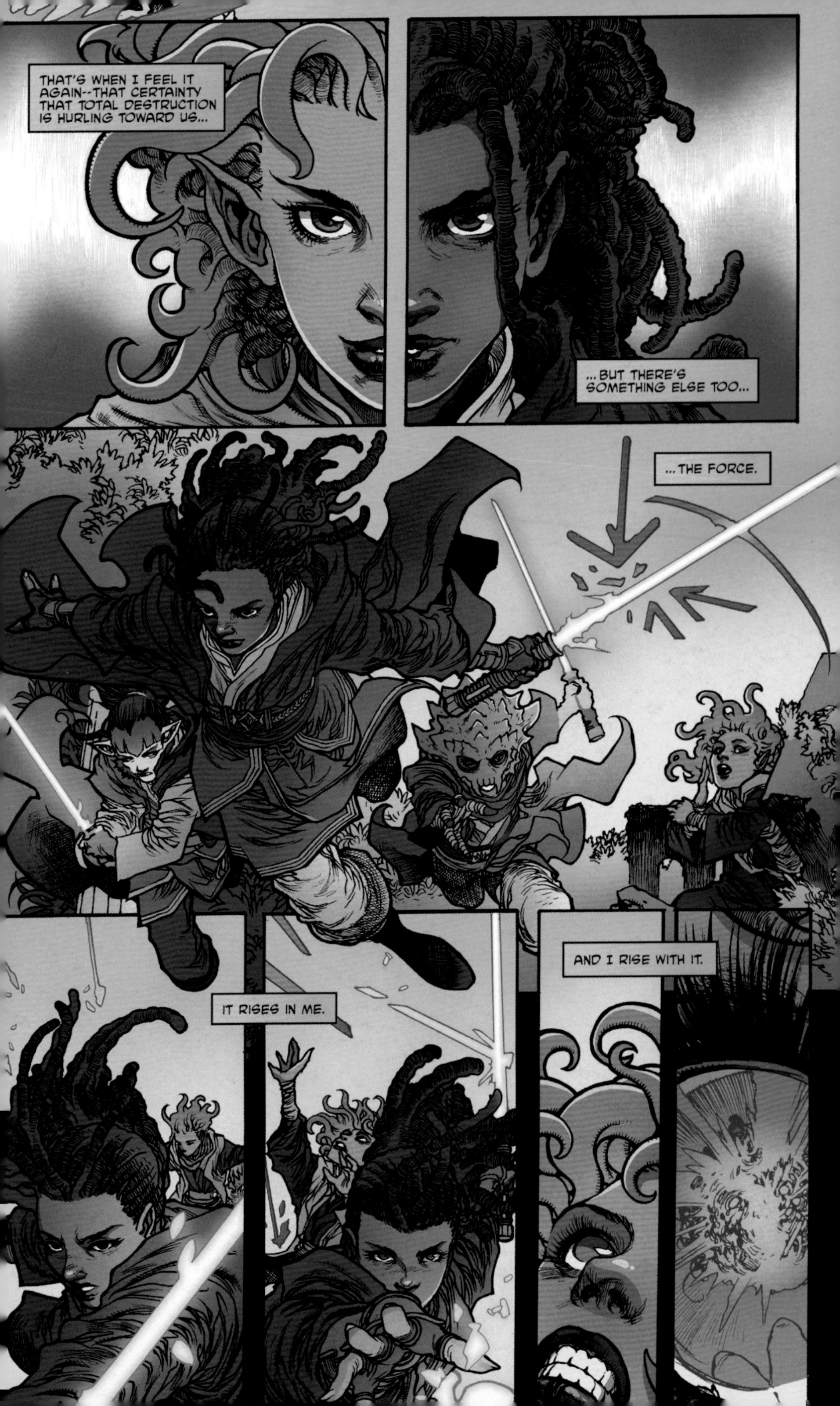
THAT'S WHEN I FEEL IT AGAIN--THAT CERTAINTY THAT TOTAL DESTRUCTION IS HURLING TOWARD US...
...BUT THERE'S SOMETHING ELSE TOO...
...THE FORCE.
IT RISES IN ME.
AND I RISE WITH IT.

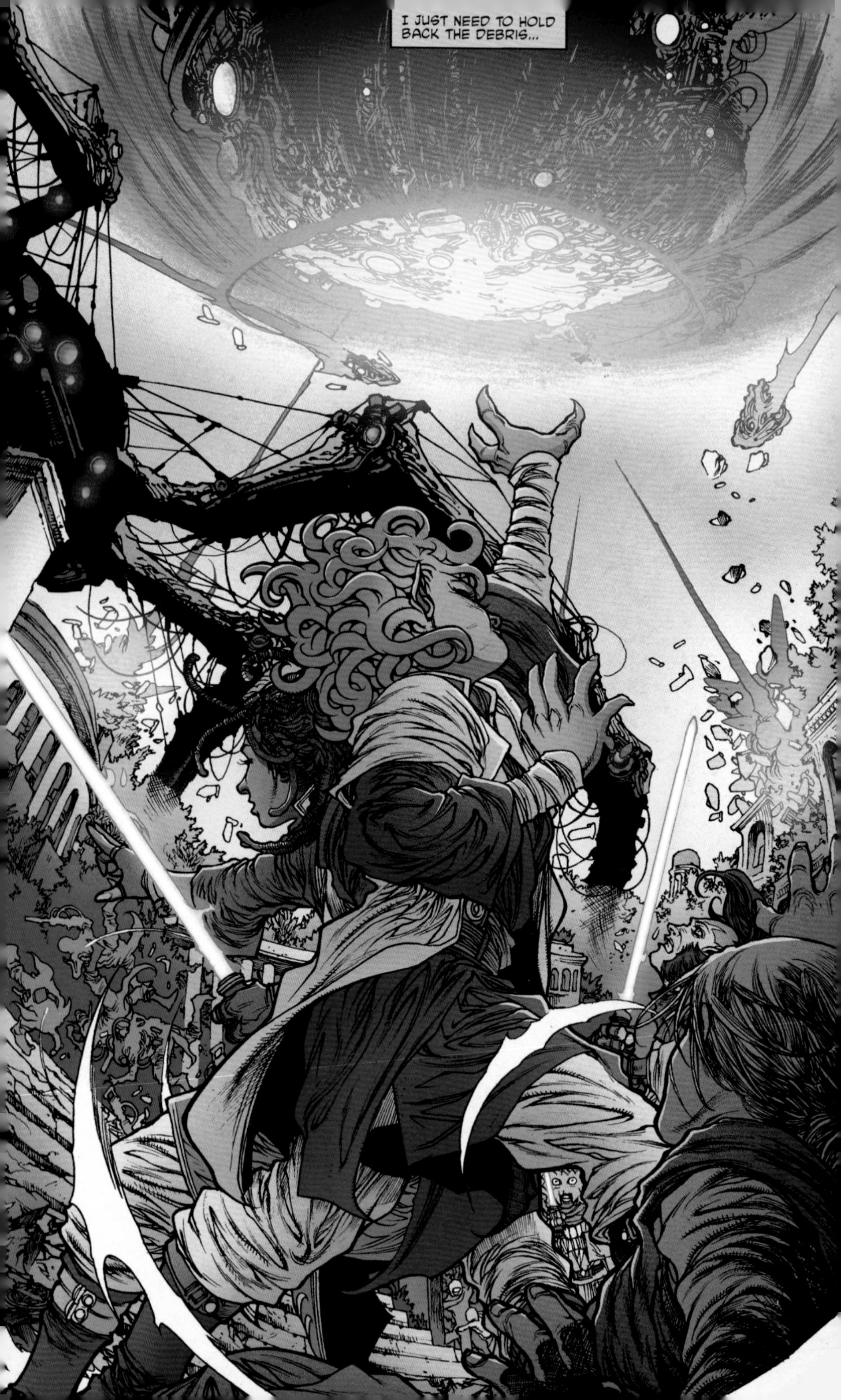
I JUST NEED TO HOLD BACK THE DEBRIS...

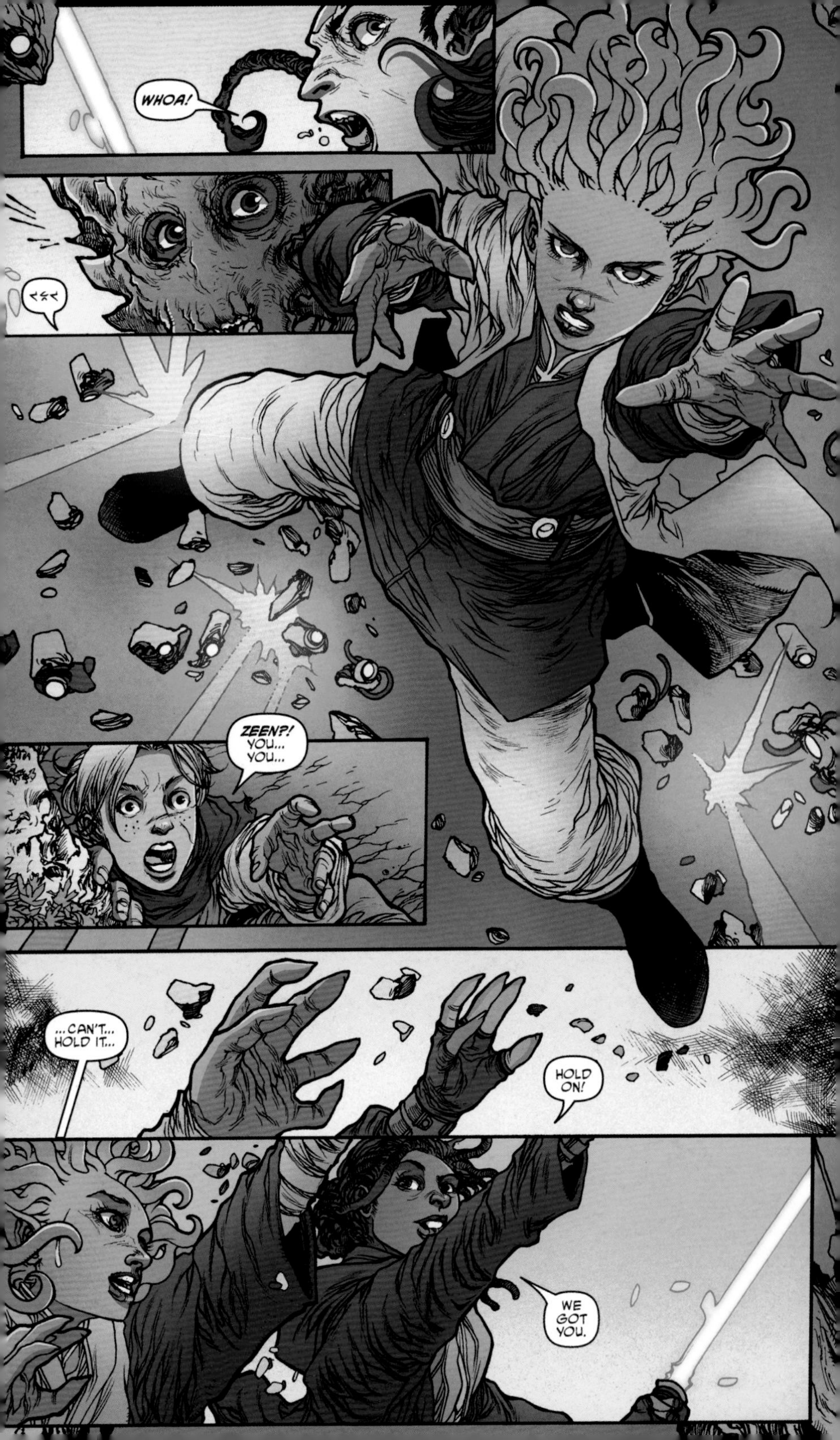
WHOA!
ZEEN?! YOU... YOU...
...CAN'T... HOLD IT...
HOLD ON!
WE GOT YOU.

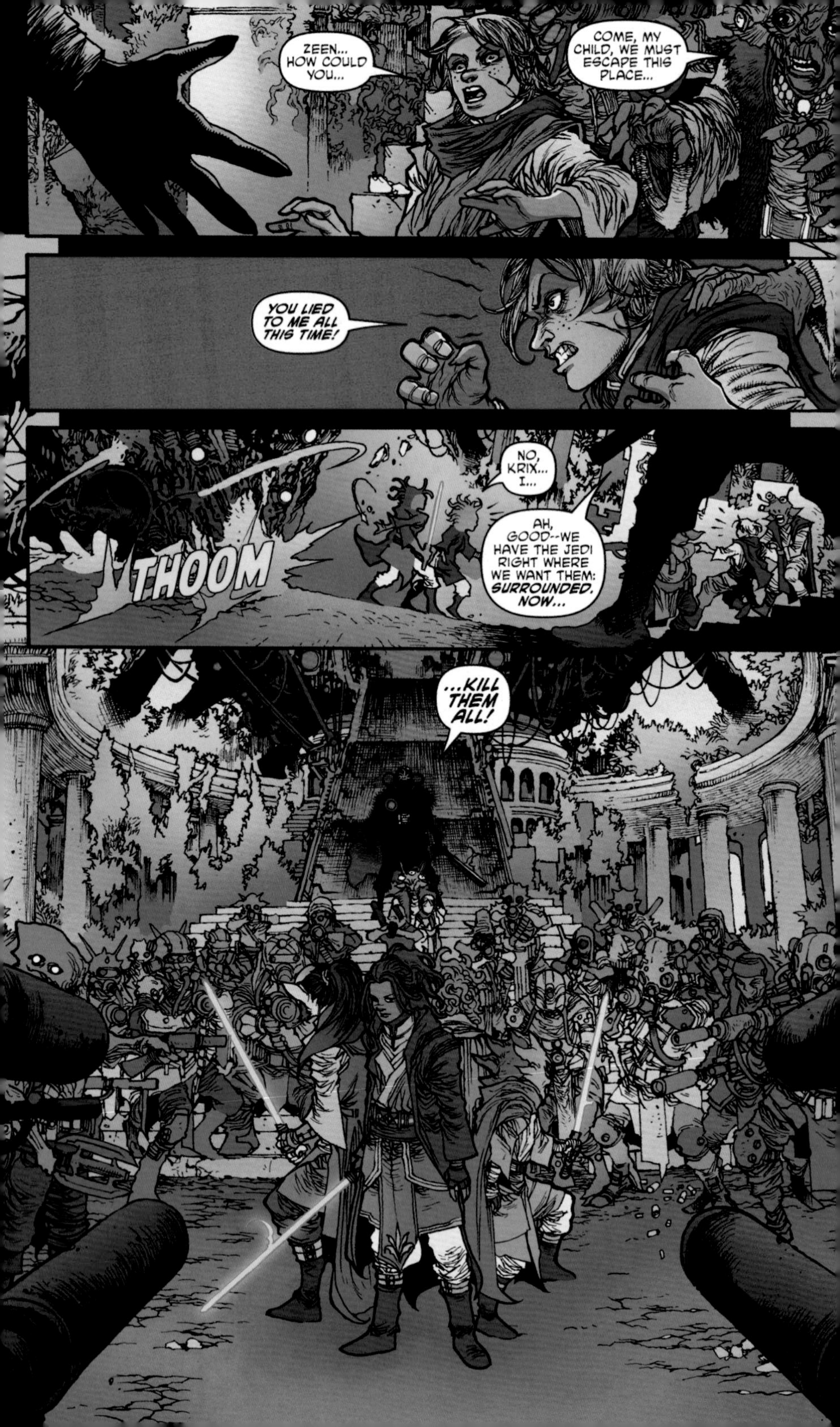
ZEEN... HOW COULD YOU...
COME, MY CHILD, WE MUST ESCAPE THIS PLACE...
YOU LIED TO ME ALL THIS TIME!
THOOM
NO, KRIX... I...
AH, GOOD--WE HAVE THE JEDI RIGHT WHERE WE WANT THEM: SURROUNDED. NOW...
...KILL THEM ALL!

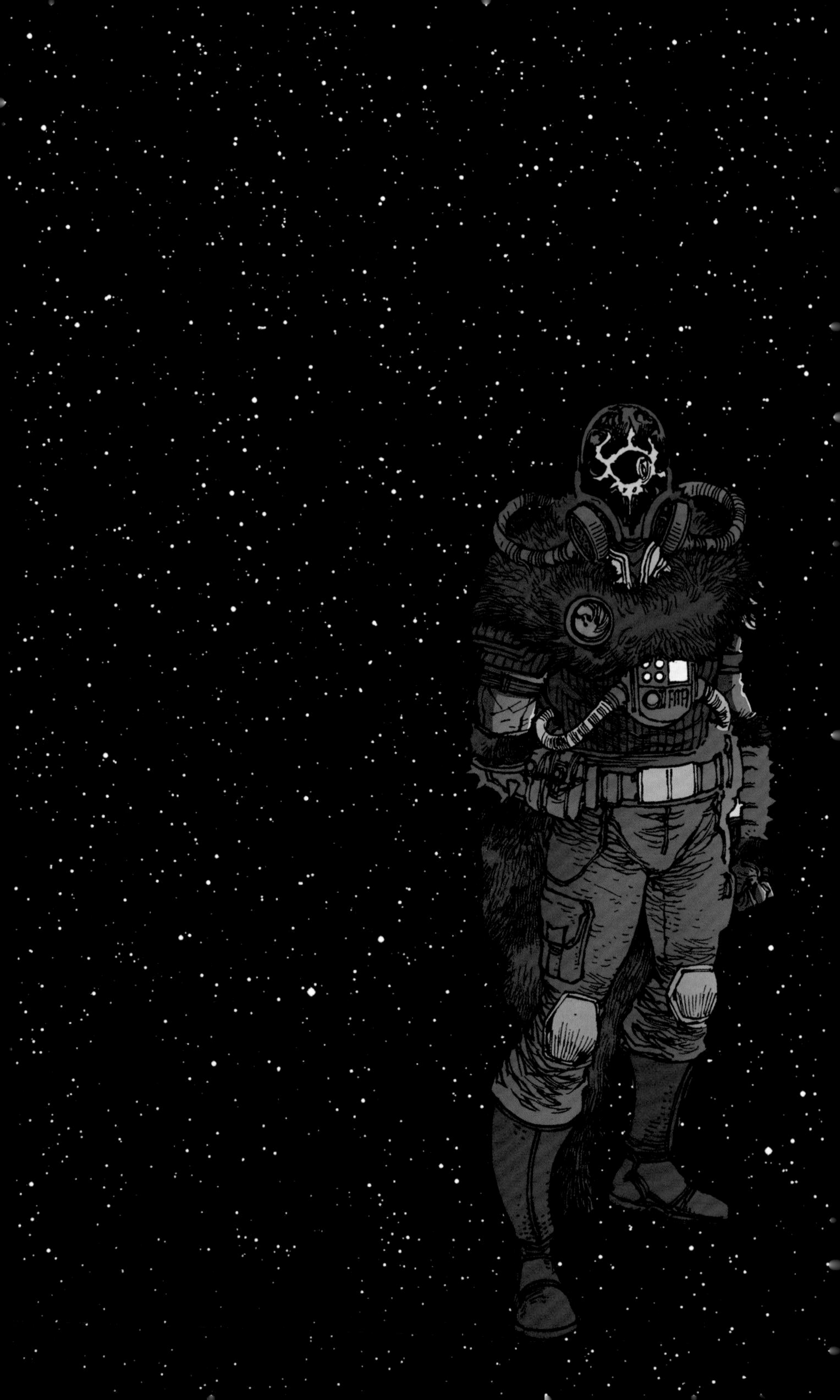

PART 2: BRALANAK CITY SMACKDOWN

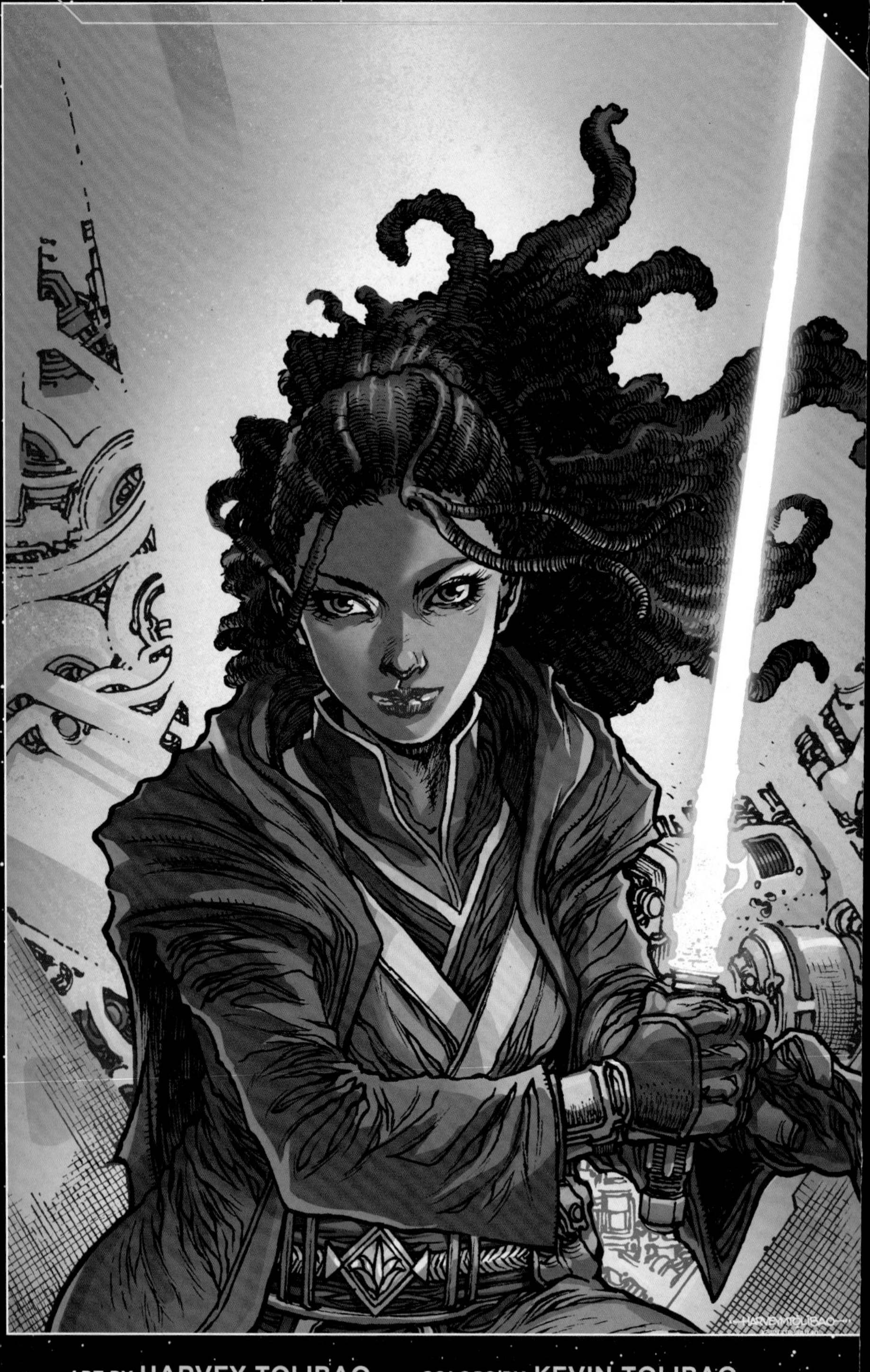

ART BY **HARVEY TOLIBAO** *COLORS BY* **KEVIN TOLIBAO**

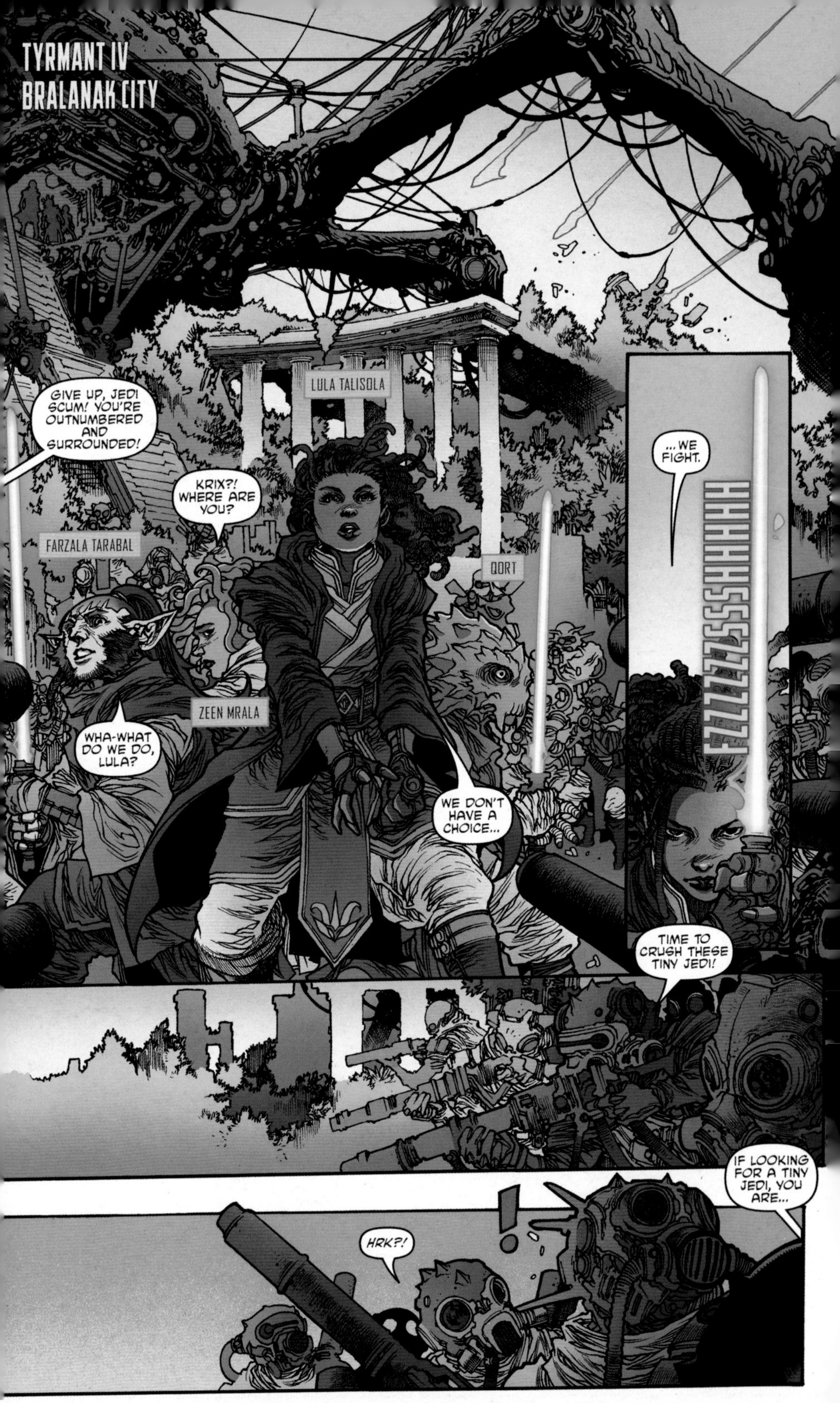
TYRMANT IV
BRALANAK CITY
LULA TALISOLA
GIVE UP, JEDI SCUM! YOU'RE OUTNUMBERED AND SURROUNDED!
KRIX?! WHERE ARE YOU?
FARZALA TARABAL
QORT
ZEEN MRALA
WHA-WHAT DO WE DO, LULA?
WE DON'T HAVE A CHOICE...
...WE FIGHT.
FZZZZZZSSSSHHHHHH
TIME TO CRUSH THESE TINY JEDI!
IF LOOKING FOR A TINY JEDI, YOU ARE...
HRK?!
!

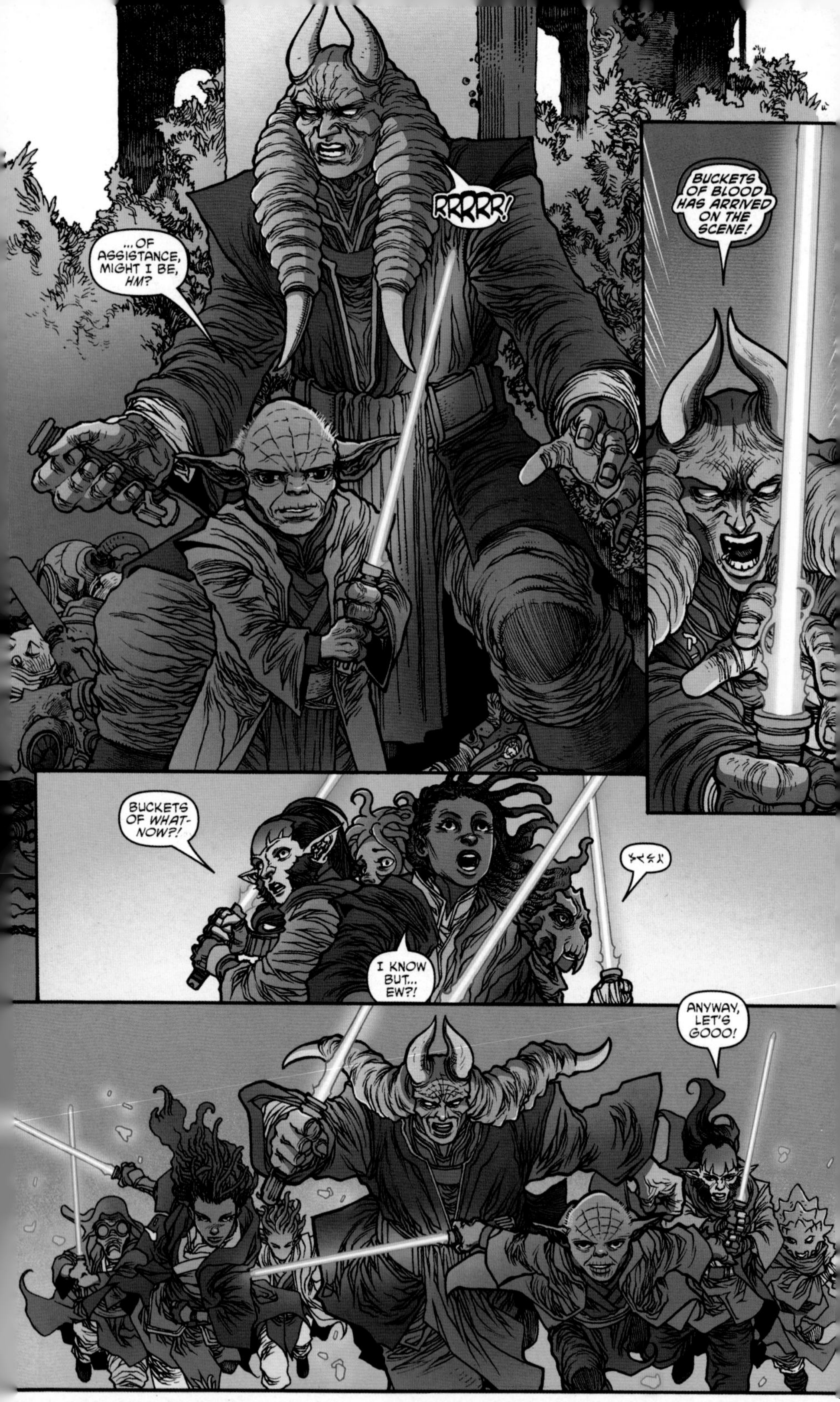
...OF ASSISTANCE, MIGHT I BE, HM?
RRRRR!
BUCKETS OF BLOOD HAS ARRIVED ON THE SCENE!
BUCKETS OF WHAT-NOW?!
I KNOW BUT... EW?!
ANYWAY, LET'S GOOO!

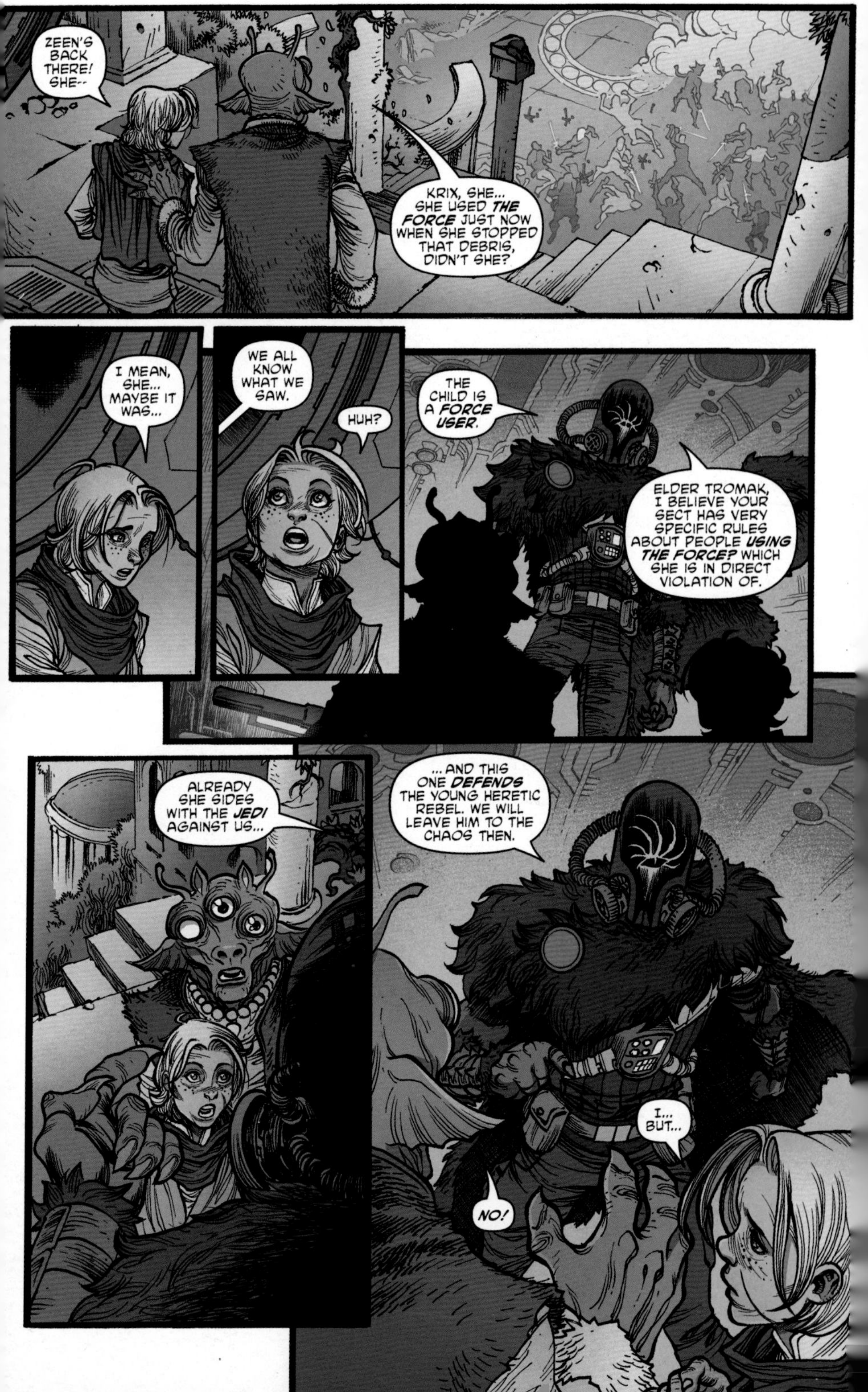
ZEEN'S BACK THERE! SHE--
KRIX, SHE... SHE USED *THE FORCE* JUST NOW WHEN SHE STOPPED THAT DEBRIS, DIDN'T SHE?
I MEAN, SHE... MAYBE IT WAS...
WE ALL KNOW WHAT WE SAW.
HUH?
THE CHILD IS A *FORCE USER*.
ELDER TROMAK, I BELIEVE YOUR SECT HAS VERY SPECIFIC RULES ABOUT PEOPLE *USING THE FORCE?* WHICH SHE IS IN DIRECT VIOLATION OF.
ALREADY SHE SIDES WITH THE *JEDI* AGAINST US...
...AND THIS ONE *DEFENDS* THE YOUNG HERETIC REBEL. WE WILL LEAVE HIM TO THE CHAOS THEN.
I... BUT...
NO!

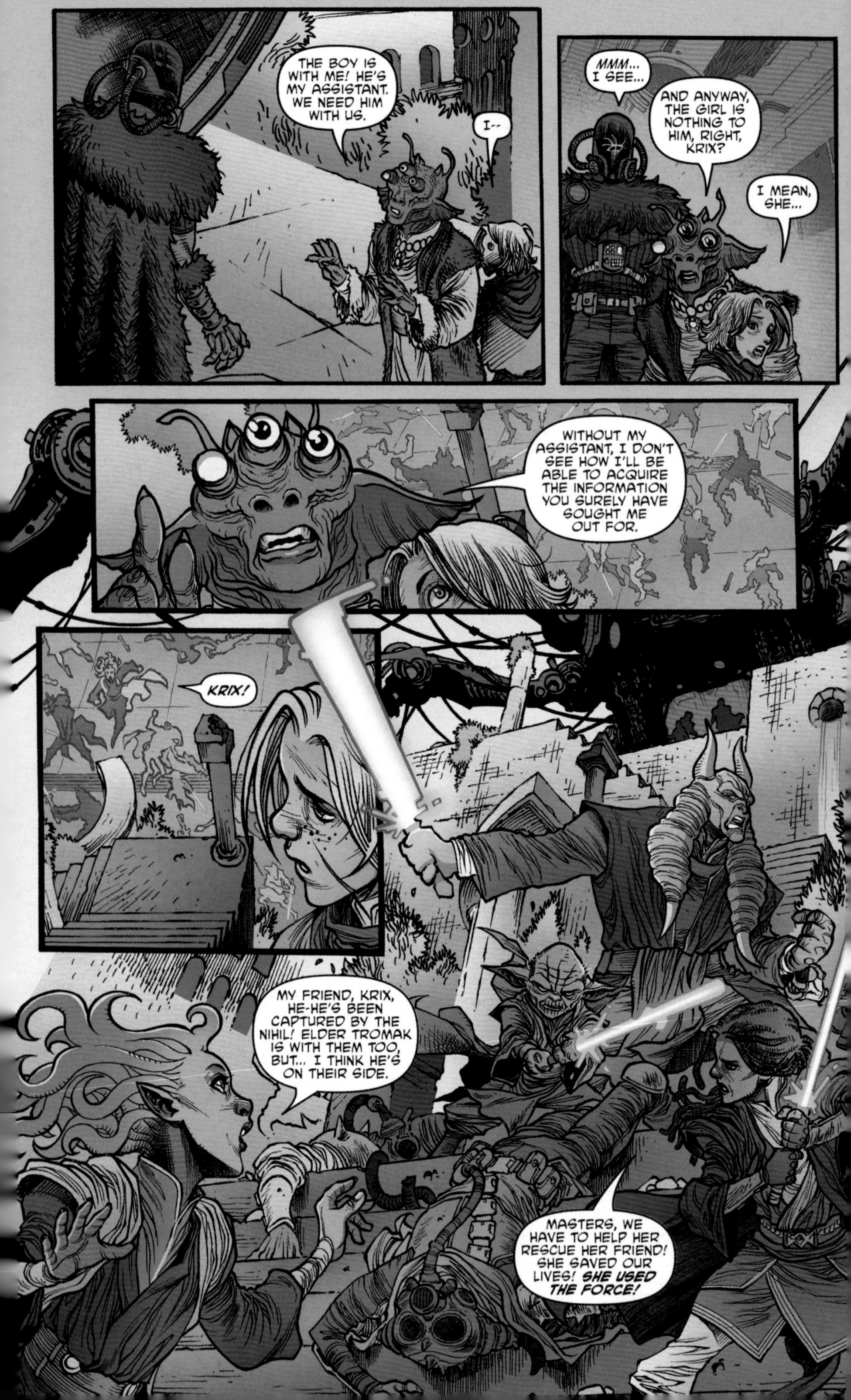
THE BOY IS WITH ME! HE'S MY ASSISTANT. WE NEED HIM WITH US.
I--
MMM... I SEE...
AND ANYWAY, THE GIRL IS NOTHING TO HIM, RIGHT, KRIX?
I MEAN, SHE...
WITHOUT MY ASSISTANT, I DON'T SEE HOW I'LL BE ABLE TO ACQUIRE THE INFORMATION YOU SURELY HAVE SOUGHT ME OUT FOR.
KRIX!
MY FRIEND, KRIX, HE-HE'S BEEN CAPTURED BY THE NIHIL! ELDER TROMAK IS WITH THEM TOO, BUT... I THINK HE'S ON THEIR SIDE.
MASTERS, WE HAVE TO HELP HER RESCUE HER FRIEND! SHE SAVED OUR LIVES! SHE USED THE FORCE!

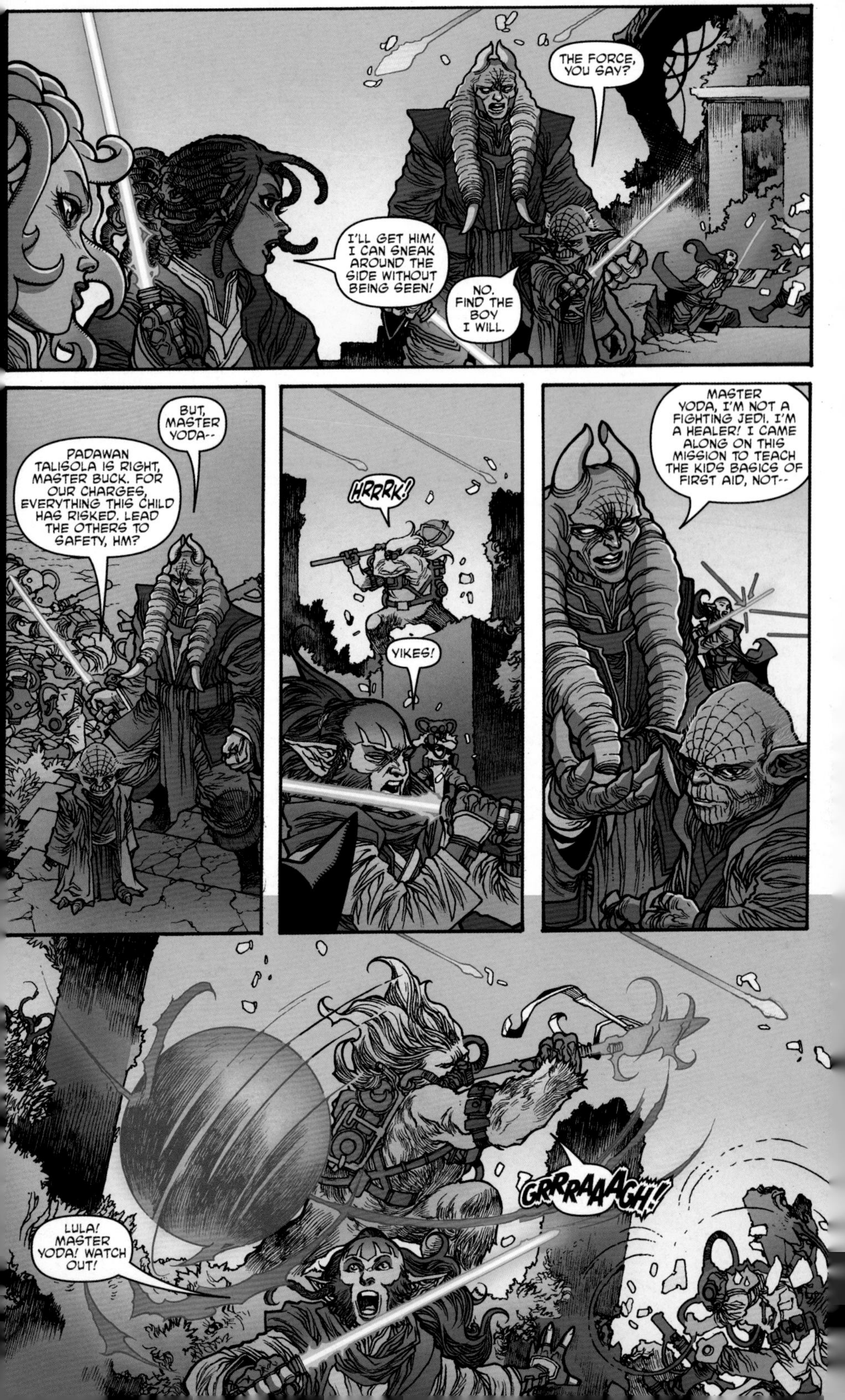
THE FORCE, YOU SAY?
I'LL GET HIM! I CAN SNEAK AROUND THE SIDE WITHOUT BEING SEEN!
NO. FIND THE BOY I WILL.
BUT, MASTER YODA--
PADAWAN TALISOLA IS RIGHT, MASTER BUCK. FOR OUR CHARGES, EVERYTHING THIS CHILD HAS RISKED. LEAD THE OTHERS TO SAFETY, HM?
HRRRK!
YIKES!
MASTER YODA, I'M NOT A FIGHTING JEDI. I'M A HEALER! I CAME ALONG ON THIS MISSION TO TEACH THE KIDS BASICS OF FIRST AID, NOT--
GRRRAAAGH!
LULA! MASTER YODA! WATCH OUT!

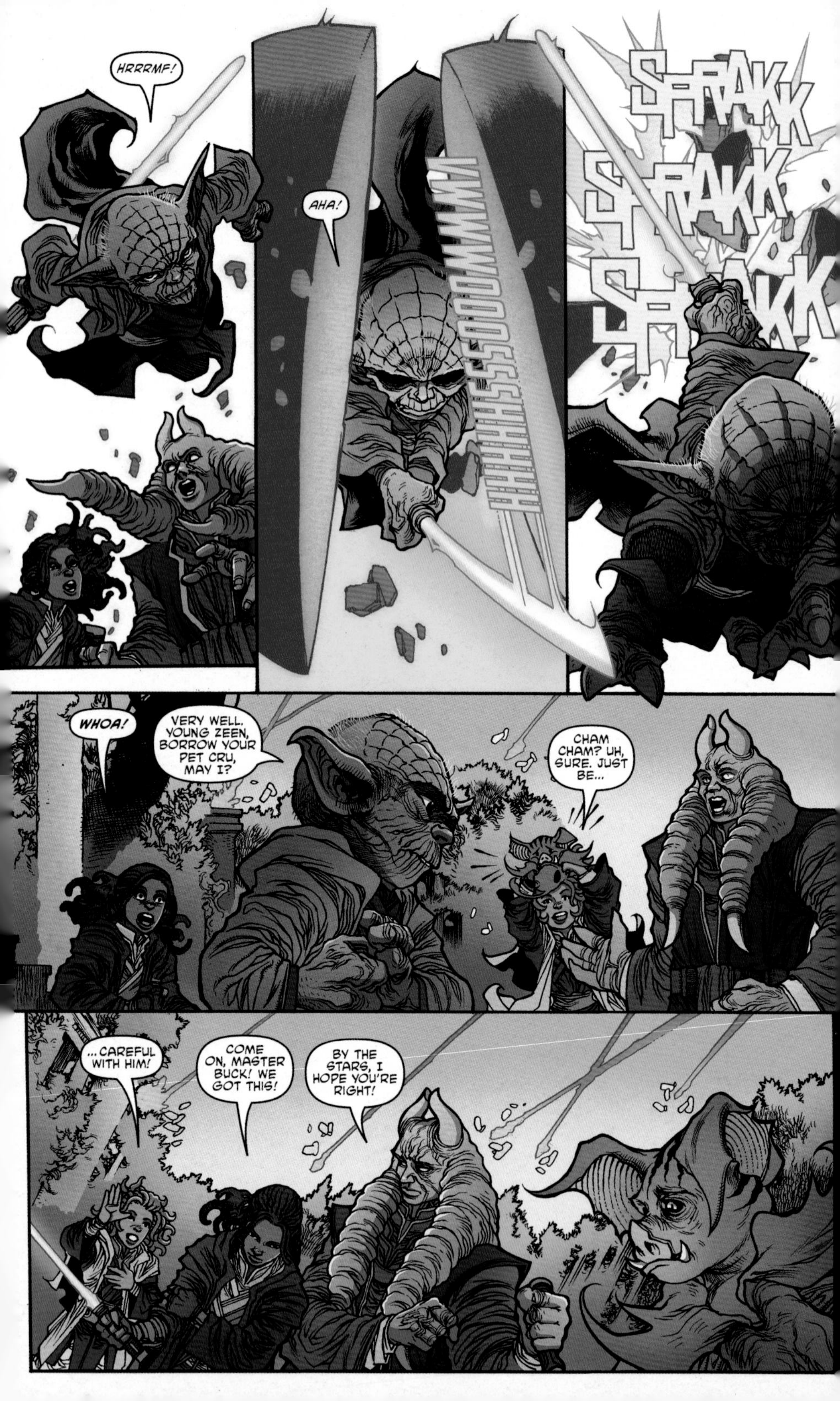
HRRRMF!
AHA!
VVVVVVOOOSSSHHHHHH
SPRAKK
SPRAKK
SPRAKK
WHOA!
VERY WELL. YOUNG ZEEN, BORROW YOUR PET CRU, MAY I?
CHAM CHAM? UH, SURE. JUST BE...
...CAREFUL WITH HIM!
COME ON, MASTER BUCK! WE GOT THIS!
BY THE STARS, I HOPE YOU'RE RIGHT!

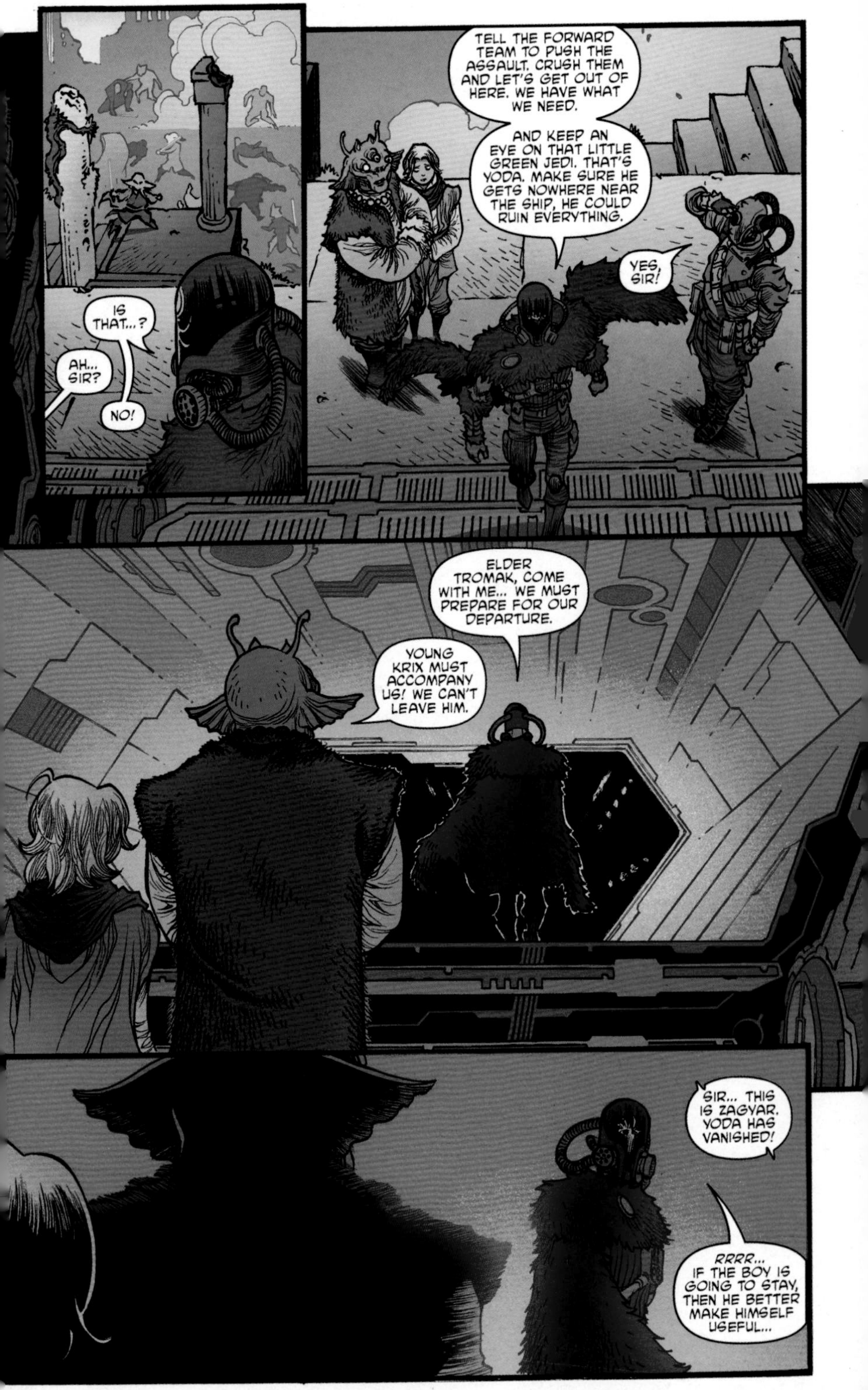
IS THAT...?
AH... SIR?
NO!
TELL THE FORWARD TEAM TO PUSH THE ASSAULT. CRUSH THEM AND LET'S GET OUT OF HERE. WE HAVE WHAT WE NEED.
AND KEEP AN EYE ON THAT LITTLE GREEN JEDI. THAT'S YODA. MAKE SURE HE GETS NOWHERE NEAR THE SHIP, HE COULD RUIN EVERYTHING.
YES, SIR!
ELDER TROMAK, COME WITH ME... WE MUST PREPARE FOR OUR DEPARTURE.
YOUNG KRIX MUST ACCOMPANY US! WE CAN'T LEAVE HIM.
SIR... THIS IS ZAGYAR. YODA HAS VANISHED!
RRRR... IF THE BOY IS GOING TO STAY, THEN HE BETTER MAKE HIMSELF USEFUL...

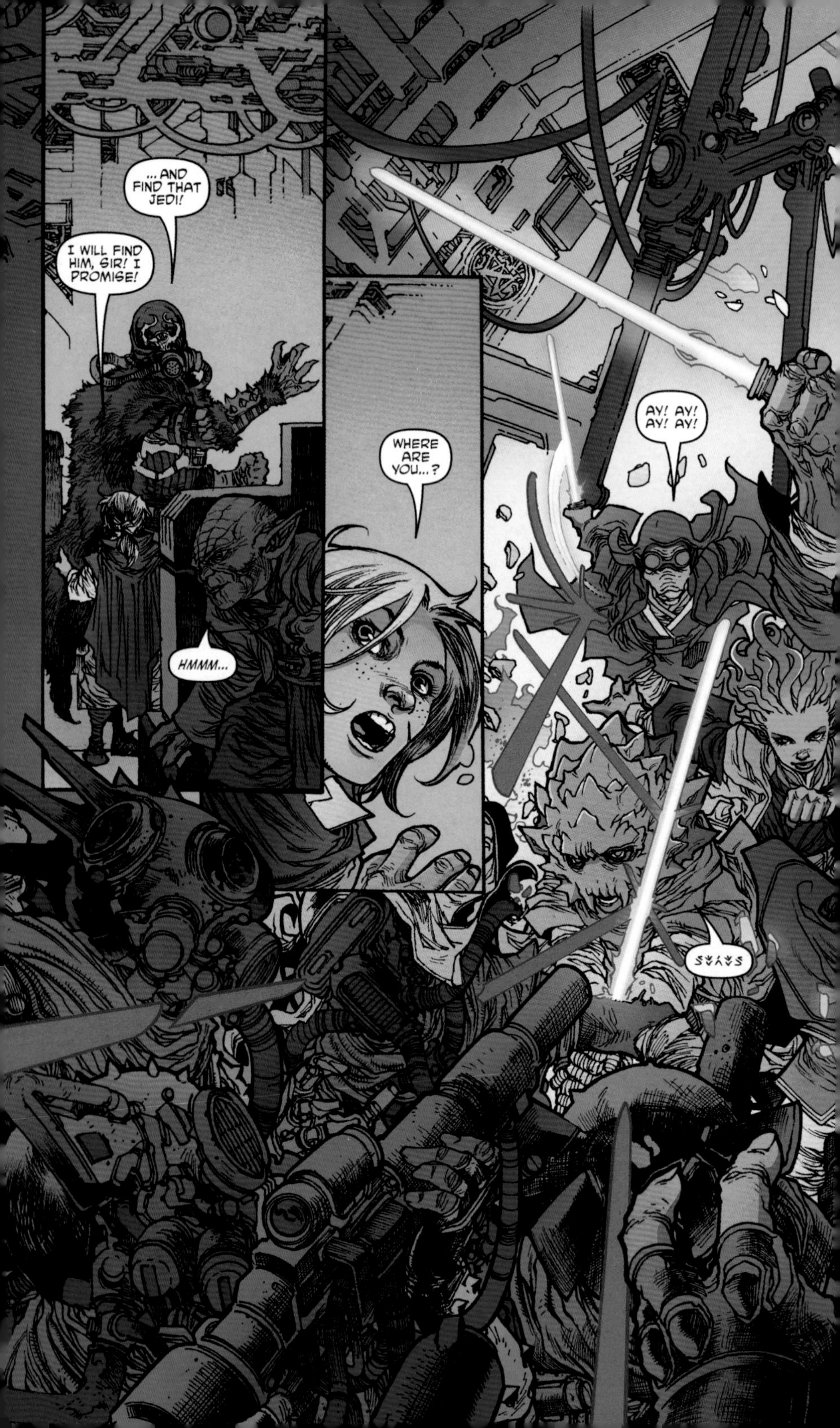
...AND FIND THAT JEDI!
I WILL FIND HIM, SIR! I PROMISE!
HMMM...
WHERE ARE YOU...?
AY! AY! AY! AY!

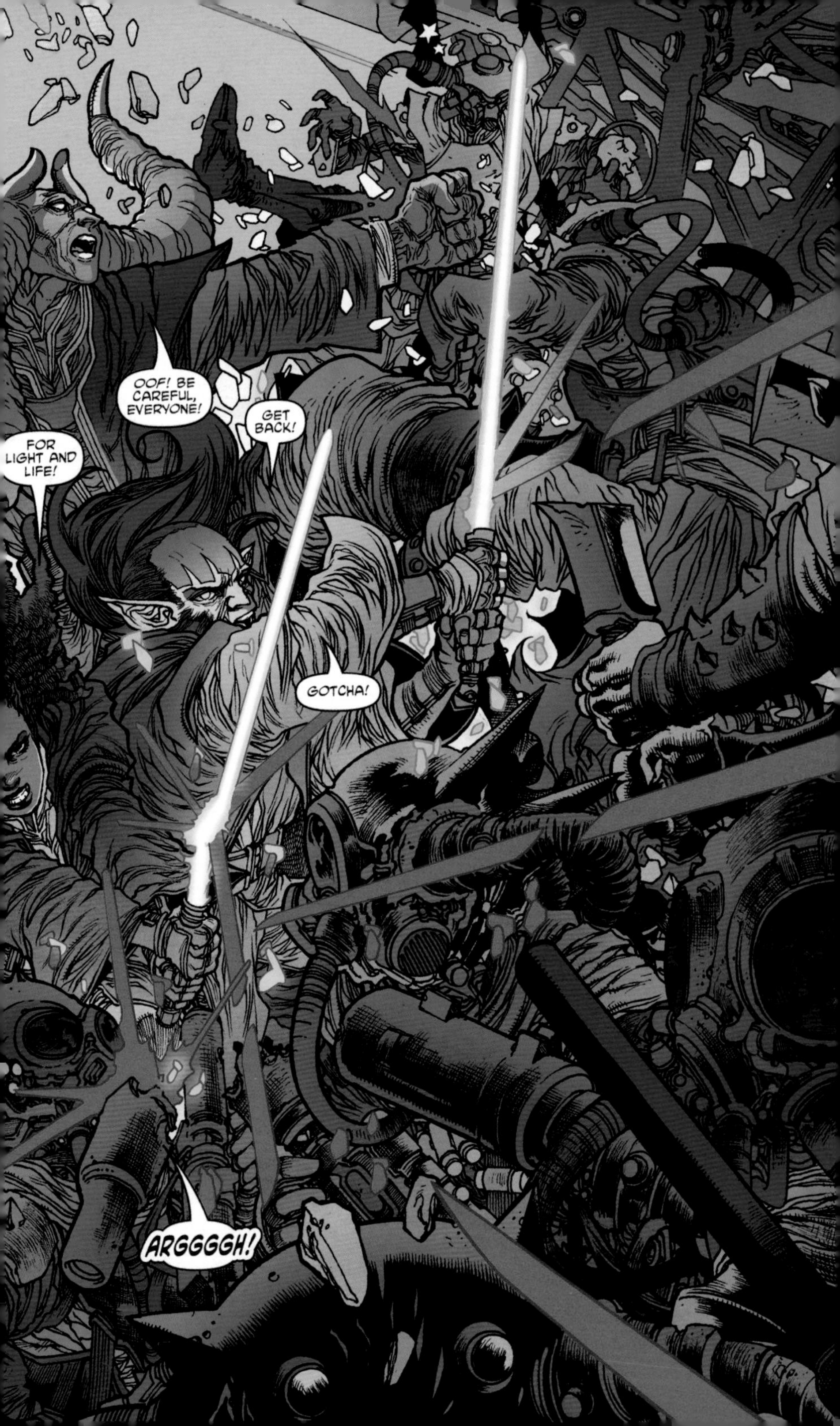
OOF! BE CAREFUL, EVERYONE!
FOR LIGHT AND LIFE!
GET BACK!
GOTCHA!
ARGGGGH!

GALACTIC DATA FILE

SHIPS OF THE HIGH REPUBLIC ERA

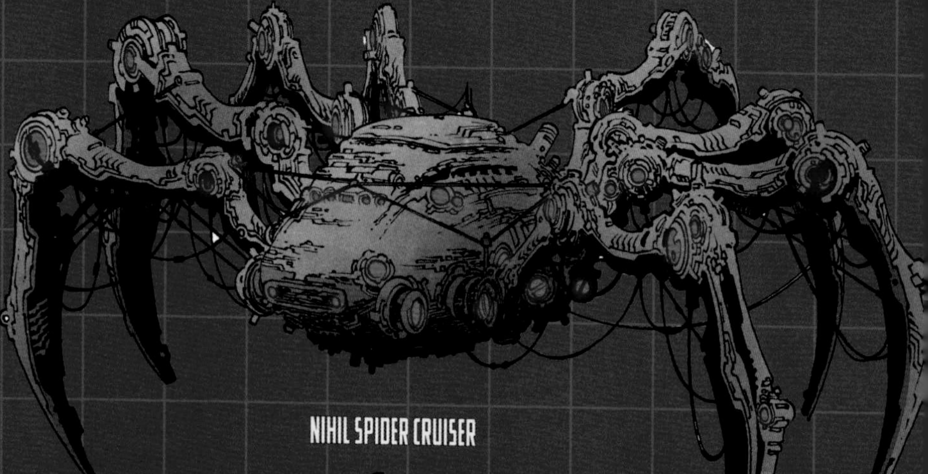

NIHIL SPIDER CRUISER

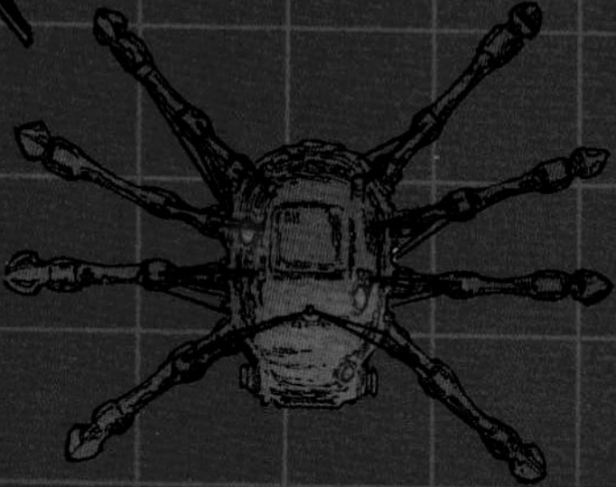

NIHIL AIR AND GROUND TRANSPORT
LENGTH: 18 METERS
CREW: 20 (2 TO FLY)
HYPERSPACE CAPABILITIES: YES

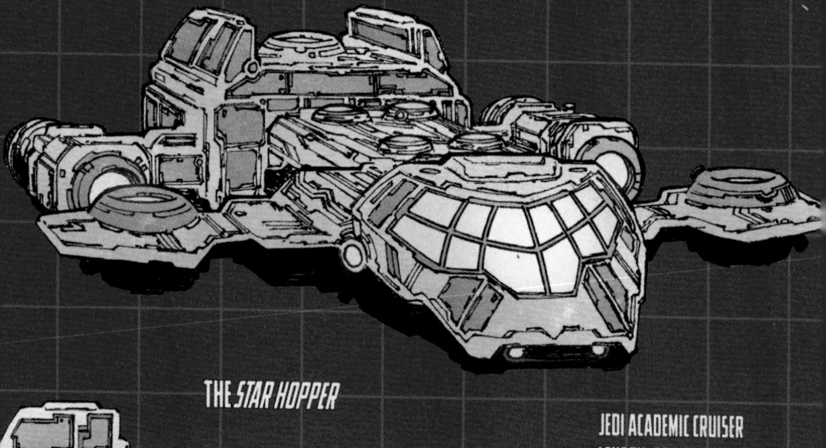

THE *STAR HOPPER*

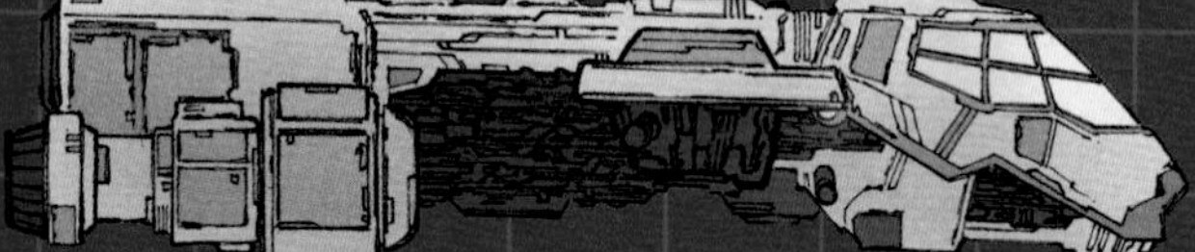

JEDI ACADEMIC CRUISER
LENGTH: 30 METERS
CREW: 18 (4 TO FLY)
HYPERSPACE CAPABILITIES: YES

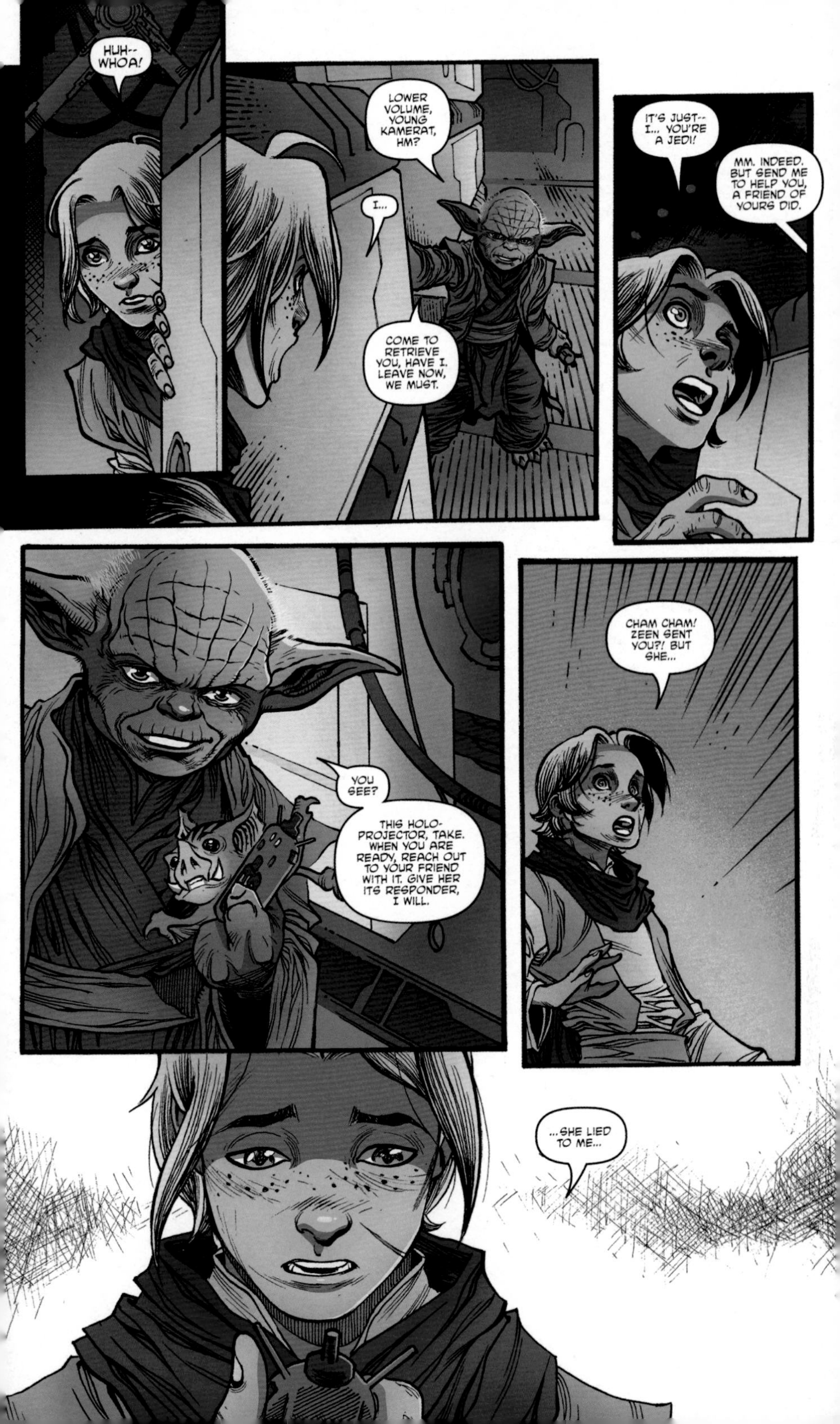
HUH--
WHOA!
LOWER VOLUME, YOUNG KAMERAT, HM?
I...
COME TO RETRIEVE YOU, HAVE I. LEAVE NOW, WE MUST.
IT'S JUST-- I... YOU'RE A JEDI!
MM. INDEED. BUT SEND ME TO HELP YOU, A FRIEND OF YOURS DID.
YOU SEE?
THIS HOLO-PROJECTOR, TAKE. WHEN YOU ARE READY, REACH OUT TO YOUR FRIEND WITH IT. GIVE HER ITS RESPONDER, I WILL.
CHAM CHAM! ZEEN SENT YOU?! BUT SHE...
...SHE LIED TO ME...

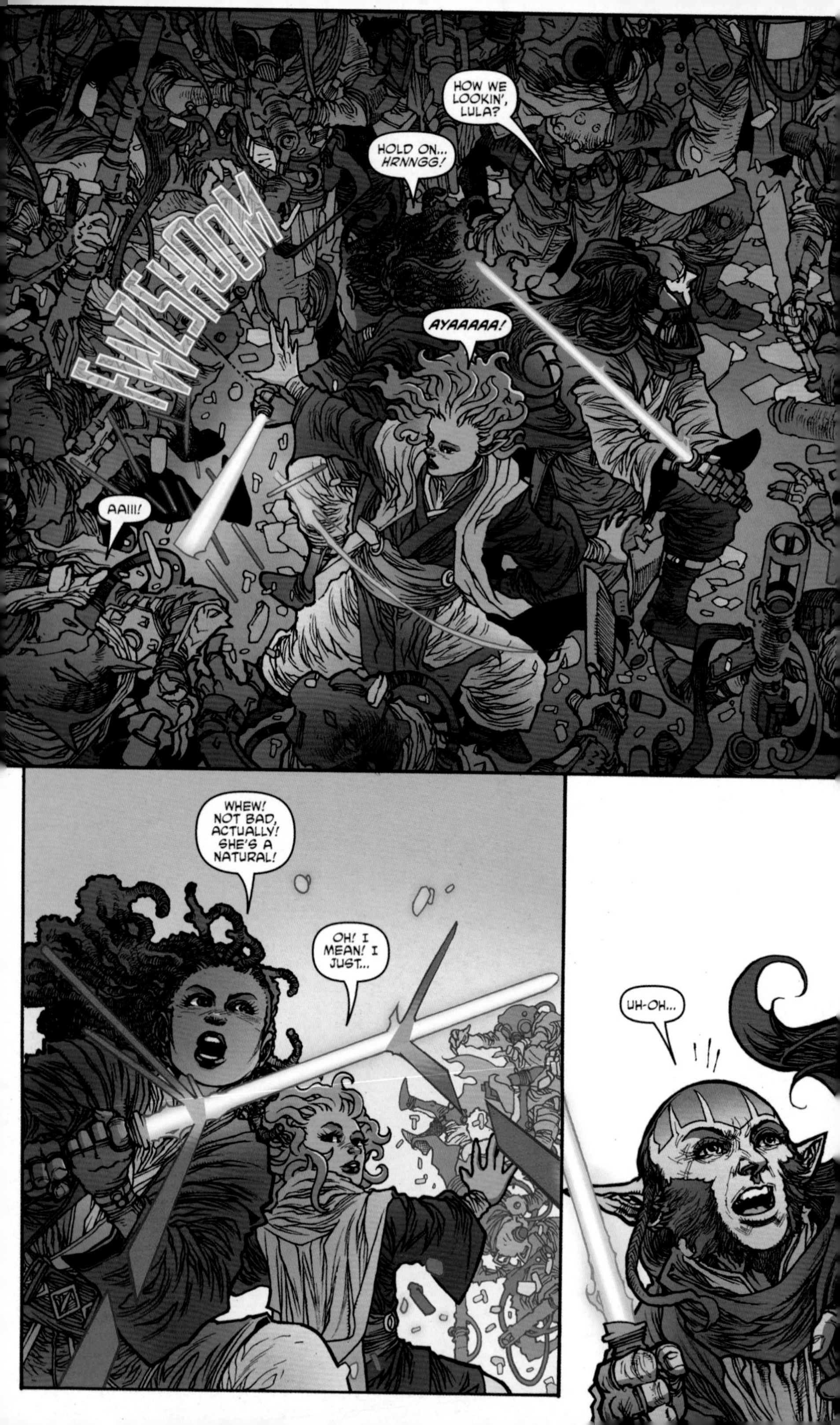
HOW WE LOOKIN', LULA?
HOLD ON... HRNNGG!
FWSHOOM
AYAAAAA!
AAIII!
WHEW! NOT BAD, ACTUALLY! SHE'S A NATURAL!
OH! I MEAN! I JUST...
UH-OH...

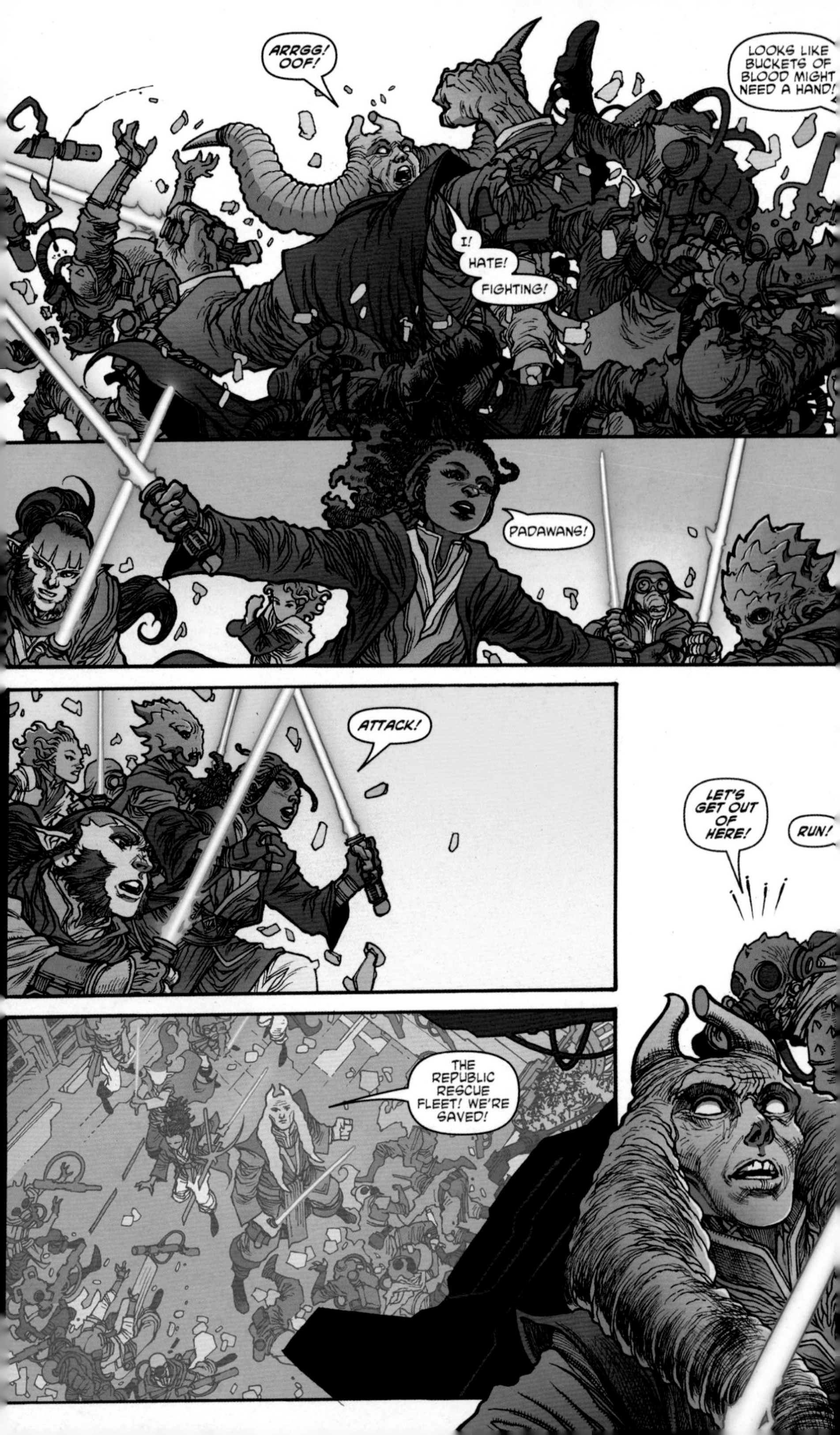
ARRGG! OOF!
LOOKS LIKE BUCKETS OF BLOOD MIGHT NEED A HAND!
I!
HATE!
FIGHTING!
PADAWANS!
ATTACK!
LET'S GET OUT OF HERE!
RUN!
THE REPUBLIC RESCUE FLEET! WE'RE SAVED!

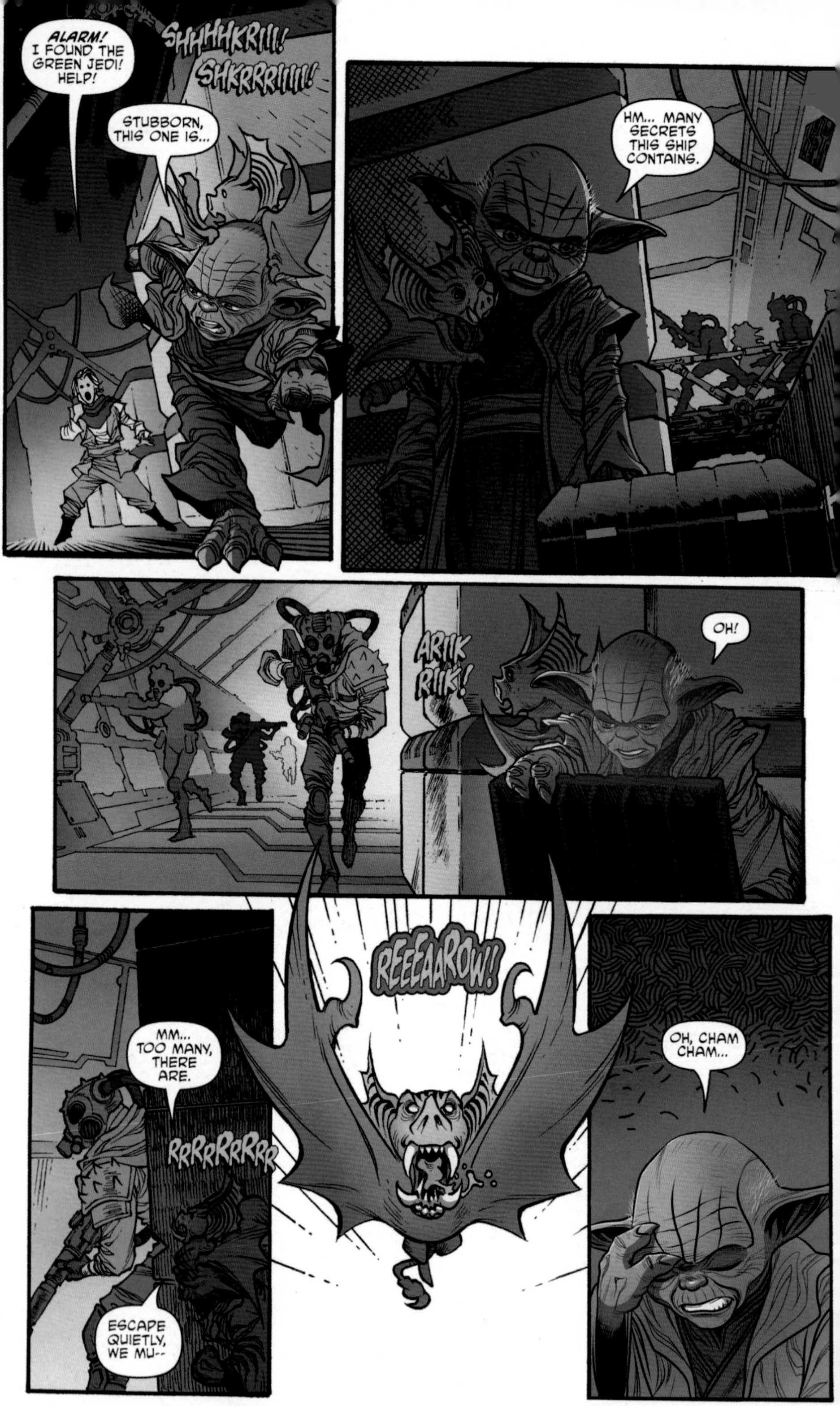
ALARM! I FOUND THE GREEN JEDI! HELP!
SHHHHKRIII!
SHKRRRIIIII!
STUBBORN, THIS ONE IS...
HM... MANY SECRETS THIS SHIP CONTAINS.
ARIIK RIIK!
OH!
MM... TOO MANY, THERE ARE.
RRRRRRRR
ESCAPE QUIETLY, WE MU--
REEEAAROW!
OH, CHAM CHAM...

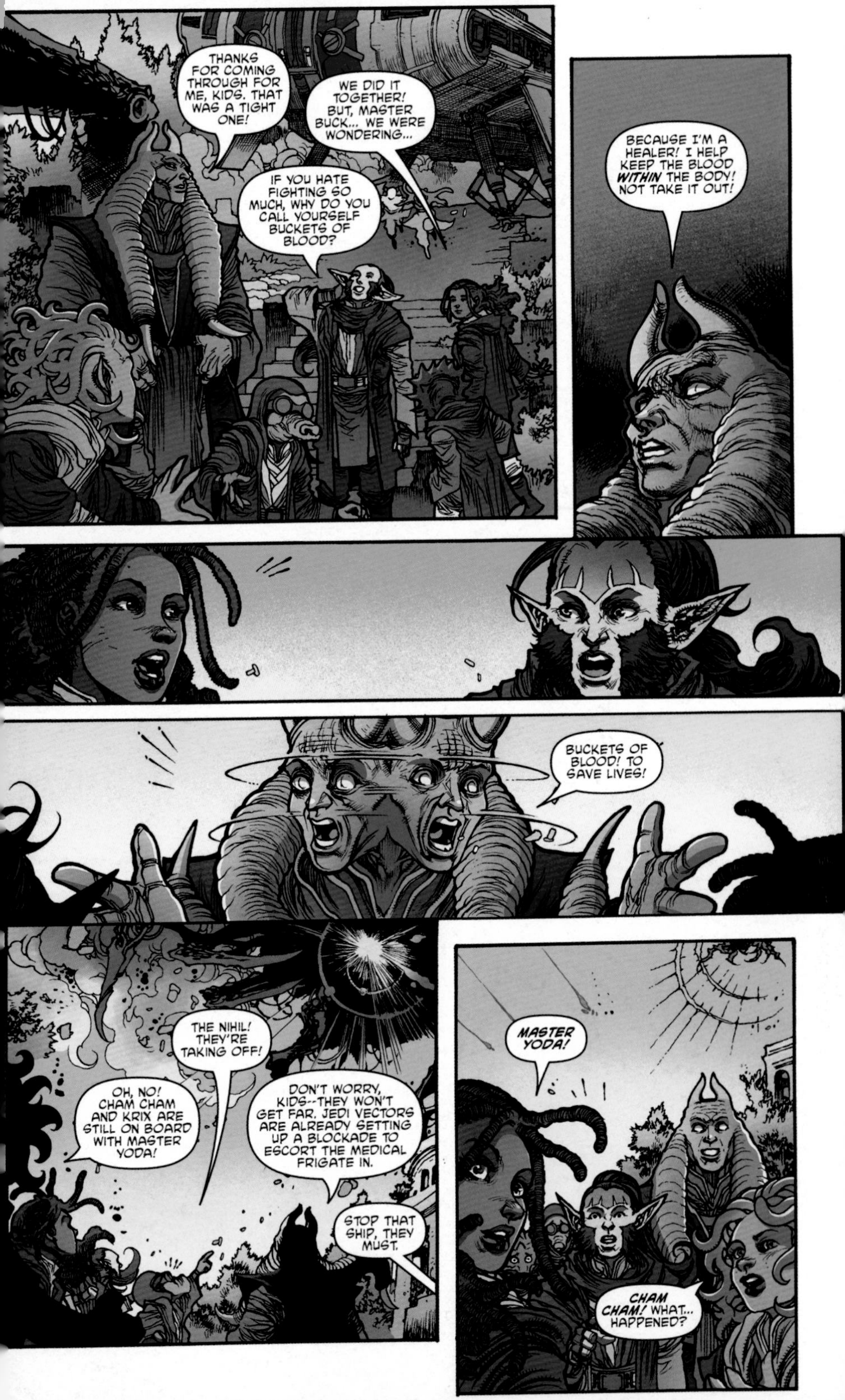
THANKS FOR COMING THROUGH FOR ME, KIDS. THAT WAS A TIGHT ONE!
WE DID IT TOGETHER! BUT, MASTER BUCK... WE WERE WONDERING...
IF YOU HATE FIGHTING SO MUCH, WHY DO YOU CALL YOURSELF BUCKETS OF BLOOD?
BECAUSE I'M A HEALER! I HELP KEEP THE BLOOD *WITHIN* THE BODY! NOT TAKE IT OUT!
BUCKETS OF BLOOD! TO SAVE LIVES!
THE NIHIL! THEY'RE TAKING OFF!
OH, NO! CHAM CHAM AND KRIX ARE STILL ON BOARD WITH MASTER YODA!
DON'T WORRY, KIDS--THEY WON'T GET FAR. JEDI VECTORS ARE ALREADY SETTING UP A BLOCKADE TO ESCORT THE MEDICAL FRIGATE IN.
STOP THAT SHIP, THEY MUST.
MASTER YODA!
CHAM CHAM! WHAT... HAPPENED?

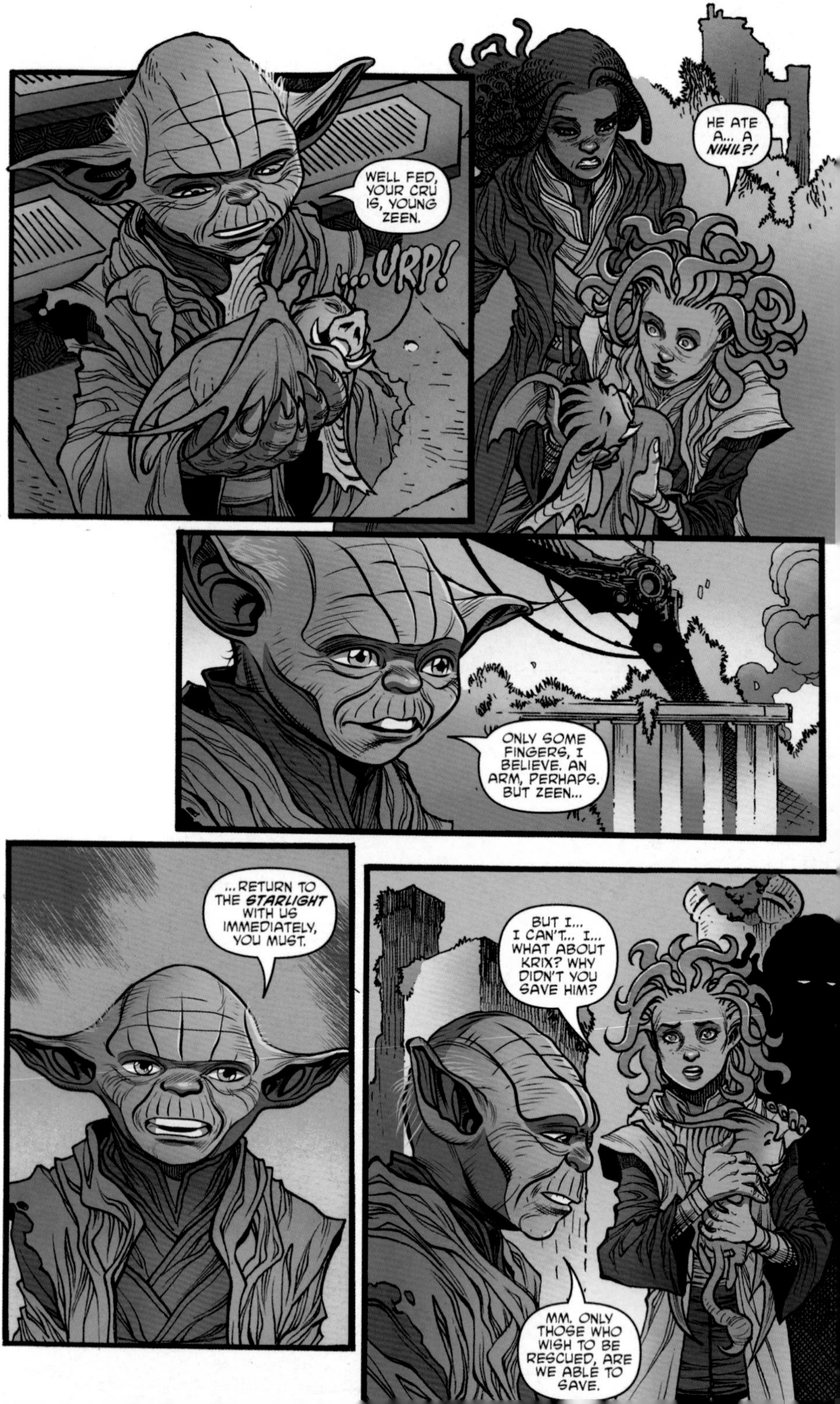
WELL FED, YOUR CRU IS, YOUNG ZEEN.
...URP!
HE ATE A... A *NIHIL?!*
ONLY SOME FINGERS, I BELIEVE. AN ARM, PERHAPS. BUT ZEEN...
...RETURN TO THE *STARLIGHT* WITH US IMMEDIATELY, YOU MUST.
BUT I... I CAN'T... I... WHAT ABOUT KRIX? WHY DIDN'T YOU SAVE HIM?
MM. ONLY THOSE WHO WISH TO BE RESCUED, ARE WE ABLE TO SAVE.

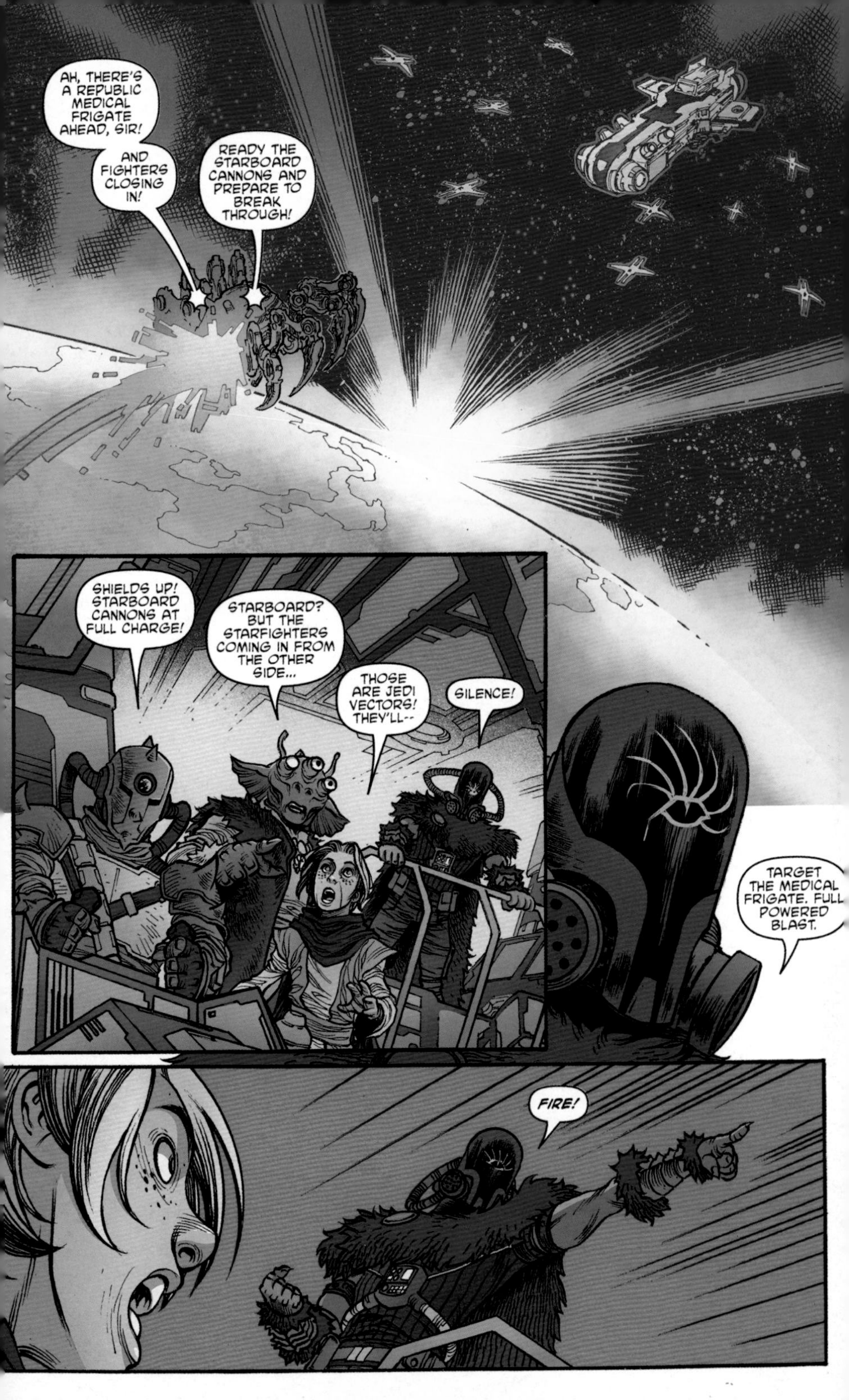
AH, THERE'S A REPUBLIC MEDICAL FRIGATE AHEAD, SIR!
AND FIGHTERS CLOSING IN!
READY THE STARBOARD CANNONS AND PREPARE TO BREAK THROUGH!
SHIELDS UP! STARBOARD CANNONS AT FULL CHARGE!
STARBOARD? BUT THE STARFIGHTERS COMING IN FROM THE OTHER SIDE...
THOSE ARE JEDI VECTORS! THEY'LL--
SILENCE!
TARGET THE MEDICAL FRIGATE. FULL POWERED BLAST.
FIRE!

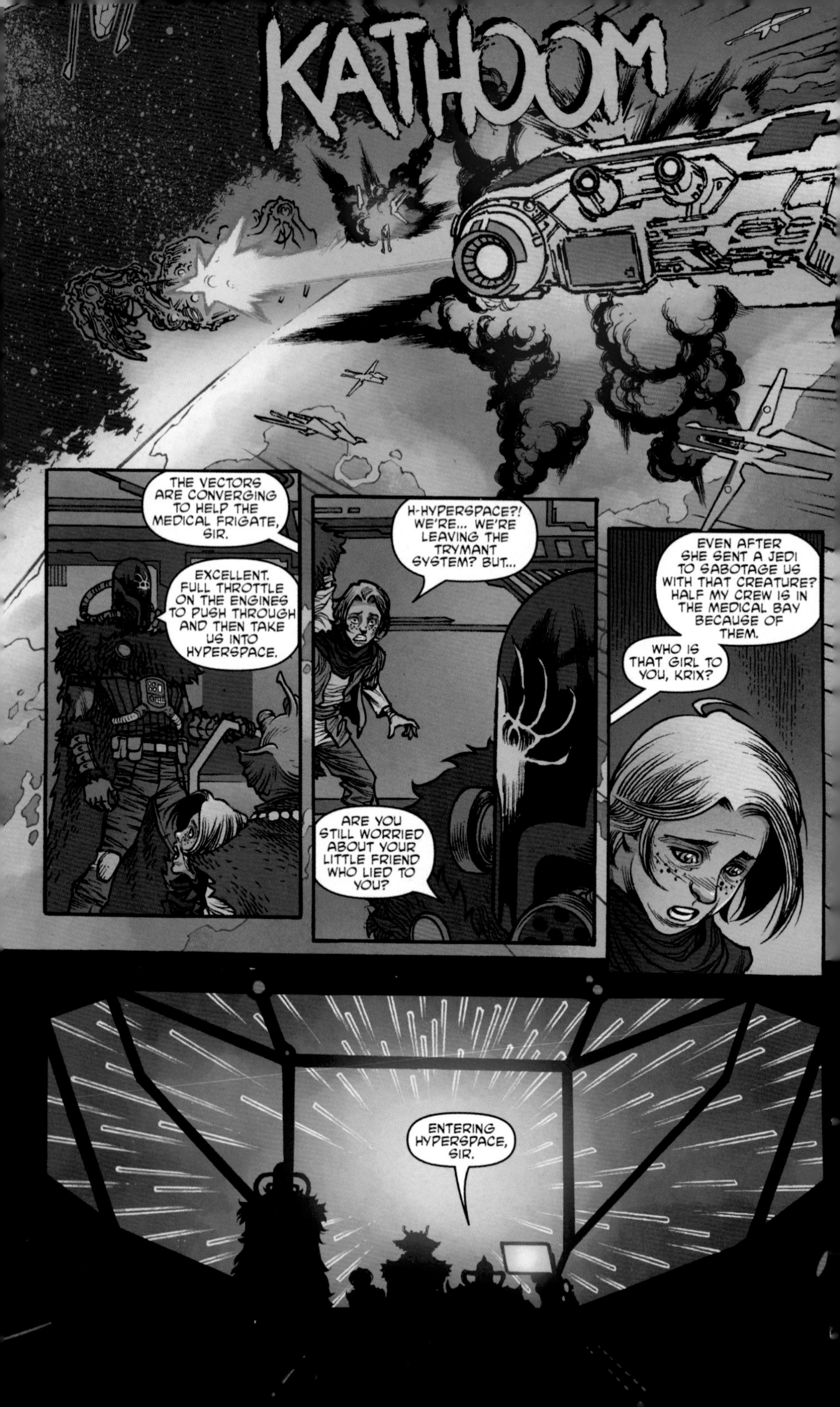
KATHOOM
THE VECTORS ARE CONVERGING TO HELP THE MEDICAL FRIGATE, SIR.
EXCELLENT. FULL THROTTLE ON THE ENGINES TO PUSH THROUGH AND THEN TAKE US INTO HYPERSPACE.
H-HYPERSPACE?! WE'RE... WE'RE LEAVING THE TRYMANT SYSTEM? BUT...
ARE YOU STILL WORRIED ABOUT YOUR LITTLE FRIEND WHO LIED TO YOU?
EVEN AFTER SHE SENT A JEDI TO SABOTAGE US WITH THAT CREATURE? HALF MY CREW IS IN THE MEDICAL BAY BECAUSE OF THEM.
WHO IS THAT GIRL TO YOU, KRIX?
ENTERING HYPERSPACE, SIR.

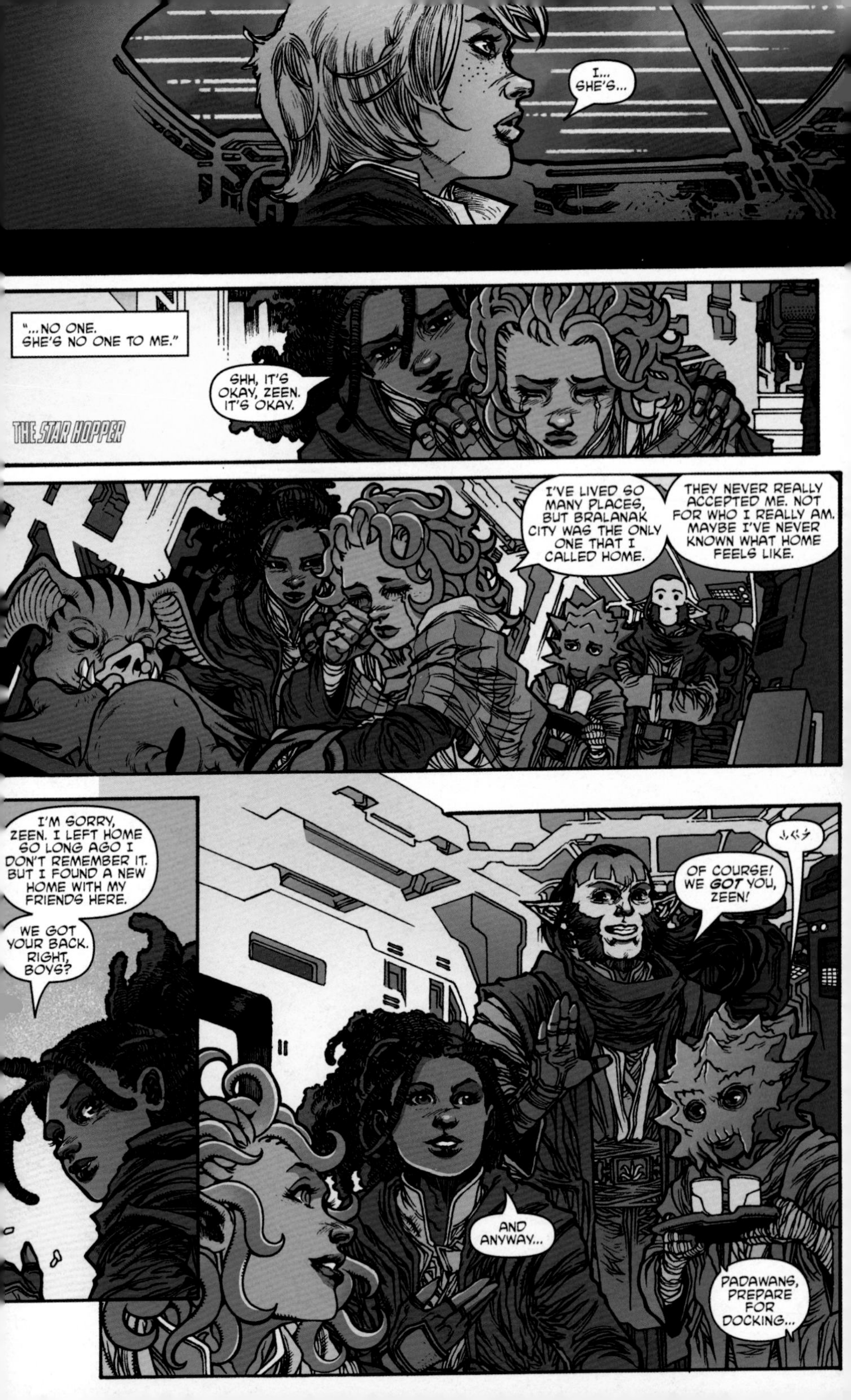
I... SHE'S...
"...NO ONE. SHE'S NO ONE TO ME."
SHH, IT'S OKAY, ZEEN. IT'S OKAY.
THE STAR HOPPER
I'VE LIVED SO MANY PLACES, BUT BRALANAK CITY WAS THE ONLY ONE THAT I CALLED HOME.
THEY NEVER REALLY ACCEPTED ME. NOT FOR WHO I REALLY AM. MAYBE I'VE NEVER KNOWN WHAT HOME FEELS LIKE.
I'M SORRY, ZEEN. I LEFT HOME SO LONG AGO I DON'T REMEMBER IT. BUT I FOUND A NEW HOME WITH MY FRIENDS HERE.
WE GOT YOUR BACK. RIGHT, BOYS?
OF COURSE! WE *GOT* YOU, ZEEN!
AND ANYWAY...
PADAWANS, PREPARE FOR DOCKING...

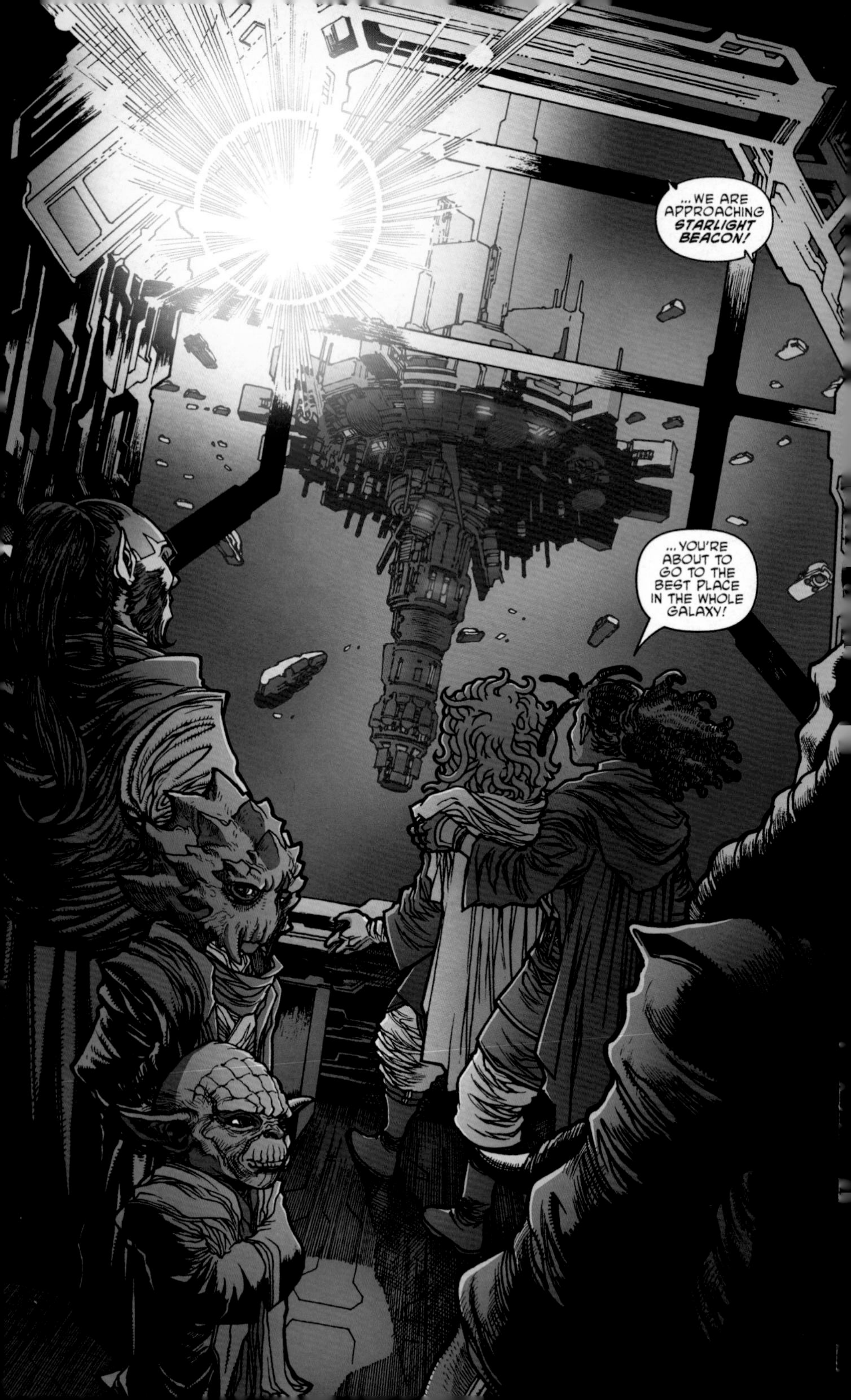
...WE ARE APPROACHING STARLIGHT BEACON!
...YOU'RE ABOUT TO GO TO THE BEST PLACE IN THE WHOLE GALAXY!

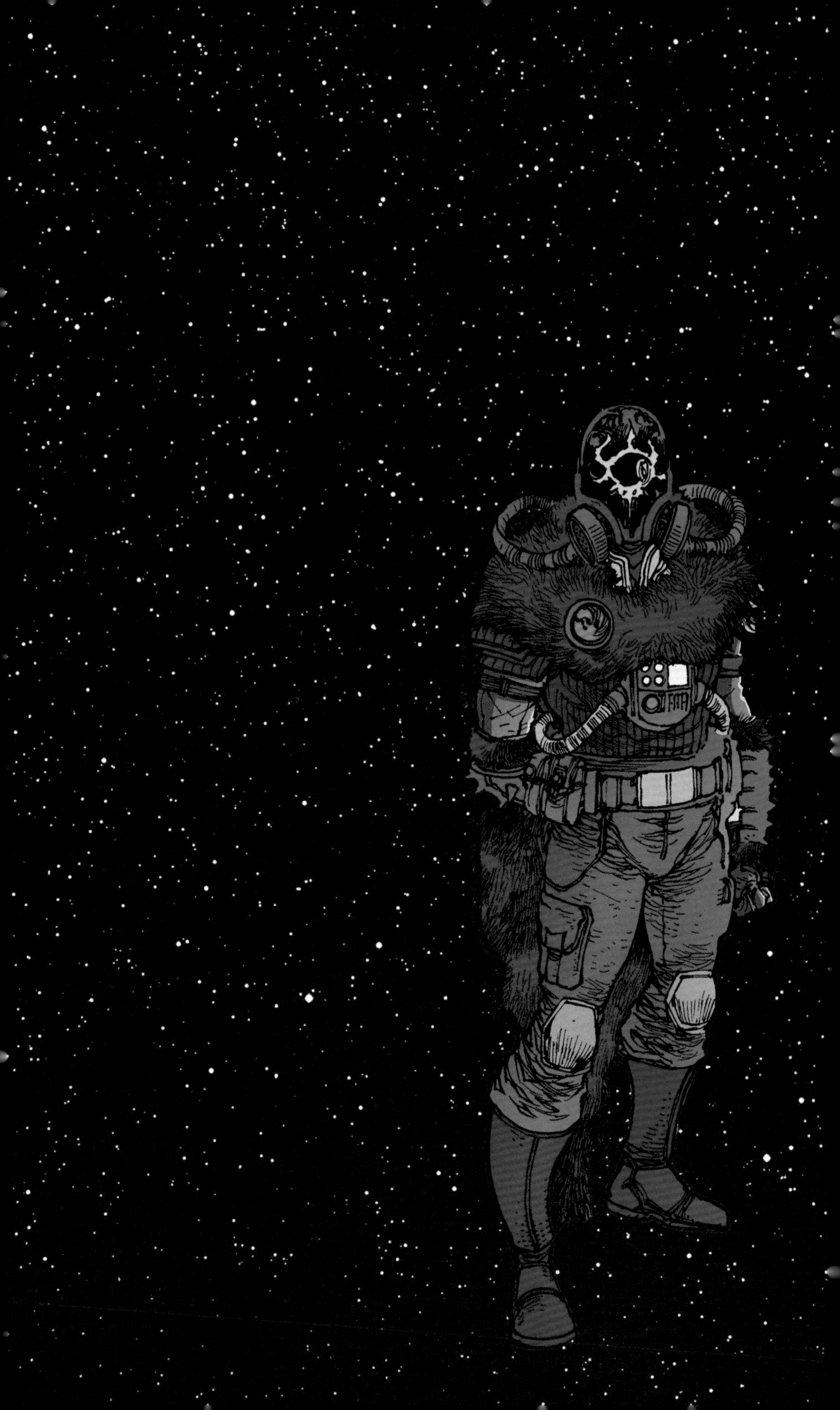

PART 3: STARLIGHT

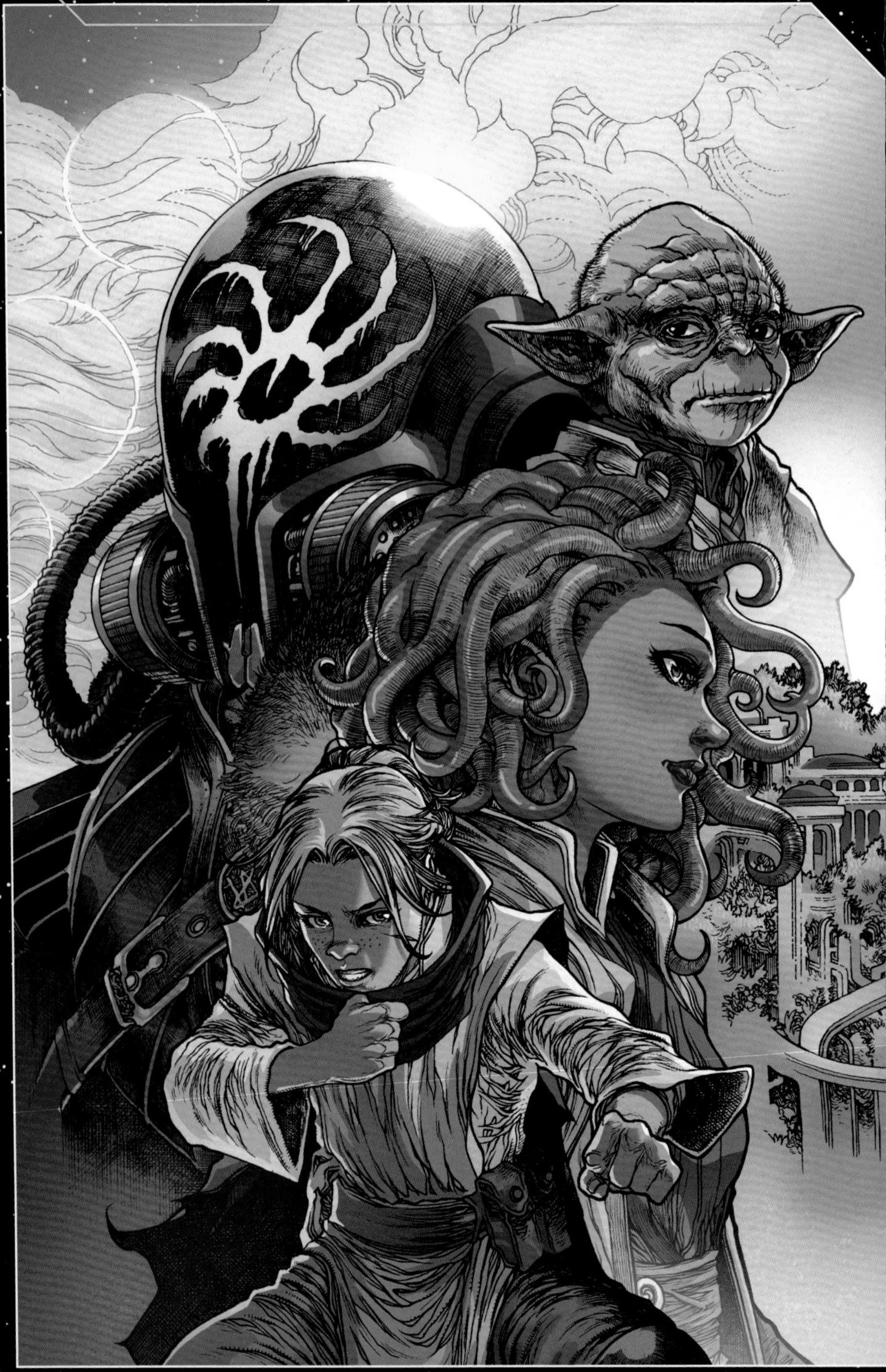

ART BY HARVEY TOLIBAO   COLORS BY KEVIN TOLIBAO

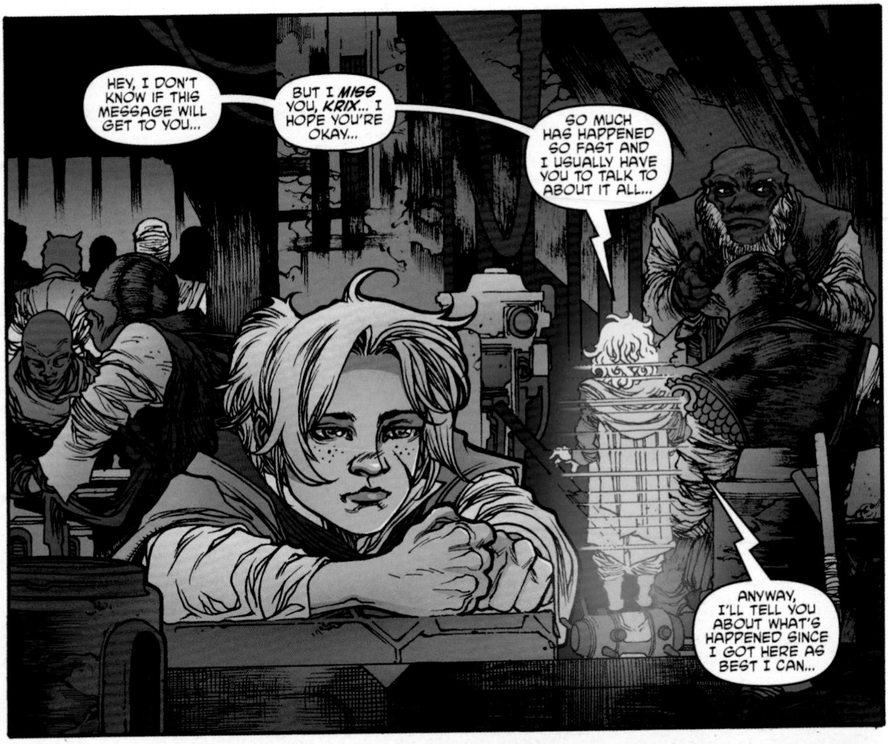
HEY, I DON'T KNOW IF THIS MESSAGE WILL GET TO YOU...
BUT I MISS YOU, KRIX... I HOPE YOU'RE OKAY...
SO MUCH HAS HAPPENED SO FAST AND I USUALLY HAVE YOU TO TALK TO ABOUT IT ALL...
ANYWAY, I'LL TELL YOU ABOUT WHAT'S HAPPENED SINCE I GOT HERE AS BEST I CAN...
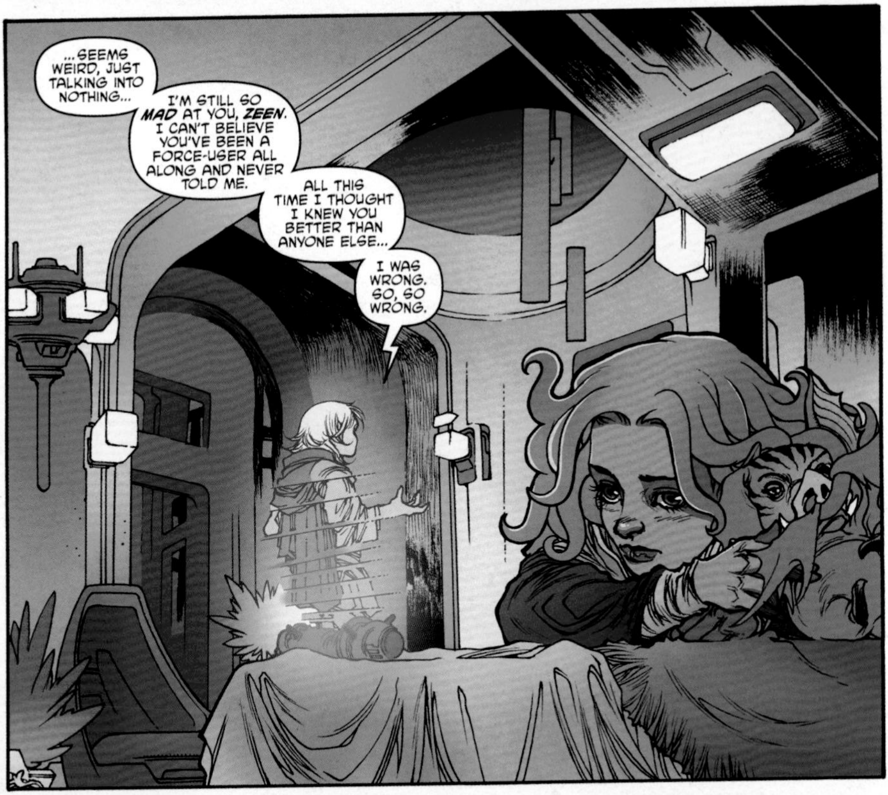
...SEEMS WEIRD, JUST TALKING INTO NOTHING...
I'M STILL SO MAD AT YOU, ZEEN. I CAN'T BELIEVE YOU'VE BEEN A FORCE-USER ALL ALONG AND NEVER TOLD ME.
ALL THIS TIME I THOUGHT I KNEW YOU BETTER THAN ANYONE ELSE...
I WAS WRONG. SO, SO WRONG.

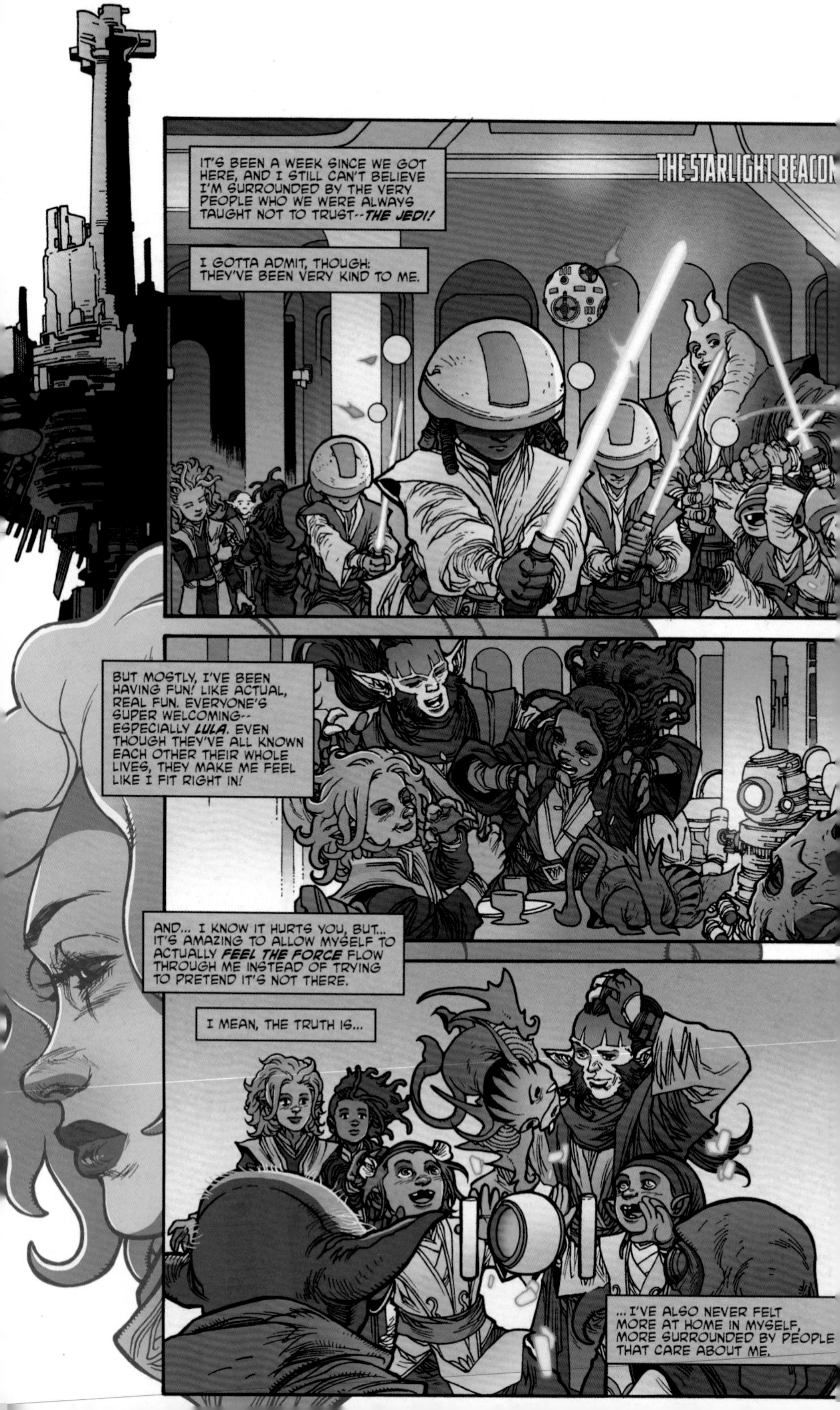
THE STARLIGHT BEACON
IT'S BEEN A WEEK SINCE WE GOT HERE, AND I STILL CAN'T BELIEVE I'M SURROUNDED BY THE VERY PEOPLE WHO WE WERE ALWAYS TAUGHT NOT TO TRUST--THE JEDI!
I GOTTA ADMIT, THOUGH: THEY'VE BEEN VERY KIND TO ME.
BUT MOSTLY, I'VE BEEN HAVING FUN! LIKE ACTUAL, REAL FUN. EVERYONE'S SUPER WELCOMING--ESPECIALLY LULA. EVEN THOUGH THEY'VE ALL KNOWN EACH OTHER THEIR WHOLE LIVES, THEY MAKE ME FEEL LIKE I FIT RIGHT IN!
AND... I KNOW IT HURTS YOU, BUT... IT'S AMAZING TO ALLOW MYSELF TO ACTUALLY FEEL THE FORCE FLOW THROUGH ME INSTEAD OF TRYING TO PRETEND IT'S NOT THERE.
I MEAN, THE TRUTH IS...
...I'VE ALSO NEVER FELT MORE AT HOME IN MYSELF, MORE SURROUNDED BY PEOPLE THAT CARE ABOUT ME.

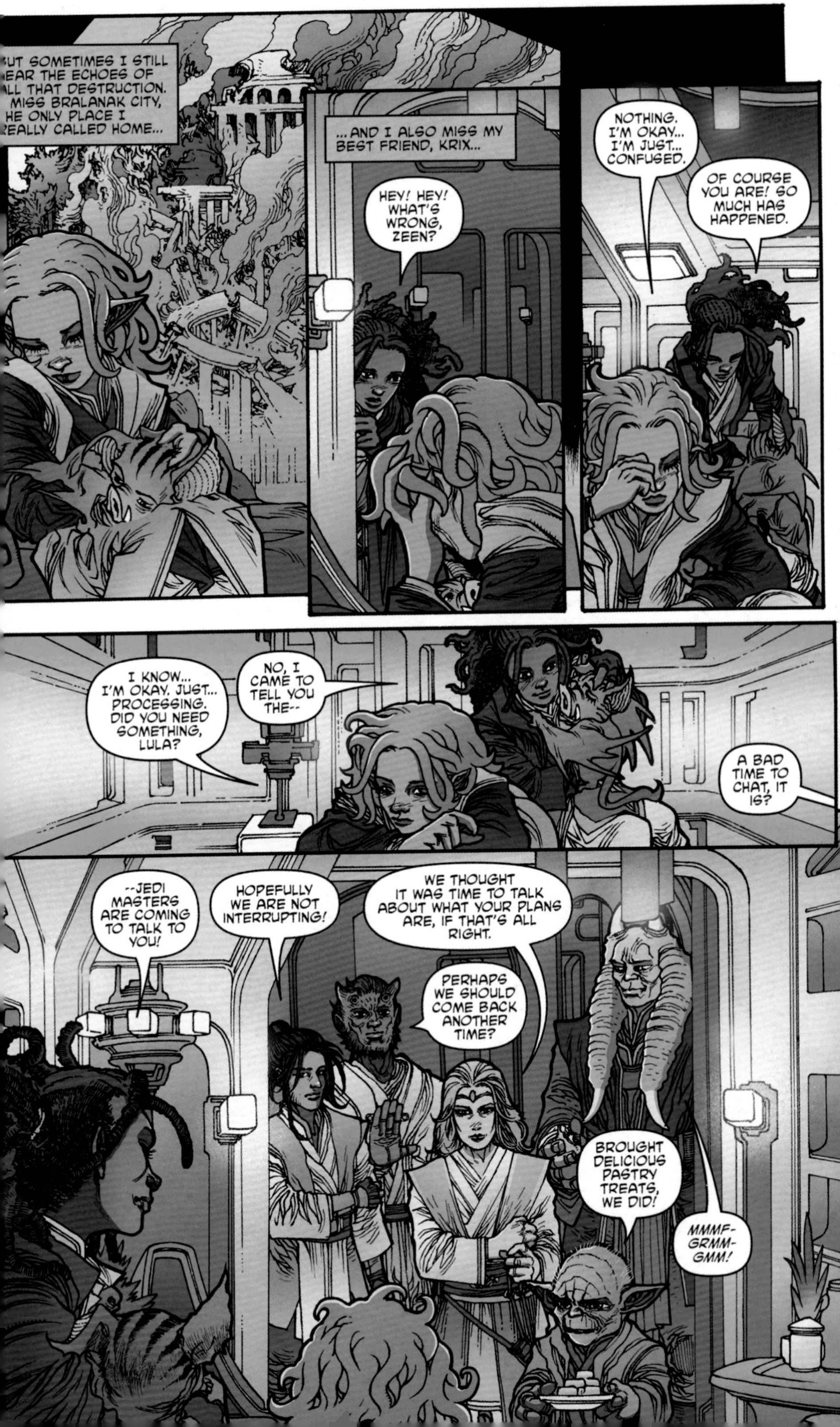
BUT SOMETIMES I STILL HEAR THE ECHOES OF ALL THAT DESTRUCTION. I MISS BRALANAK CITY, THE ONLY PLACE I REALLY CALLED HOME...
...AND I ALSO MISS MY BEST FRIEND, KRIX...
HEY! HEY! WHAT'S WRONG, ZEEN?
NOTHING. I'M OKAY... I'M JUST... CONFUSED.
OF COURSE YOU ARE! SO MUCH HAS HAPPENED.
I KNOW... I'M OKAY. JUST... PROCESSING. DID YOU NEED SOMETHING, LULA?
NO, I CAME TO TELL YOU THE--
A BAD TIME TO CHAT, IT IS?
--JEDI MASTERS ARE COMING TO TALK TO YOU!
HOPEFULLY WE ARE NOT INTERRUPTING!
WE THOUGHT IT WAS TIME TO TALK ABOUT WHAT YOUR PLANS ARE, IF THAT'S ALL RIGHT.
PERHAPS WE SHOULD COME BACK ANOTHER TIME?
BROUGHT DELICIOUS PASTRY TREATS, WE DID!
MMMF-GRMM-GMM!

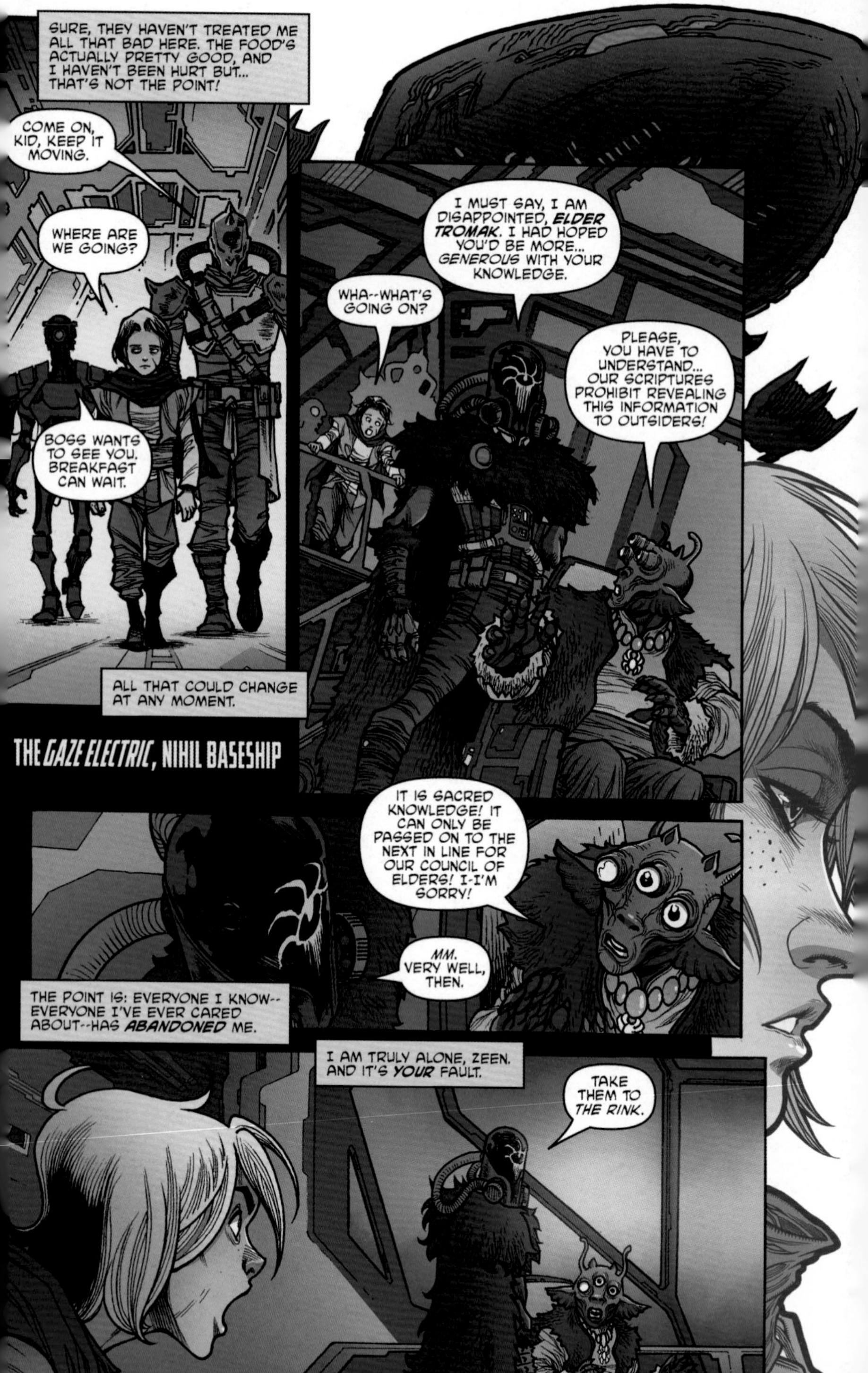
SURE, THEY HAVEN'T TREATED ME ALL THAT BAD HERE. THE FOOD'S ACTUALLY PRETTY GOOD, AND I HAVEN'T BEEN HURT BUT... THAT'S NOT THE POINT!
COME ON, KID, KEEP IT MOVING.
WHERE ARE WE GOING?
BOSS WANTS TO SEE YOU. BREAKFAST CAN WAIT.
ALL THAT COULD CHANGE AT ANY MOMENT.
THE *GAZE ELECTRIC*, NIHIL BASESHIP
I MUST SAY, I AM DISAPPOINTED, ***ELDER TROMAK***. I HAD HOPED YOU'D BE MORE... *GENEROUS* WITH YOUR KNOWLEDGE.
WHA--WHAT'S GOING ON?
PLEASE, YOU HAVE TO UNDERSTAND... OUR SCRIPTURES PROHIBIT REVEALING THIS INFORMATION TO OUTSIDERS!
IT IS SACRED KNOWLEDGE! IT CAN ONLY BE PASSED ON TO THE NEXT IN LINE FOR OUR COUNCIL OF ELDERS! I-I'M SORRY!
MM. VERY WELL, THEN.
THE POINT IS: EVERYONE I KNOW-- EVERYONE I'VE EVER CARED ABOUT--HAS ***ABANDONED*** ME.
I AM TRULY ALONE, ZEEN. AND IT'S ***YOUR*** FAULT.
TAKE THEM TO *THE RINK*.

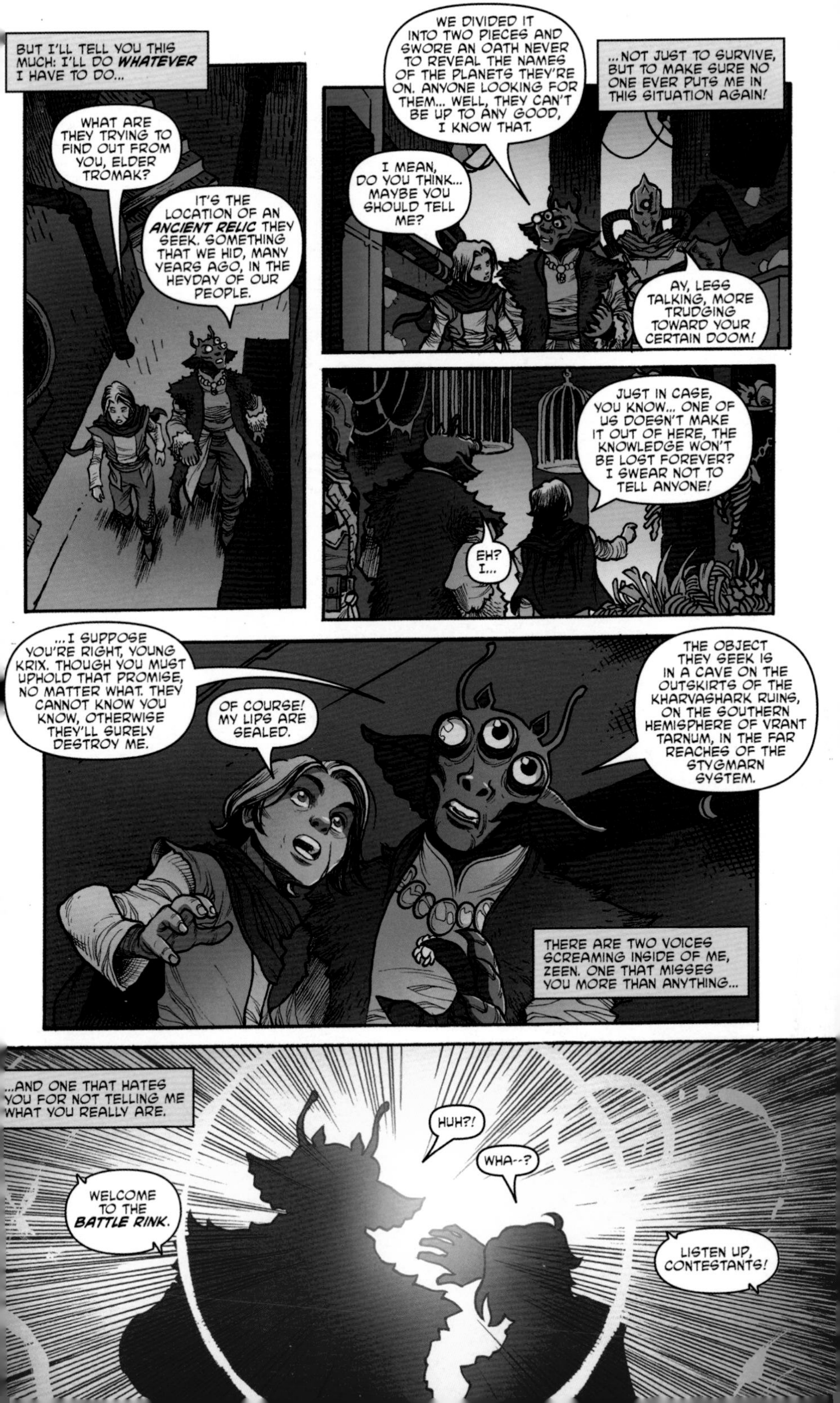

BUT I'LL TELL YOU THIS MUCH: I'LL DO WHATEVER I HAVE TO DO...
WHAT ARE THEY TRYING TO FIND OUT FROM YOU, ELDER TROMAK?
IT'S THE LOCATION OF AN ANCIENT RELIC THEY SEEK. SOMETHING THAT WE HID, MANY YEARS AGO, IN THE HEYDAY OF OUR PEOPLE.
WE DIVIDED IT INTO TWO PIECES AND SWORE AN OATH NEVER TO REVEAL THE NAMES OF THE PLANETS THEY'RE ON. ANYONE LOOKING FOR THEM... WELL, THEY CAN'T BE UP TO ANY GOOD, I KNOW THAT.
...NOT JUST TO SURVIVE, BUT TO MAKE SURE NO ONE EVER PUTS ME IN THIS SITUATION AGAIN!
I MEAN, DO YOU THINK... MAYBE YOU SHOULD TELL ME?
AY, LESS TALKING, MORE TRUDGING TOWARD YOUR CERTAIN DOOM!
JUST IN CASE, YOU KNOW... ONE OF US DOESN'T MAKE IT OUT OF HERE, THE KNOWLEDGE WON'T BE LOST FOREVER? I SWEAR NOT TO TELL ANYONE!
EH? I...
...I SUPPOSE YOU'RE RIGHT, YOUNG KRIX. THOUGH YOU MUST UPHOLD THAT PROMISE, NO MATTER WHAT. THEY CANNOT KNOW YOU KNOW, OTHERWISE THEY'LL SURELY DESTROY ME.
OF COURSE! MY LIPS ARE SEALED.
THE OBJECT THEY SEEK IS IN A CAVE ON THE OUTSKIRTS OF THE KHARVASHARK RUINS, ON THE SOUTHERN HEMISPHERE OF VRANT TARNUM, IN THE FAR REACHES OF THE STYGMARN SYSTEM.
THERE ARE TWO VOICES SCREAMING INSIDE OF ME, ZEEN. ONE THAT MISSES YOU MORE THAN ANYTHING...
...AND ONE THAT HATES YOU FOR NOT TELLING ME WHAT YOU REALLY ARE.
HUH?!
WHA--?
WELCOME TO THE BATTLE RINK.
LISTEN UP, CONTESTANTS!

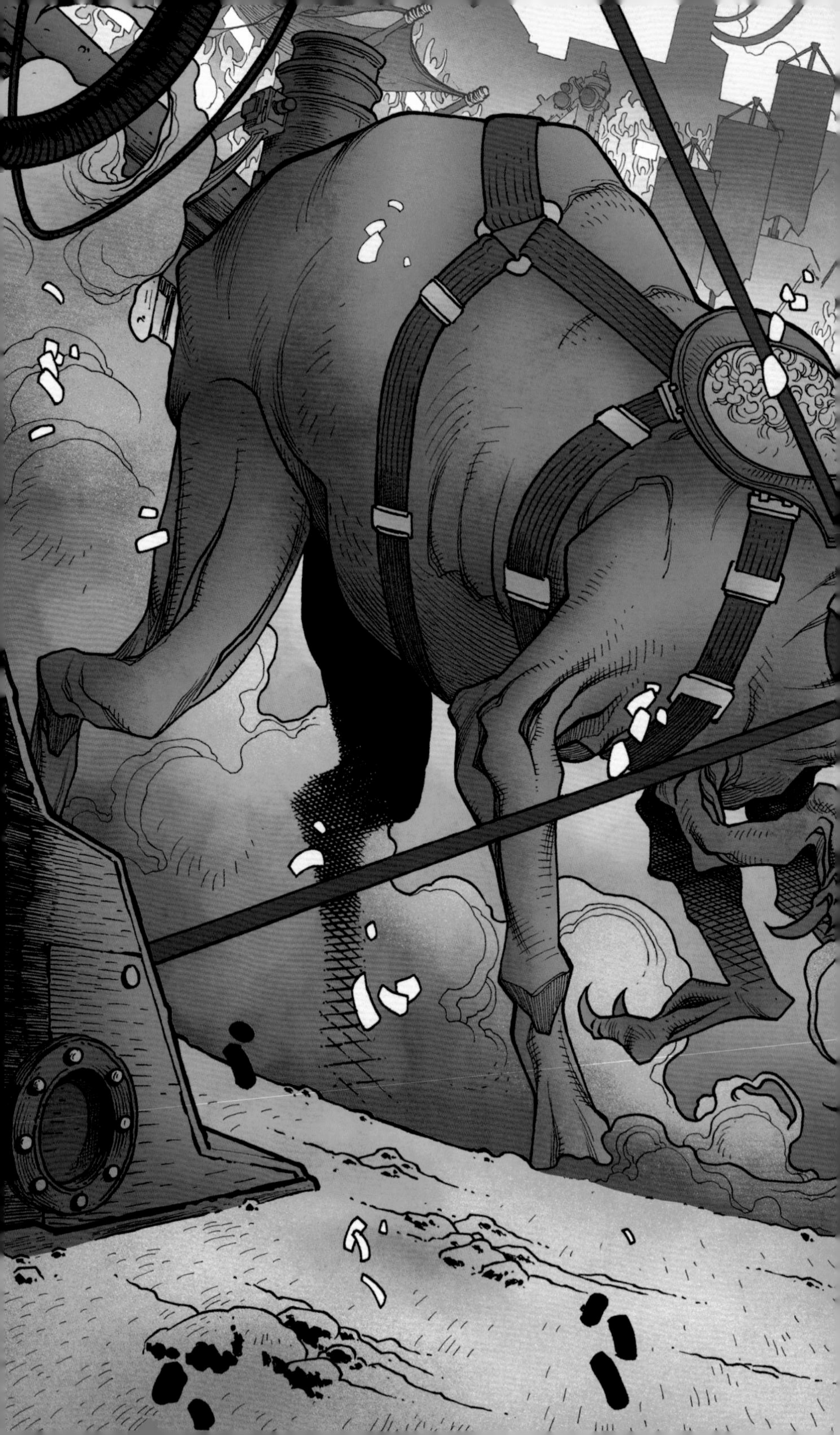

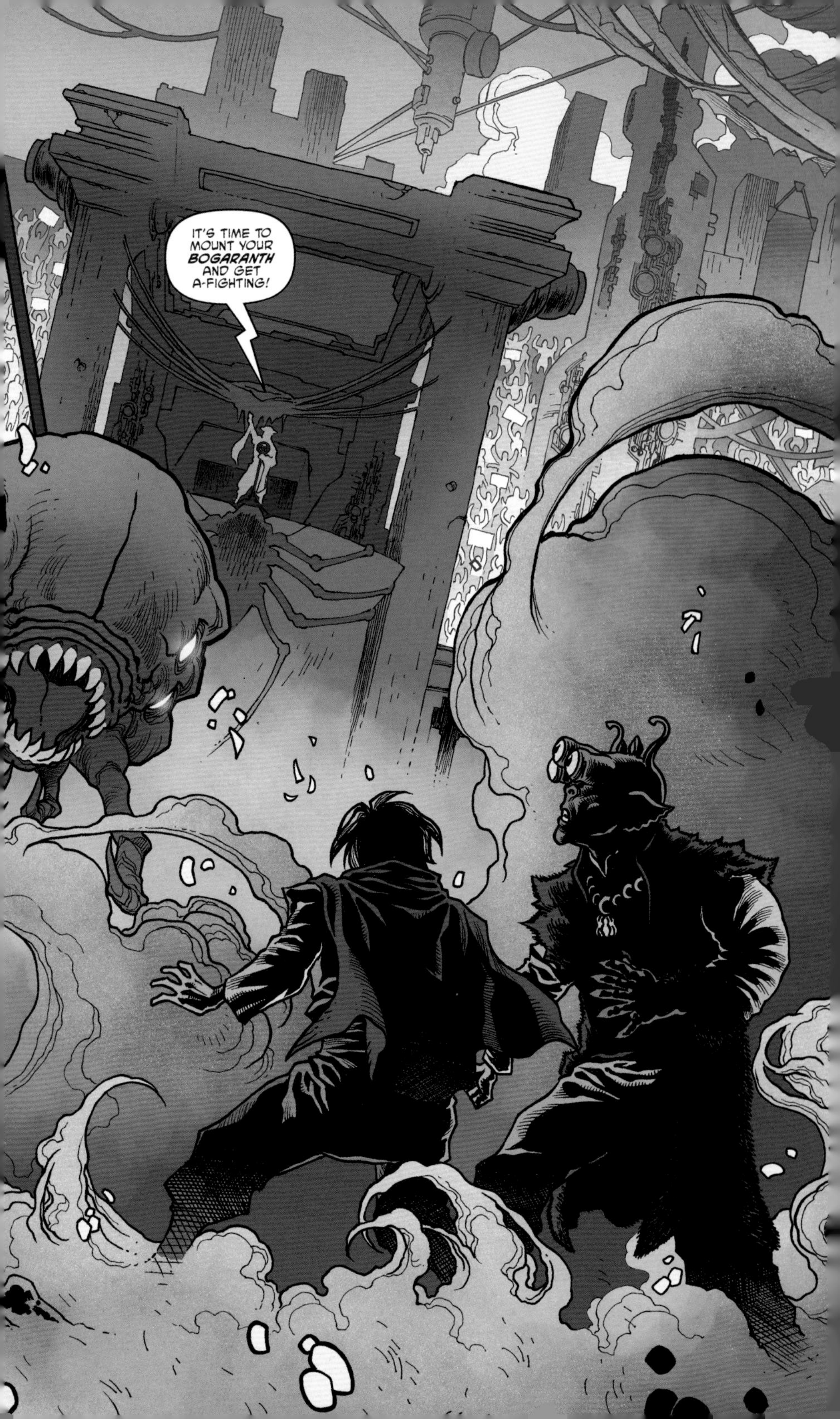
IT'S TIME TO MOUNT YOUR **BOGARANTH** AND GET A-FIGHTING!

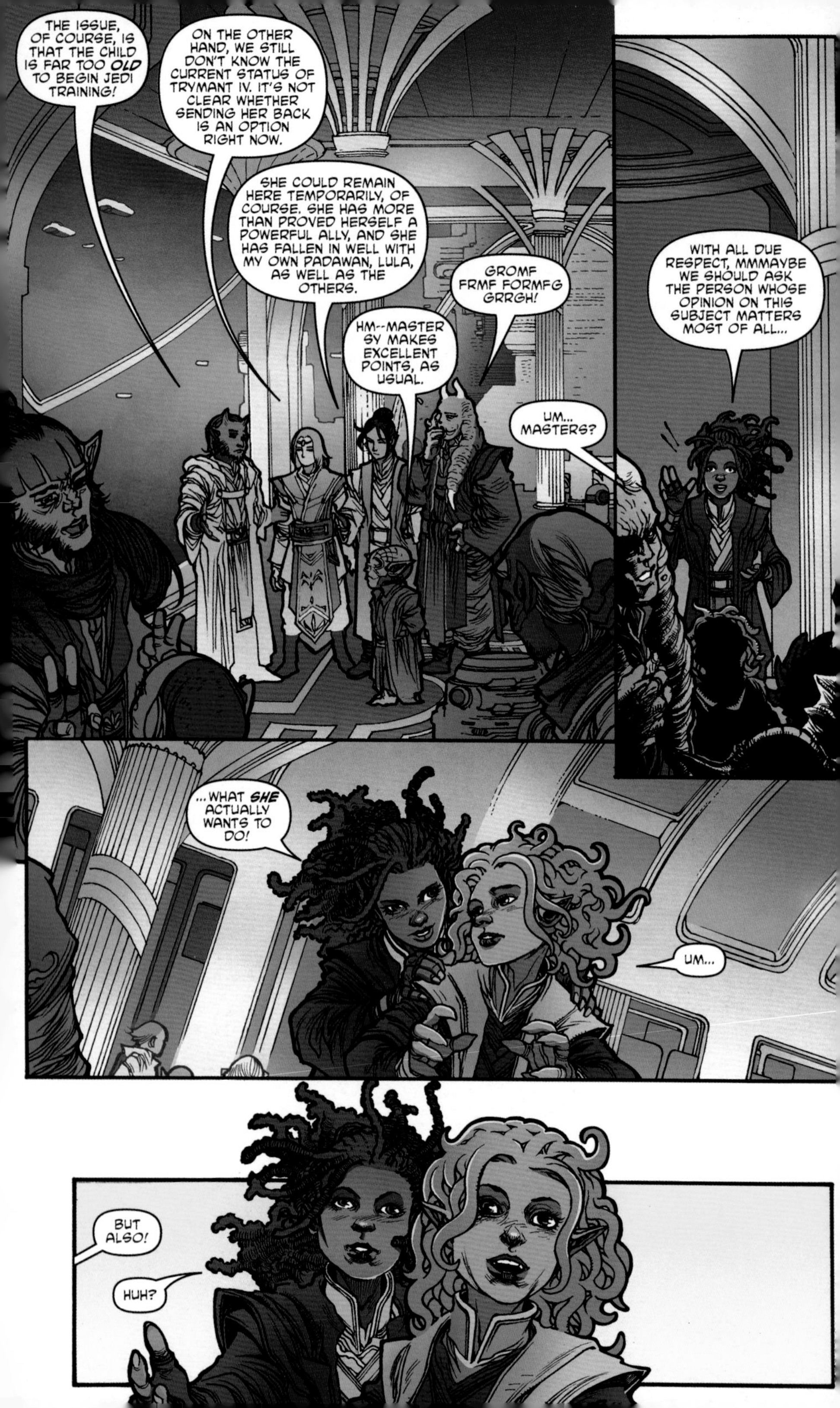
THE ISSUE, OF COURSE, IS THAT THE CHILD IS FAR TOO OLD TO BEGIN JEDI TRAINING!
ON THE OTHER HAND, WE STILL DON'T KNOW THE CURRENT STATUS OF TRYMANT IV. IT'S NOT CLEAR WHETHER SENDING HER BACK IS AN OPTION RIGHT NOW.
SHE COULD REMAIN HERE TEMPORARILY, OF COURSE. SHE HAS MORE THAN PROVED HERSELF A POWERFUL ALLY, AND SHE HAS FALLEN IN WELL WITH MY OWN PADAWAN, LULA, AS WELL AS THE OTHERS.
HM--MASTER SY MAKES EXCELLENT POINTS, AS USUAL.
GROMF FRMF FORMFG GRRGH!
UM... MASTERS?
WITH ALL DUE RESPECT, MMMAYBE WE SHOULD ASK THE PERSON WHOSE OPINION ON THIS SUBJECT MATTERS MOST OF ALL...
...WHAT SHE ACTUALLY WANTS TO DO!
UM...
BUT ALSO!
HUH?

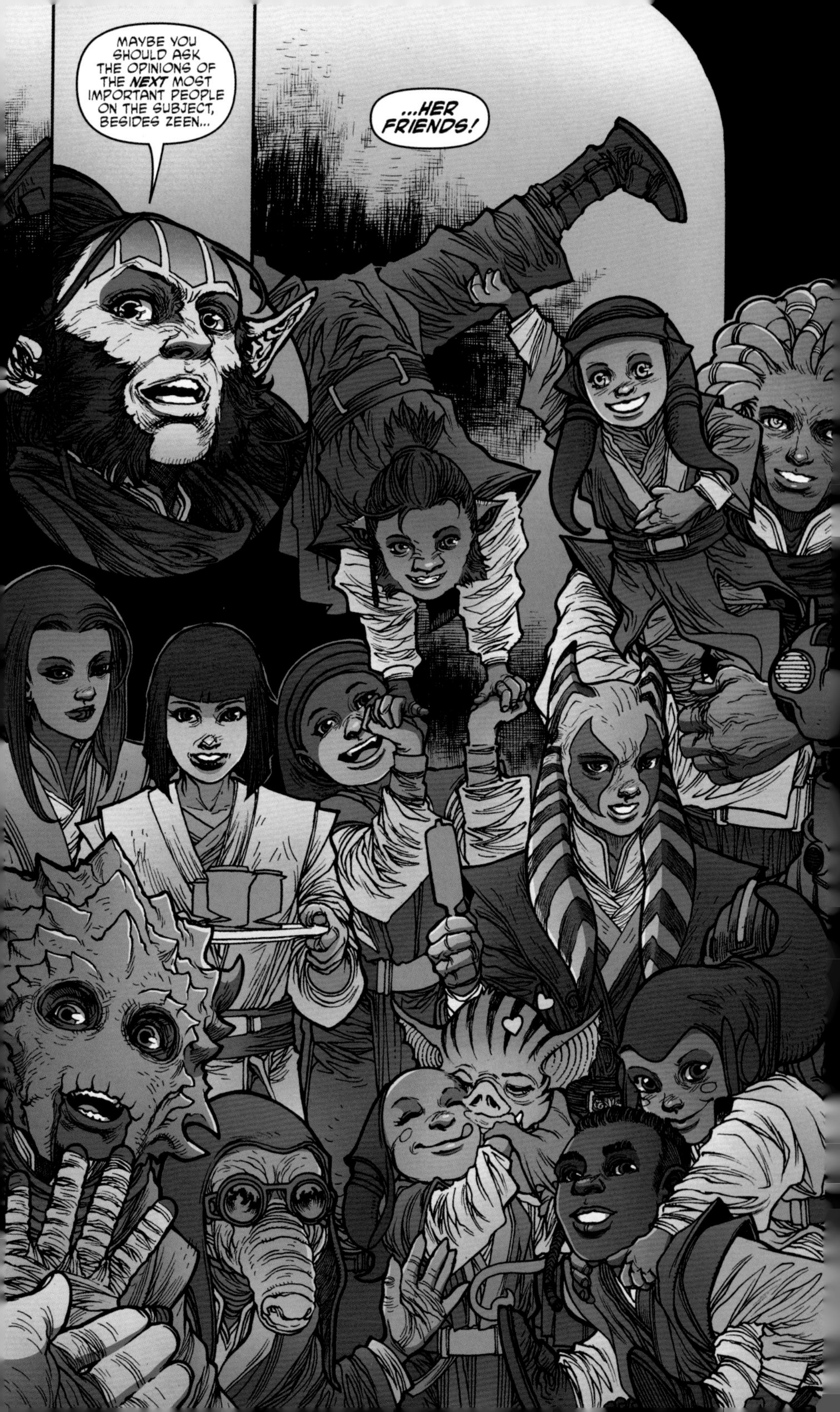
MAYBE YOU SHOULD ASK THE OPINIONS OF THE *NEXT* MOST IMPORTANT PEOPLE ON THE SUBJECT, BESIDES ZEEN...
...HER FRIENDS!

GALACTIC DATA FILE
JEDI HIERARCHY OF THE HIGH REPUBLIC

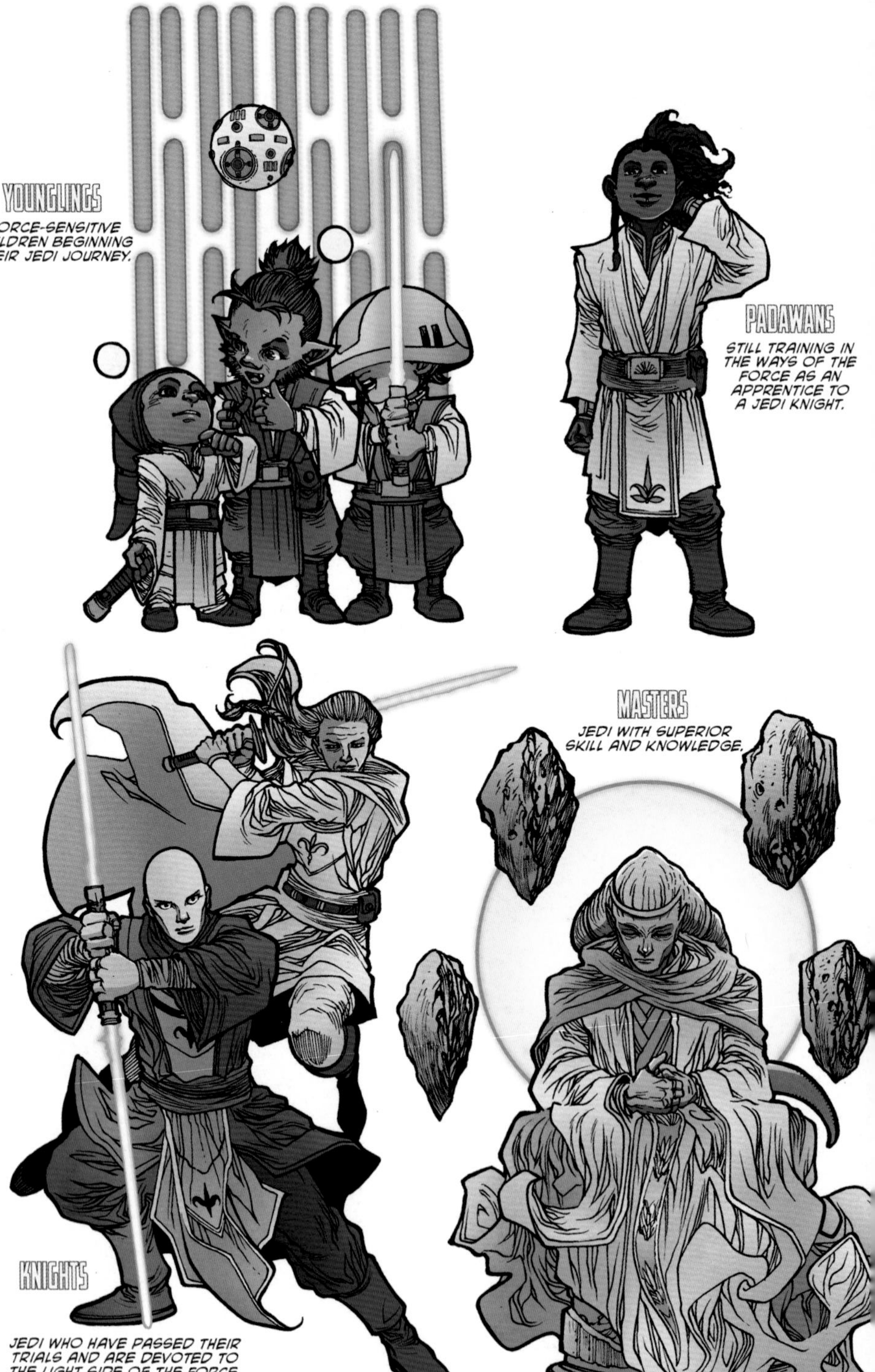

YOUNGLINGS
FORCE-SENSITIVE CHILDREN BEGINNING THEIR JEDI JOURNEY.
PADAWANS
STILL TRAINING IN THE WAYS OF THE FORCE AS AN APPRENTICE TO A JEDI KNIGHT.
MASTERS
JEDI WITH SUPERIOR SKILL AND KNOWLEDGE.
KNIGHTS
JEDI WHO HAVE PASSED THEIR TRIALS AND ARE DEVOTED TO THE LIGHT SIDE OF THE FORCE.

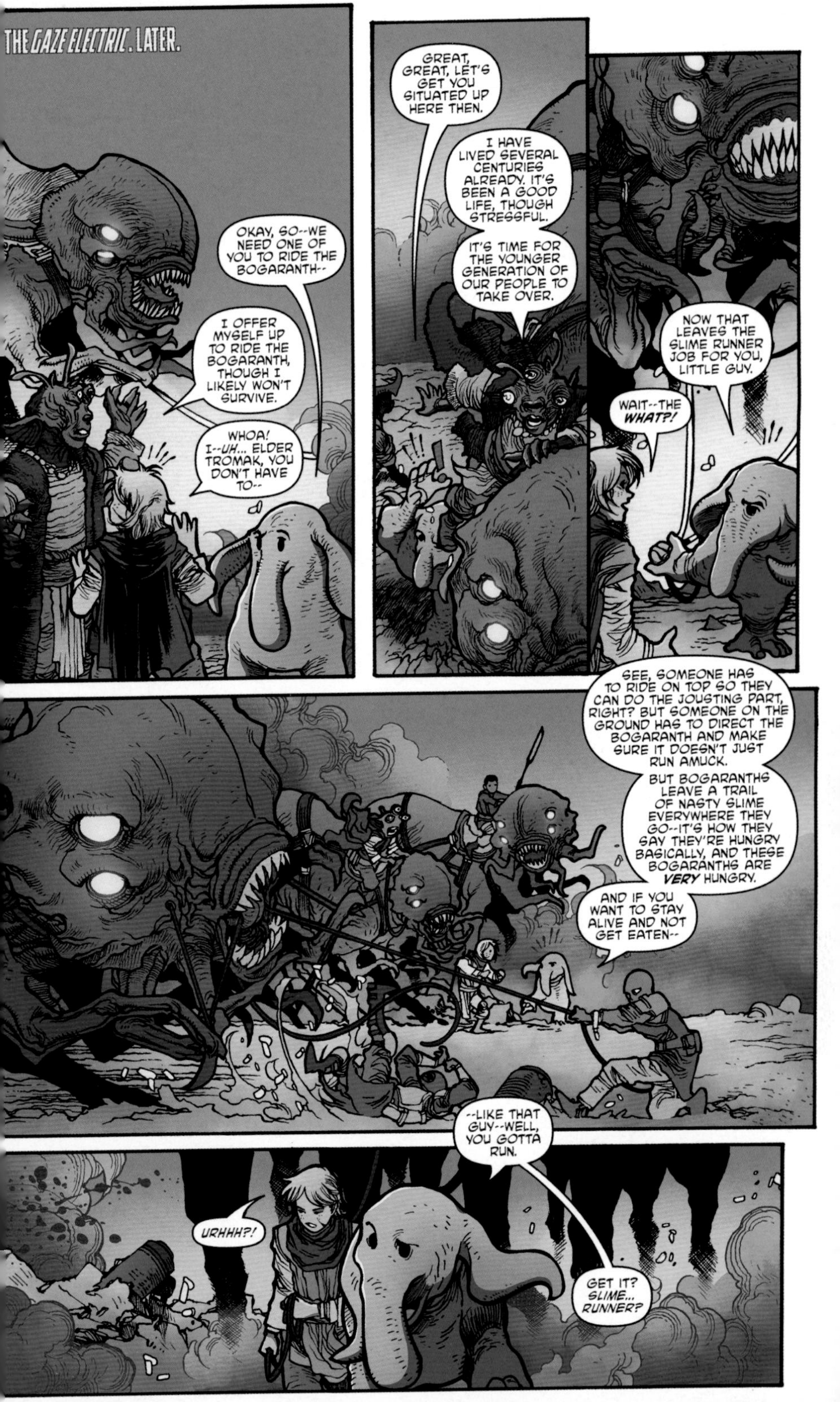
THE GAZE ELECTRIC. LATER.
OKAY, SO--WE NEED ONE OF YOU TO RIDE THE BOGARANTH--
I OFFER MYSELF UP TO RIDE THE BOGARANTH, THOUGH I LIKELY WON'T SURVIVE.
WHOA! I--UH... ELDER TROMAK, YOU DON'T HAVE TO--
GREAT, GREAT, LET'S GET YOU SITUATED UP HERE THEN.
I HAVE LIVED SEVERAL CENTURIES ALREADY. IT'S BEEN A GOOD LIFE, THOUGH STRESSFUL.
IT'S TIME FOR THE YOUNGER GENERATION OF OUR PEOPLE TO TAKE OVER.
NOW THAT LEAVES THE SLIME RUNNER JOB FOR YOU, LITTLE GUY.
WAIT--THE WHAT?!
SEE, SOMEONE HAS TO RIDE ON TOP SO THEY CAN DO THE JOUSTING PART, RIGHT? BUT SOMEONE ON THE GROUND HAS TO DIRECT THE BOGARANTH AND MAKE SURE IT DOESN'T JUST RUN AMUCK.
BUT BOGARANTHS LEAVE A TRAIL OF NASTY SLIME EVERYWHERE THEY GO--IT'S HOW THEY SAY THEY'RE HUNGRY BASICALLY, AND THESE BOGARANTHS ARE VERY HUNGRY.
AND IF YOU WANT TO STAY ALIVE AND NOT GET EATEN--
--LIKE THAT GUY--WELL, YOU GOTTA RUN.
URHHH?!
GET IT? SLIME... RUNNER?

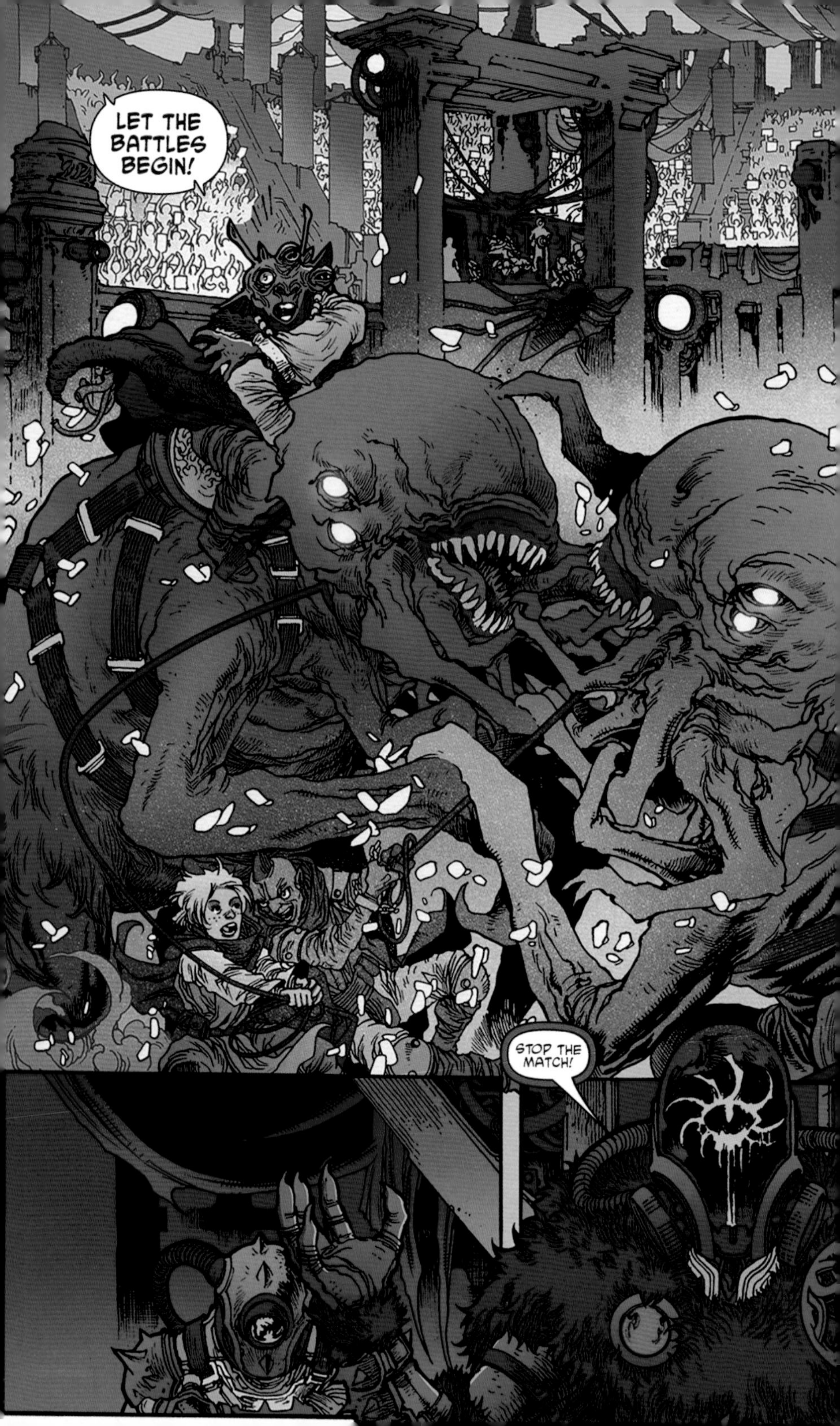
LET THE BATTLES BEGIN!
STOP THE MATCH!

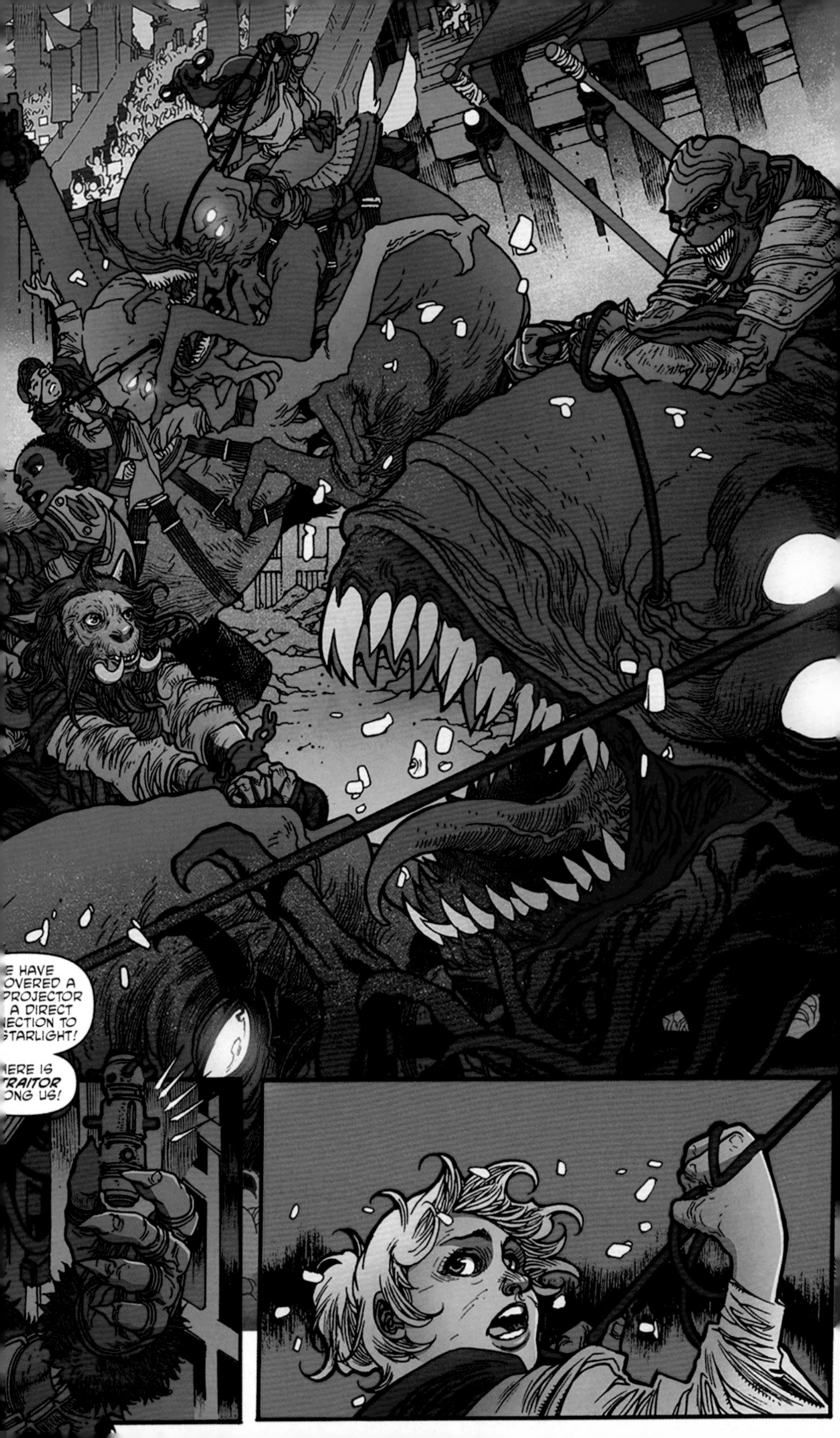
E HAVE
OVERED A
PROJECTOR
A DIRECT
ECTION TO
STARLIGHT!
ERE IS
TRAITOR
ONG US!

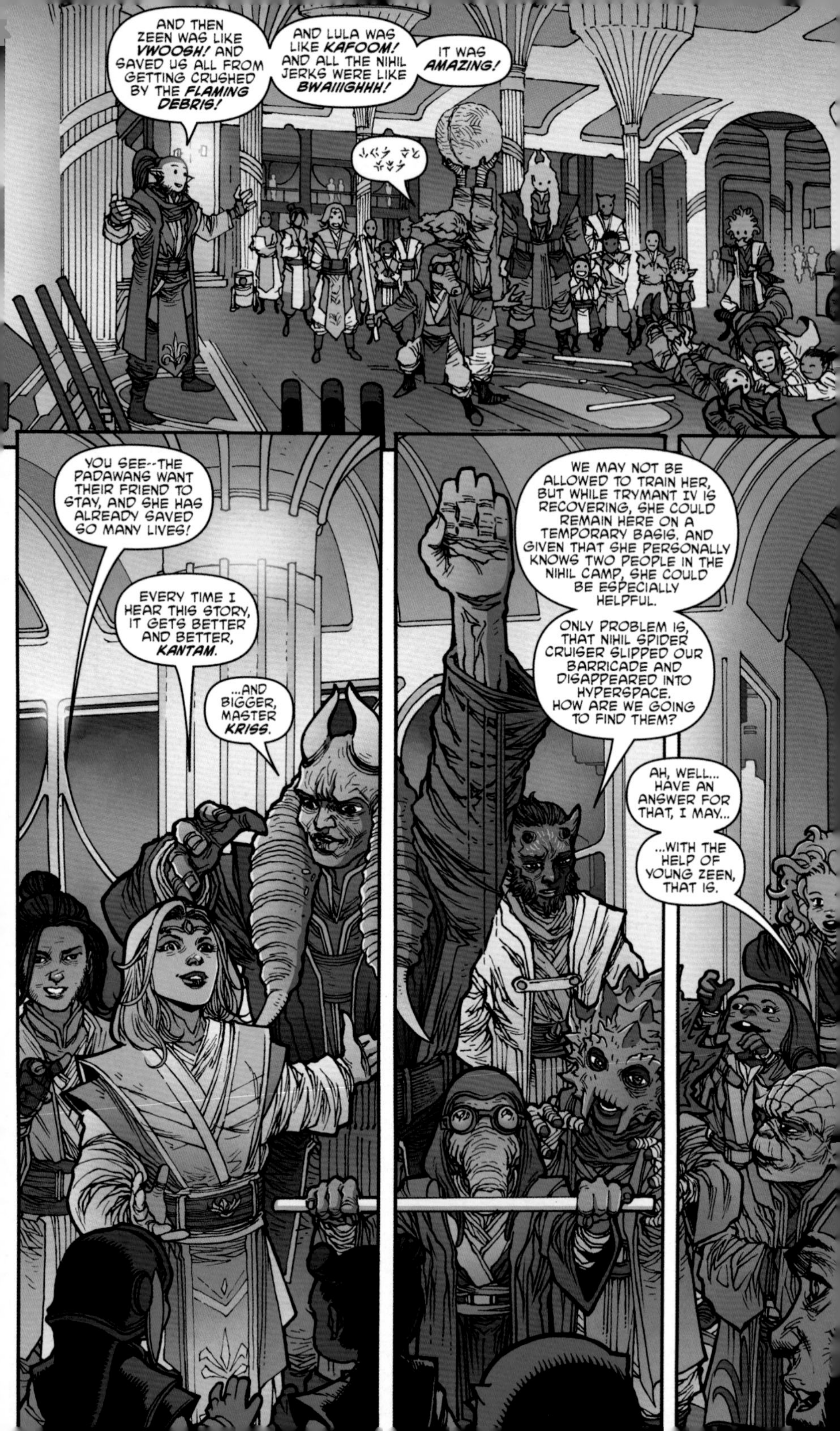
AND THEN ZEEN WAS LIKE VWOOSH! AND SAVED US ALL FROM GETTING CRUSHED BY THE FLAMING DEBRIS!
AND LULA WAS LIKE KAFOOM! AND ALL THE NIHIL JERKS WERE LIKE BWAIIIGHHH!
IT WAS AMAZING!
YOU SEE--THE PADAWANS WANT THEIR FRIEND TO STAY, AND SHE HAS ALREADY SAVED SO MANY LIVES!
EVERY TIME I HEAR THIS STORY, IT GETS BETTER AND BETTER, KANTAM.
...AND BIGGER, MASTER KRISS.
WE MAY NOT BE ALLOWED TO TRAIN HER, BUT WHILE TRYMANT IV IS RECOVERING, SHE COULD REMAIN HERE ON A TEMPORARY BASIS. AND GIVEN THAT SHE PERSONALLY KNOWS TWO PEOPLE IN THE NIHIL CAMP, SHE COULD BE ESPECIALLY HELPFUL.
ONLY PROBLEM IS, THAT NIHIL SPIDER CRUISER SLIPPED OUR BARRICADE AND DISAPPEARED INTO HYPERSPACE. HOW ARE WE GOING TO FIND THEM?
AH, WELL... HAVE AN ANSWER FOR THAT, I MAY...
...WITH THE HELP OF YOUNG ZEEN, THAT IS.

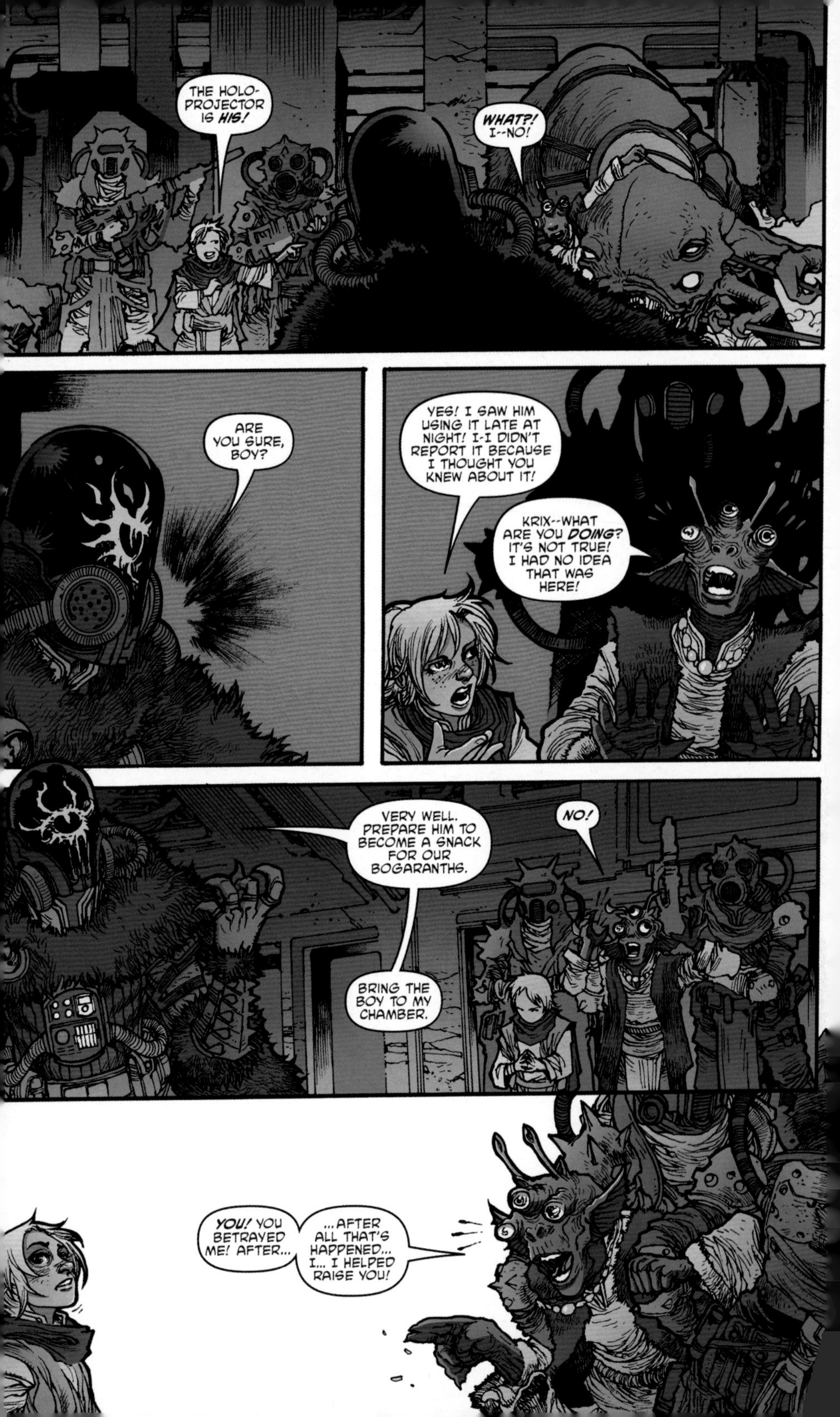
THE HOLO-PROJECTOR IS HIS!
WHAT?! I--NO!
ARE YOU SURE, BOY?
YES! I SAW HIM USING IT LATE AT NIGHT! I-I DIDN'T REPORT IT BECAUSE I THOUGHT YOU KNEW ABOUT IT!
KRIX--WHAT ARE YOU DOING? IT'S NOT TRUE! I HAD NO IDEA THAT WAS HERE!
VERY WELL. PREPARE HIM TO BECOME A SNACK FOR OUR BOGARANTHS.
BRING THE BOY TO MY CHAMBER.
NO!
YOU! YOU BETRAYED ME! AFTER...
...AFTER ALL THAT'S HAPPENED... I... I HELPED RAISE YOU!

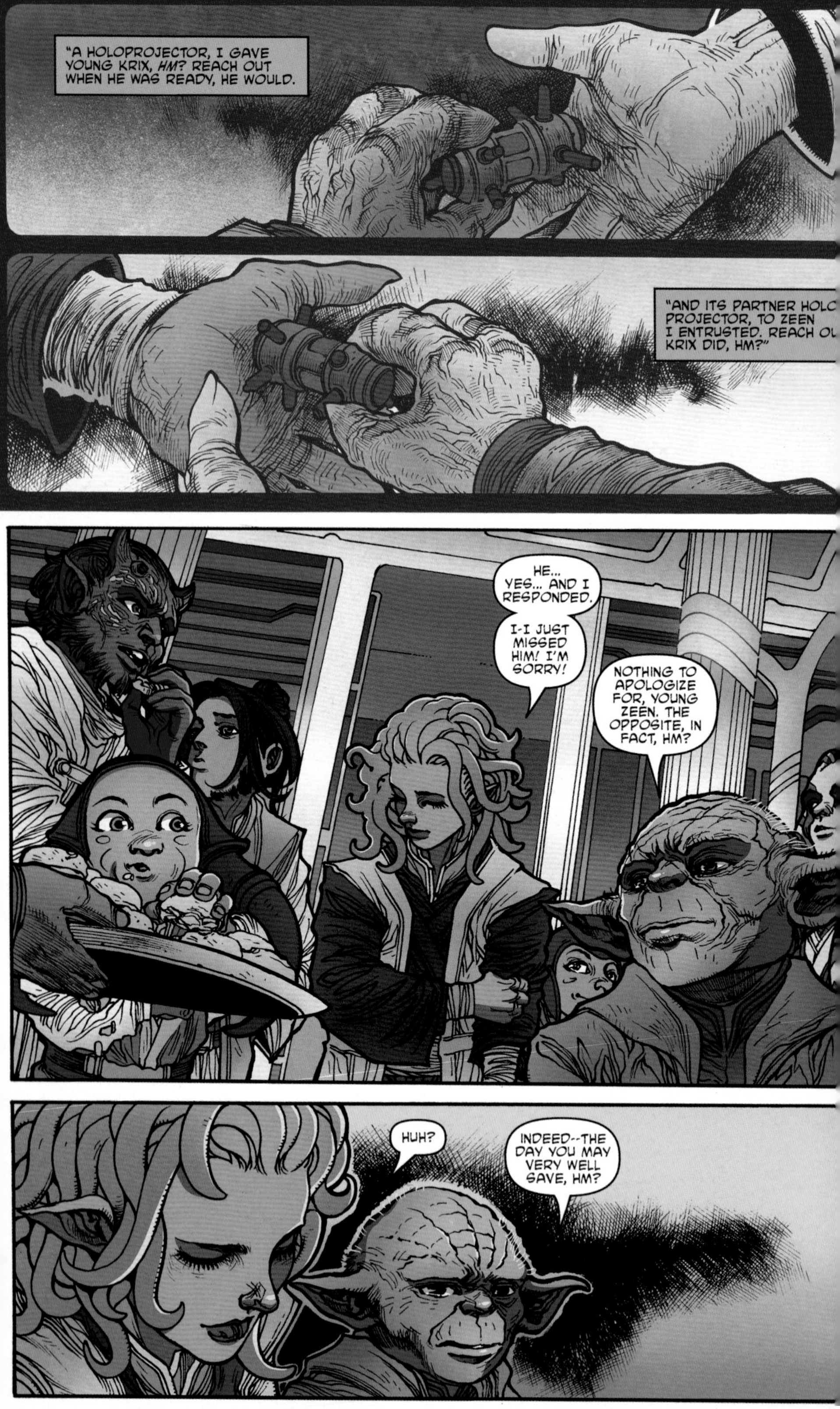
"A HOLOPROJECTOR, I GAVE YOUNG KRIX, HM? REACH OUT WHEN HE WAS READY, HE WOULD.
"AND ITS PARTNER HOLO PROJECTOR, TO ZEEN I ENTRUSTED. REACH OU KRIX DID, HM?"
HE... YES... AND I RESPONDED.
I-I JUST MISSED HIM! I'M SORRY!
NOTHING TO APOLOGIZE FOR, YOUNG ZEEN. THE OPPOSITE, IN FACT, HM?
HUH?
INDEED--THE DAY YOU MAY VERY WELL SAVE, HM?

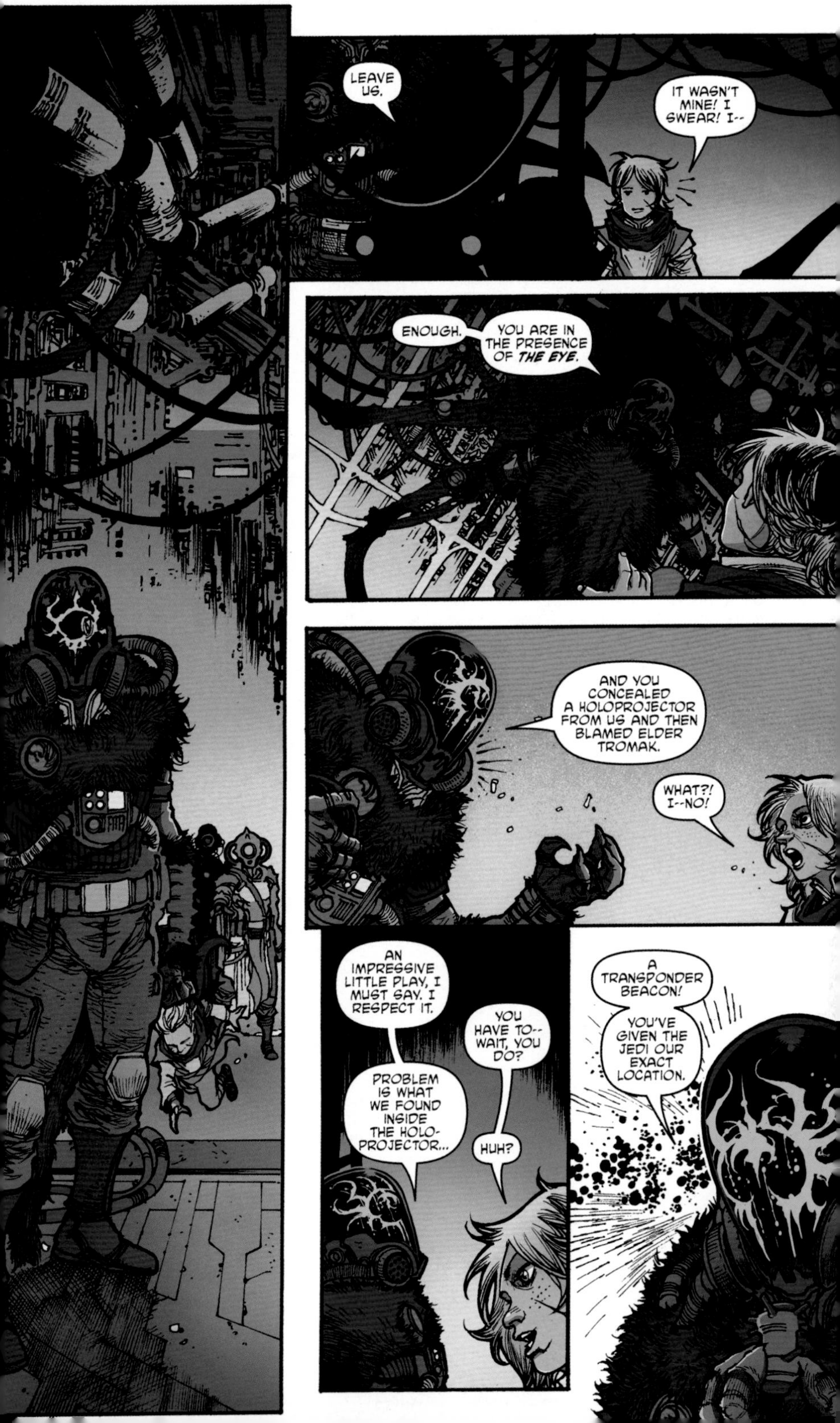
LEAVE US.
IT WASN'T MINE! I SWEAR! I--
ENOUGH.
YOU ARE IN THE PRESENCE OF *THE EYE*.
AND YOU CONCEALED A HOLOPROJECTOR FROM US AND THEN BLAMED ELDER TROMAK.
WHAT?! I--NO!
AN IMPRESSIVE LITTLE PLAY, I MUST SAY. I RESPECT IT.
YOU HAVE TO--WAIT, YOU DO?
PROBLEM IS WHAT WE FOUND INSIDE THE HOLO-PROJECTOR...
HUH?
A TRANSPONDER BEACON!
YOU'VE GIVEN THE JEDI OUR EXACT LOCATION.

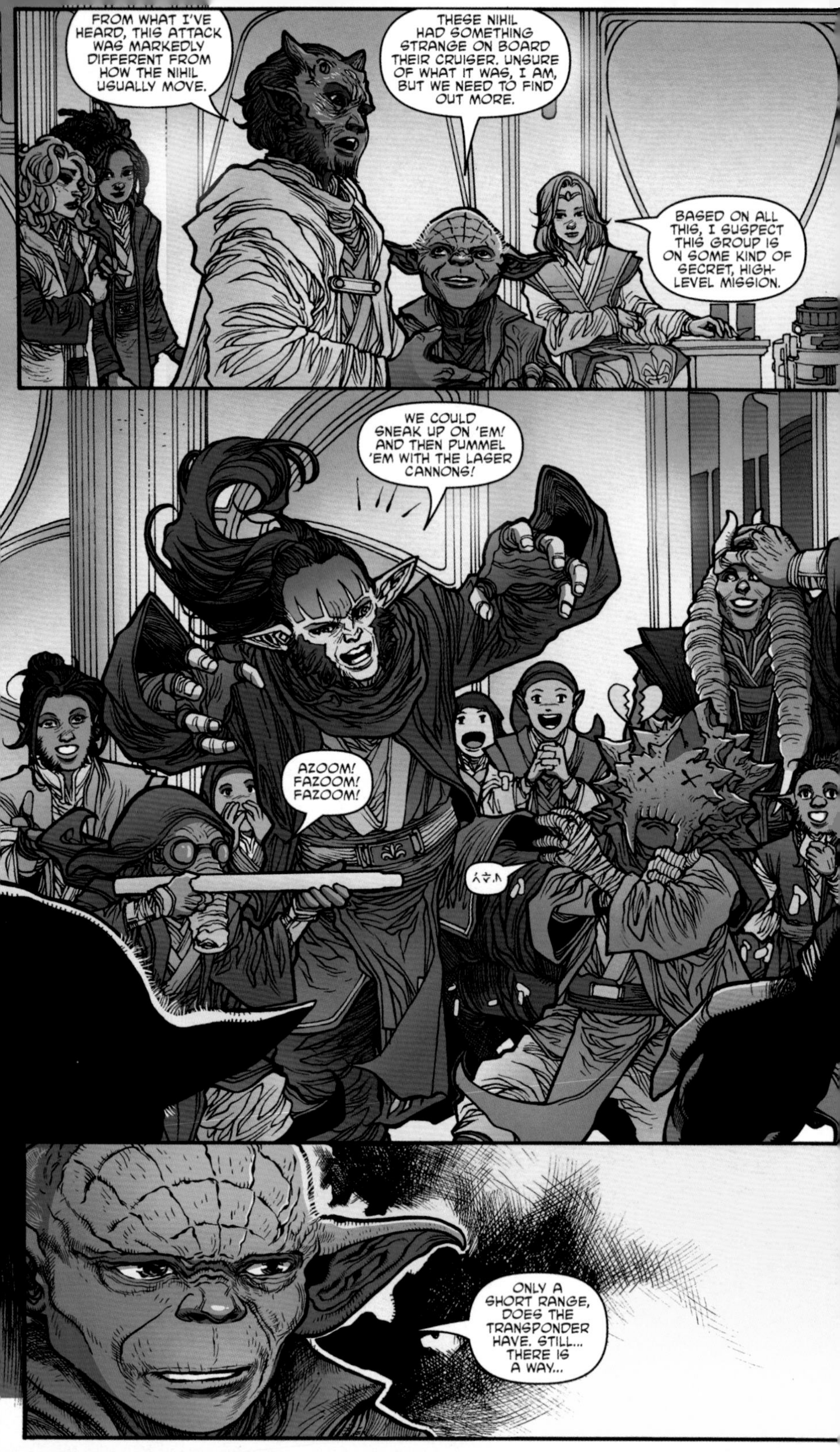
FROM WHAT I'VE HEARD, THIS ATTACK WAS MARKEDLY DIFFERENT FROM HOW THE NIHIL USUALLY MOVE.
THESE NIHIL HAD SOMETHING STRANGE ON BOARD THEIR CRUISER. UNSURE OF WHAT IT WAS, I AM, BUT WE NEED TO FIND OUT MORE.
BASED ON ALL THIS, I SUSPECT THIS GROUP IS ON SOME KIND OF SECRET, HIGH-LEVEL MISSION.
WE COULD SNEAK UP ON 'EM! AND THEN PUMMEL 'EM WITH THE LASER CANNONS!
AZOOM! FAZOOM! FAZOOM!
ONLY A SHORT RANGE, DOES THE TRANSPONDER HAVE. STILL... THERE IS A WAY...

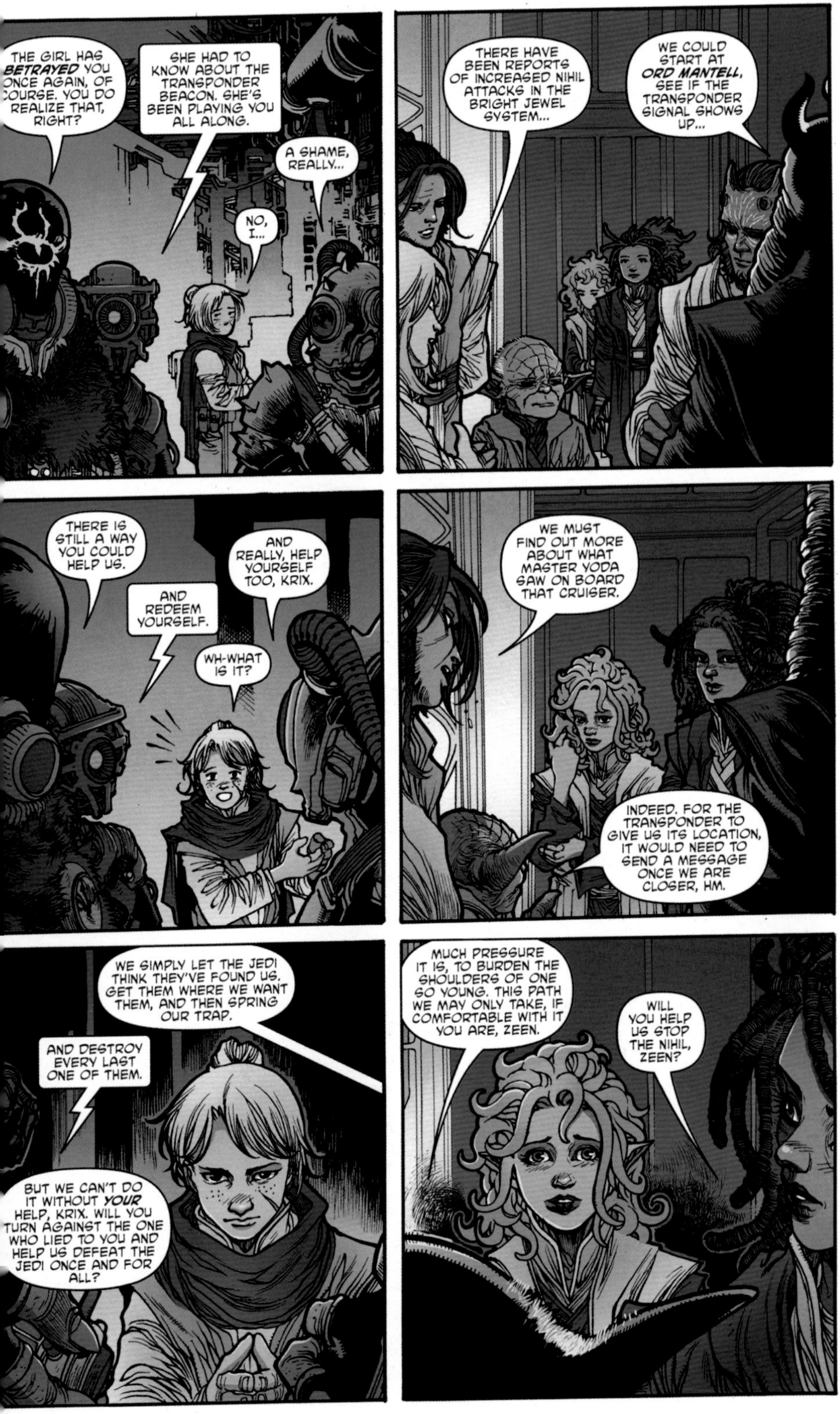
THE GIRL HAS BETRAYED YOU ONCE AGAIN, OF COURSE. YOU DO REALIZE THAT, RIGHT?
SHE HAD TO KNOW ABOUT THE TRANSPONDER BEACON. SHE'S BEEN PLAYING YOU ALL ALONG.
A SHAME, REALLY...
NO, I...
THERE HAVE BEEN REPORTS OF INCREASED NIHIL ATTACKS IN THE BRIGHT JEWEL SYSTEM...
WE COULD START AT ORD MANTELL, SEE IF THE TRANSPONDER SIGNAL SHOWS UP...
THERE IS STILL A WAY YOU COULD HELP US.
AND REDEEM YOURSELF.
AND REALLY, HELP YOURSELF TOO, KRIX.
WH-WHAT IS IT?
WE MUST FIND OUT MORE ABOUT WHAT MASTER YODA SAW ON BOARD THAT CRUISER.
INDEED. FOR THE TRANSPONDER TO GIVE US ITS LOCATION, IT WOULD NEED TO SEND A MESSAGE ONCE WE ARE CLOSER, HM.
WE SIMPLY LET THE JEDI THINK THEY'VE FOUND US. GET THEM WHERE WE WANT THEM, AND THEN SPRING OUR TRAP.
AND DESTROY EVERY LAST ONE OF THEM.
BUT WE CAN'T DO IT WITHOUT YOUR HELP, KRIX. WILL YOU TURN AGAINST THE ONE WHO LIED TO YOU AND HELP US DEFEAT THE JEDI ONCE AND FOR ALL?
MUCH PRESSURE IT IS, TO BURDEN THE SHOULDERS OF ONE SO YOUNG. THIS PATH WE MAY ONLY TAKE, IF COMFORTABLE WITH IT YOU ARE, ZEEN.
WILL YOU HELP US STOP THE NIHIL, ZEEN?

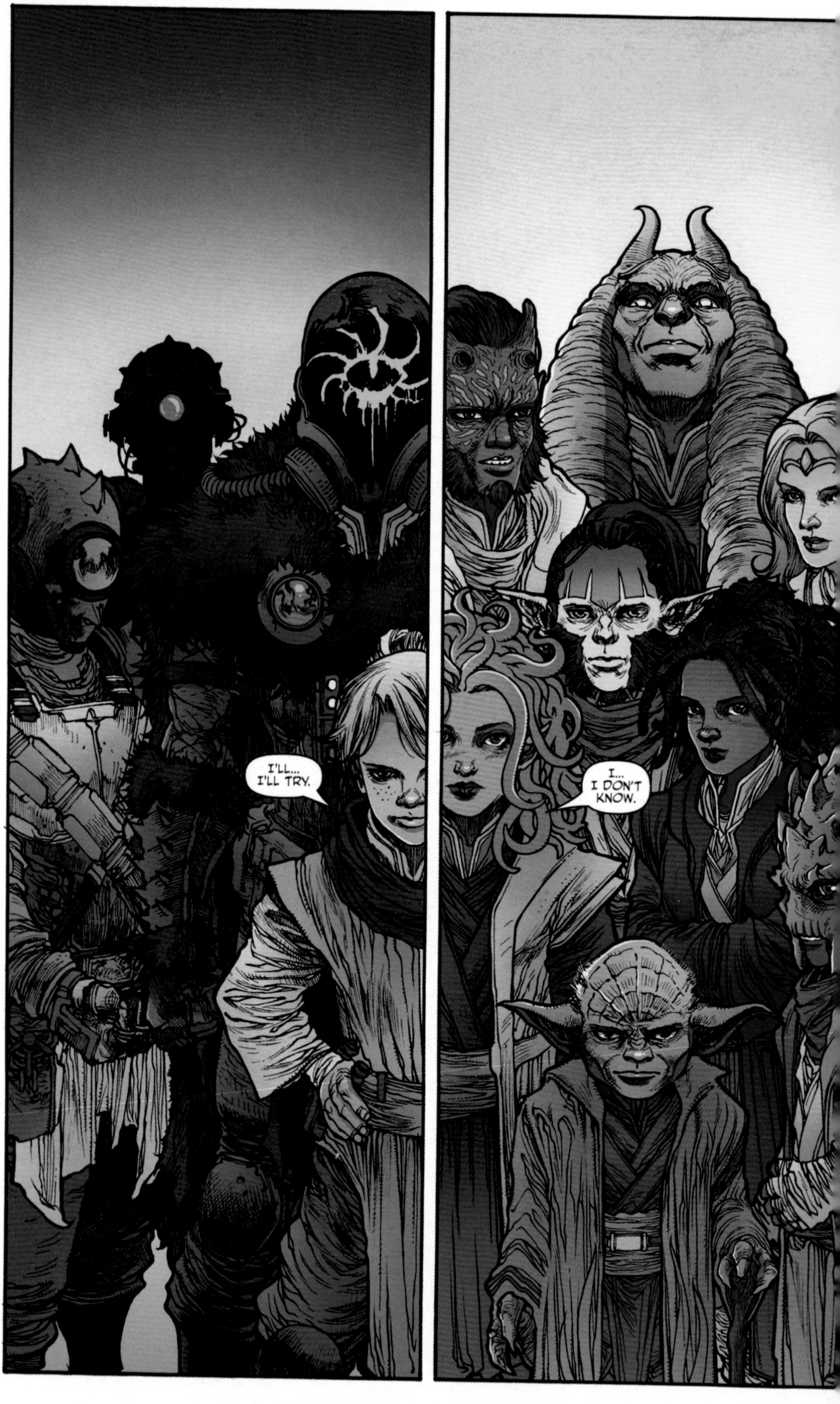
I'LL... I'LL TRY.
I... I DON'T KNOW.

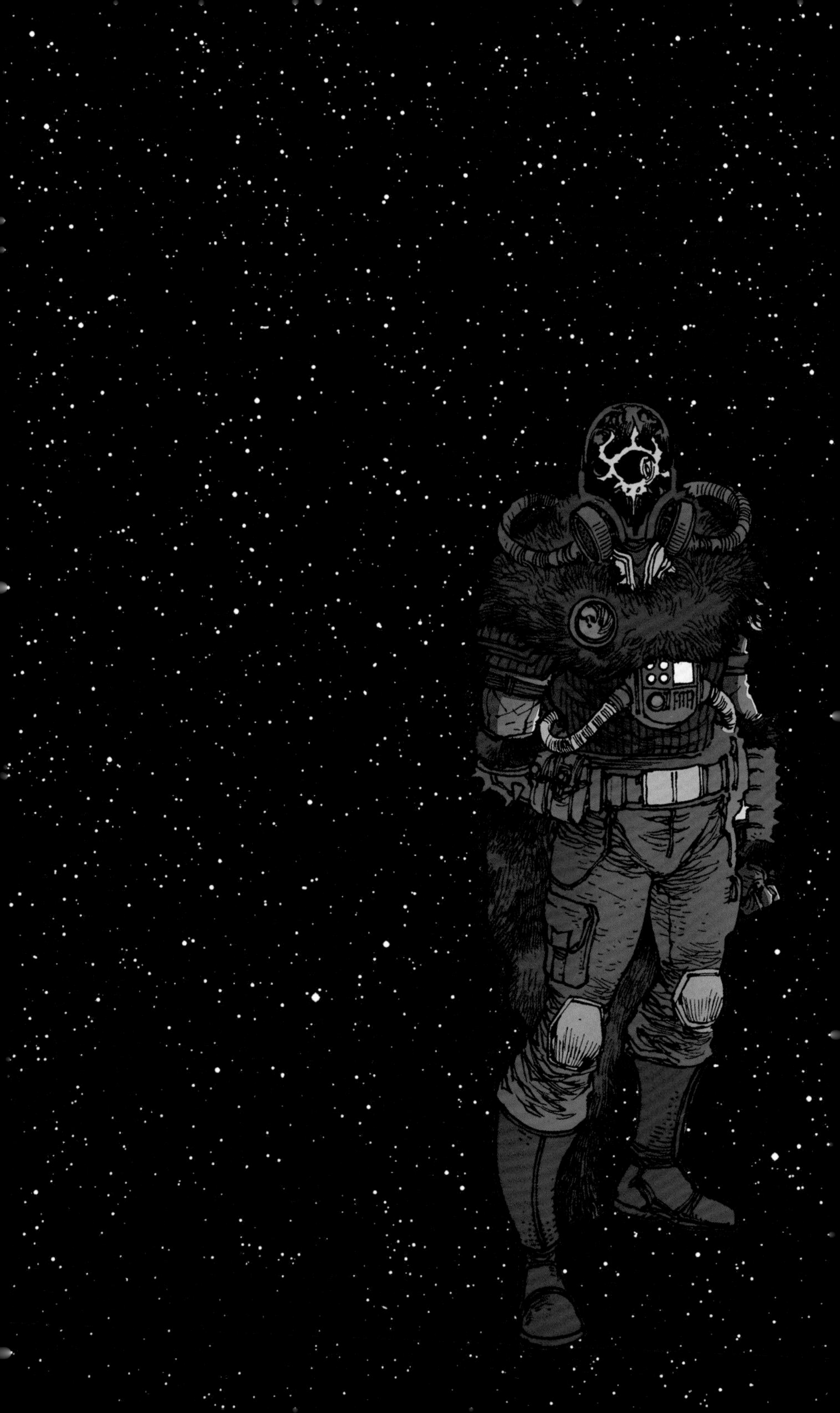

PART 4: THE MOUNTAIN

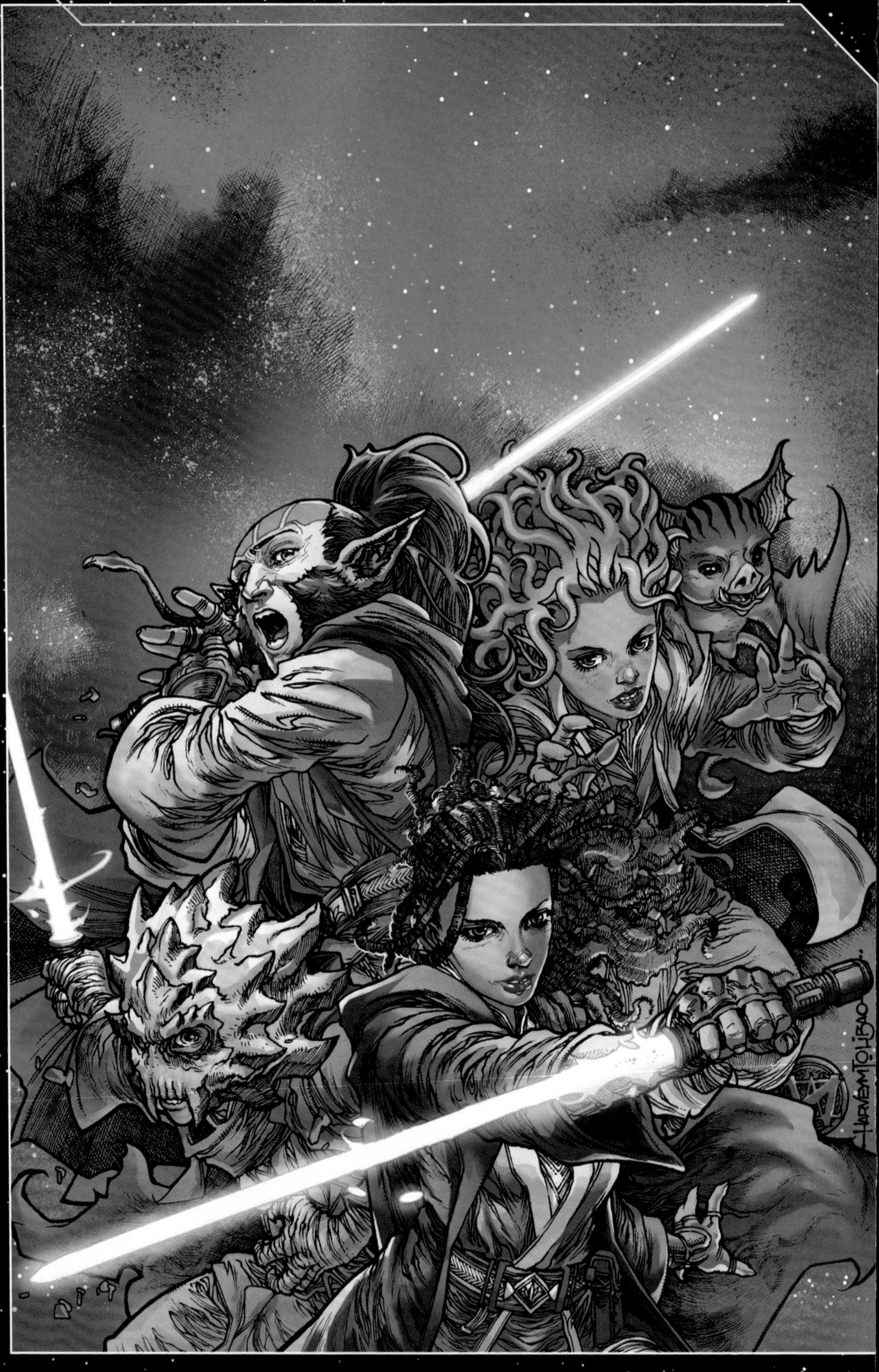

ART BY HARVEY TOLIBAO **COLORS BY** KEVIN TOLIBAO

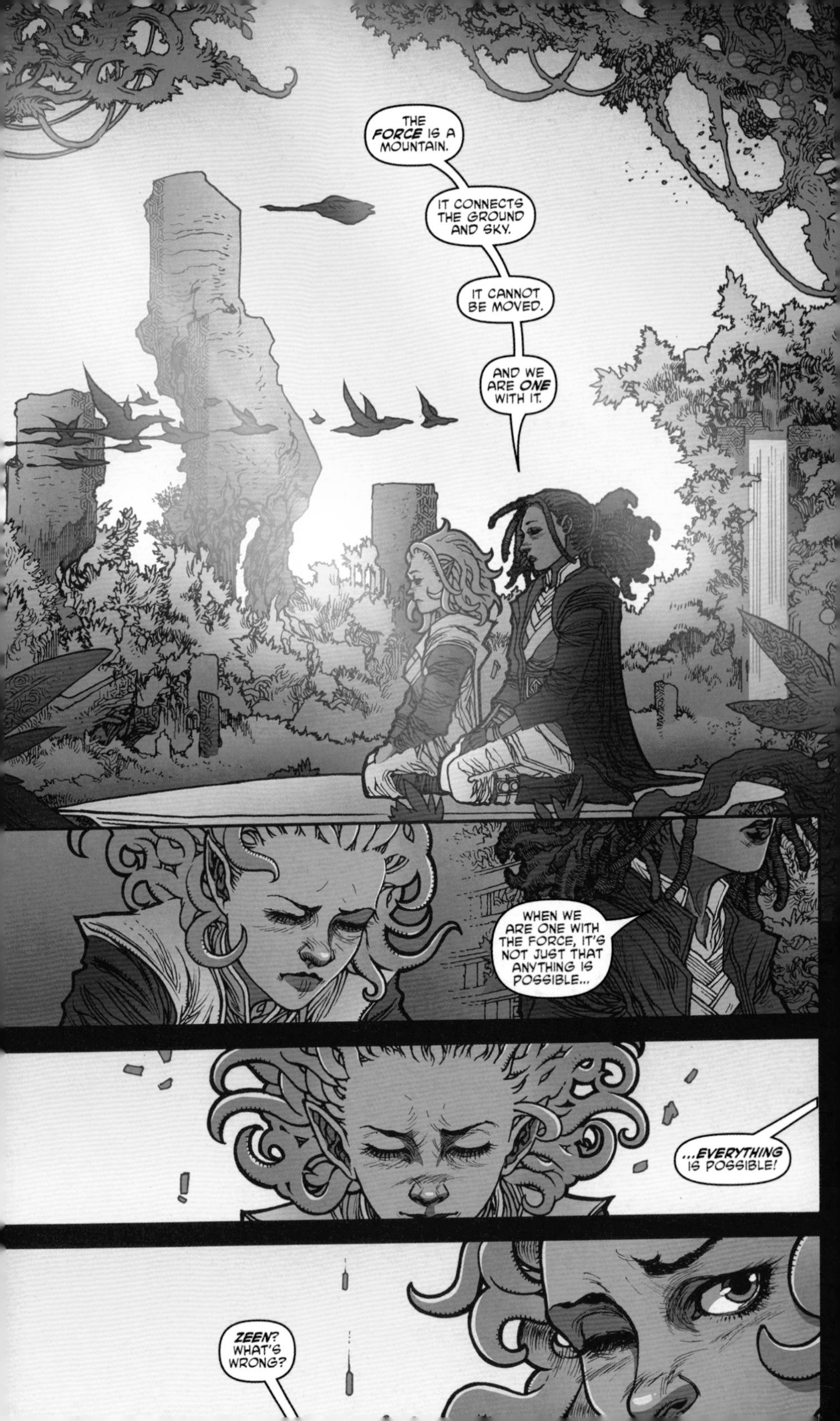
THE FORCE IS A MOUNTAIN.
IT CONNECTS THE GROUND AND SKY.
IT CANNOT BE MOVED.
AND WE ARE ONE WITH IT.
WHEN WE ARE ONE WITH THE FORCE, IT'S NOT JUST THAT ANYTHING IS POSSIBLE...
...EVERYTHING IS POSSIBLE!
ZEEN? WHAT'S WRONG?

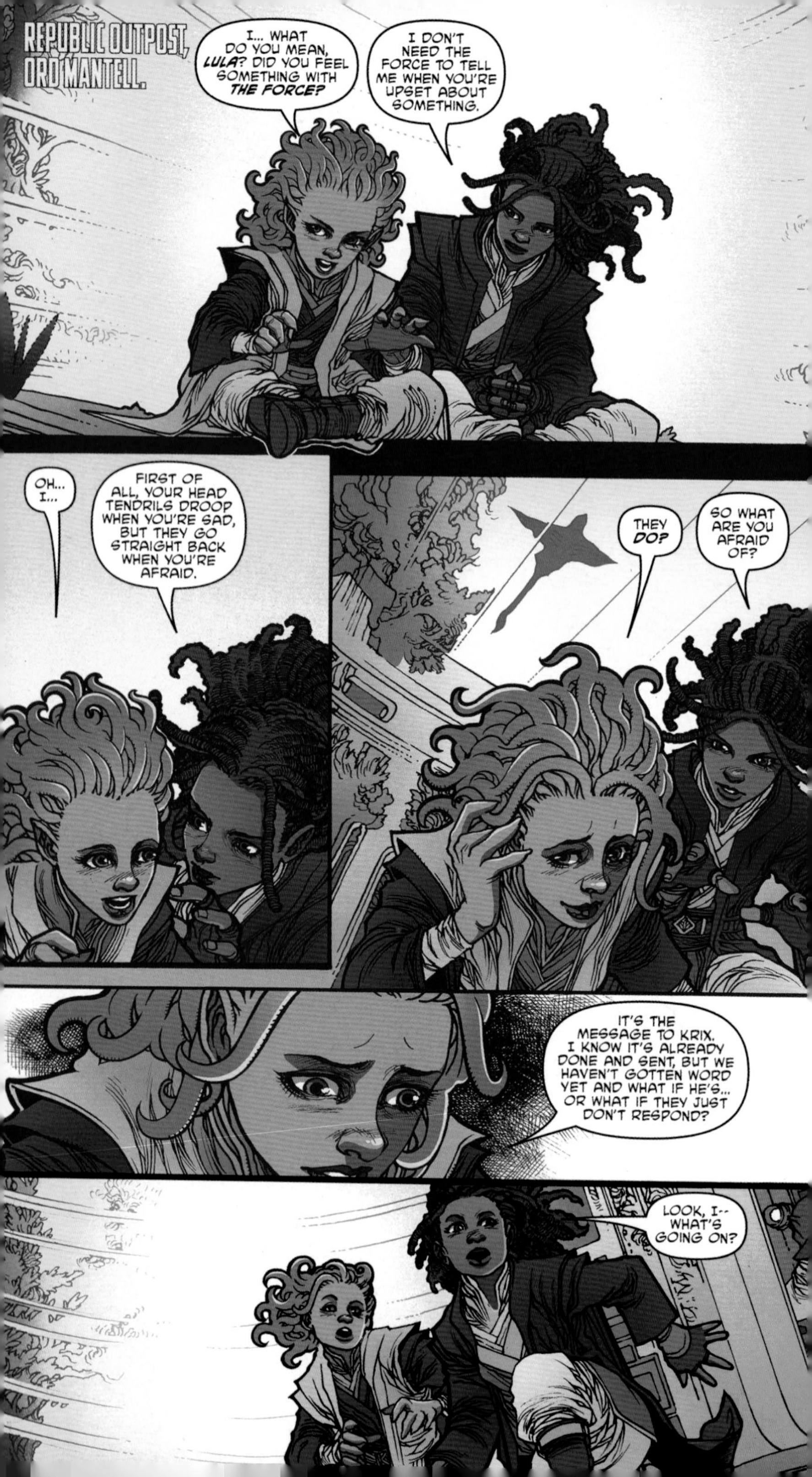
REPUBLIC OUTPOST, ORD MANTELL.
I... WHAT DO YOU MEAN, LULA? DID YOU FEEL SOMETHING WITH THE FORCE?
I DON'T NEED THE FORCE TO TELL ME WHEN YOU'RE UPSET ABOUT SOMETHING.
OH... I...
FIRST OF ALL, YOUR HEAD TENDRILS DROOP WHEN YOU'RE SAD, BUT THEY GO STRAIGHT BACK WHEN YOU'RE AFRAID.
THEY DO?
SO WHAT ARE YOU AFRAID OF?
IT'S THE MESSAGE TO KRIX. I KNOW IT'S ALREADY DONE AND SENT, BUT WE HAVEN'T GOTTEN WORD YET AND WHAT IF HE'S... OR WHAT IF THEY JUST DON'T RESPOND?
LOOK, I-- WHAT'S GOING ON?

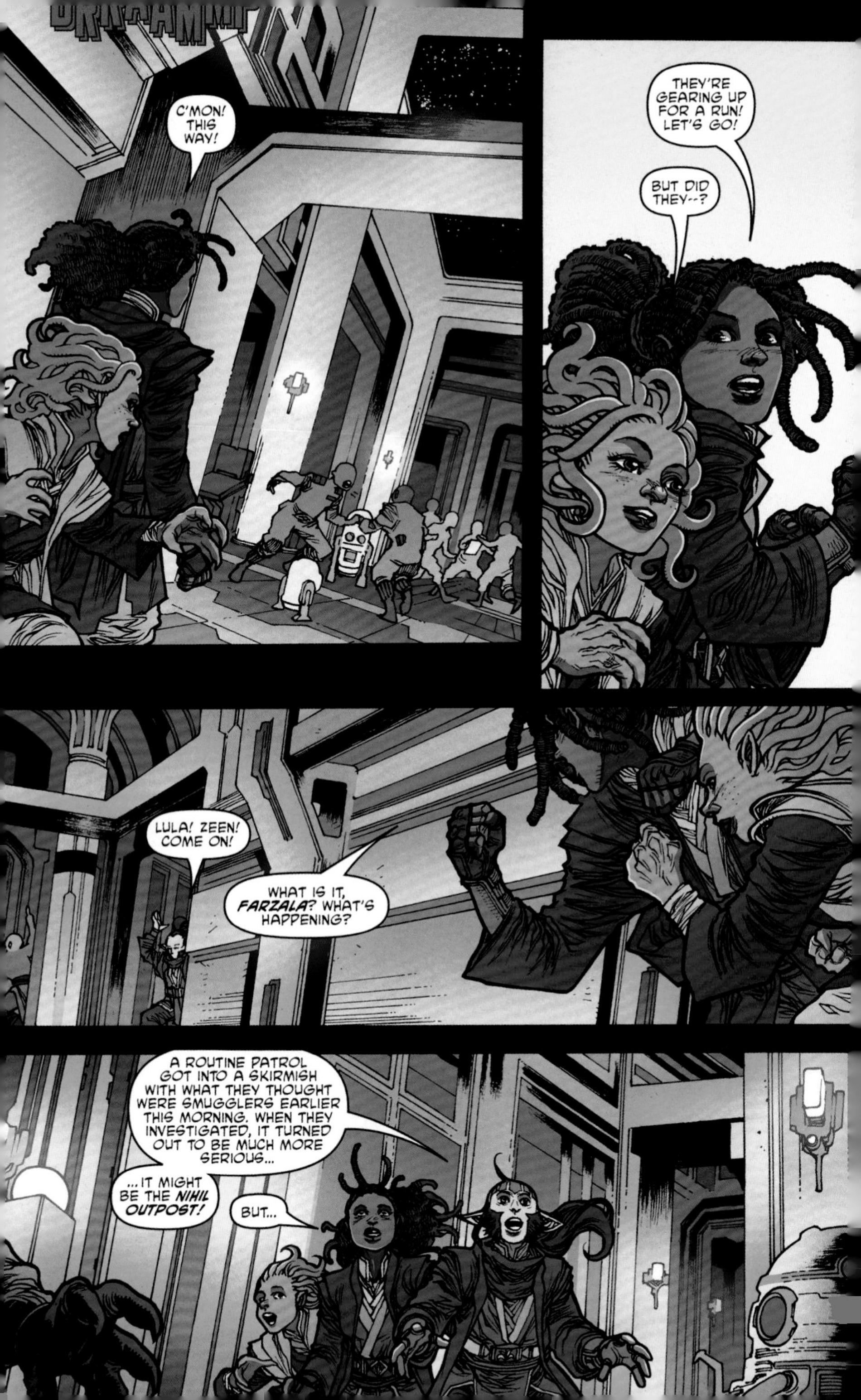

DRRAAMMP
C'MON! THIS WAY!
THEY'RE GEARING UP FOR A RUN! LET'S GO!
BUT DID THEY--?
LULA! ZEEN! COME ON!
WHAT IS IT, FARZALA? WHAT'S HAPPENING?
A ROUTINE PATROL GOT INTO A SKIRMISH WITH WHAT THEY THOUGHT WERE SMUGGLERS EARLIER THIS MORNING. WHEN THEY INVESTIGATED, IT TURNED OUT TO BE MUCH MORE SERIOUS...
...IT MIGHT BE THE NIHIL OUTPOST!
BUT...

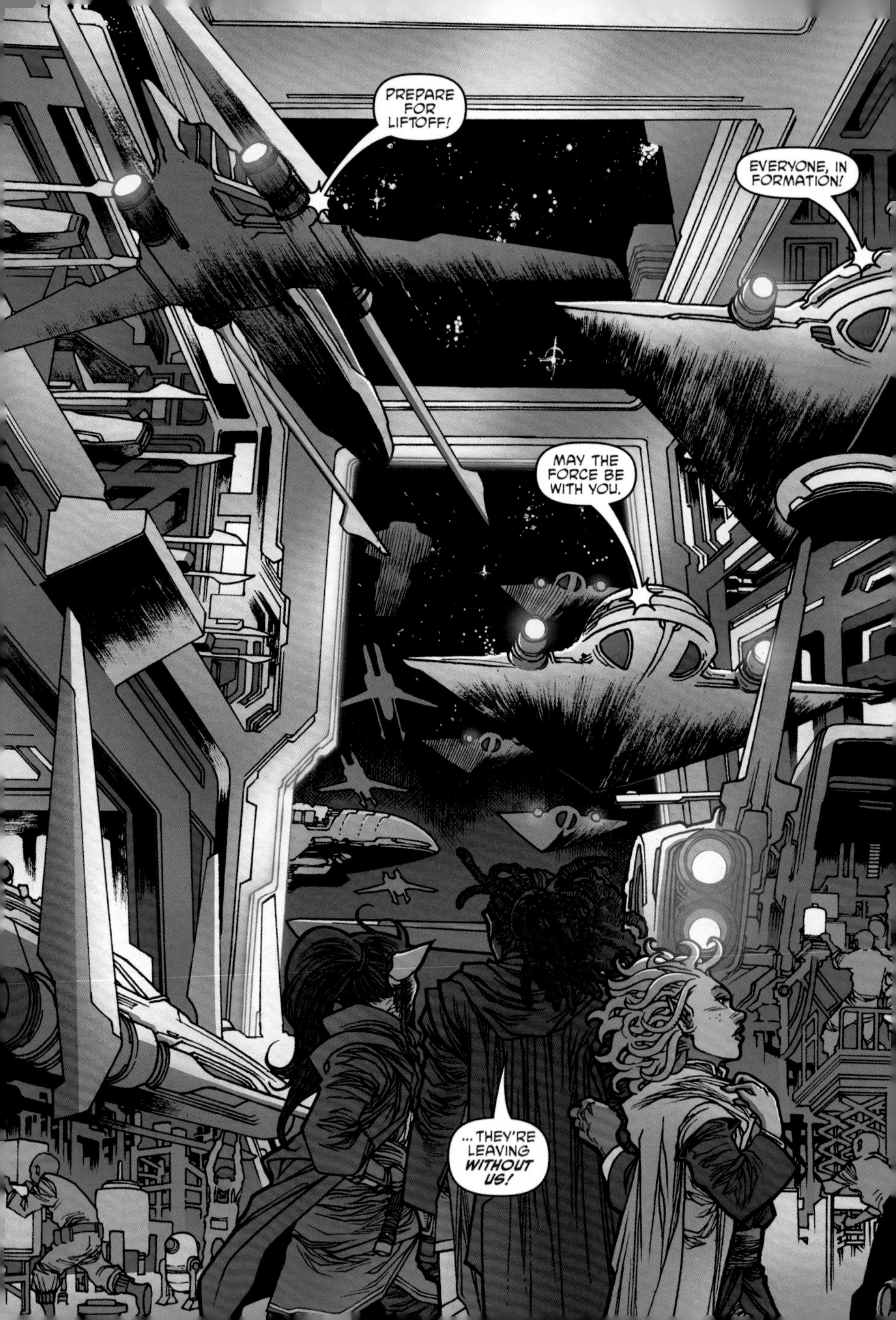
PREPARE FOR LIFTOFF!
EVERYONE, IN FORMATION!
MAY THE FORCE BE WITH YOU.
...THEY'RE LEAVING *WITHOUT* *US!*

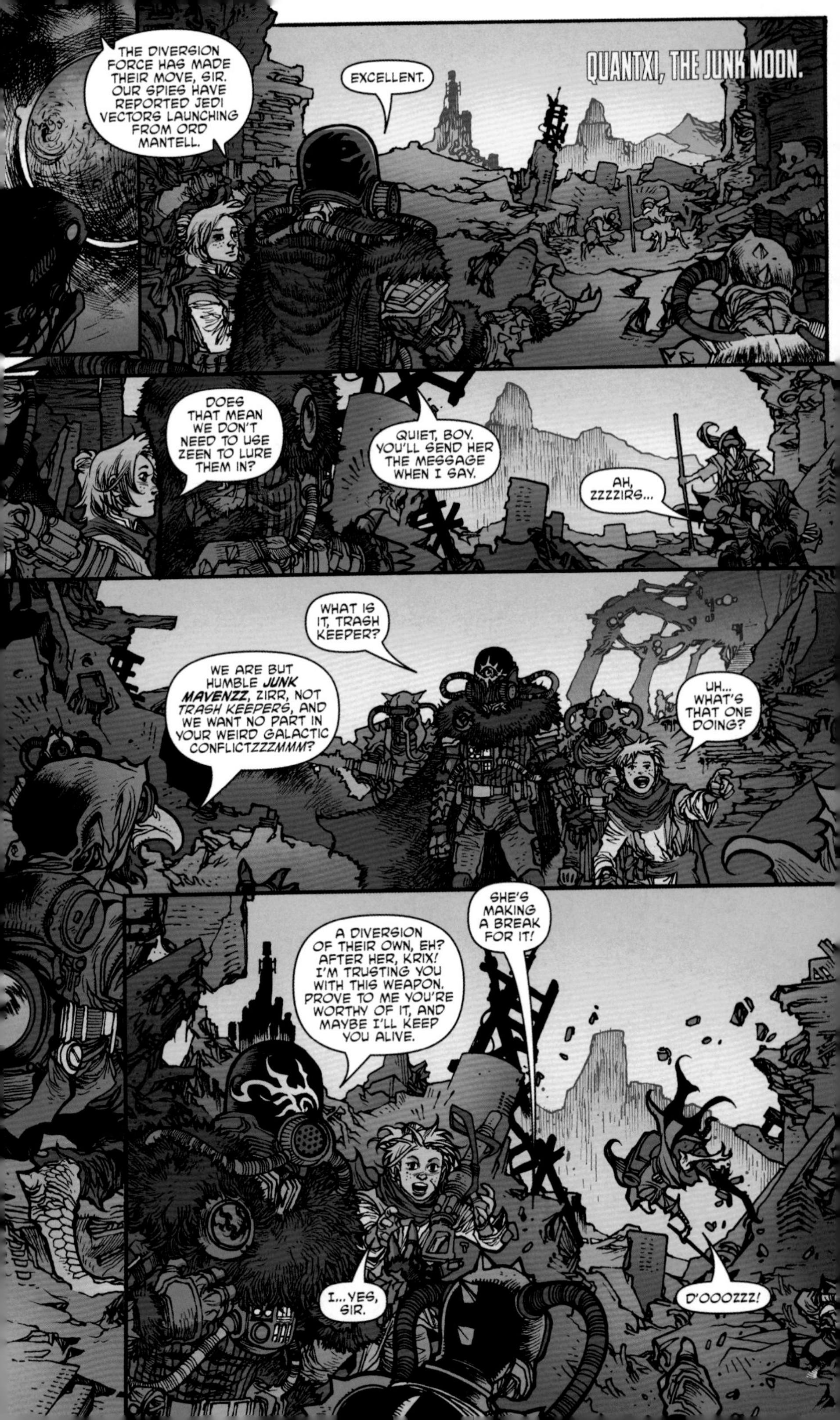
QUANTXI, THE JUNK MOON.
THE DIVERSION FORCE HAS MADE THEIR MOVE, SIR. OUR SPIES HAVE REPORTED JEDI VECTORS LAUNCHING FROM ORD MANTELL.
EXCELLENT.
DOES THAT MEAN WE DON'T NEED TO USE ZEEN TO LURE THEM IN?
QUIET, BOY. YOU'LL SEND HER THE MESSAGE WHEN I SAY.
AH, ZZZZIRS...
WHAT IS IT, TRASH KEEPER?
WE ARE BUT HUMBLE *JUNK MAVENZZ*, ZIRR, NOT *TRASH KEEPERS*, AND WE WANT NO PART IN YOUR WEIRD GALACTIC CONFLICTZZZMMM?
UH... WHAT'S THAT ONE DOING?
SHE'S MAKING A BREAK FOR IT!
A DIVERSION OF THEIR OWN, EH? AFTER HER, KRIX! I'M TRUSTING YOU WITH THIS WEAPON. PROVE TO ME YOU'RE WORTHY OF IT, AND MAYBE I'LL KEEP YOU ALIVE.
I... YES, SIR.
D'OOOZZZ!

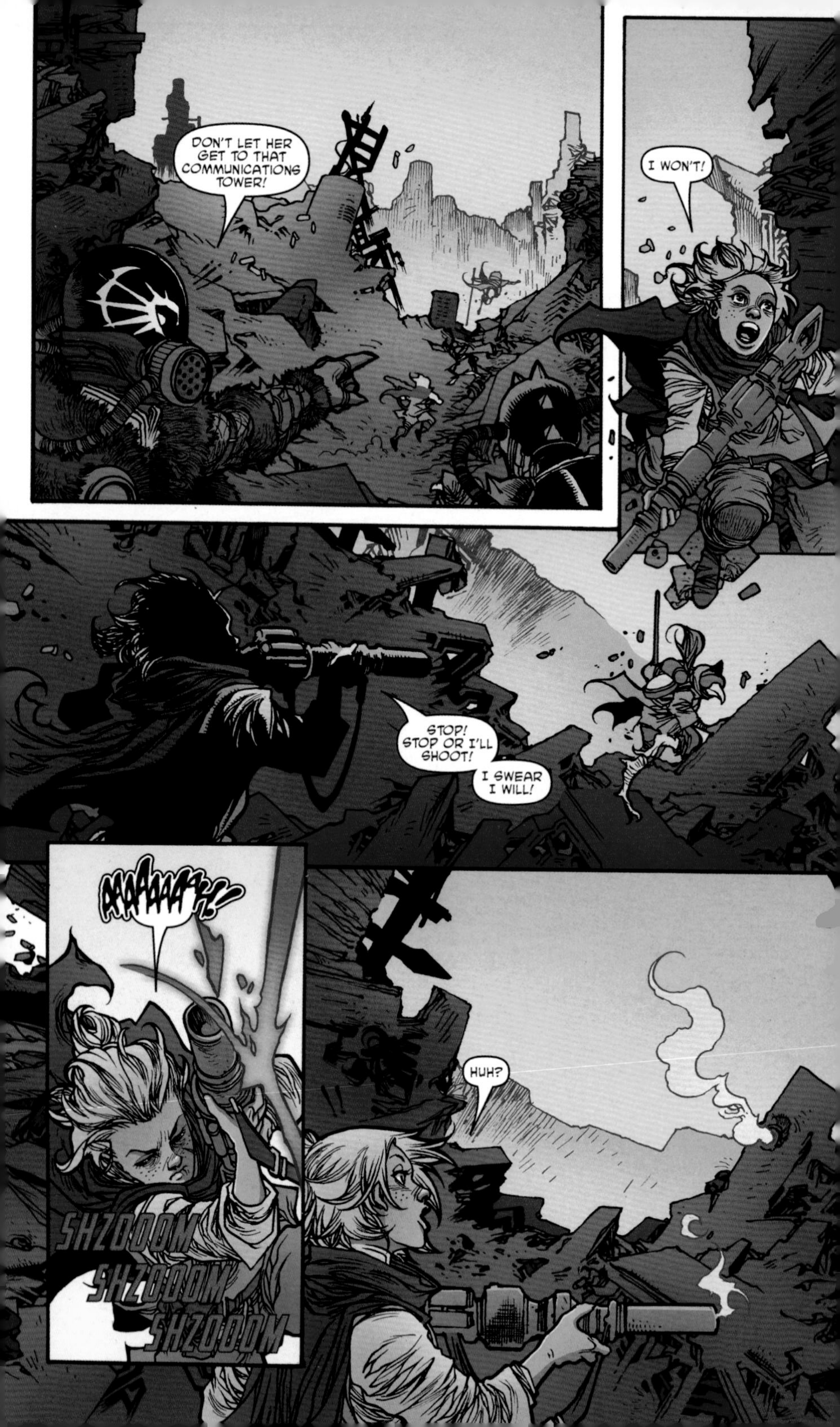
DON'T LET HER GET TO THAT COMMUNICATIONS TOWER!
I WON'T!
STOP! STOP OR I'LL SHOOT!
I SWEAR I WILL!
HUH?
SHZOOOM
SHZOOOM
SHZOOOM

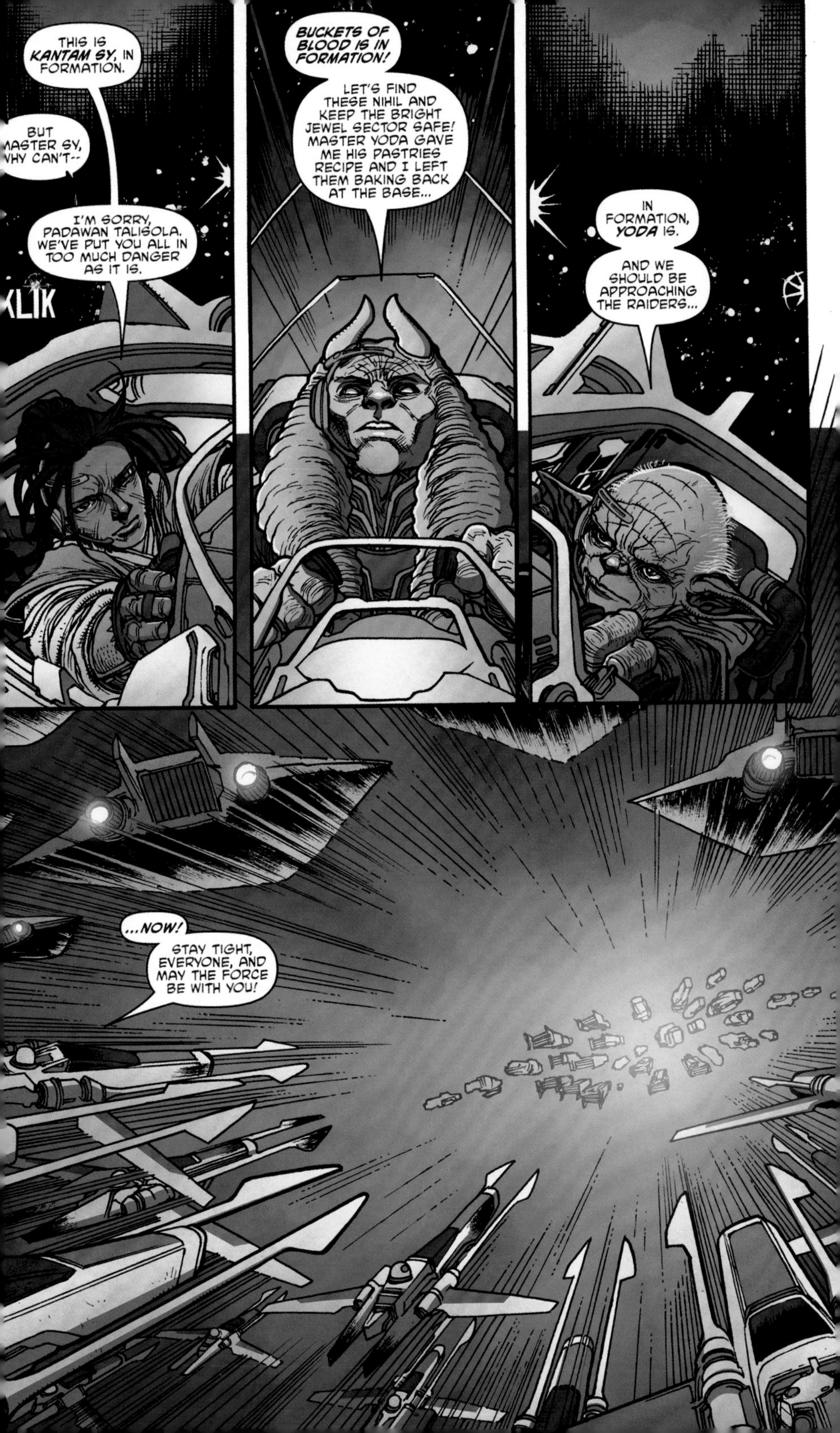
THIS IS KANTAM SY, IN FORMATION.
BUT MASTER SY, WHY CAN'T--
I'M SORRY, PADAWAN TALISOLA. WE'VE PUT YOU ALL IN TOO MUCH DANGER AS IT IS.
KLIK
BUCKETS OF BLOOD IS IN FORMATION!
LET'S FIND THESE NIHIL AND KEEP THE BRIGHT JEWEL SECTOR SAFE! MASTER YODA GAVE ME HIS PASTRIES RECIPE AND I LEFT THEM BAKING BACK AT THE BASE...
IN FORMATION, YODA IS.
AND WE SHOULD BE APPROACHING THE RAIDERS...
...NOW!
STAY TIGHT, EVERYONE, AND MAY THE FORCE BE WITH YOU!

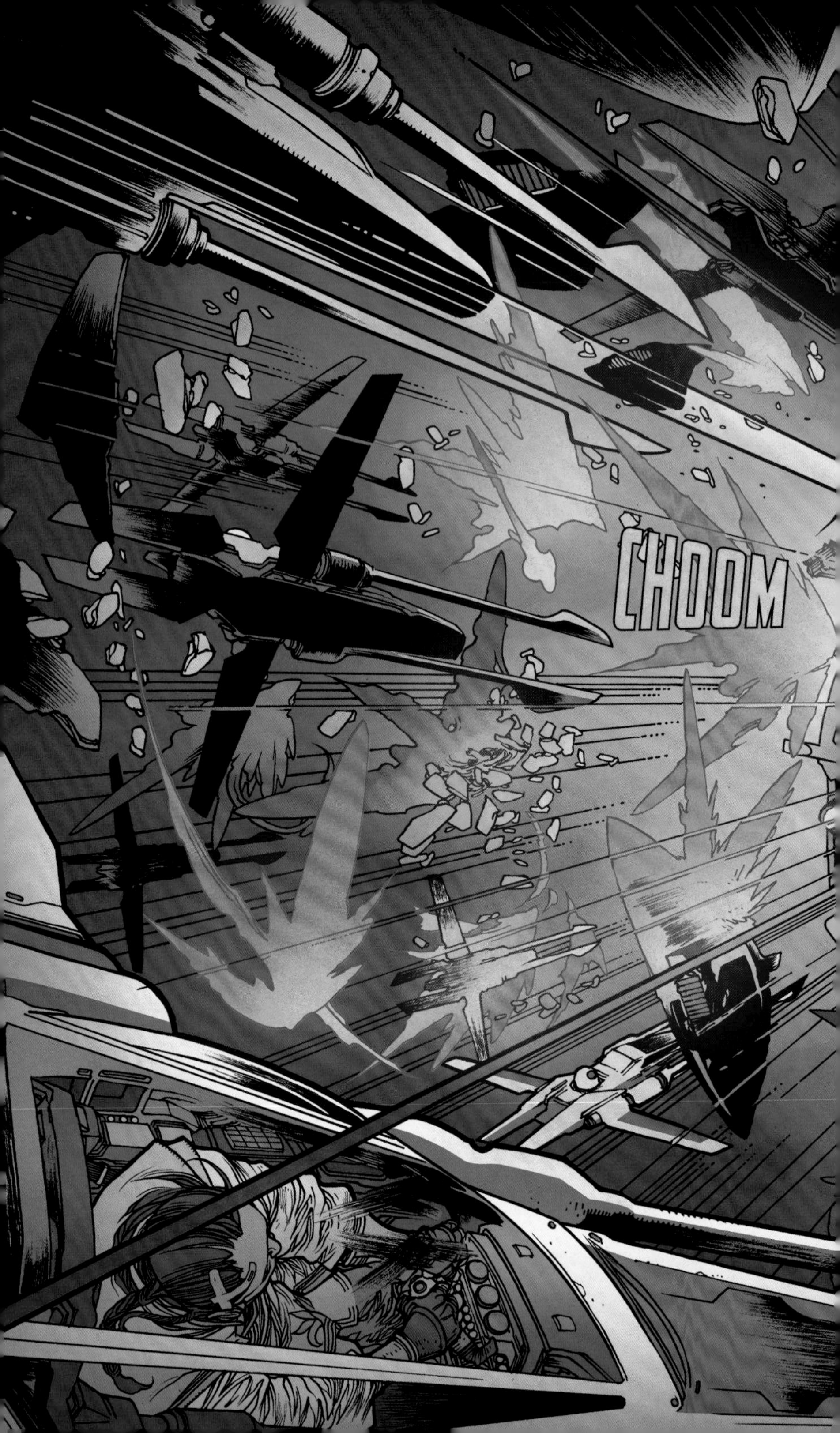
CHOOM

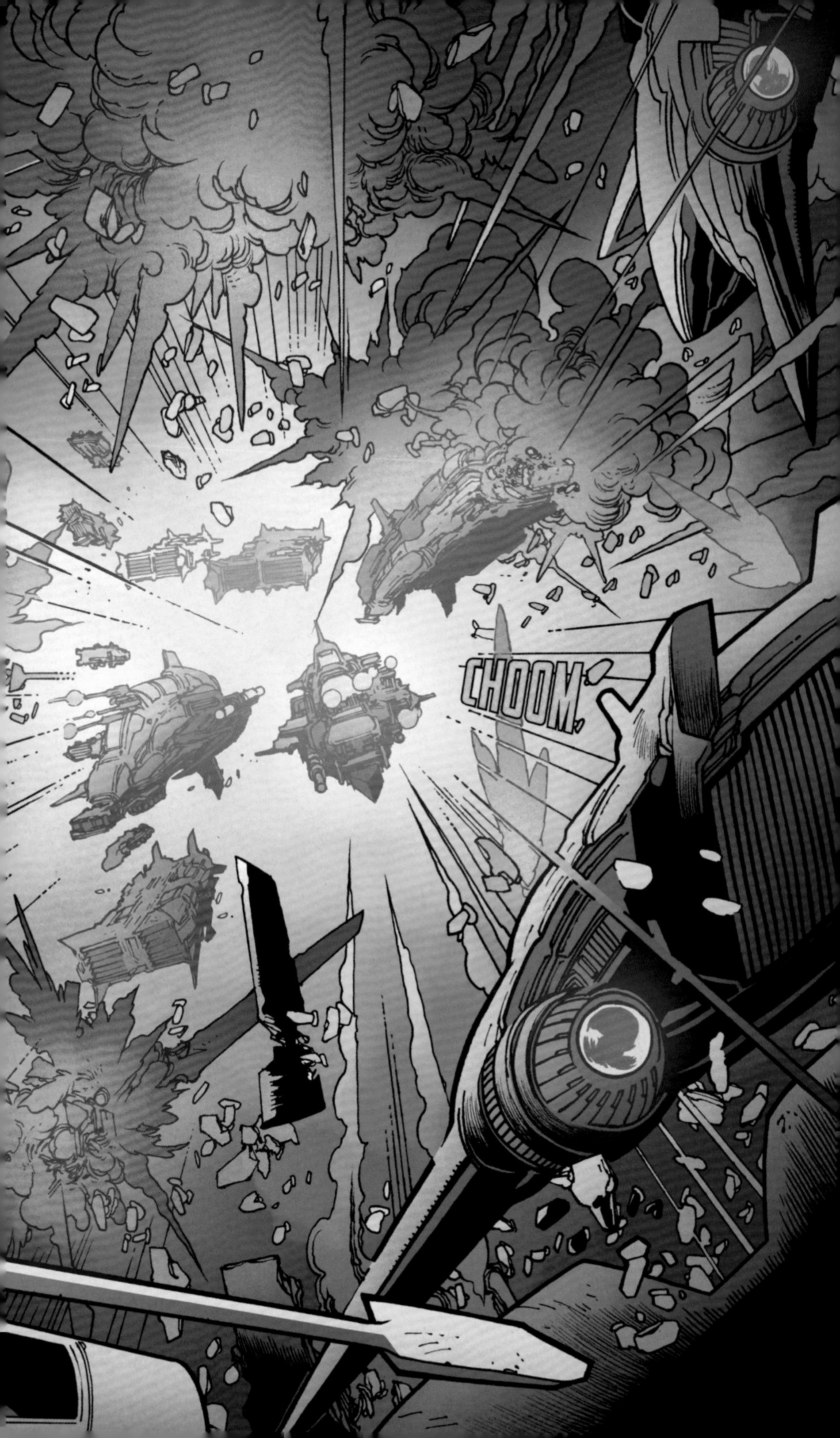
CHOOM

GALACTIC DATA FILE LIGHTSABERS OF THE HIGH REPUBLIC

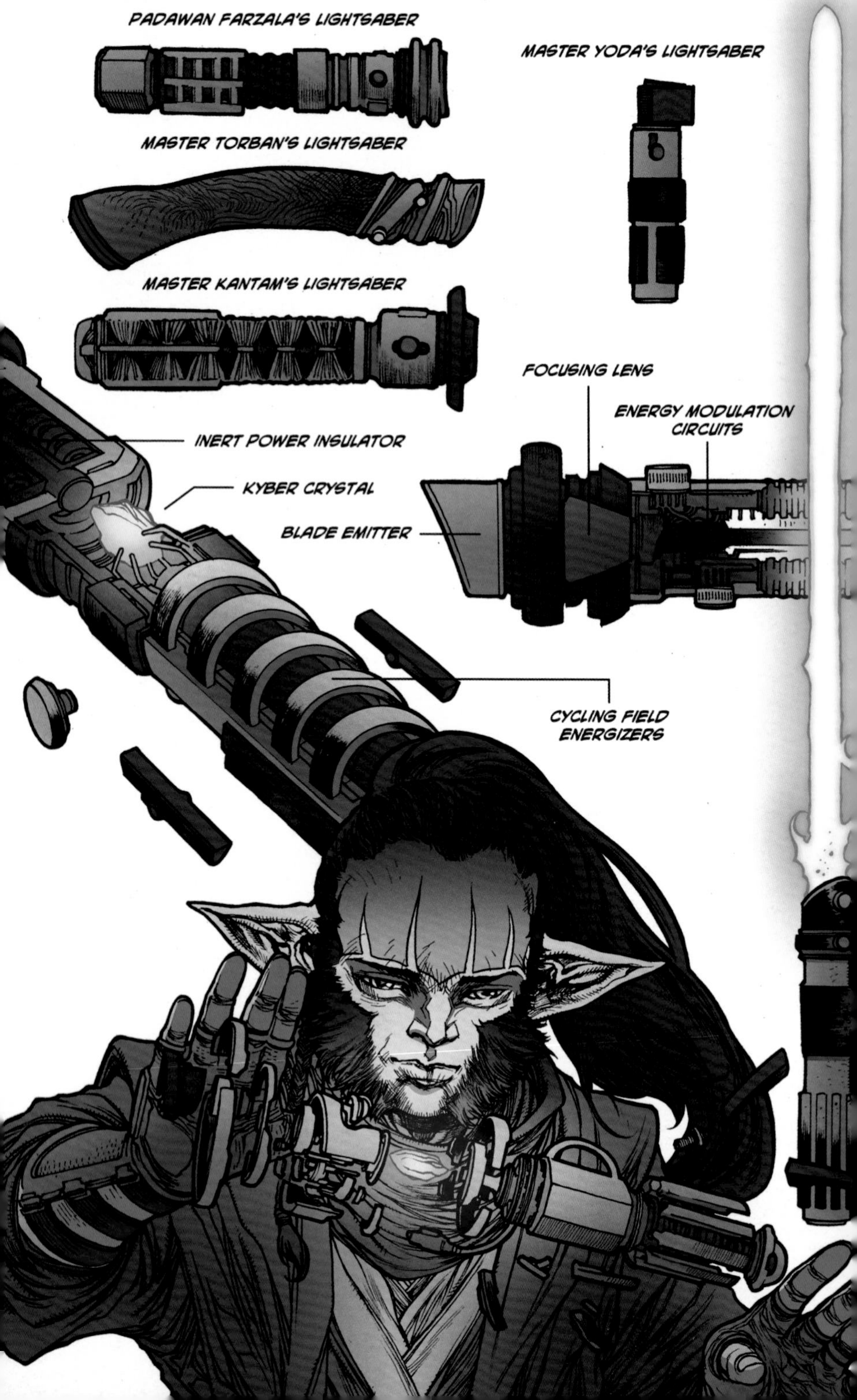

PADAWAN FARZALA'S LIGHTSABER
MASTER YODA'S LIGHTSABER
MASTER TORBAN'S LIGHTSABER
MASTER KANTAM'S LIGHTSABER
FOCUSING LENS
ENERGY MODULATION CIRCUITS
INERT POWER INSULATOR
KYBER CRYSTAL
BLADE EMITTER
CYCLING FIELD ENERGIZERS

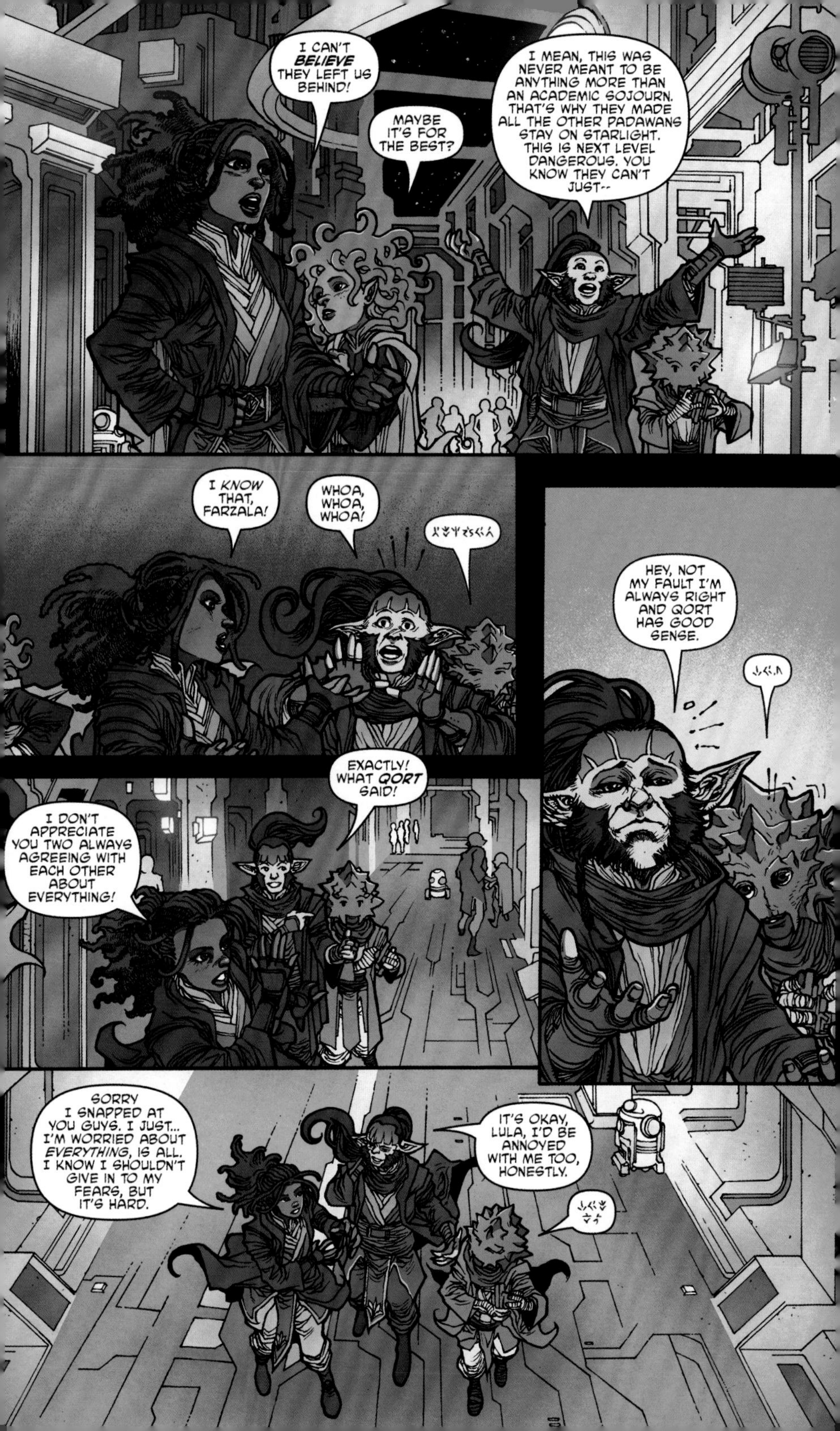
I CAN'T *BELIEVE* THEY LEFT US BEHIND!
MAYBE IT'S FOR THE BEST?
I MEAN, THIS WAS NEVER MEANT TO BE ANYTHING MORE THAN AN ACADEMIC SOJOURN. THAT'S WHY THEY MADE ALL THE OTHER PADAWANS STAY ON STARLIGHT. THIS IS NEXT LEVEL DANGEROUS. YOU KNOW THEY CAN'T JUST--
I *KNOW* THAT, FARZALA!
WHOA, WHOA, WHOA!
HEY, NOT MY FAULT I'M ALWAYS RIGHT AND QORT HAS GOOD SENSE.
EXACTLY! WHAT *QORT* SAID!
I DON'T APPRECIATE YOU TWO ALWAYS AGREEING WITH EACH OTHER ABOUT EVERYTHING!
SORRY I SNAPPED AT YOU GUYS. I JUST... I'M WORRIED ABOUT *EVERYTHING*, IS ALL. I KNOW I SHOULDN'T GIVE IN TO MY FEARS, BUT IT'S HARD.
IT'S OKAY, LULA, I'D BE ANNOYED WITH ME TOO, HONESTLY.

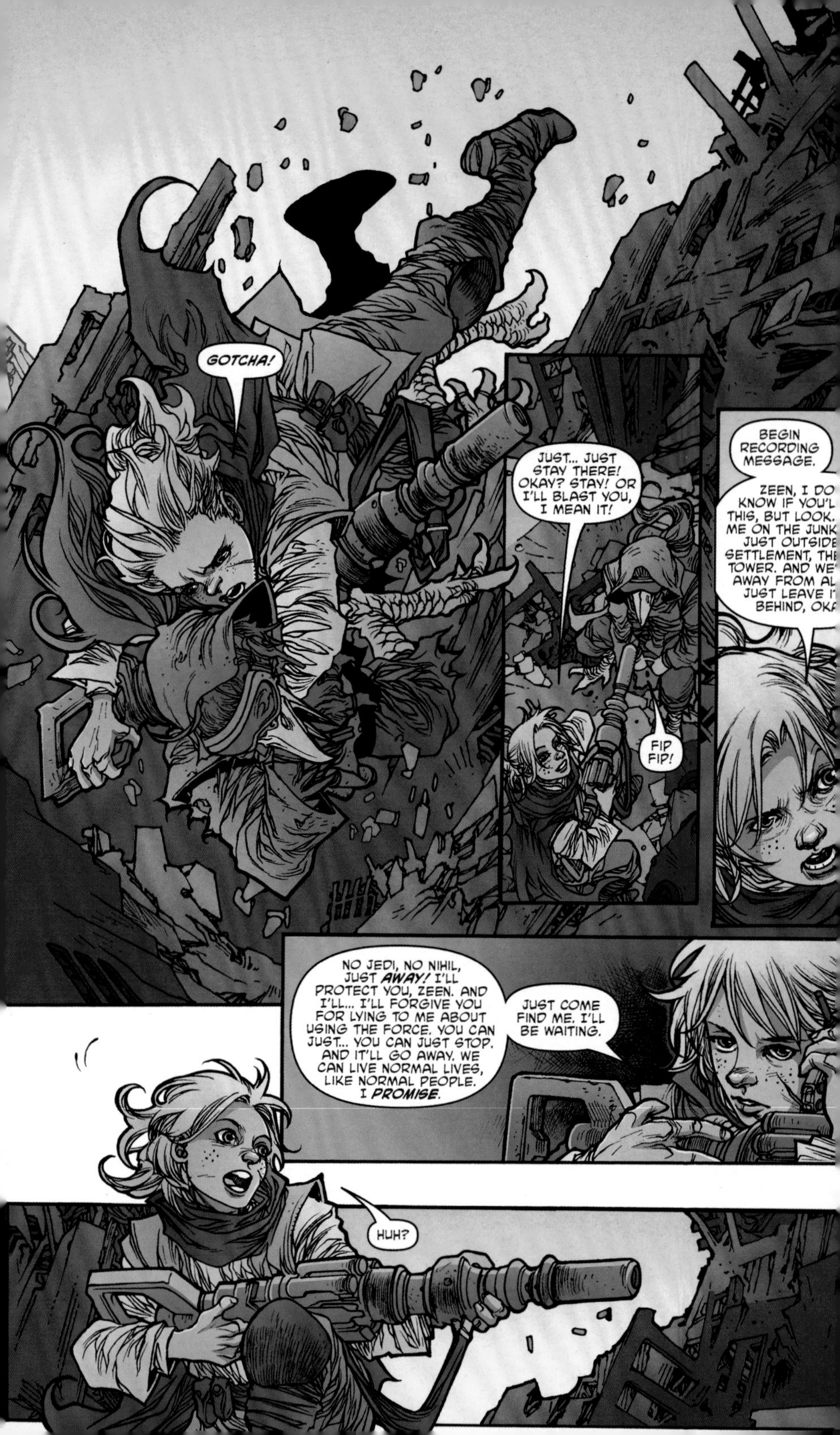
GOTCHA!
JUST... JUST STAY THERE! OKAY? STAY! OR I'LL BLAST YOU, I MEAN IT!
FIP FIP!
BEGIN RECORDING MESSAGE.
ZEEN, I DO
KNOW IF YOU'L
THIS, BUT LOOK.
ME ON THE JUNK
JUST OUTSIDE
SETTLEMENT, THE
TOWER. AND WE'
AWAY FROM AL
JUST LEAVE IT
BEHIND, OKA
NO JEDI, NO NIHIL, JUST AWAY! I'LL PROTECT YOU, ZEEN. AND I'LL... I'LL FORGIVE YOU FOR LYING TO ME ABOUT USING THE FORCE. YOU CAN JUST... YOU CAN JUST STOP. AND IT'LL GO AWAY. WE CAN LIVE NORMAL LIVES, LIKE NORMAL PEOPLE. I PROMISE.
JUST COME FIND ME. I'LL BE WAITING.
HUH?

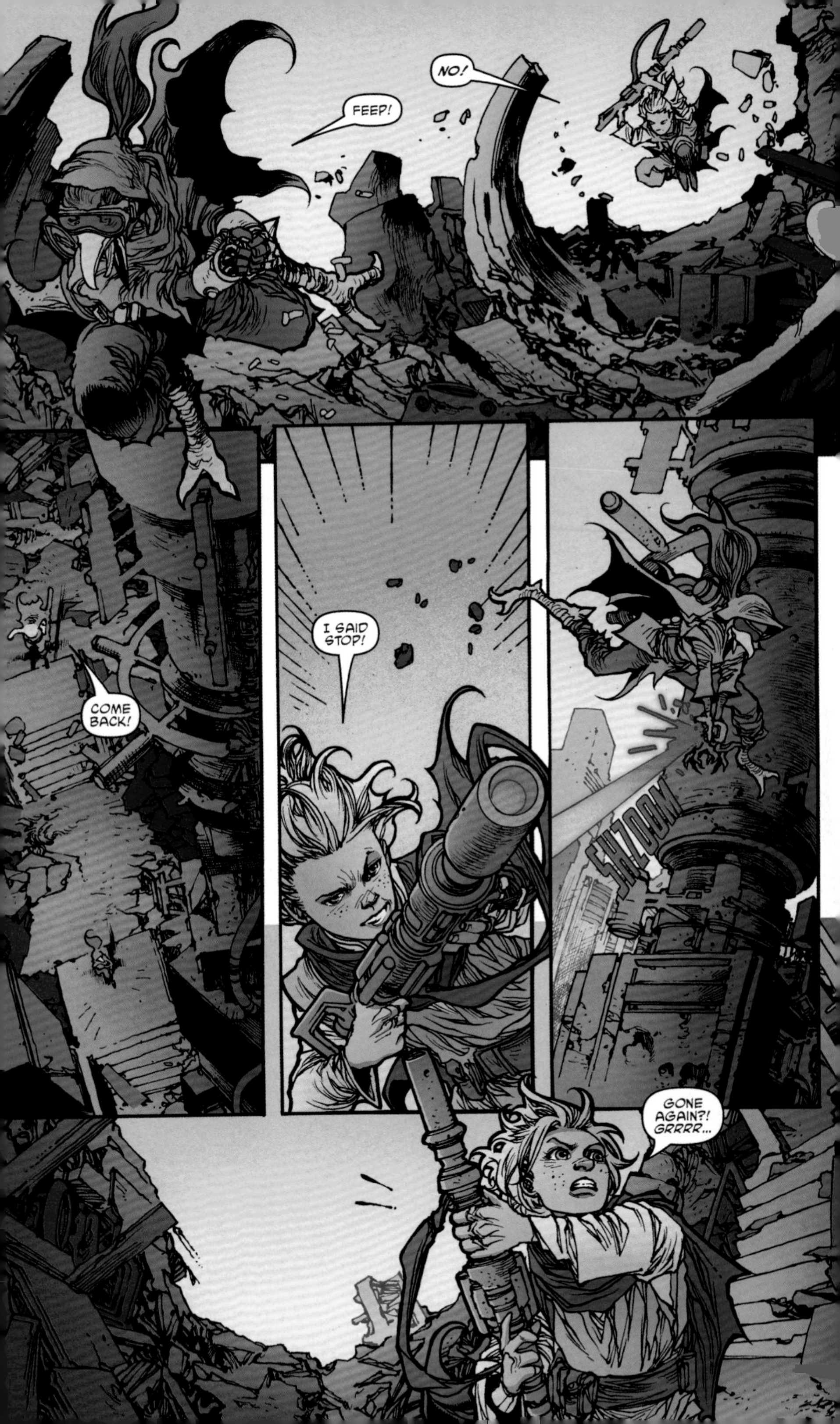
NO!
FEEP!
COME BACK!
I SAID STOP!
SHZOOM
GONE AGAIN?! GRRRR...

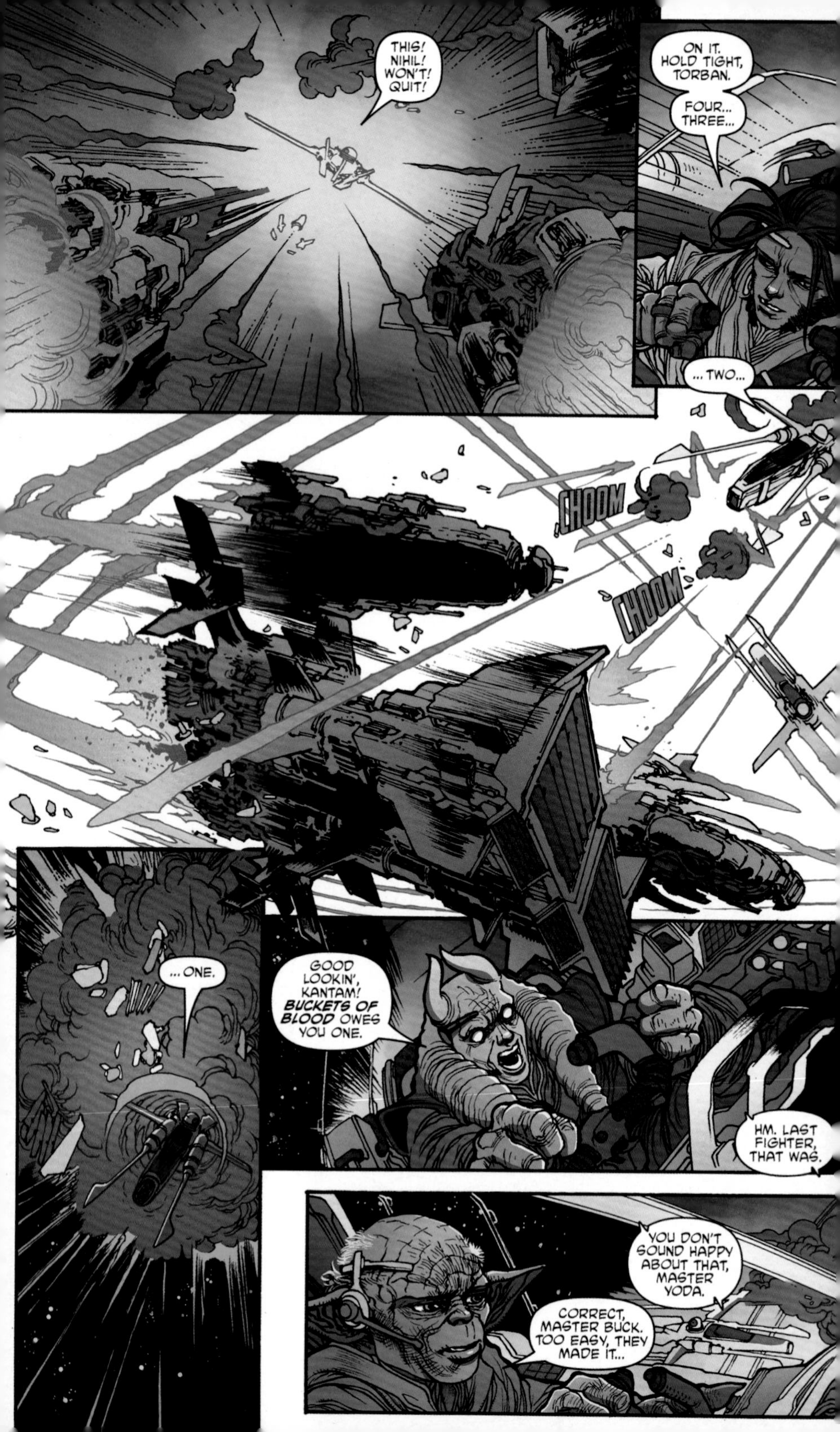
THIS! NIHIL! WON'T! QUIT!
ON IT. HOLD TIGHT, TORBAN.
FOUR... THREE...
... TWO...
CHOOM
CHOOM
... ONE.
GOOD LOOKIN', KANTAM! BUCKETS OF BLOOD OWES YOU ONE.
HM. LAST FIGHTER, THAT WAS.
YOU DON'T SOUND HAPPY ABOUT THAT, MASTER YODA.
CORRECT, MASTER BUCK. TOO EASY, THEY MADE IT...

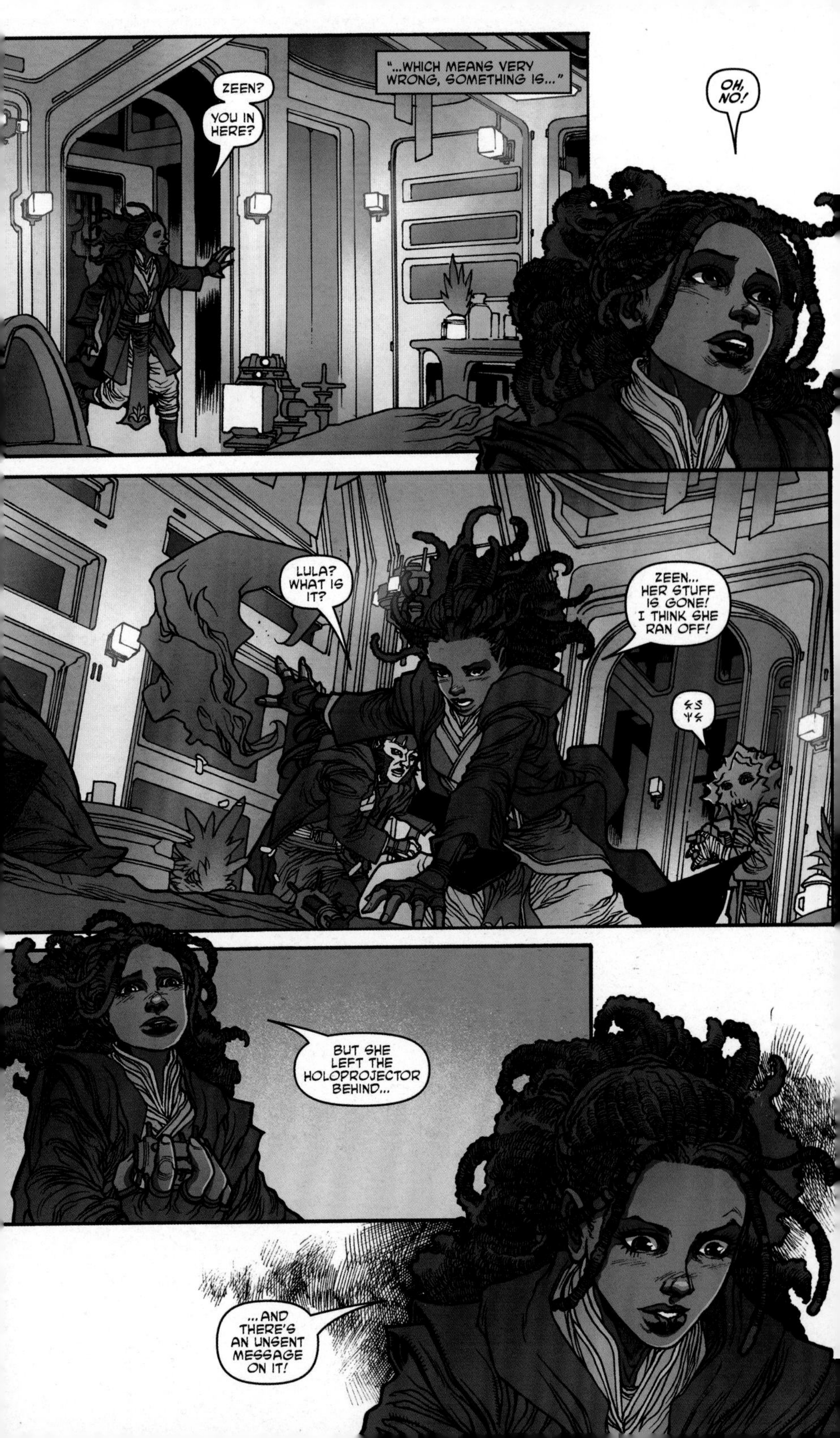
"...WHICH MEANS VERY WRONG, SOMETHING IS..."
ZEEN?
YOU IN HERE?
OH, NO!
LULA? WHAT IS IT?
ZEEN... HER STUFF IS GONE! I THINK SHE RAN OFF!
BUT SHE LEFT THE HOLOPROJECTOR BEHIND...
...AND THERE'S AN UNSENT MESSAGE ON IT!

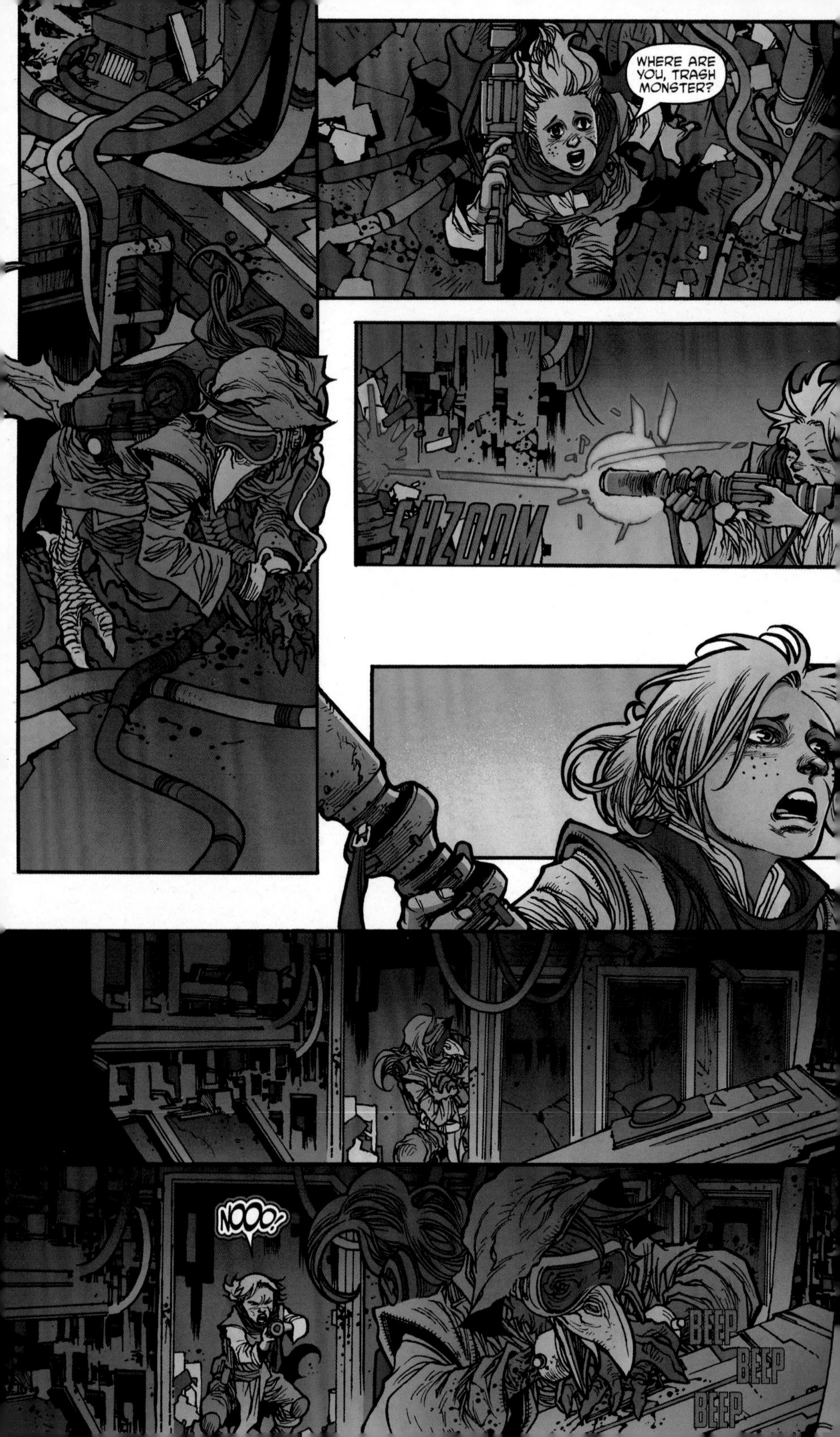
WHERE ARE YOU, TRASH MONSTER?
SHZOOM
NOOO!
BEEP
BEEP
BEEP

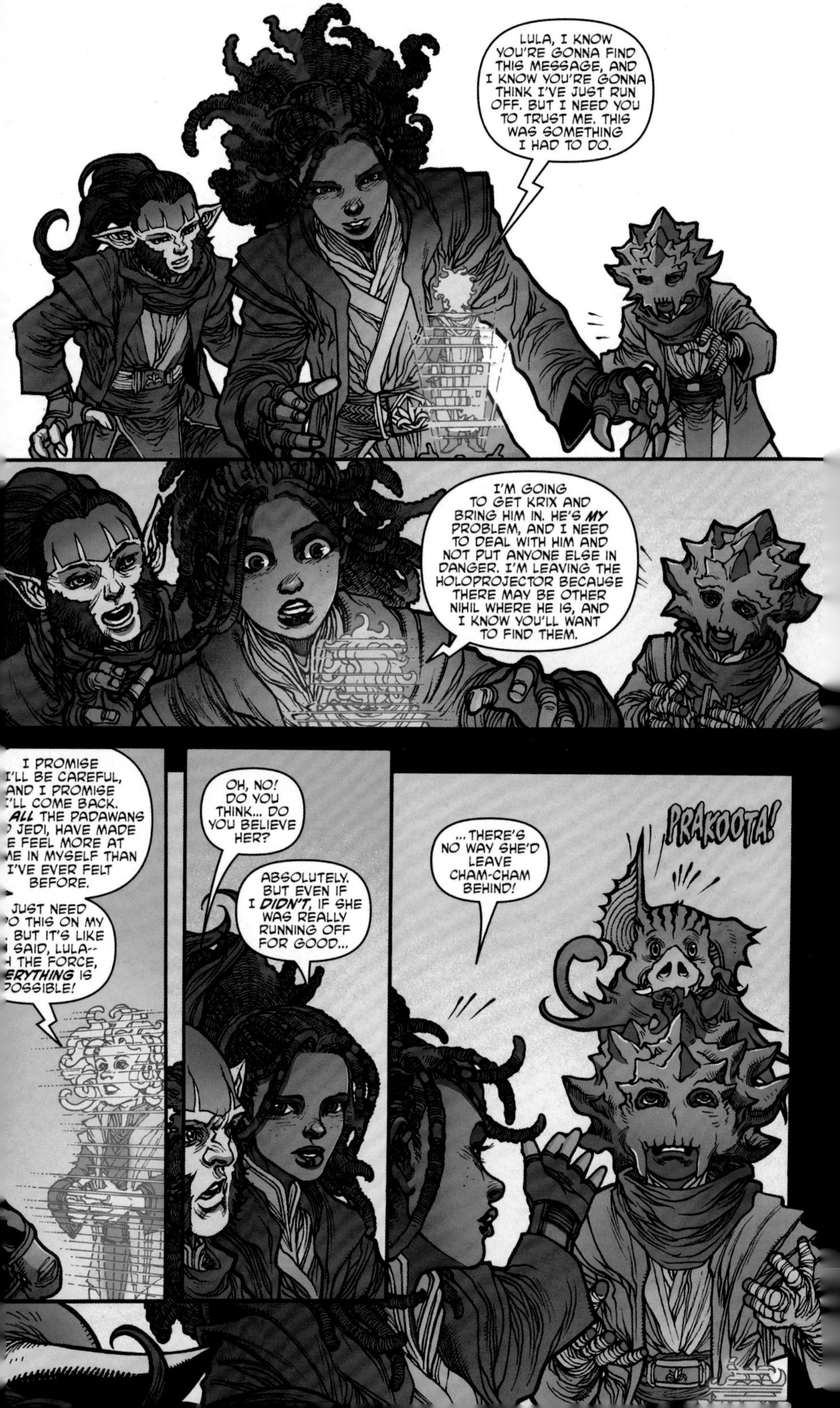
LULA, I KNOW YOU'RE GONNA FIND THIS MESSAGE, AND I KNOW YOU'RE GONNA THINK I'VE JUST RUN OFF. BUT I NEED YOU TO TRUST ME. THIS WAS SOMETHING I HAD TO DO.
I'M GOING TO GET KRIX AND BRING HIM IN. HE'S *MY* PROBLEM, AND I NEED TO DEAL WITH HIM AND NOT PUT ANYONE ELSE IN DANGER. I'M LEAVING THE HOLOPROJECTOR BECAUSE THERE MAY BE OTHER NIHIL WHERE HE IS, AND I KNOW YOU'LL WANT TO FIND THEM.
I PROMISE I'LL BE CAREFUL, AND I PROMISE I'LL COME BACK. *ALL* THE PADAWANS JEDI, HAVE MADE E FEEL MORE AT ME IN MYSELF THAN I'VE EVER FELT BEFORE.
JUST NEED O THIS ON MY . BUT IT'S LIKE SAID, LULA-- H THE FORCE, *ERYTHING* IS POSSIBLE!
OH, NO! DO YOU THINK... DO YOU BELIEVE HER?
ABSOLUTELY. BUT EVEN IF I *DIDN'T*, IF SHE WAS REALLY RUNNING OFF FOR GOOD...
...THERE'S NO WAY SHE'D LEAVE CHAM-CHAM BEHIND!
PRAKOOTA!

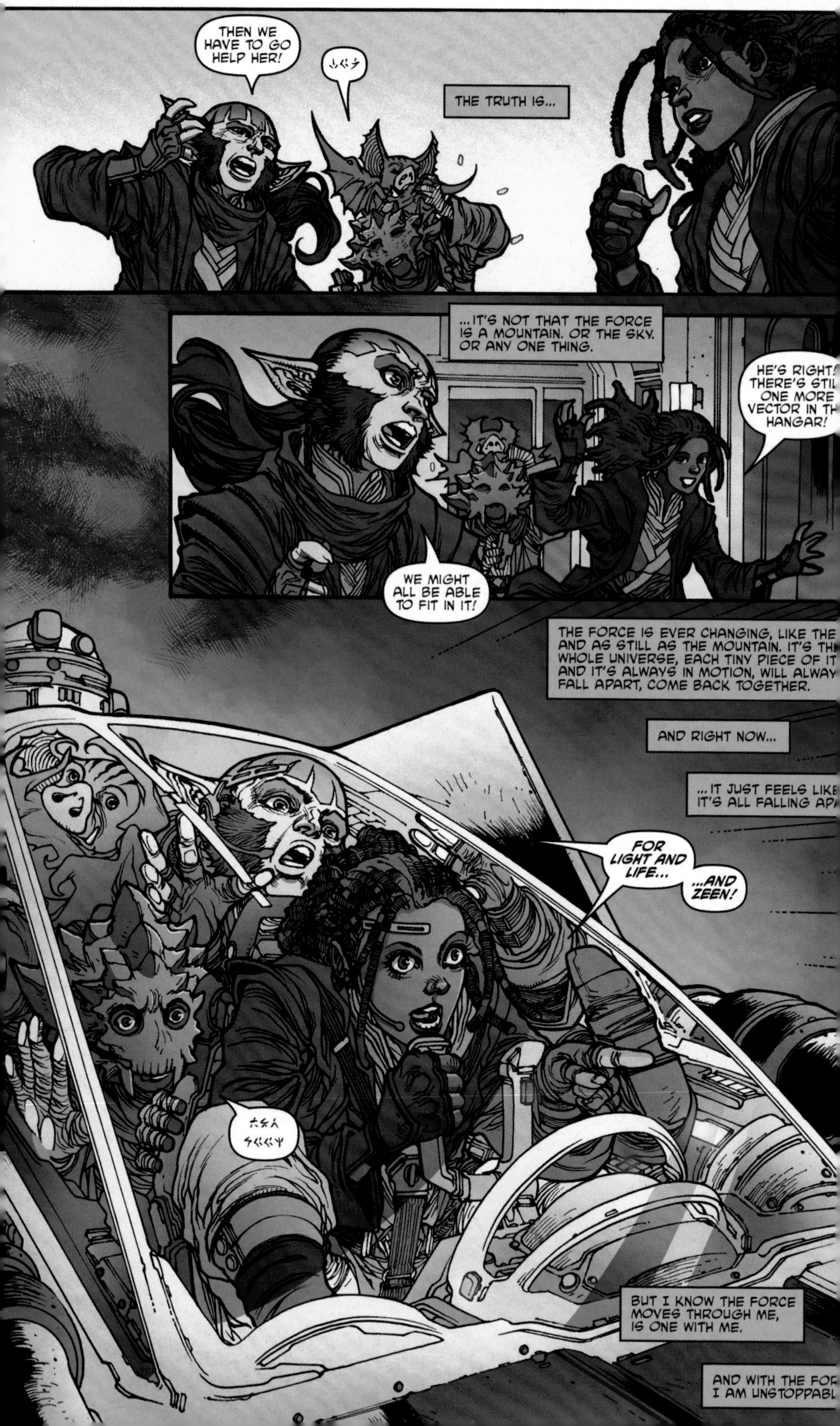
THEN WE HAVE TO GO HELP HER!
THE TRUTH IS...
...IT'S NOT THAT THE FORCE IS A MOUNTAIN. OR THE SKY. OR ANY ONE THING.
HE'S RIGHT! THERE'S STIL ONE MORE VECTOR IN TH HANGAR!
WE MIGHT ALL BE ABLE TO FIT IN IT!
THE FORCE IS EVER CHANGING, LIKE THE AND AS STILL AS THE MOUNTAIN. IT'S TH WHOLE UNIVERSE, EACH TINY PIECE OF IT AND IT'S ALWAYS IN MOTION, WILL ALWAY FALL APART, COME BACK TOGETHER.
AND RIGHT NOW...
...IT JUST FEELS LIKE IT'S ALL FALLING AP
FOR LIGHT AND LIFE...
...AND ZEEN!
BUT I KNOW THE FORCE MOVES THROUGH ME, IS ONE WITH ME.
AND WITH THE FOR I AM UNSTOPPABL

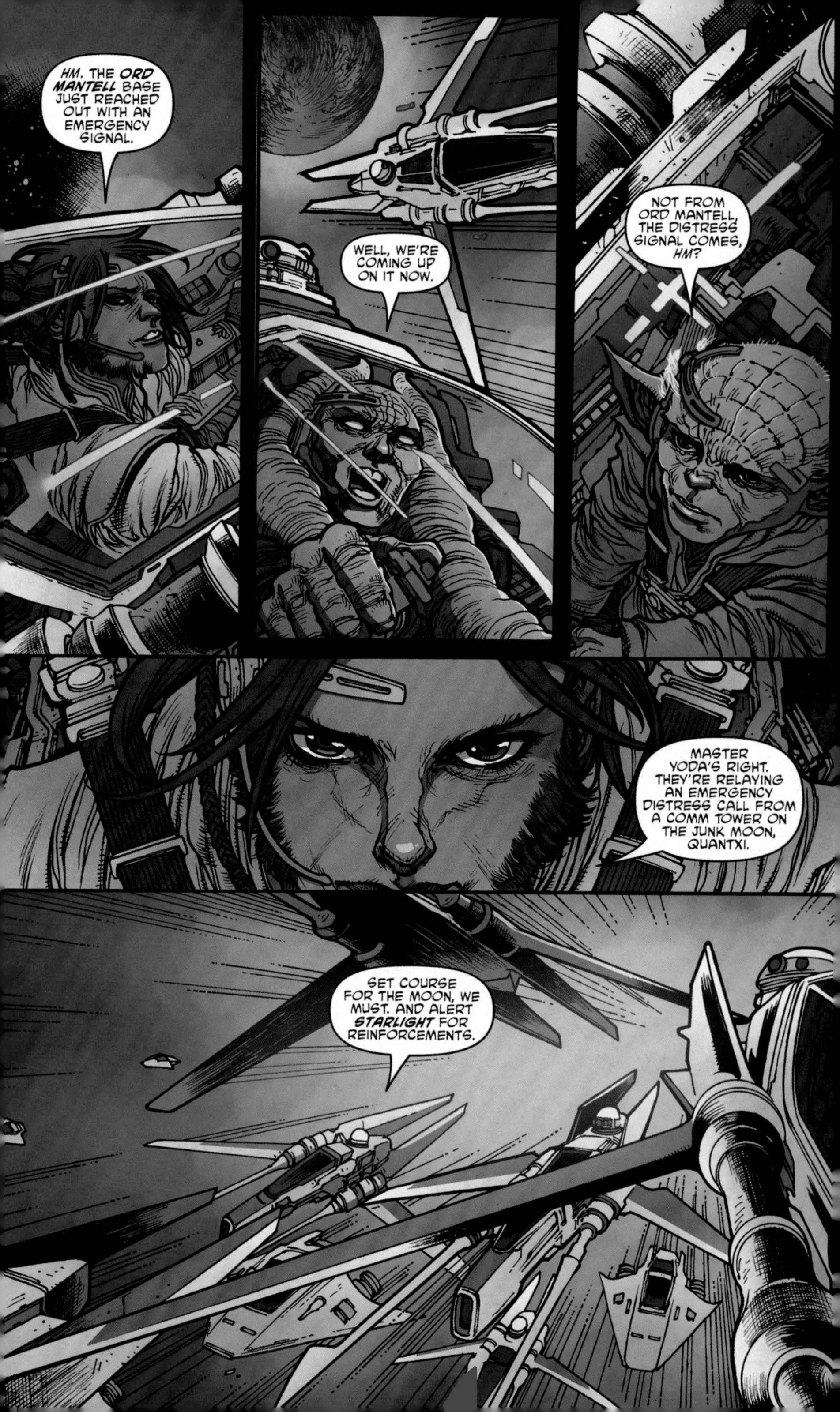
HM. THE ORD MANTELL BASE JUST REACHED OUT WITH AN EMERGENCY SIGNAL.
WELL, WE'RE COMING UP ON IT NOW.
NOT FROM ORD MANTELL, THE DISTRESS SIGNAL COMES, HM?
MASTER YODA'S RIGHT. THEY'RE RELAYING AN EMERGENCY DISTRESS CALL FROM A COMM TOWER ON THE JUNK MOON, QUANTXI.
SET COURSE FOR THE MOON, WE MUST. AND ALERT STARLIGHT FOR REINFORCEMENTS.

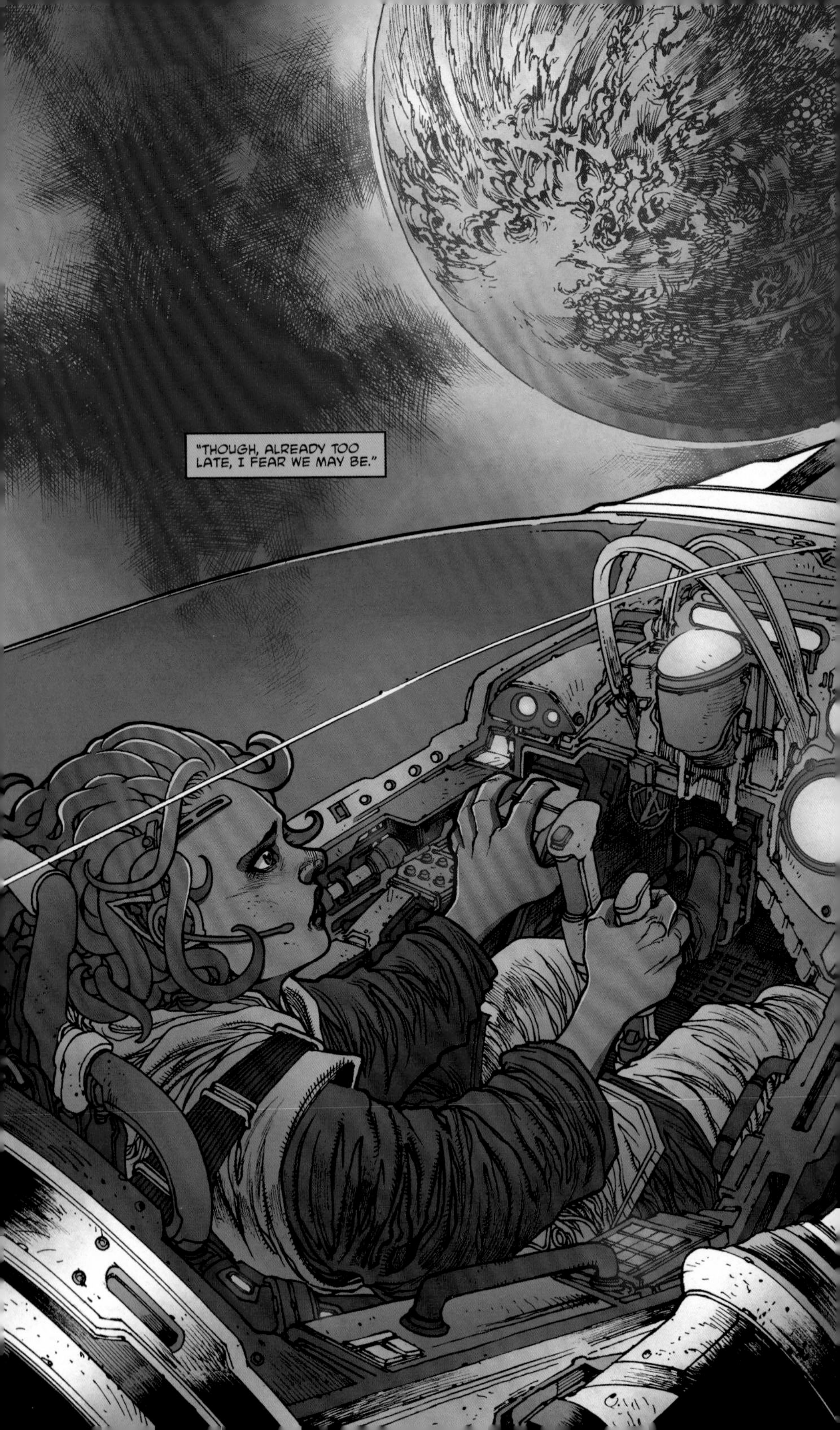
"THOUGH, ALREADY TOO LATE, I FEAR WE MAY BE."

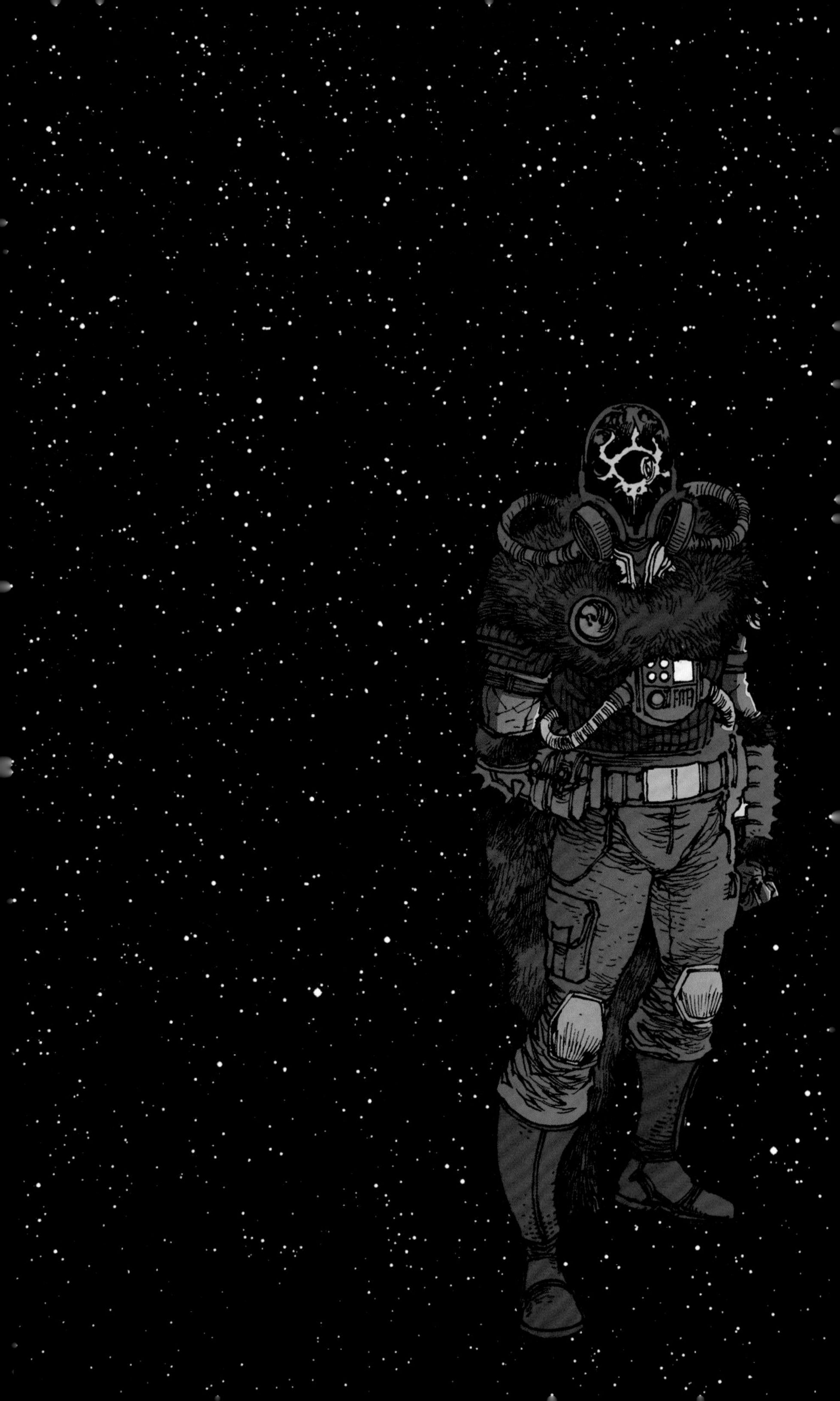

PART 5: SHOWDOWN ON THE JUNK MOON

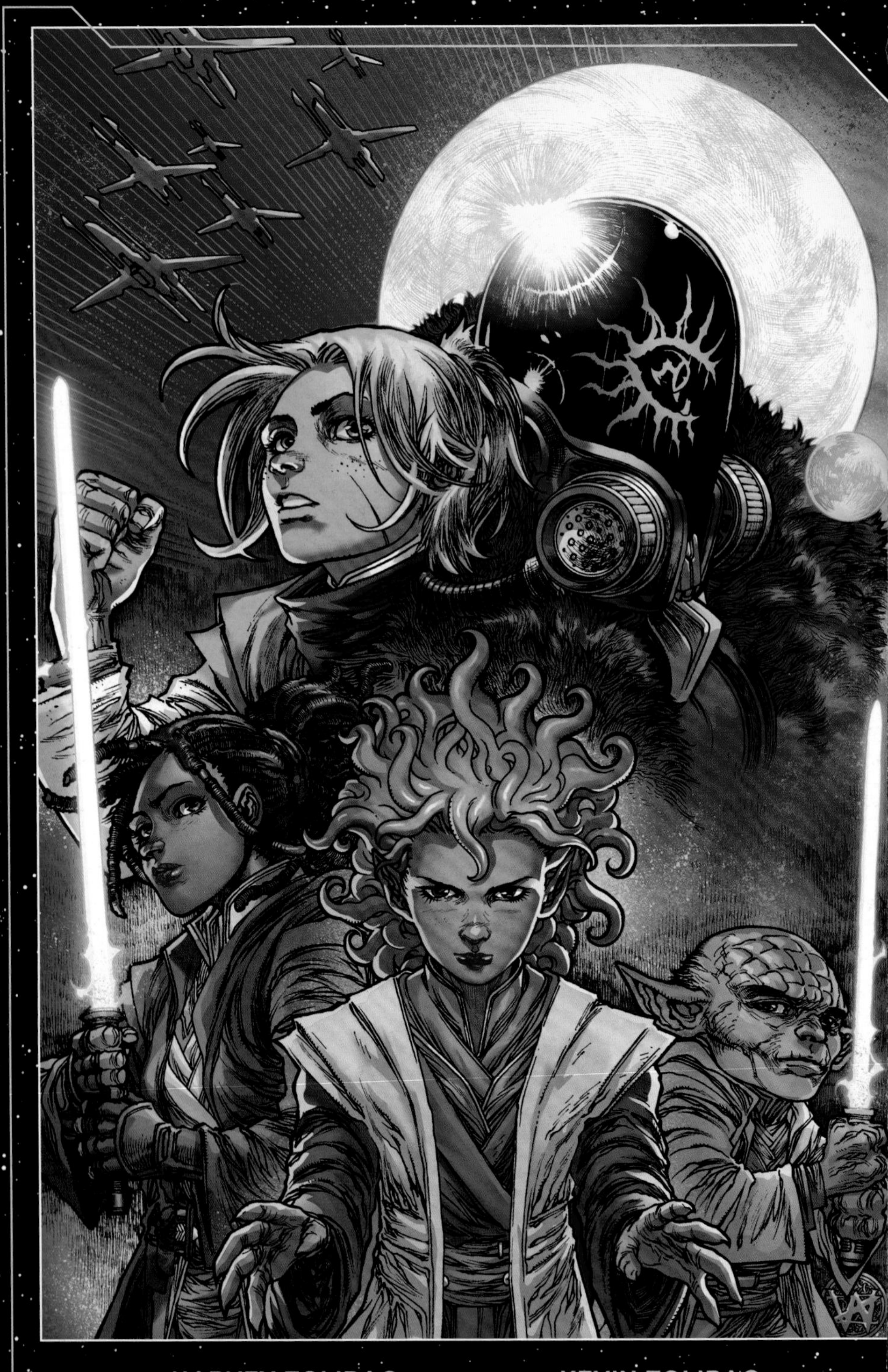

ART BY HARVEY TOLIBAO COLORS BY KEVIN TOLIBAO

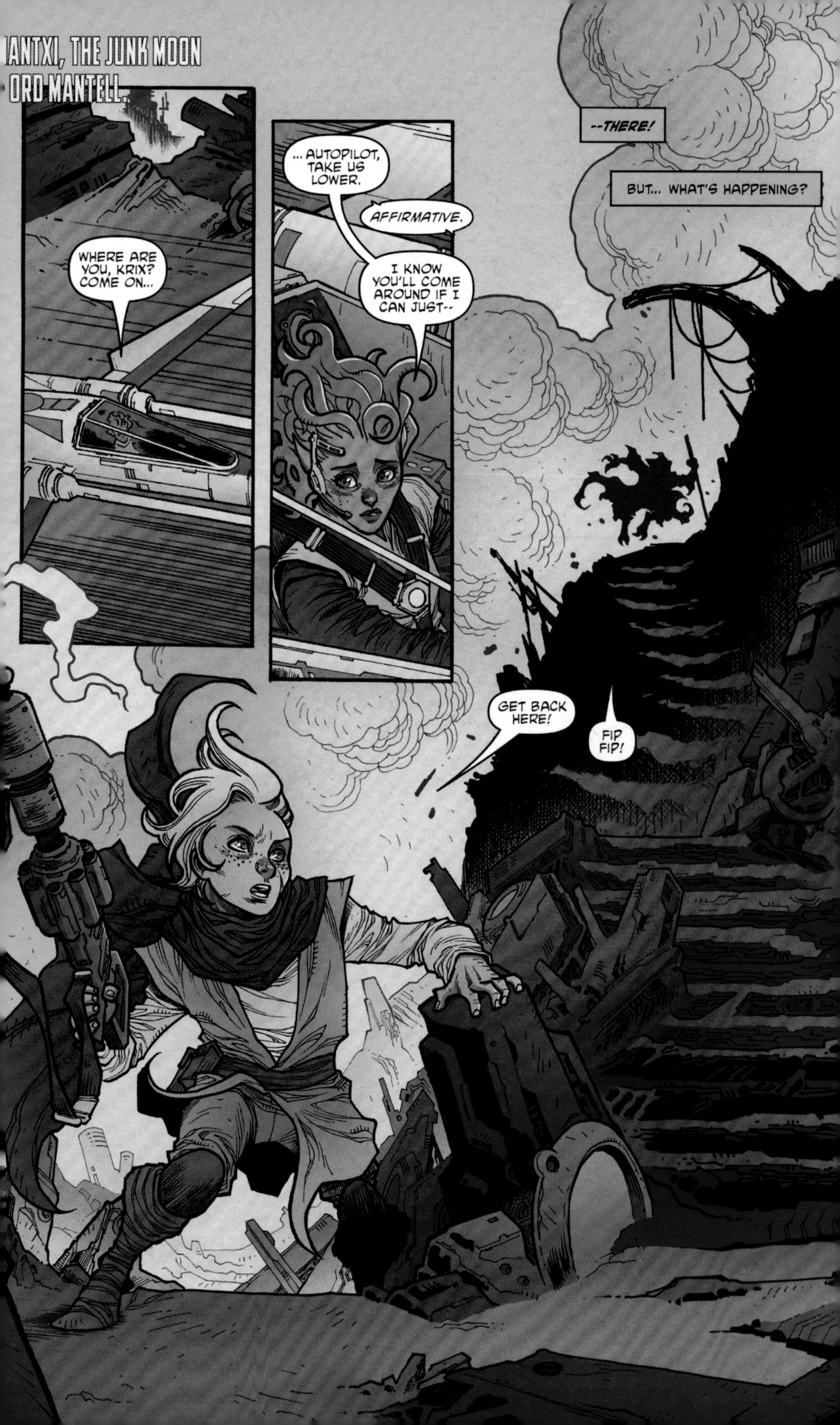
ANTXI, THE JUNK MOON
ORD MANTELL.
WHERE ARE YOU, KRIX? COME ON...
...AUTOPILOT, TAKE US LOWER.
AFFIRMATIVE.
I KNOW YOU'LL COME AROUND IF I CAN JUST--
--THERE!
BUT... WHAT'S HAPPENING?
GET BACK HERE!
FIP FIP!

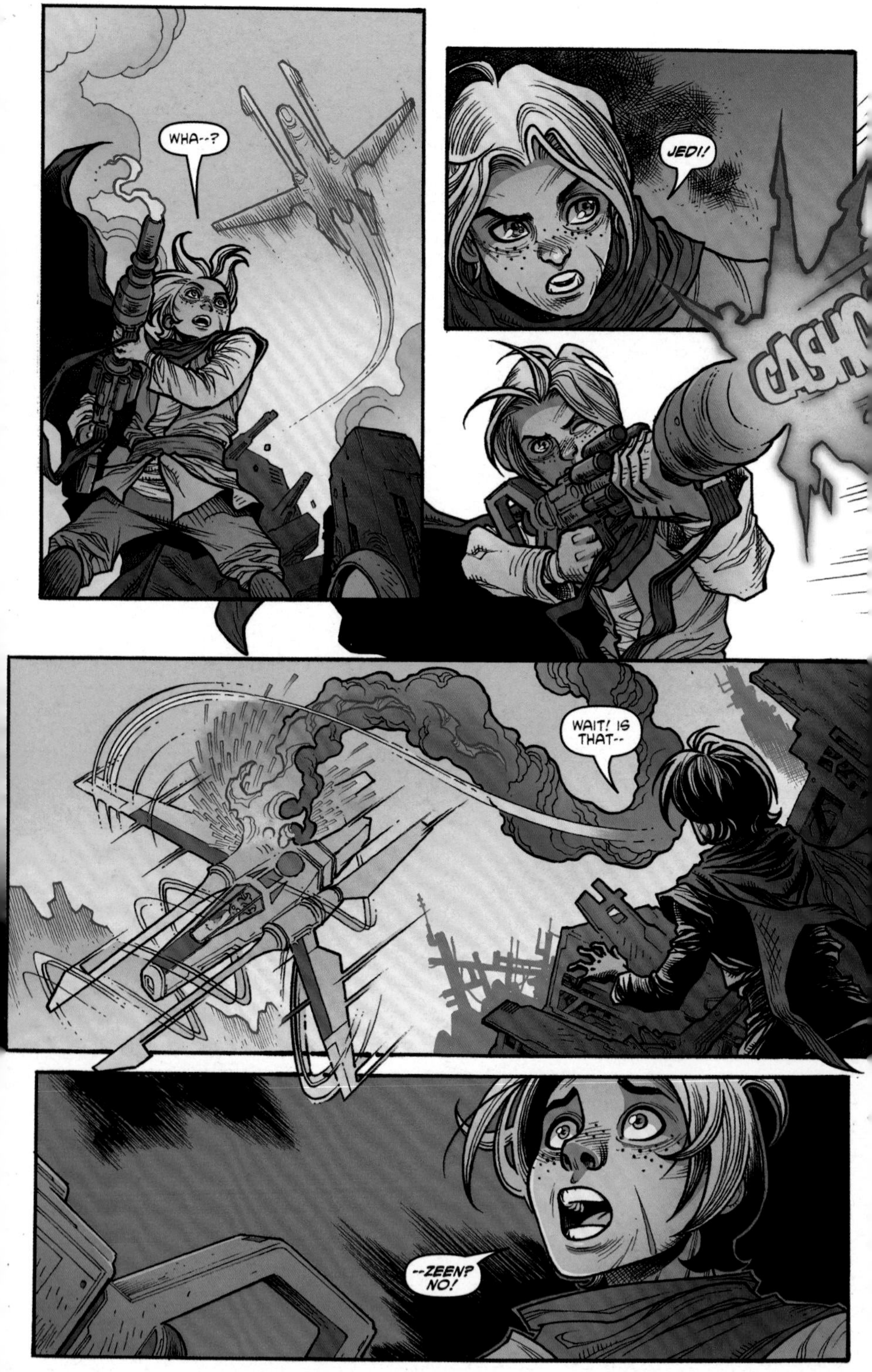
WHA--?
JEDI!
GASH
WAIT! IS THAT--
--ZEEN? NO!

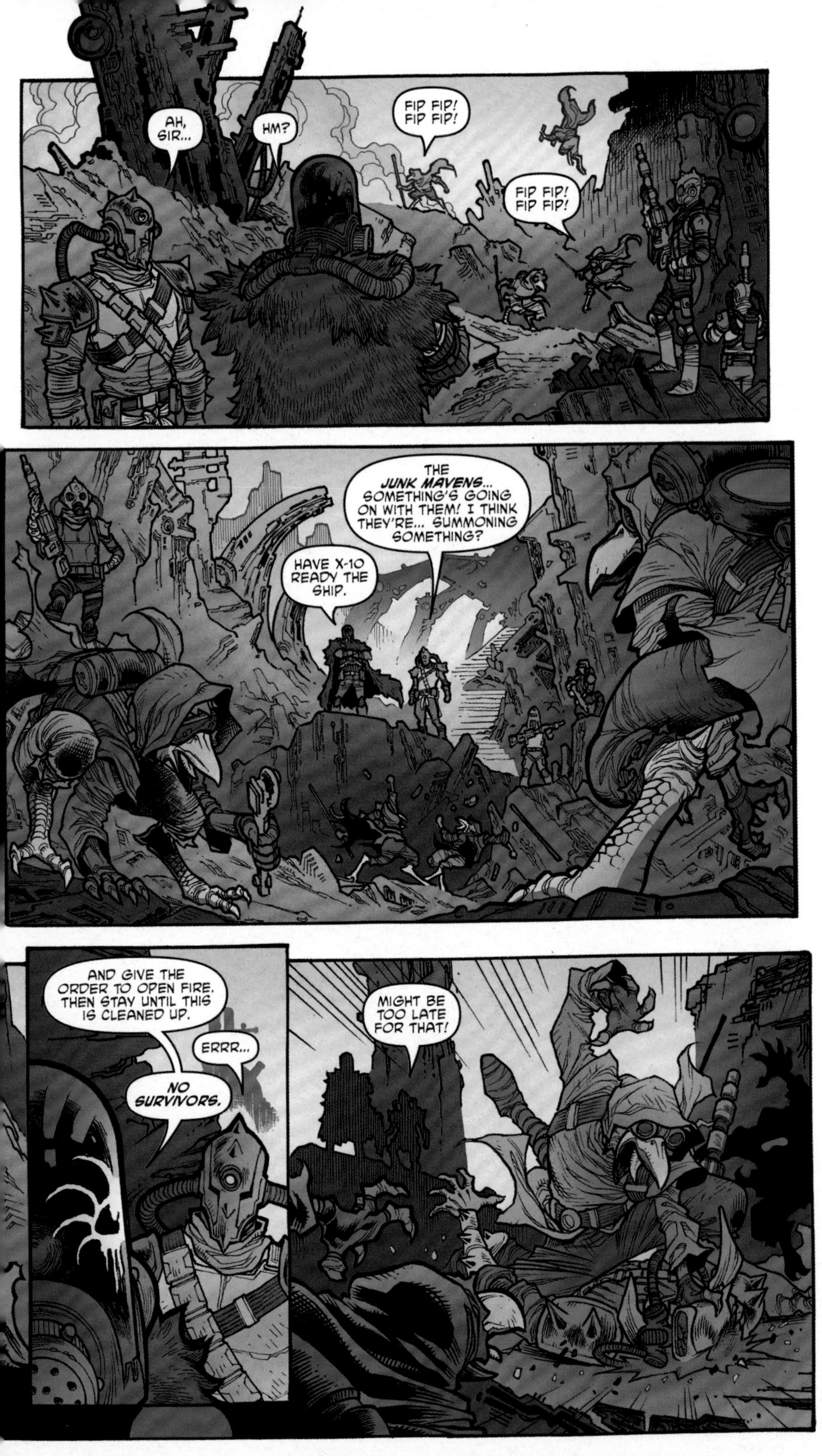
AH, SIR...
HM?
FIP FIP! FIP FIP!
FIP FIP! FIP FIP!
THE *JUNK MAVENS*... SOMETHING'S GOING ON WITH THEM! I THINK THEY'RE... SUMMONING SOMETHING?
HAVE X-10 READY THE SHIP.
AND GIVE THE ORDER TO OPEN FIRE. THEN STAY UNTIL THIS IS CLEANED UP.
ERRR...
NO SURVIVORS.
MIGHT BE TOO LATE FOR THAT!

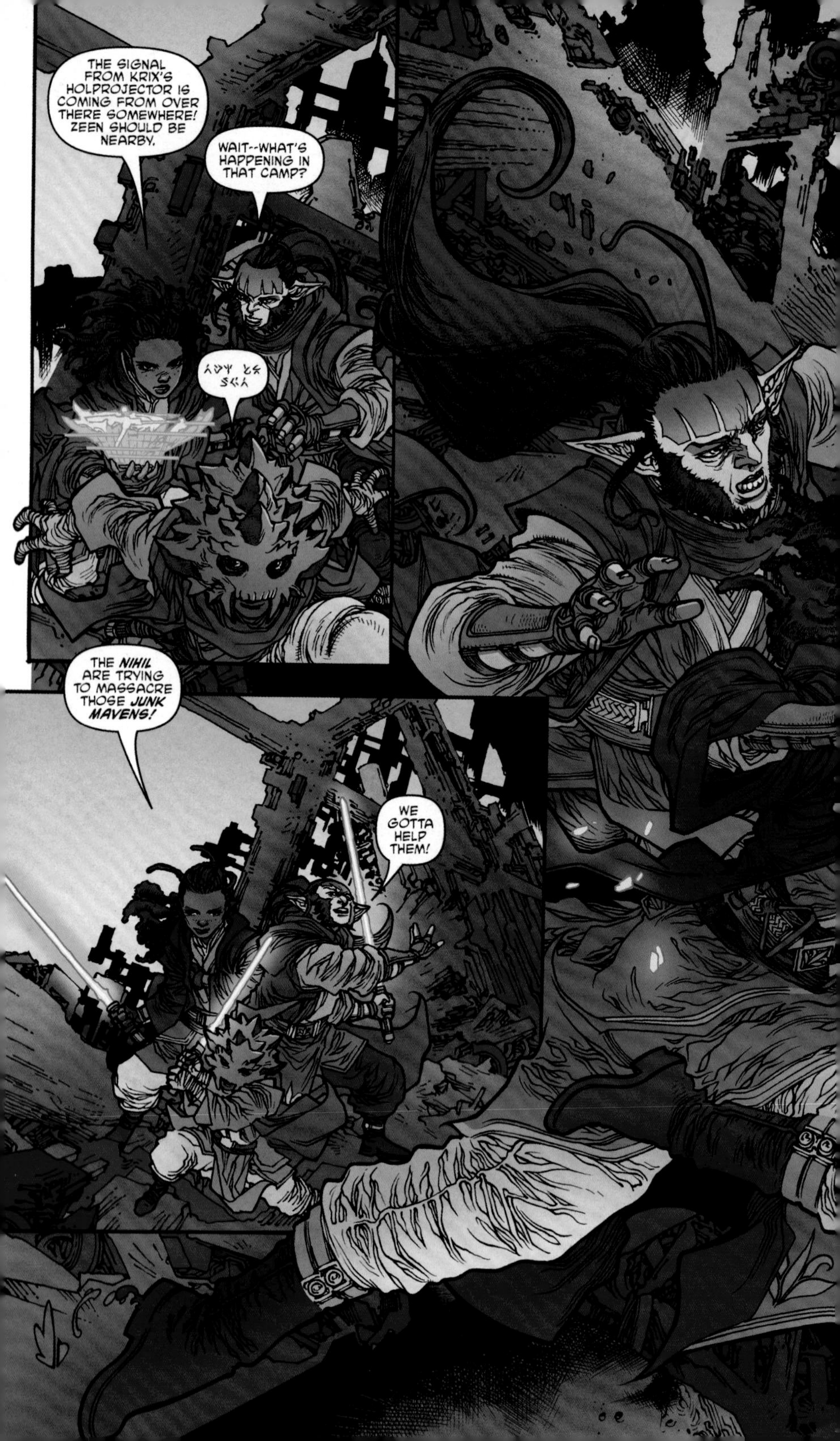
THE SIGNAL FROM KRIX'S HOLPROJECTOR IS COMING FROM OVER THERE SOMEWHERE! ZEEN SHOULD BE NEARBY.
WAIT--WHAT'S HAPPENING IN THAT CAMP?
THE *NIHIL* ARE TRYING TO MASSACRE THOSE *JUNK MAVENS!*
WE GOTTA HELP THEM!

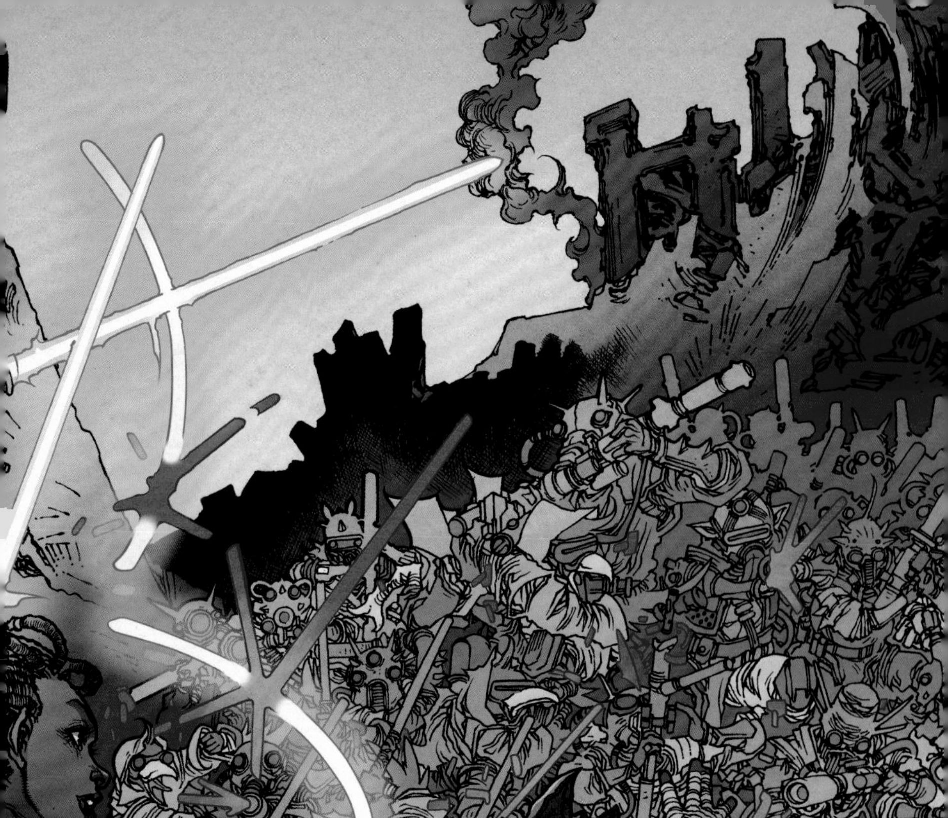
FOR LIGHT AND LIFE!

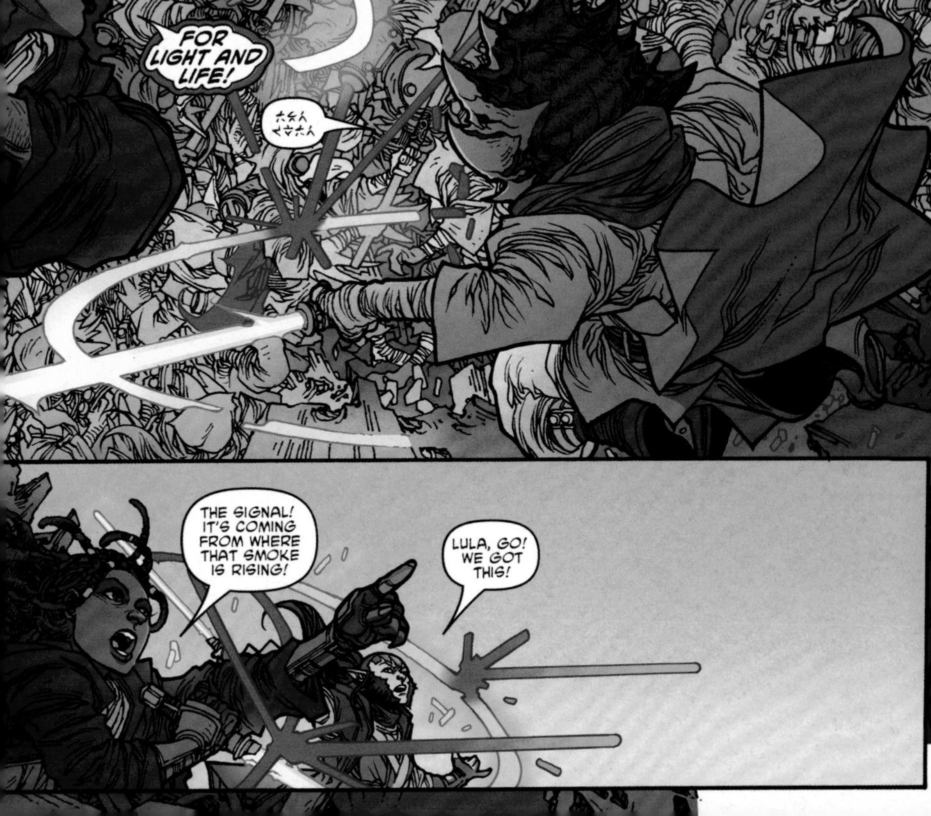
THE SIGNAL! IT'S COMING FROM WHERE THAT SMOKE IS RISING!
LULA, GO! WE GOT THIS!

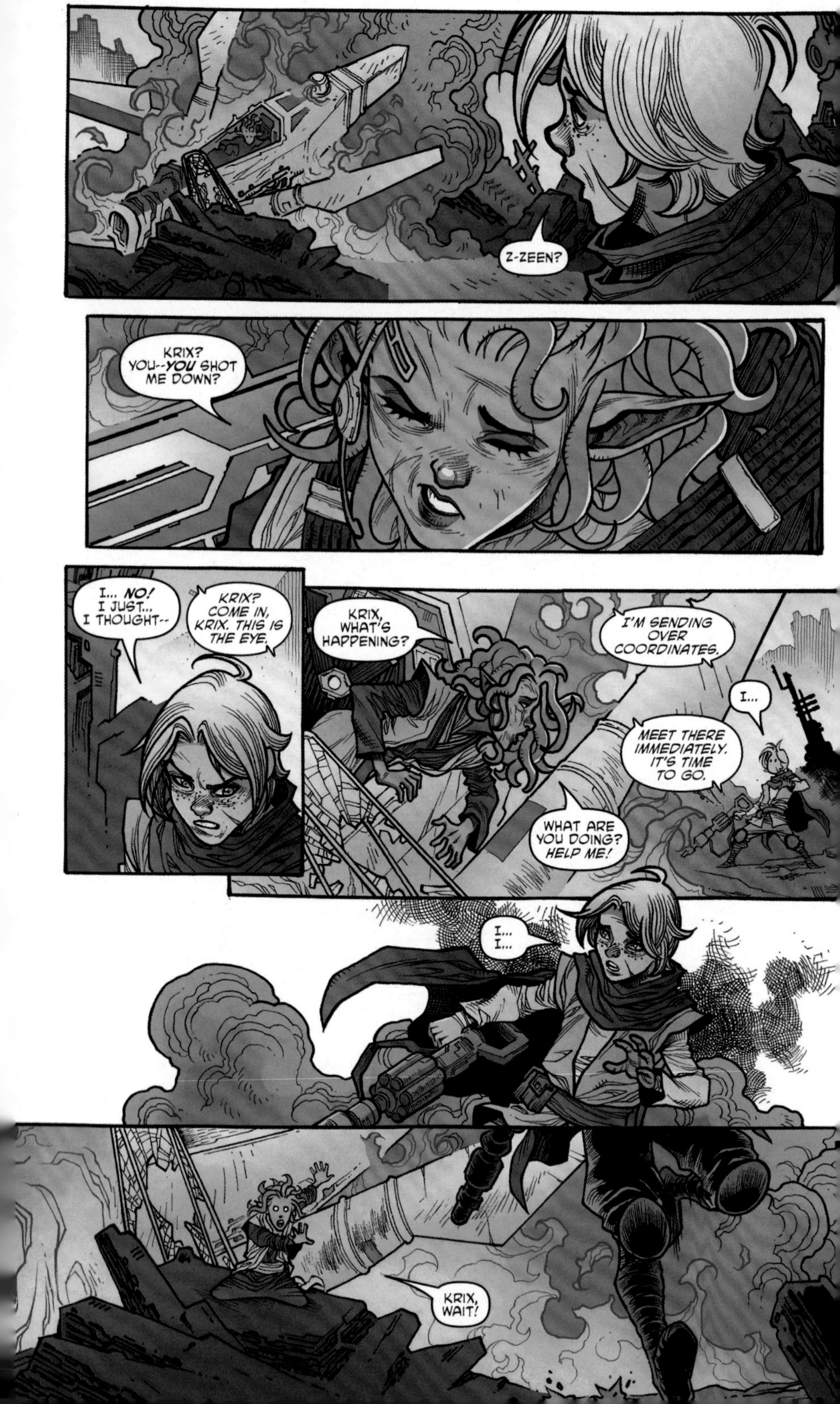
Z-ZEEN?
KRIX? YOU--*YOU* SHOT ME DOWN?
I... *NO!* I JUST... I THOUGHT--
KRIX? COME IN, KRIX. THIS IS THE EYE.
KRIX, WHAT'S HAPPENING?
I'M SENDING OVER COORDINATES.
I...
MEET THERE IMMEDIATELY. IT'S TIME TO GO.
WHAT ARE YOU DOING? *HELP ME!*
I... I...
KRIX, WAIT!

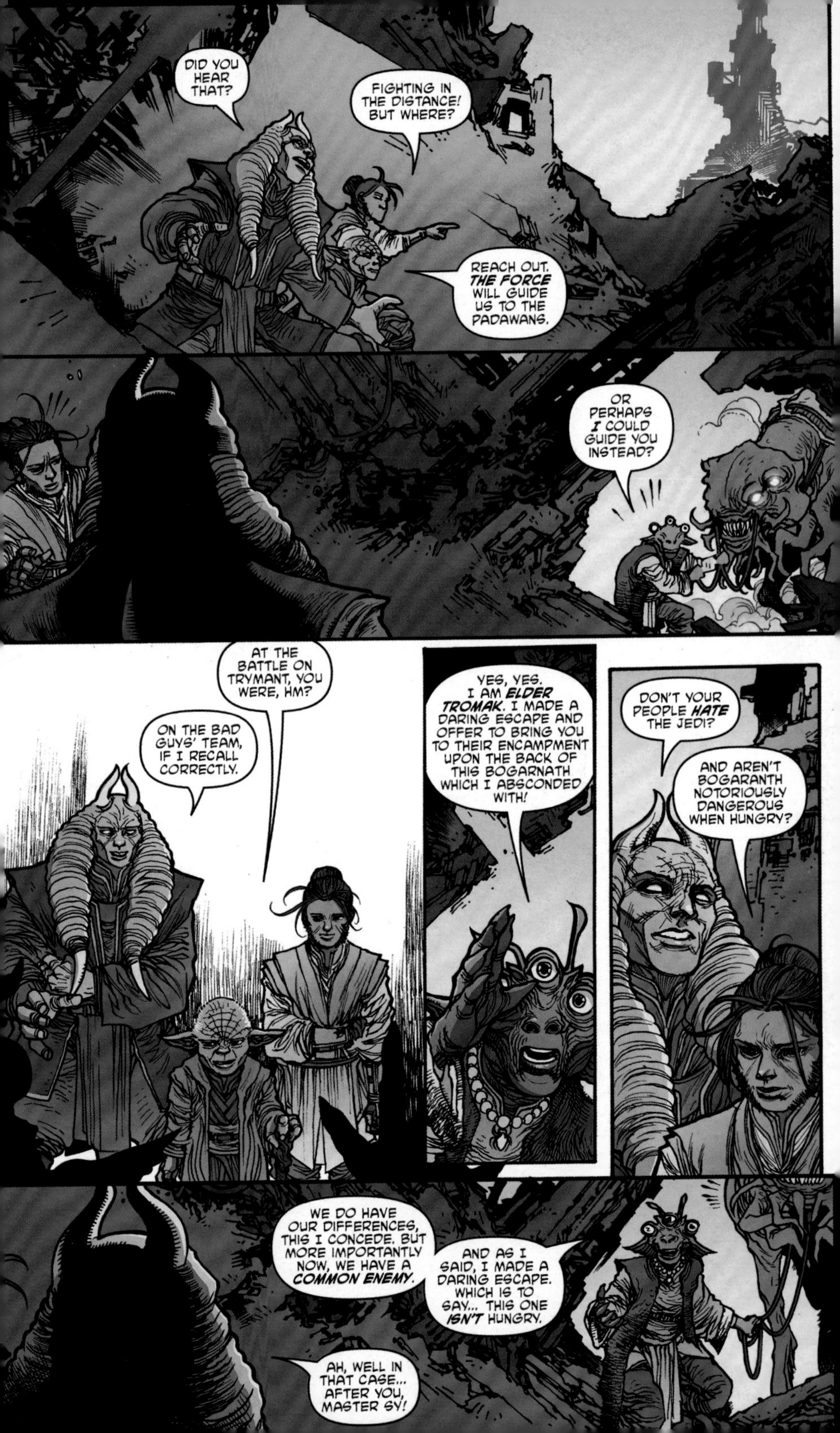
DID YOU HEAR THAT?
FIGHTING IN THE DISTANCE! BUT WHERE?
REACH OUT. THE FORCE WILL GUIDE US TO THE PADAWANS.
OR PERHAPS I COULD GUIDE YOU INSTEAD?
AT THE BATTLE ON TRYMANT, YOU WERE, HM?
ON THE BAD GUYS' TEAM, IF I RECALL CORRECTLY.
YES, YES. I AM ELDER TROMAK. I MADE A DARING ESCAPE AND OFFER TO BRING YOU TO THEIR ENCAMPMENT UPON THE BACK OF THIS BOGARNATH WHICH I ABSCONDED WITH!
DON'T YOUR PEOPLE HATE THE JEDI?
AND AREN'T BOGARANTH NOTORIOUSLY DANGEROUS WHEN HUNGRY?
WE DO HAVE OUR DIFFERENCES, THIS I CONCEDE. BUT MORE IMPORTANTLY NOW, WE HAVE A COMMON ENEMY.
AND AS I SAID, I MADE A DARING ESCAPE. WHICH IS TO SAY... THIS ONE ISN'T HUNGRY.
AH, WELL IN THAT CASE... AFTER YOU, MASTER SY!

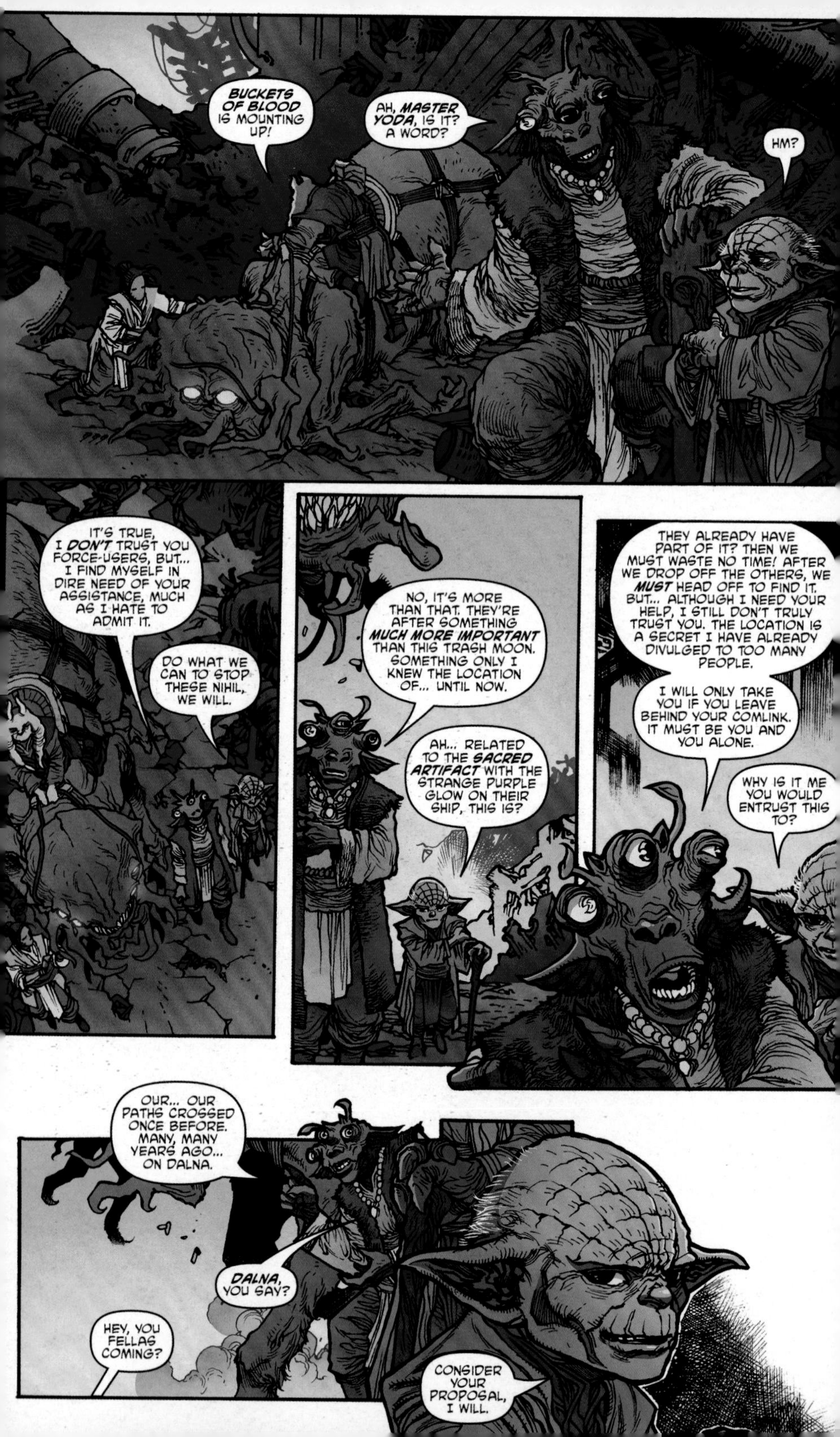
BUCKETS OF BLOOD IS MOUNTING UP!
AH, MASTER YODA, IS IT? A WORD?
HM?
IT'S TRUE, I DON'T TRUST YOU FORCE-USERS, BUT... I FIND MYSELF IN DIRE NEED OF YOUR ASSISTANCE, MUCH AS I HATE TO ADMIT IT.
DO WHAT WE CAN TO STOP THESE NIHIL, WE WILL.
NO, IT'S MORE THAN THAT. THEY'RE AFTER SOMETHING MUCH MORE IMPORTANT THAN THIS TRASH MOON. SOMETHING ONLY I KNEW THE LOCATION OF... UNTIL NOW.
AH... RELATED TO THE SACRED ARTIFACT WITH THE STRANGE PURPLE GLOW ON THEIR SHIP, THIS IS?
THEY ALREADY HAVE PART OF IT? THEN WE MUST WASTE NO TIME! AFTER WE DROP OFF THE OTHERS, WE MUST HEAD OFF TO FIND IT. BUT... ALTHOUGH I NEED YOUR HELP, I STILL DON'T TRULY TRUST YOU. THE LOCATION IS A SECRET I HAVE ALREADY DIVULGED TO TOO MANY PEOPLE.
I WILL ONLY TAKE YOU IF YOU LEAVE BEHIND YOUR COMLINK. IT MUST BE YOU AND YOU ALONE.
WHY IS IT ME YOU WOULD ENTRUST THIS TO?
OUR... OUR PATHS CROSSED ONCE BEFORE. MANY, MANY YEARS AGO... ON DALNA.
DALNA, YOU SAY?
HEY, YOU FELLAS COMING?
CONSIDER YOUR PROPOSAL, I WILL.

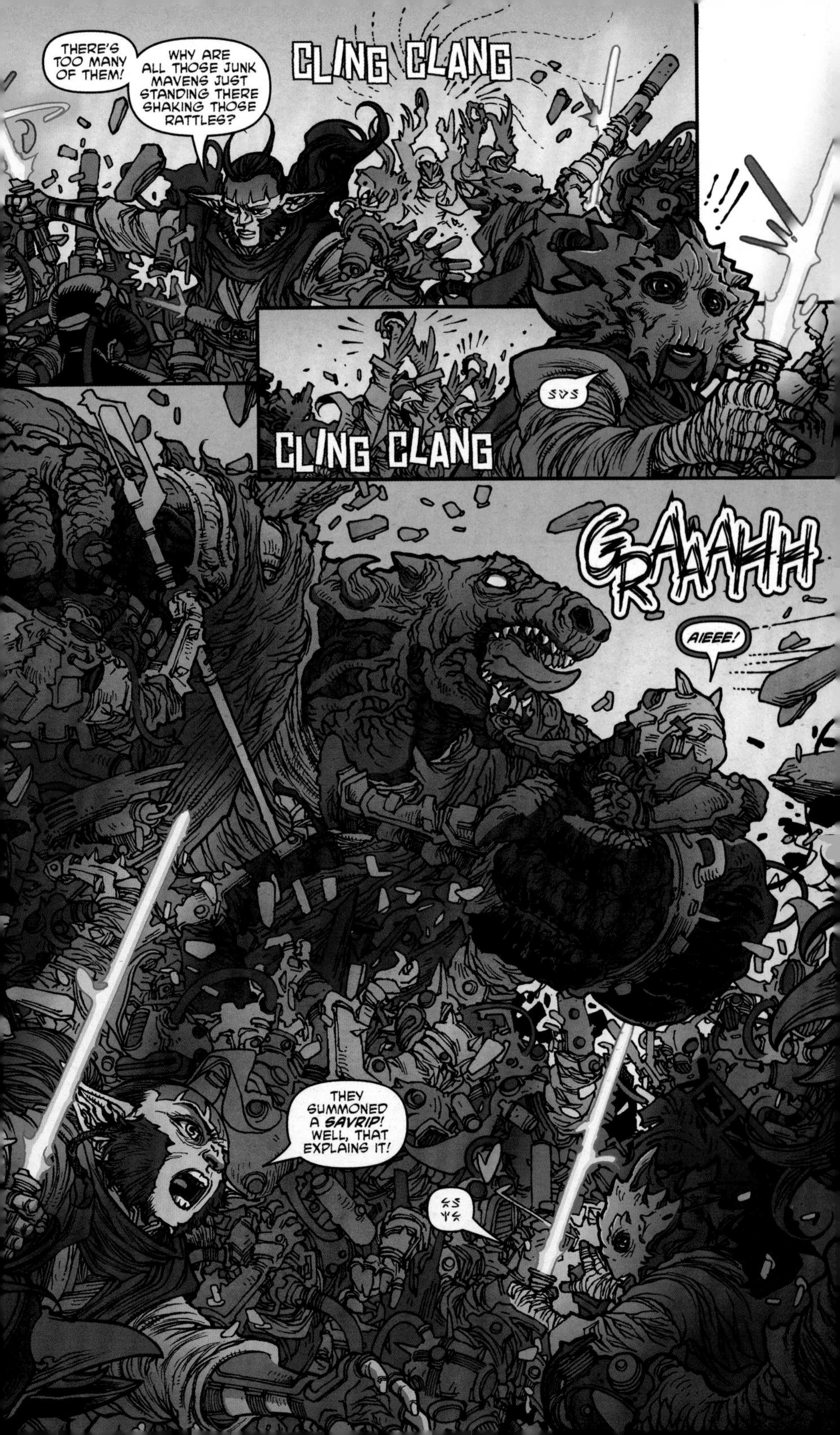
THERE'S TOO MANY OF THEM!
WHY ARE ALL THOSE JUNK MAVENS JUST STANDING THERE SHAKING THOSE RATTLES?
CLING CLANG
CLING CLANG
GRAAAHH
AIEEE!
THEY SUMMONED A *SAVRIP!* WELL, THAT EXPLAINS IT!

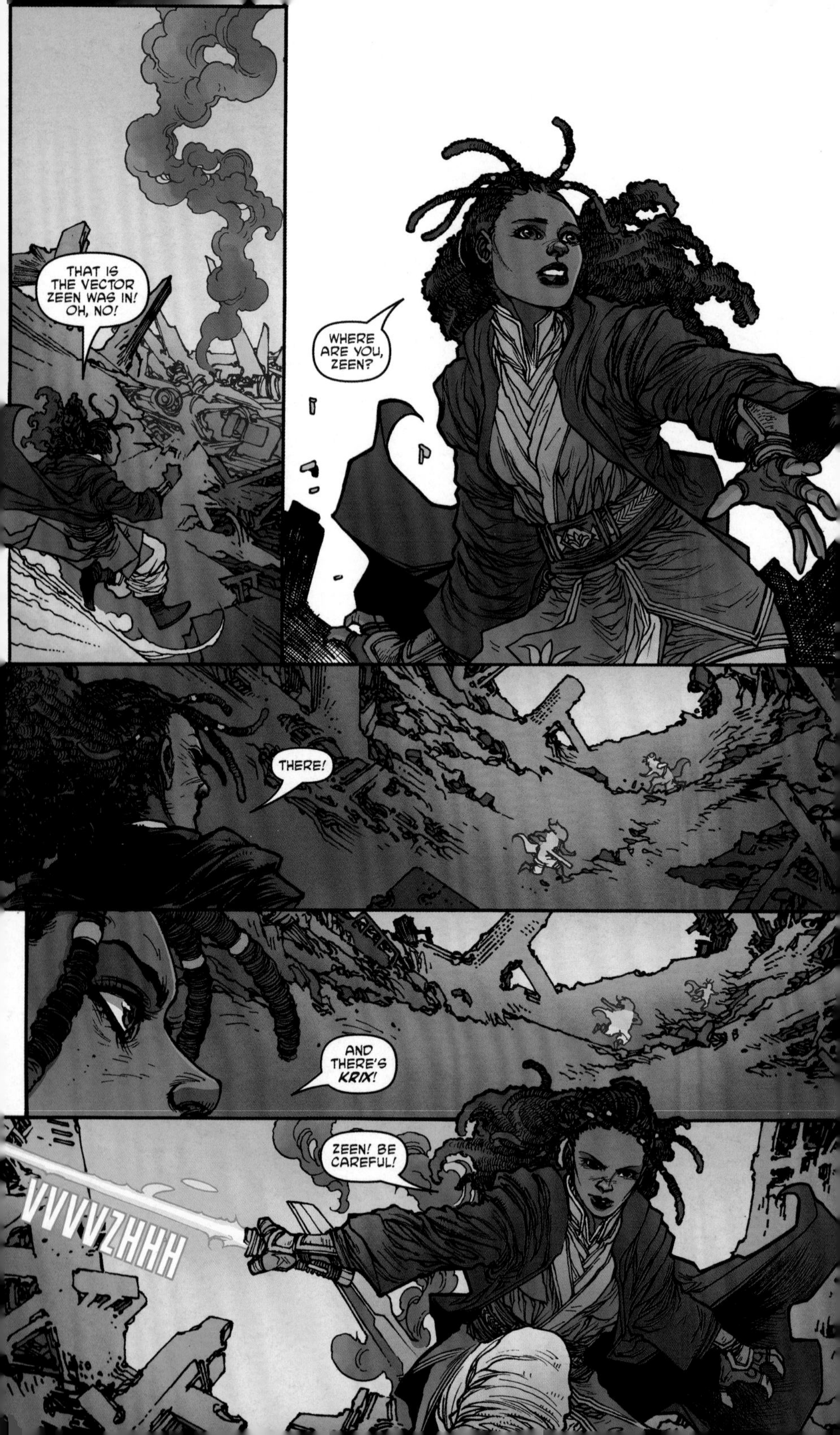
THAT IS THE VECTOR ZEEN WAS IN! OH, NO!
WHERE ARE YOU, ZEEN?
THERE!
AND THERE'S *KRIX*!
ZEEN! BE CAREFUL!
VVVVZHHH

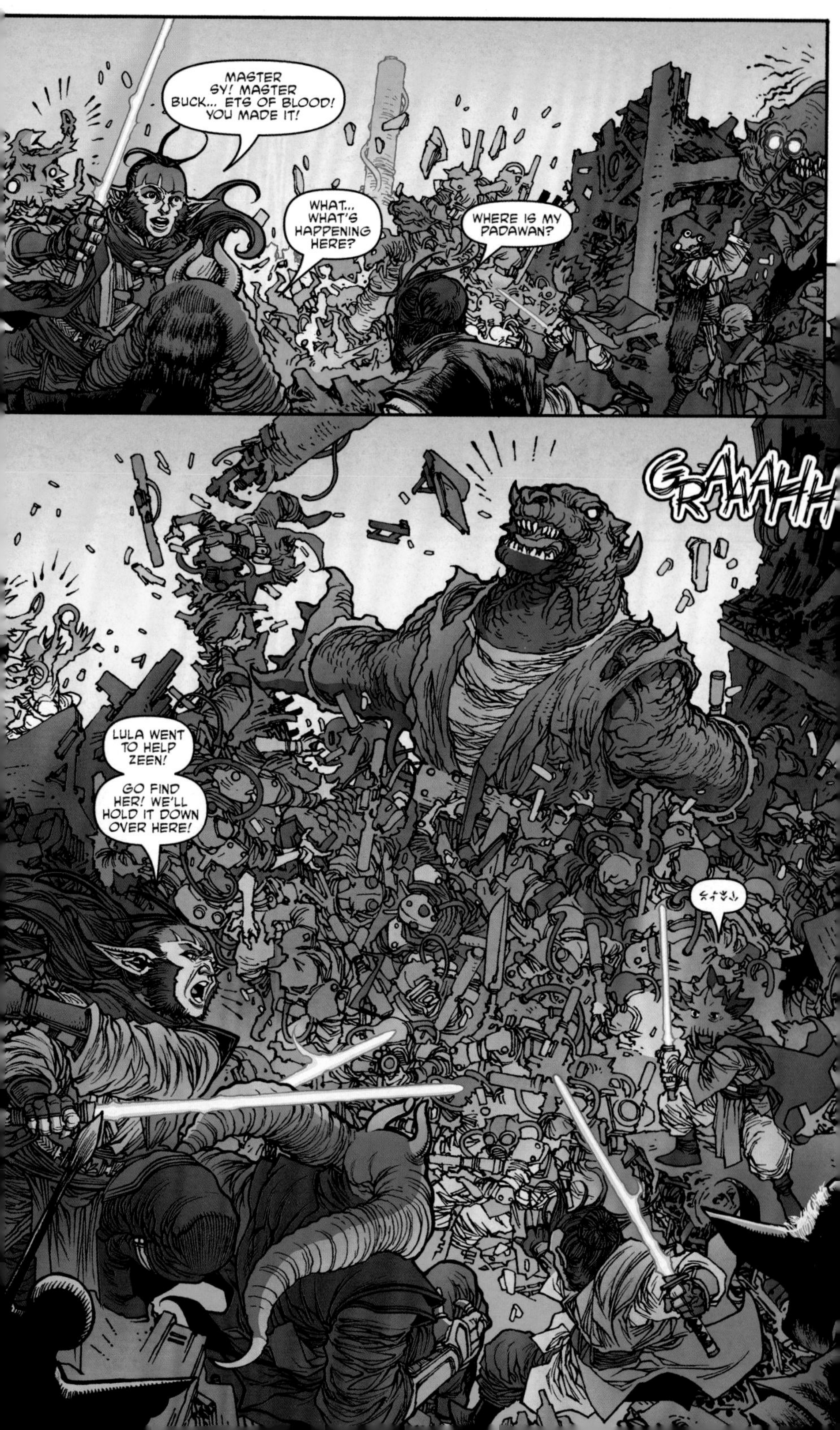
MASTER SY! MASTER BUCK... ETS OF BLOOD! YOU MADE IT!
WHAT... WHAT'S HAPPENING HERE?
WHERE IS MY PADAWAN?
GRAAAHH
LULA WENT TO HELP ZEEN!
GO FIND HER! WE'LL HOLD IT DOWN OVER HERE!

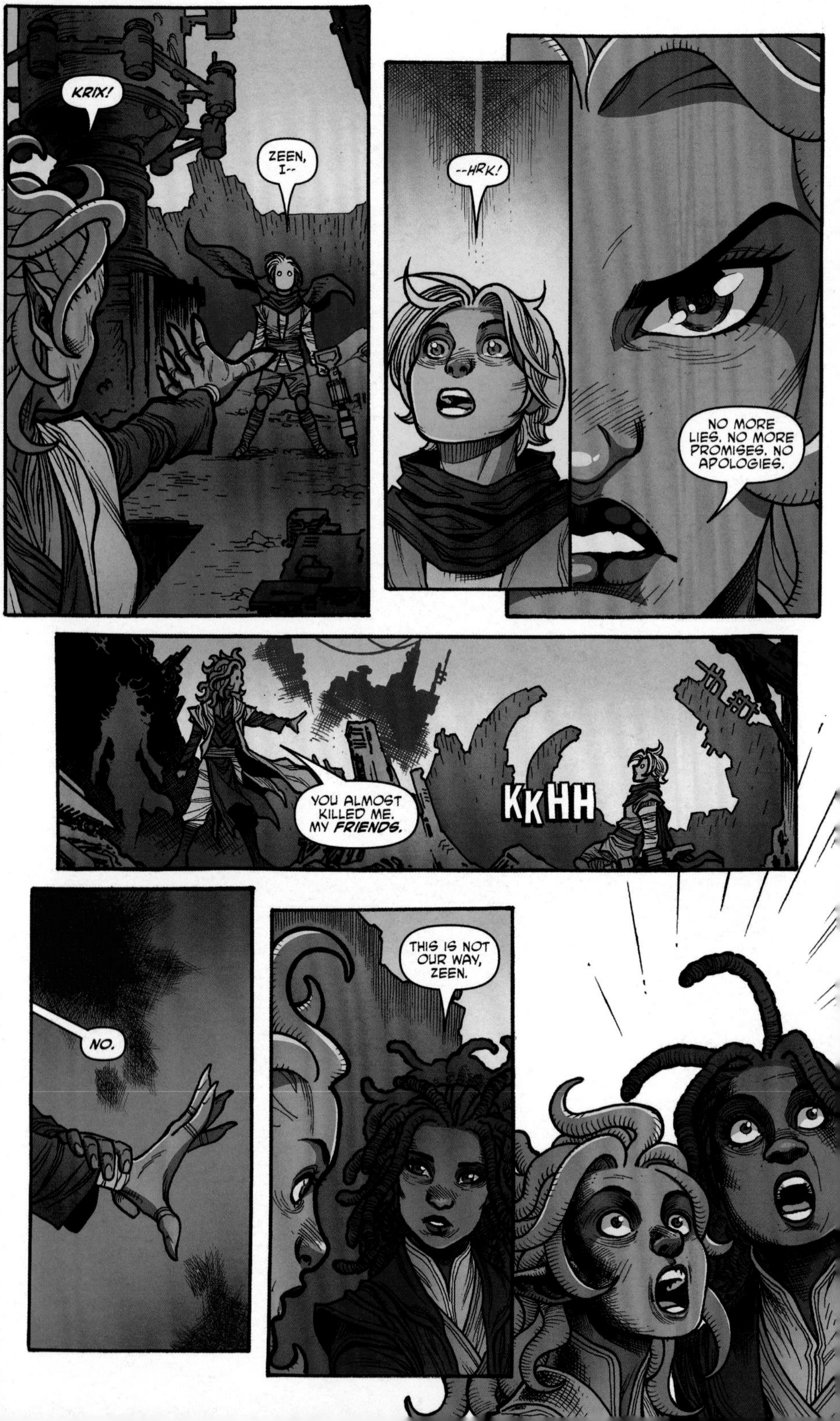
KRIX!
ZEEN, I--
--HRK!
NO MORE LIES. NO MORE PROMISES. NO APOLOGIES.
YOU ALMOST KILLED ME. MY FRIENDS.
KKHH
NO.
THIS IS NOT OUR WAY, ZEEN.

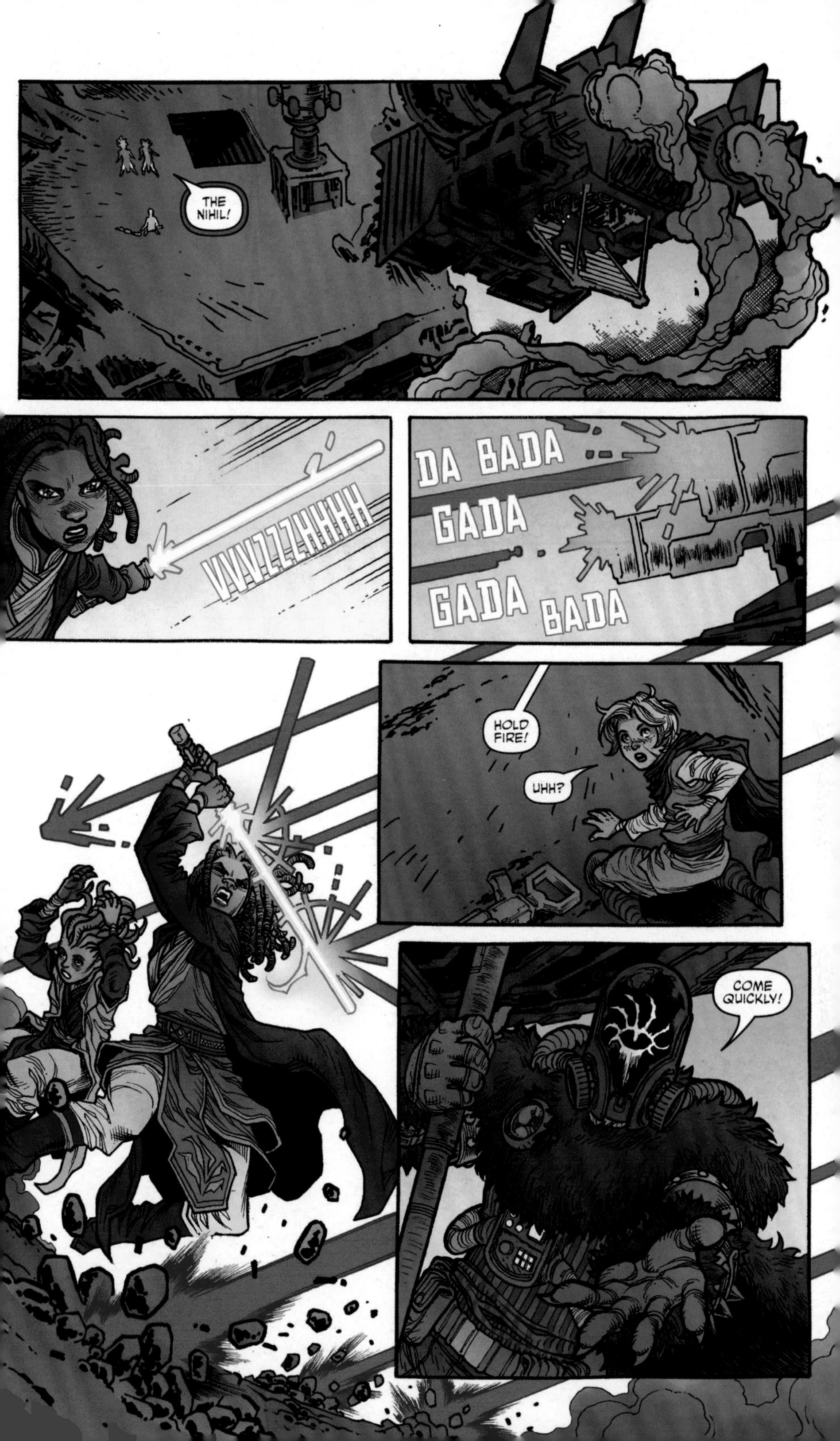
THE NIHIL!
VVVZZZHHHHH
DA BADA
GADA
GADA BADA
HOLD FIRE!
UHH?
COME QUICKLY!

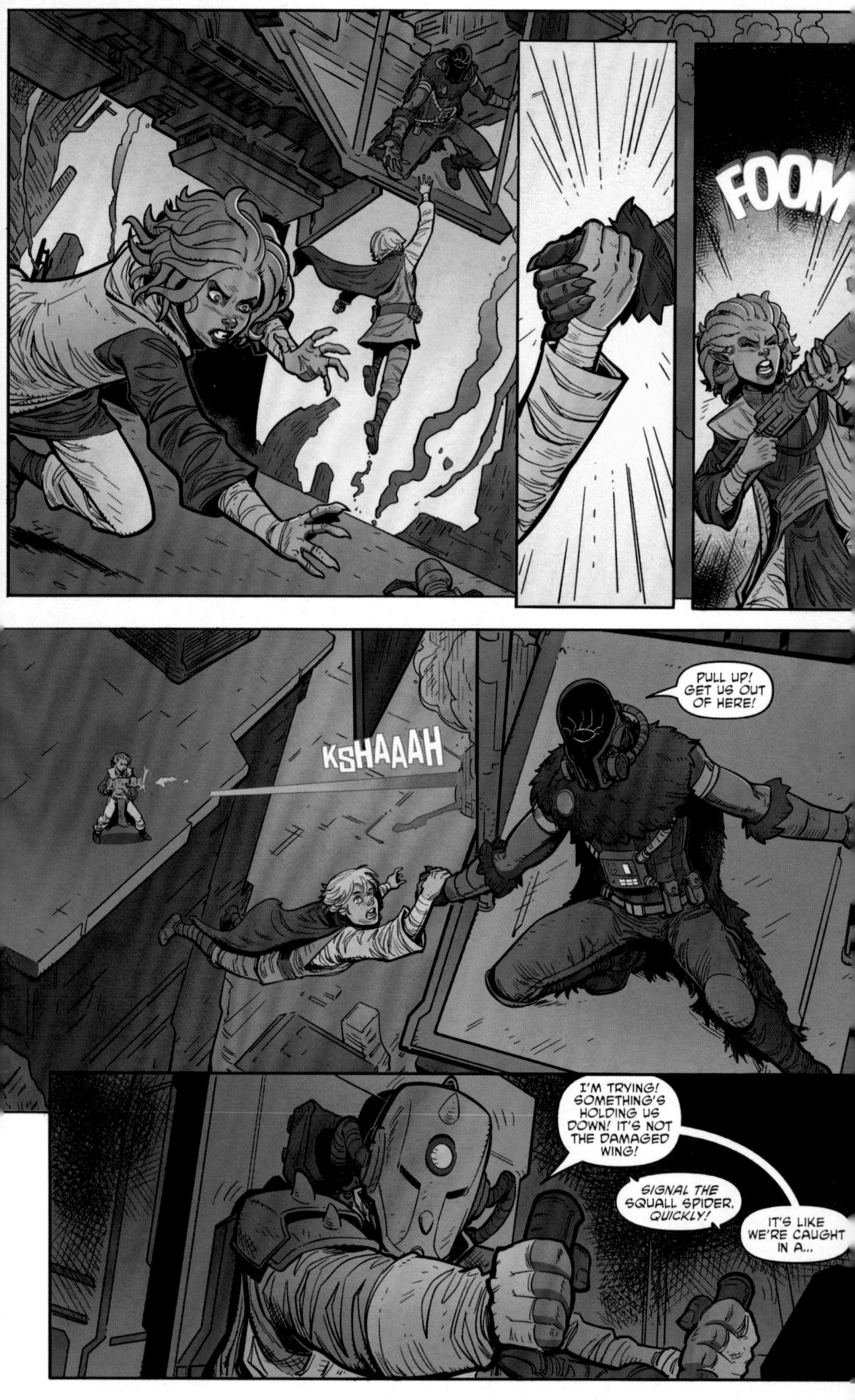
FOOM
PULL UP! GET US OUT OF HERE!
KSHAAAH
I'M TRYING! SOMETHING'S HOLDING US DOWN! IT'S NOT THE DAMAGED WING!
SIGNAL THE SQUALL SPIDER. QUICKLY!
IT'S LIKE WE'RE CAUGHT IN A...

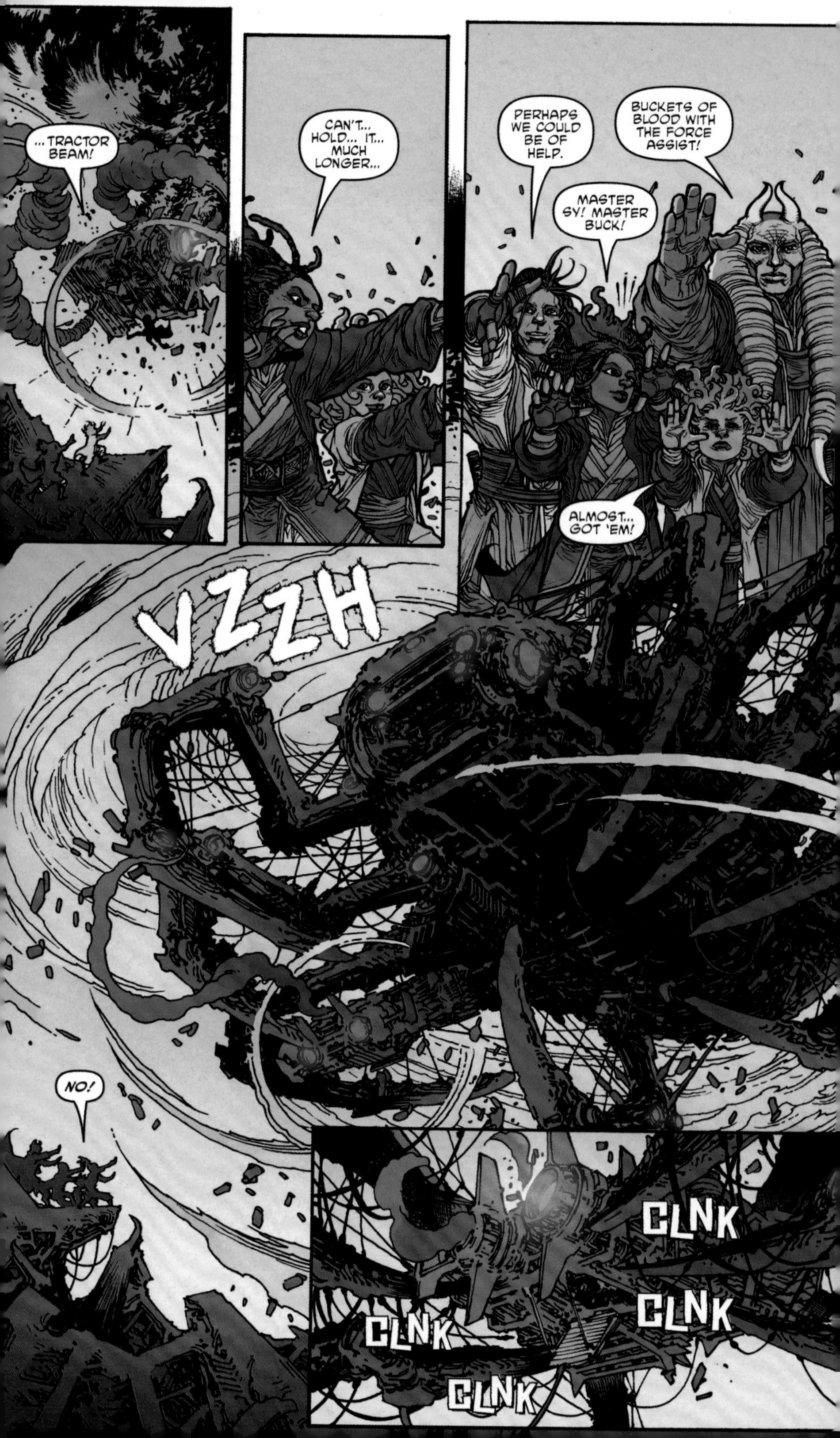
...TRACTOR BEAM!
CAN'T... HOLD... IT... MUCH LONGER...
PERHAPS WE COULD BE OF HELP.
BUCKETS OF BLOOD WITH THE FORCE ASSIST!
MASTER SY! MASTER BUCK!
ALMOST... GOT 'EM!
VZZH
NO!
CLNK
CLNK
CLNK
CLNK

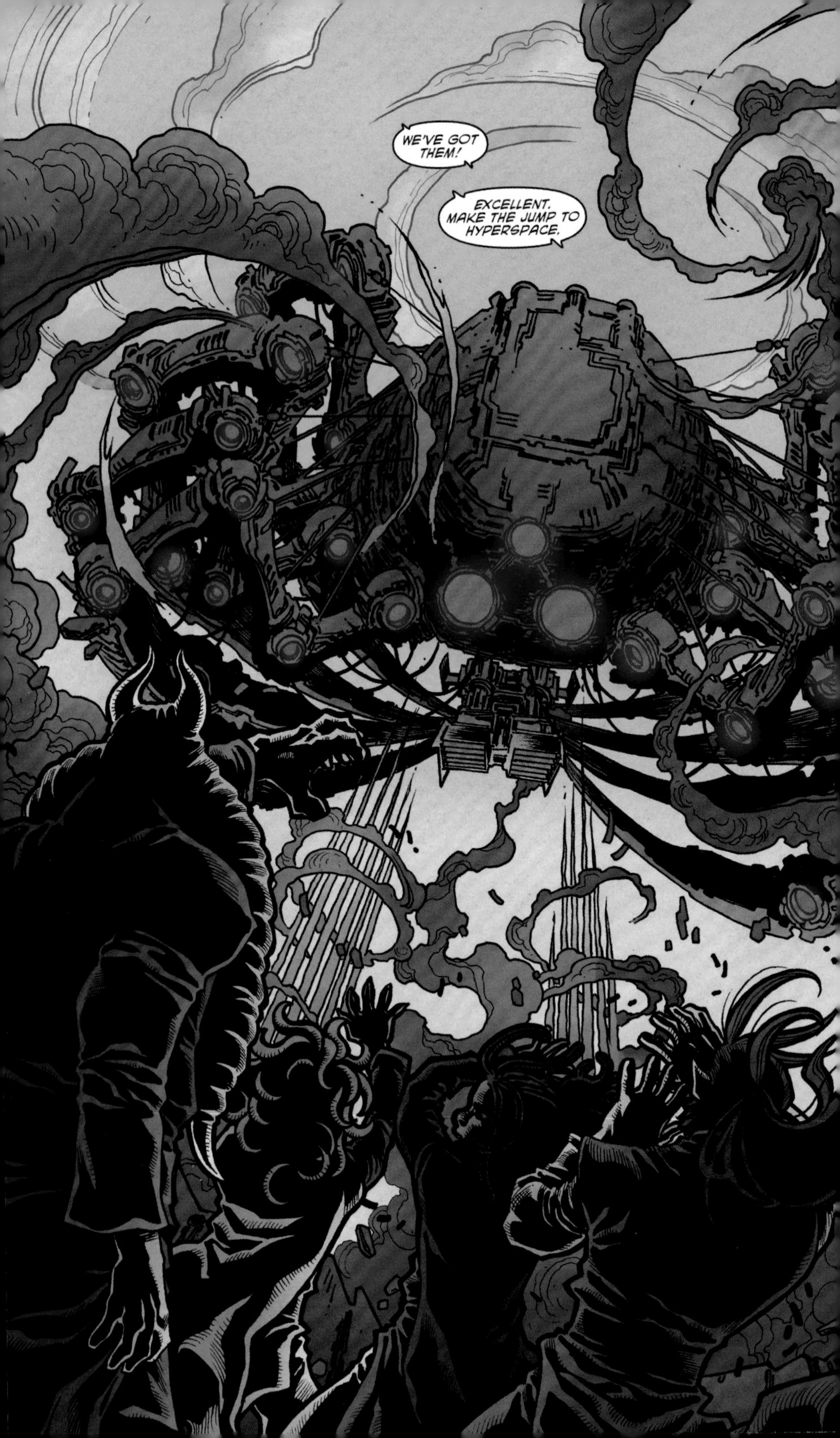
WE'VE GOT THEM!
EXCELLENT. MAKE THE JUMP TO HYPERSPACE.

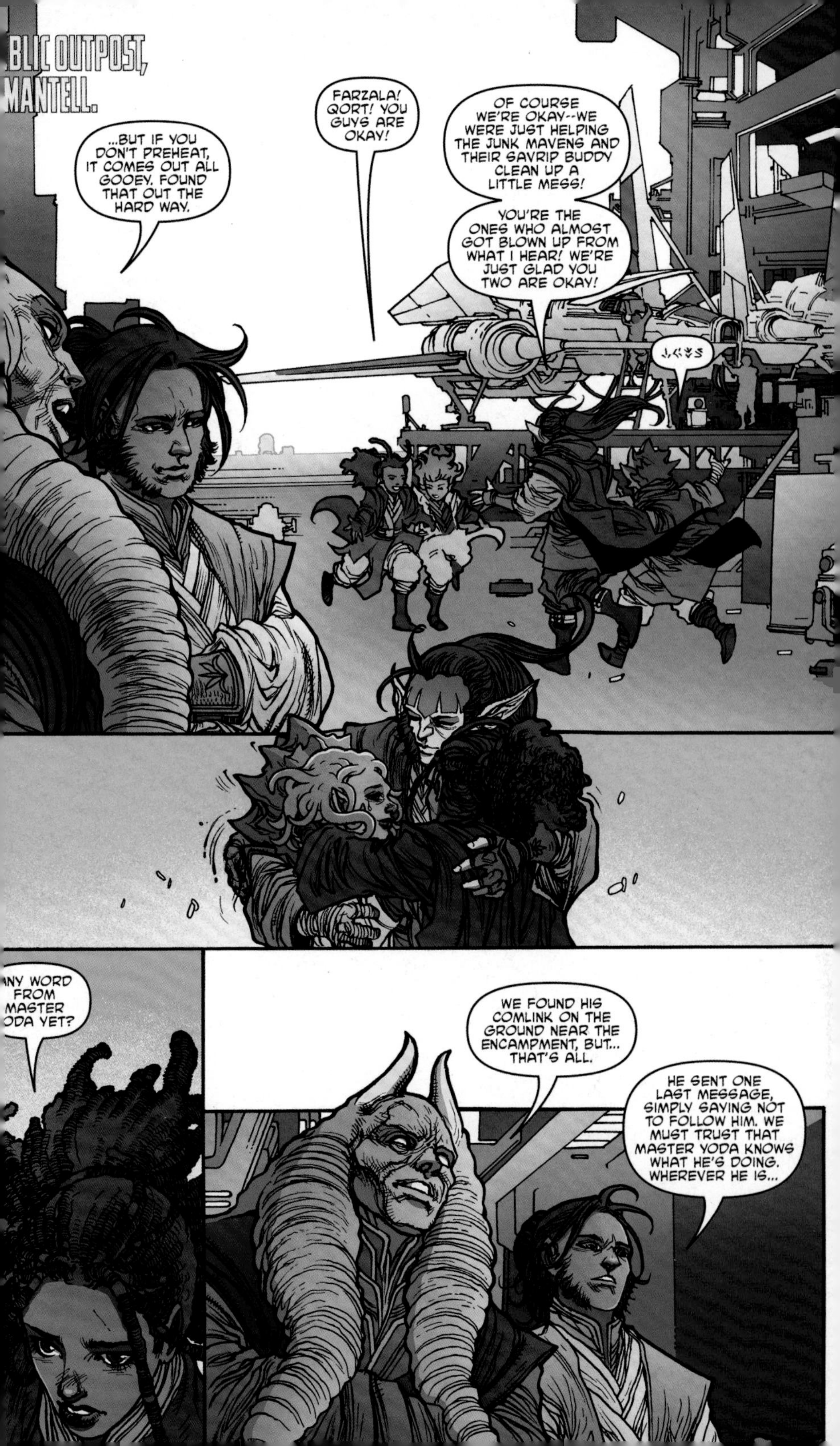
BLIC OUTPOST,
MANTELL.
...BUT IF YOU DON'T PREHEAT, IT COMES OUT ALL GOOEY. FOUND THAT OUT THE HARD WAY.
FARZALA! QORT! YOU GUYS ARE OKAY!
OF COURSE WE'RE OKAY--WE WERE JUST HELPING THE JUNK MAVENS AND THEIR SAVRIP BUDDY CLEAN UP A LITTLE MESS!
YOU'RE THE ONES WHO ALMOST GOT BLOWN UP FROM WHAT I HEAR! WE'RE JUST GLAD YOU TWO ARE OKAY!
ANY WORD FROM MASTER ODA YET?
WE FOUND HIS COMLINK ON THE GROUND NEAR THE ENCAMPMENT, BUT... THAT'S ALL.
HE SENT ONE LAST MESSAGE, SIMPLY SAYING NOT TO FOLLOW HIM. WE MUST TRUST THAT MASTER YODA KNOWS WHAT HE'S DOING. WHEREVER HE IS...

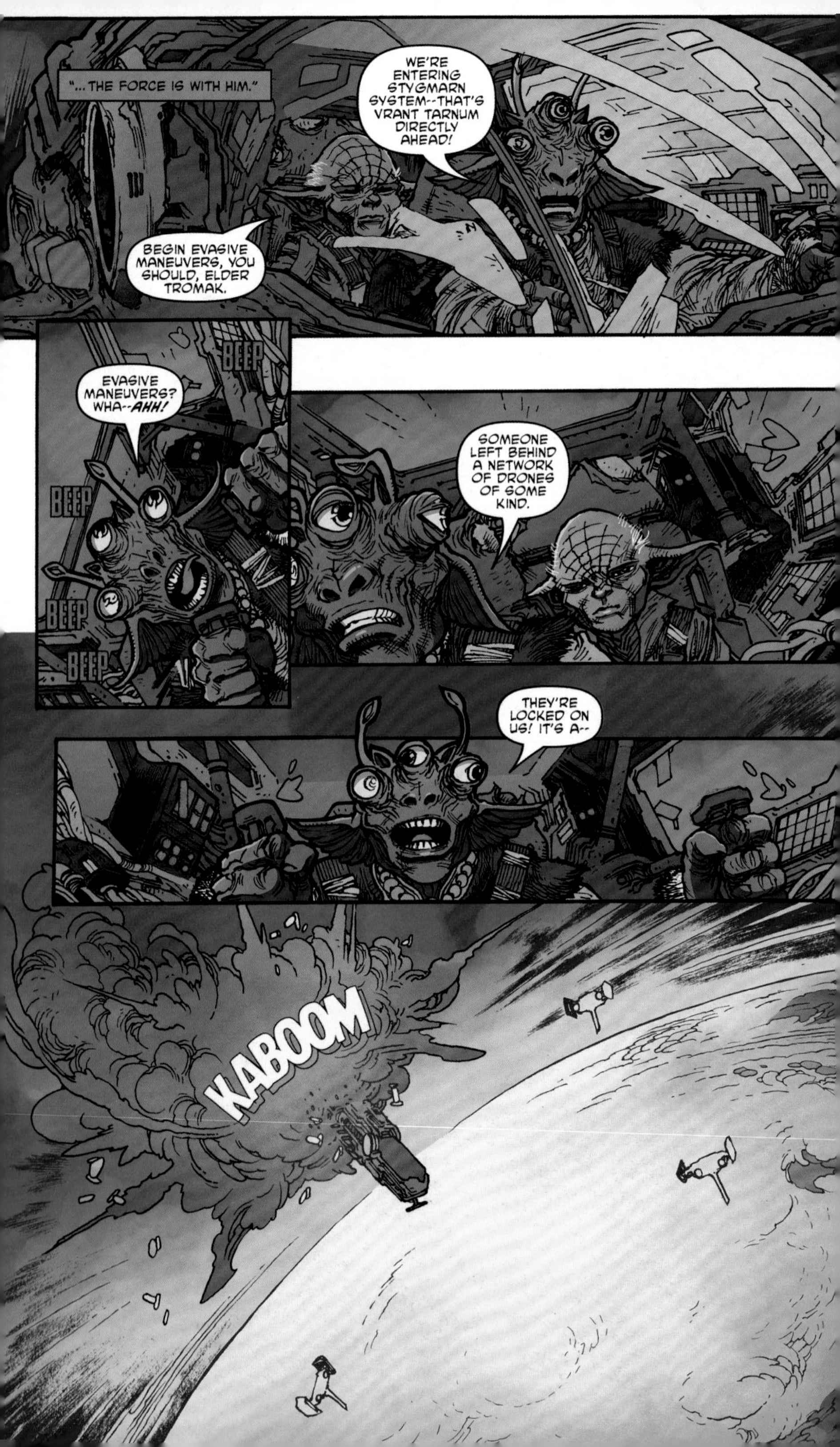
"...THE FORCE IS WITH HIM."
WE'RE ENTERING STYGMARN SYSTEM--THAT'S VRANT TARNUM DIRECTLY AHEAD!
BEGIN EVASIVE MANEUVERS, YOU SHOULD, ELDER TROMAK.
BEEP
EVASIVE MANEUVERS? WHA--AHH!
BEEP
BEEP
BEEP
SOMEONE LEFT BEHIND A NETWORK OF DRONES OF SOME KIND.
THEY'RE LOCKED ON US! IT'S A--
KABOOM

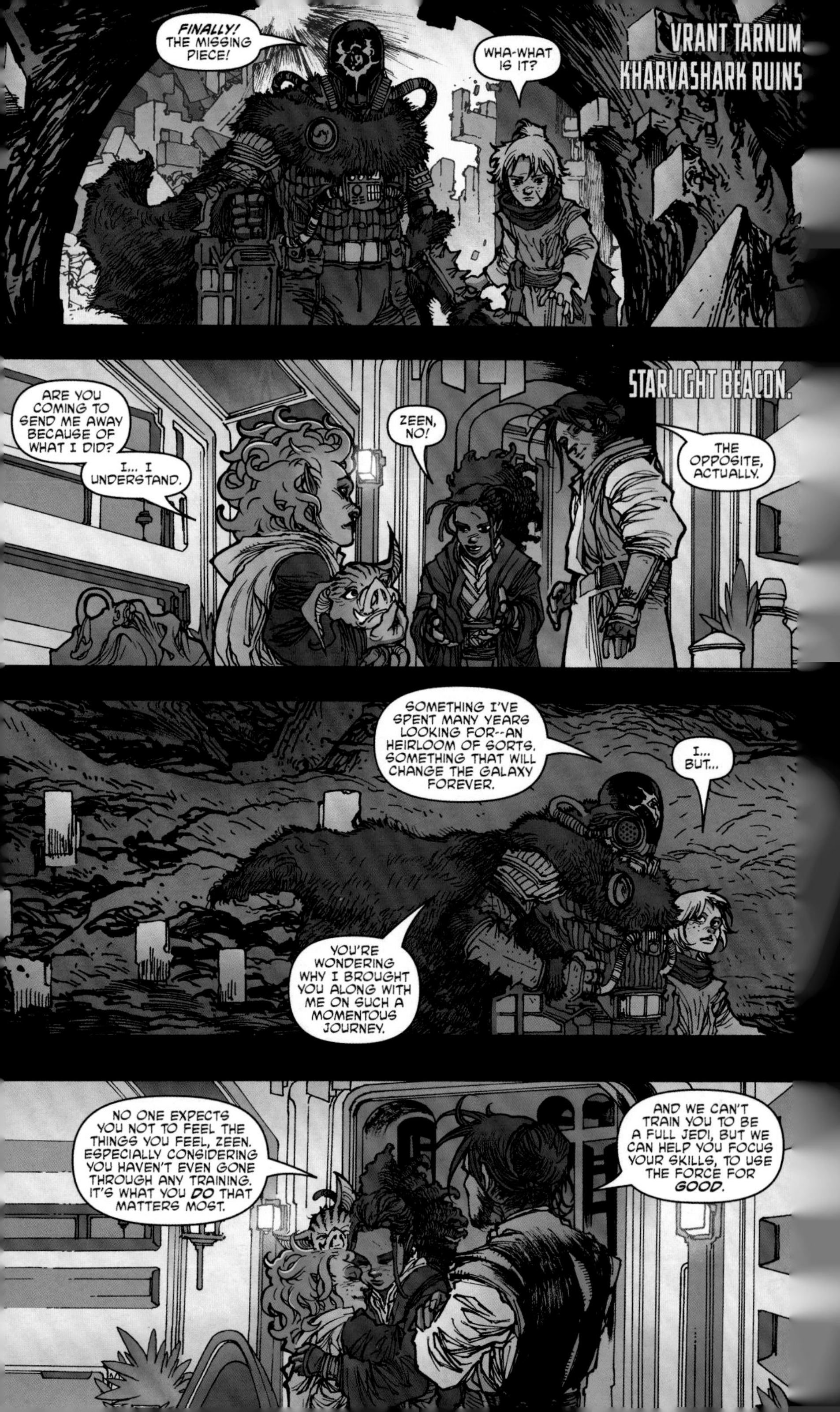

VRANT TARNUM
KHARVASHARK RUINS
FINALLY! THE MISSING PIECE!
WHA-WHAT IS IT?
STARLIGHT BEACON.
ARE YOU COMING TO SEND ME AWAY BECAUSE OF WHAT I DID?
I... I UNDERSTAND.
ZEEN, NO!
THE OPPOSITE, ACTUALLY.
SOMETHING I'VE SPENT MANY YEARS LOOKING FOR--AN HEIRLOOM OF SORTS. SOMETHING THAT WILL CHANGE THE GALAXY FOREVER.
I... BUT...
YOU'RE WONDERING WHY I BROUGHT YOU ALONG WITH ME ON SUCH A MOMENTOUS JOURNEY.
NO ONE EXPECTS YOU NOT TO FEEL THE THINGS YOU FEEL, ZEEN. ESPECIALLY CONSIDERING YOU HAVEN'T EVEN GONE THROUGH ANY TRAINING. IT'S WHAT YOU DO THAT MATTERS MOST.
AND WE CAN'T TRAIN YOU TO BE A FULL JEDI, BUT WE CAN HELP YOU FOCUS YOUR SKILLS, TO USE THE FORCE FOR GOOD.

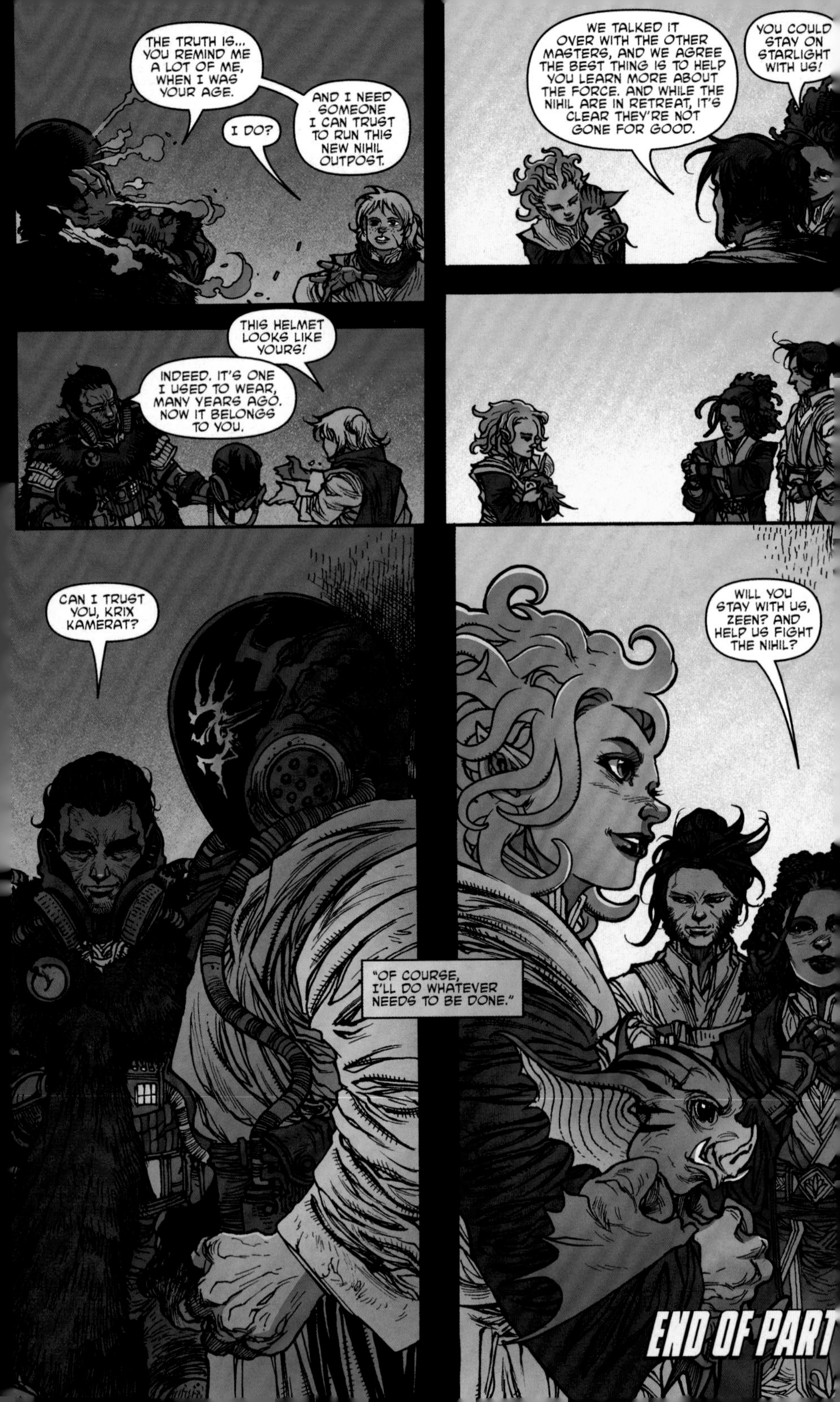
THE TRUTH IS... YOU REMIND ME A LOT OF ME, WHEN I WAS YOUR AGE.
I DO?
AND I NEED SOMEONE I CAN TRUST TO RUN THIS NEW NIHIL OUTPOST.
THIS HELMET LOOKS LIKE YOURS!
INDEED. IT'S ONE I USED TO WEAR, MANY YEARS AGO. NOW IT BELONGS TO YOU.
CAN I TRUST YOU, KRIX KAMERAT?
"OF COURSE, I'LL DO WHATEVER NEEDS TO BE DONE."
WE TALKED IT OVER WITH THE OTHER MASTERS, AND WE AGREE THE BEST THING IS TO HELP YOU LEARN MORE ABOUT THE FORCE. AND WHILE THE NIHIL ARE IN RETREAT, IT'S CLEAR THEY'RE NOT GONE FOR GOOD.
YOU COULD STAY ON STARLIGHT WITH US!
WILL YOU STAY WITH US, ZEEN? AND HELP US FIGHT THE NIHIL?
END OF PART

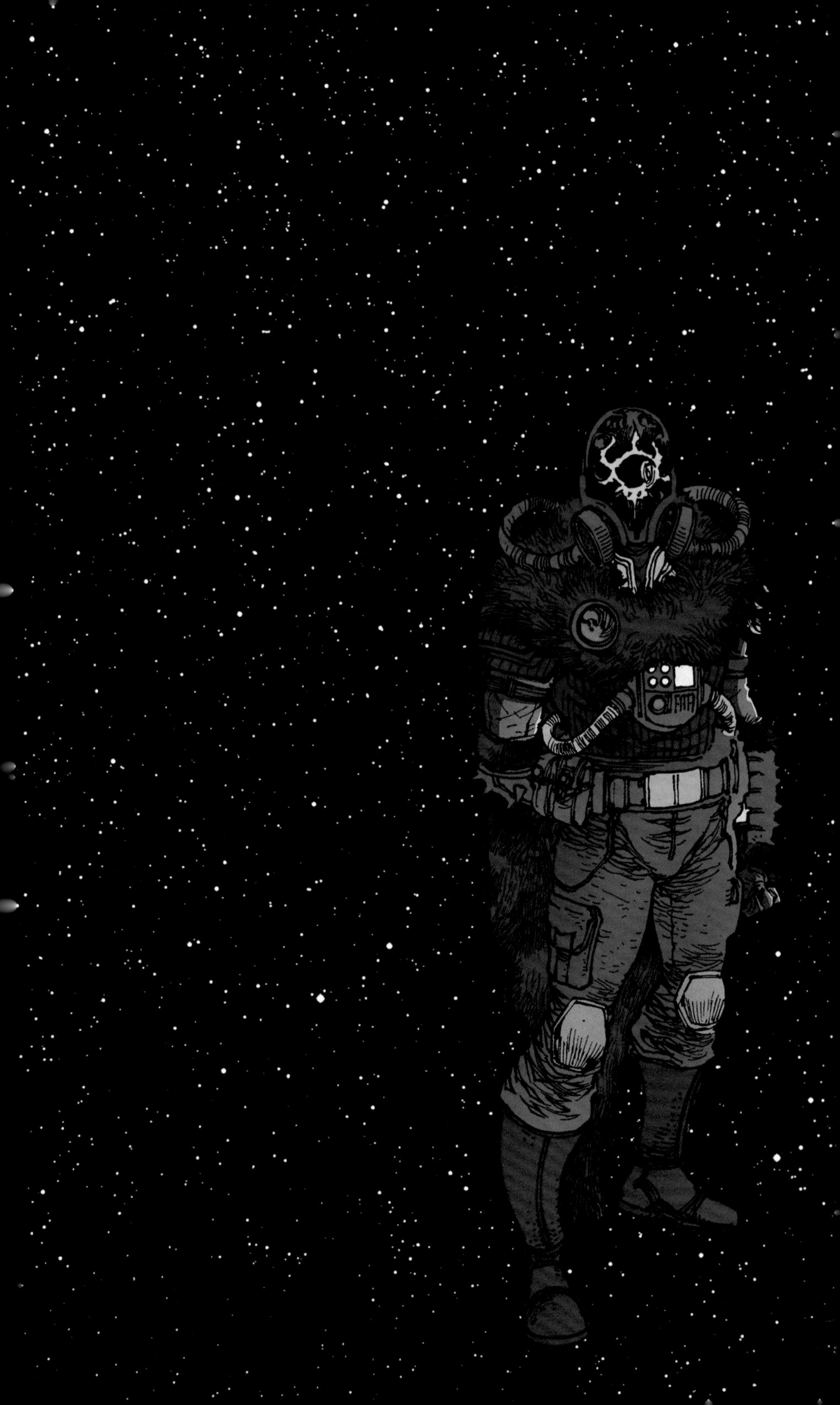

ART BY YAEL NATHAN

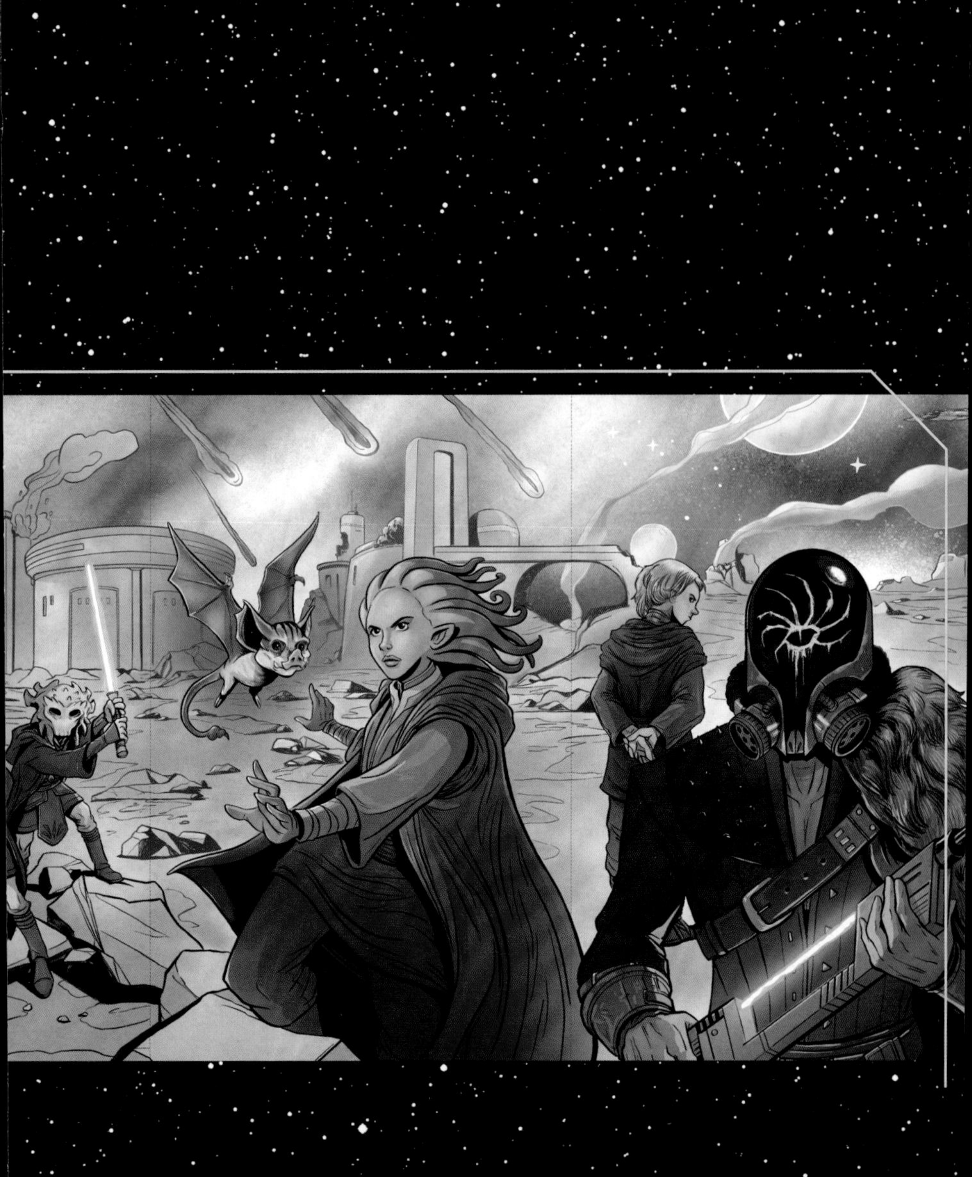

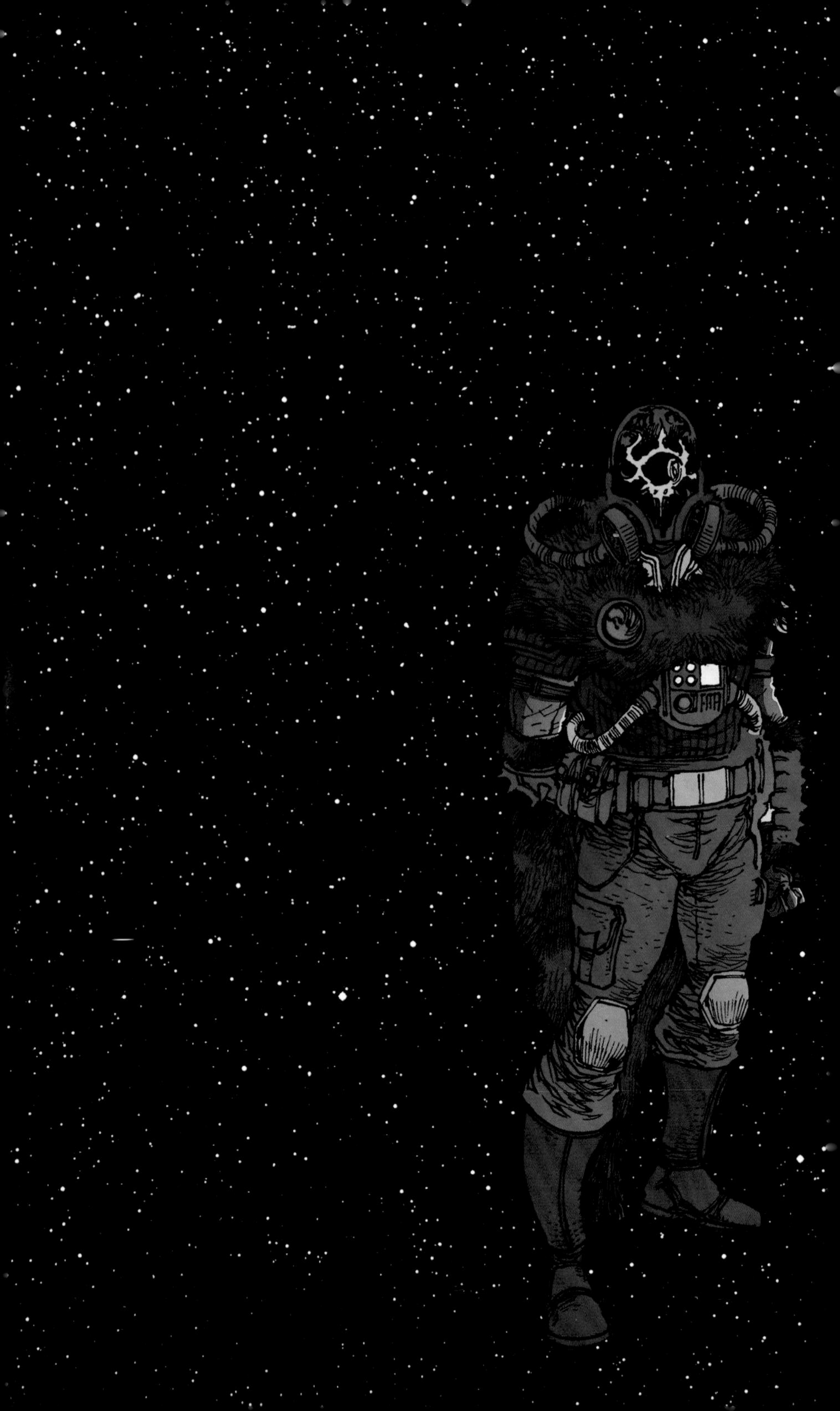